To Protect & Serve

To save others' lives, they will risk their own

Staci Stallings

Spirit Light Publishing

To Protect & Serve
Copyright © 2012 by Staci Stallings
All Rights Reserved

Cover Design: Allan Kristopher Palor
Contact info: allan.palor@yahoo.com
Interior Formatting: Ellen C. Maze, The Author's Mentor,
    www.theauthorsmentor.com
Author Website: http://www.stacistallings.com

Spirit Light Publishing
ISBN-13: 978-0615654300 (Custom Universal)
ISBN-10: 0615654304
Also available in eBook publication

Spirit Light Publishing

PRINTED IN THE UNITED STATES OF AMERICA

To all those who are called to risk their lives to save others—

You are all my heroes!

May God bless you and keep you safe always!

~*~

One

"I promise concern for others, and a willingness to help those in need," Jeff Taylor said as he stood, hands clasped behind his back, shoulder-to-shoulder with 28 of Houston's finest. His chest swelled with the words he had committed to memory in anticipation of this very moment more than ten years before. "I promise strength... strength of heart to bear whatever burdens might be placed upon me..."

He closed his eyes and breathed the words into his soul. This pledge would change his life in ways he could hardly even imagine at the moment. Where would it lead? Up flights of steps as others fled the other direction? Into the mouth of hell to pluck a single life back? Those images from the future coupled with the words making it difficult to so much as breathe them, and yet somehow his voice managed far more than that.

Strong, with a strength he had gained and a strength he would have to find in himself to do this job, his voice came. A solemn vow to all those his life would touch. "...I promise to protect and serve to the best of my ability. I promise the wisdom to lead, the compassion to comfort, and the love to serve unselfishly whenever I am called."

A moment of silence for them all to breathe, one more moment affording a final opportunity to turn back. But like the image of those steps, he knew he never would. If someone needed him, Jeff Taylor, now standing at the door to his destiny, was ready and willing to help.

"I said I needed those reports by two! What? Were you hoping my desk would blow up and I wouldn't notice they weren't here?" Lisa

Matheson asked in fury as the phone shook in her hand. "I don't need excuses. I'm tired of excuses. I want them here in five minutes—or you can pack your things and I'll find someone who can actually do this job."

Without bothering to say good-bye, she slammed the phone down, and her gaze swept the desk stacked a foot high. How was it possible that every single incompetent moron found their way into her office? They were everywhere—and each one had more excuses than the last one did. One carefully manicured set of nails sifted through the files on her desk, but without the latest sales reports, this information was useless.

She hit the intercom button. "Sherie, did Kamden call yet?"

"About ten minutes ago. He's on his way."

"Terrific," Lisa breathed as she let go of the intercom button. More bad news. Kamden was sure to jump ship the second he figured out her little agency couldn't even get a simple set of sales figures together. She had given her blood, sweat, and tears for the better part of a year to land the Kamden Foods account. Now, she had it, and it was going to be gone before she so much as had a shot at really promoting it. It never ceased to amaze her how long it took to build something and how very quickly it simply crashed down around her. One finger hit the intercom button. "When Joel gets here with those reports, send him in."

"Sure thing."

If she could just get organized before the next disaster hit, it would be nice. It would also be nice if she could sweep one hand across her desk and dump all of the problems there into the garbage. With a frustrated sigh, she reached for the folder she had been compiling since that morning just as Joel not so much walked but fell into her office.

"Nice of you to make it," she said icily. She held out a hand for the information in his. "It's all there?"

"The last three months," he said, nodding.

However, when she opened the folder, her gaze fell across the tallies. "No, this is last quarter. I've already got this. I need the newest quarter."

"Yeah, well, the newest quarter isn't over yet, so..."

"No." Lisa lowered her tone as her gaze skewered through him. "I need the figures for the newest quarter. Now!"

"Well, you said the quarter. I thought you meant..."

2

Her head was really starting to hurt. "Do you have the figures for this quarter or not?"

"For last month," Joel hedged as he pushed his black glasses up on his nose. "This month isn't..."

"Then get me the figures for last month."

"But that's not..."

"Get them!"

"O... okay," Joel said, and although he looked like he wanted to add another excuse, one more look at her told him a quick exit would be best. "I'll be back."

In frustration Lisa twirled the single strand of auburn-brunette hair that framed her face in a perfect arch. "Okay, this isn't so bad. I've got the newest mock-ups. I'll just show him those. I could probably wing the sales figures too if I had to..."

The intercom beeped. "Haley's on line two."

"No, no, no," Lisa moaned as she reached for the phone. "I don't have time for this!" The phone was at her ear in one motion, and she breathed one quick breath to squelch all of her frustration. "Hey, Haley-girl, what's up?"

"I just wanted to make sure my maid of honor hasn't forgotten about our little shindig tonight," the sweet voice of Lisa's younger sister said, sounding even sweeter couched in the middle of the most magical month of her life.

"No, I didn't forget, but I am a little busy trying to get away in time."

"I can come by and get you if you want," Haley said. "Bryn and Chandra are going to meet us there."

"I've got my car."

"I know, but I also know you're liable to get buried six feet deep in that paperwork of yours and forget."

"I wouldn't..."

"Be careful where you go with that statement. This is the same sister who sat at the airport for six hours waiting for you when you decided to drive from Dallas that time."

"Okay, okay. Come get me, but I wouldn't have forgotten this."

Joel slipped into the room, and Lisa looked up at him, dreading the bad news he was obviously bringing.

"Listen, Hal, I've got to go."

"Six."

3

"Yeah, six," Lisa replied, feeling the full weight of the duty fall on her shoulders. If she made it that long, life could only go up from there. With that promise, she hung up.

Carefully Joel handed her the folder. "Here they are, and I've got the ones for this month in there too."

With her brain going in seven directions at once, Lisa opened the folder and tried to focus on what she was looking at just as the intercom buzzed.

"Mr. Kamden is in the conference room," Sherie said.

"Lovely."

Surrounded by the men who had become his best friends over the last nine months, Jeff stood, drinking punch and laughing about the exploits they had traversed together—like the time Dustin had fallen backward the first time they put the full gear on him, or when Craig got stuck in the door as he went through the obstacle course, and the time Ramsey slid down the pole holding his boots in one hand and his pants in the other.

Ramsey, who was one of the six black men in their class, had never been the most organized among them, but down deep, he had a heart as big as the Astrodome. In fact, as Jeff looked around at them, it struck him how very different each was from the others—but how well they had fit together despite their differences or maybe because of them. One strength made up for another's weakness. He only hoped that his new post would work out as well.

"Well, gentlemen." Captain Drake clapped Jeff on the back as he stepped up to the group. "It was touch and go there for awhile, but you made it."

"Yes, sir," they all chorused like a well-rehearsed kindergarten class.

"So, what's up next?"

"I'm going down to South Houston," Dustin said, speaking up first as he always did. Dustin. Cool, smooth, confident Dustin. The leader and the one Jeff would miss the most.

"I'm headed out to College Station," Ramsey said with a nod.

"God help them," Captain Drake said, and they laughed. He looked over to Craig.

"I've got two apps in. Depends who takes me," Craig said

4

with his slow Texas grin. Meticulous Craig—the guy who always the right gear at the right time. Jeff would've followed Craig into a burning building that was destined to fall at any moment. It wouldn't matter, Craig would be there with the right stuff to keep the whole thing upright until they had accomplished every last component of their mission.

"And how about you, Taylor? What're your big plans?"

The attention from the group descended on him in a flash, and Jeff ducked fully comprehending that he was now center stage.

"Oh, you know, Taylor," Dustin said after a beat. "He's just looking for the station with the best stud calendar." As though the statement needed emphasis, Dustin struck a heroic pose.

Instantly Jeff shook his head even as he buried it into his chest.

"Well, that's the only way he's ever going to get any action," Ramsey said with a laugh.

"Yeah, Lord knows, he's never going to actually ask anybody out," Craig said, joining in on the ribbing session that had been going on for more than six months.

Somehow, Jeff knew he never should've admitted he wasn't exactly an expert in the area of women. The other three, two married and one constantly on the prowl, made women seem like a subject with the difficulty of third-grade reading. However, when they taught the lessons the other guys had obviously learned, he must have been absent because as far as Jeff could tell, he was clueless on the subject.

It wasn't totally his fault. It was something about how he was wired. Around the guys it was hard enough to get a few words in, but bring a woman around, and the already errant signals from his brain to his mouth became downright unintelligible.

Captain Drake laughed with the others and patted Jeff on the back. "Well, if you need a good reference…"

"He needs more than that," Ramsey said, and they all burst out laughing again.

"Thanks, Captain." Jeff extended his hand trying to be oblivious to the joke. "It's been an honor, Sir."

"Good luck, Taylor," the captain said, and his smile spoke in terms *of I hope to see you again someday* and *take care of yourself out there.* Then the captain moved on to the next cluster of graduates.

"Hey, you know, this punch is nice and all," Ramsey said,

spinning his little cup, "but I'm thinking we really deserve a better send off than this."

"What do you have in mind?" Dustin asked as he took a drink of the punch.

"The Bar Houston?" Ramsey said quizzically. He jerked his head over to the table where the wives sat. "You can even bring them along if you want."

Craig laughed. "How generous of you."

"I try." Ramsey shrugged and downed the last of his punch. "Even though I seriously hate the thought of diluting the opportunity pool. Know what I'm saying?"

"So, you going to let my man Jeff come along too?" Dustin asked, draping an arm over Jeff's shoulders.

"Why not?" Ramsey said with a knowing smirk. "You've got to actually talk for the prospects to notice you're in the hunt."

"I don't know." Jeff shrunk away from the thought. "I'm kind of busy."

"What? Polishing your boots?" Ramsey taunted.

It was too close to the truth to deny too vehemently, and Jeff scratched the back of his ear wishing he could just disappear and be done with it. "It's been a long day."

"And what better way to relieve a long day than a little one-on-one time with some very lovely ladies?" Dustin asked. Then he looked at Jeff. "Oh, yeah. I forgot who I'm talking to."

They laughed as annoyance landed squarely on Jeff's chest. "Fine. Let's go."

"I knew it."

Lisa jumped at the sound of her sister's voice suddenly in the middle of her office; however, she kept her gaze solely on the campaign spread across her desk. "Knew what?"

"You aren't ready yet." Haley crossed her arms in irritation.

"I am." Head down, Lisa wrote out the rest of her idea. "I was just waiting on you."

"Uh-huh, and I didn't see you downstairs."

"I figured you'd come up and get me."

"Okay, so I'm here."

Lisa's gaze never lifted from the drawings. "You know, Hal, the whole bar thing really isn't my scene."

"Yeah," Haley said as she walked around the desk where she laced her arm through her sister's and tugged on her, "and if I'd let you, you'd hole up here forever and never go anywhere."

Quickly Lisa made one more mark before she allowed herself to be pulled up. "And that would be a bad thing?"

"Come on, Bryn and Chandra are waiting."

"Now this is a party!" Dustin said as he draped one arm over the shoulders of his wife, Eve, a lovely brunette who huddled in closer to him.

"I just hope the babysitter doesn't charge overtime," Craig's wife, Bridget, said looking at her watch.

"Hey, hey, hey," Ramsey said with a definite scowl. "Now, you ladies know I love you, but come on. Babysitters? You're cramping my style."

"And what style would that be, R.J.?" Eve asked teasingly.

"You know." Ramsey slid out of the booth and did a smooth slide past the table. "My style."

Eve ran her hand down Dustin's chest. "I'm just glad he didn't rub off on you while you were cooped up in that training thing with him." Lovingly Dustin turned to her and rubbed the tip of her nose with his.

"Me too."

"Yeah, yeah, yeah. While the two of you are getting all lovey-dovey on us, I'm going to go find myself a little action," Ramsey said.

"There's plenty of action right here for me," Dustin said, and as Jeff watched them from across the table, his hand on his cold Bud Lite, he couldn't help but think that in the whole general scheme of things he'd rather be where Dustin and Eve now sat than where Ramsey stood.

"I'm telling you, you're missing out," Ramsey said, shaking his head.

"You know for someone who wants action so bad, you sure don't move very fast," Craig said from his position next to Bridget.

"You just take notes, Hyatt." Pointing both forefingers at the group as he slid backward, Ramsey arched an eyebrow and disappeared into the crowd.

"I'm sure glad I don't have to do that anymore." Eve slid so close to Dustin that Jeff wondered how she didn't just disappear. "This is so much better."

"Enjoy it," Bridget, who wasn't huddled nearly so close to her husband, said. "You get a couple of kids, and you'll never get to be that close again."

Craig laughed. "Yeah, it's family night every night of the week."

Coiling her neck, Eve looked up at Dustin. "Let's not ever have kids."

"Ah," he said, smiling down at her, "I think making them sounds like fun."

"Oh, yeah," she said as a fire lit in her eyes. "Now that does sound like fun."

"Hey, hey! Hello! What are we going to have to do, hose you two down?" Craig asked.

"Well, considering you've got a hot babe sitting right next to you, I don't think I'd be so concerned with us," Dustin said, smirking.

"You know," Craig said as he turned to Bridget. "The man has a point. Do you remember how to dance, Mrs. Hyatt?"

Instantly she smiled. "I thought you'd never ask." Together they slid from the booth.

"That doesn't sound like a half-bad idea," Eve said, tracing a finger around and around on Dustin's chest.

"Well, then what are we waiting for?" Dustin asked, and they slid out the other way. Just before they stepped from the table, Dustin turned back to the lone table occupant. "Hold our seats."

Off-handedly Jeff saluted with two fingers. Somehow he wished he had just stayed home to polish his boots.

"Good grief, Lisa-girl, you've really got to get out of that office more." Bryn, one of the other bridesmaids tipped up the beer in her hand.

"What makes you say that?" Lisa asked, trying not to squirm defensively. Her own bottle of beer sat on the table without so much as a sip taken out of it.

"Look at you." Chandra frowned. "You look like you just stepped off the cover of *Working Women Today*."

"You really should learn to let your hair down a little," Bryn confirmed.

Lisa's hand went to the back of the upsweep of hair. "I didn't have time to change before Haley dragged me out here."

"Okay, I heard my name," Haley said, slipping up to the booth. "So, what? Are we going to sit here all night and drink, or did we come to enjoy ourselves a little?" Haley was moving to the beat of the pounding music like she was born in a dance club.

"Well, let's go dance already!" Bryn said, pushing Haley out in front of her.

Chandra slid out the other way and then stopped. "Lis, aren't you coming?"

"No, I think I'll just hold the table," Lisa said, waving them away.

With a shrug, Chandra followed the other two out into the crowd, swaying with every step she took. As soon as they were gone, Lisa relaxed into the soft plastic of the booth as her finger played with the ice on her beer. Haley. She was here because of Haley. Just remember that. *Put a smile on your face, and get through this.*

"Hi," a tall guy in a T-shirt and a baseball cap suddenly said, standing in front of her table. "I saw you sitting over here by yourself. I was wondering if you'd like to dance?"

The relaxation snapped right out of her spine as she sat straight up. "Oh, no. Umm, no thanks. I'm not really into dancing."

"You sure?" He flashed that false smile she'd seen so many times it sickened her now. "I'd hate for you to just be left over here all by yourself."

"No," she said, trying to smile but the effort hurt her face, "maybe later."

He held out his palms in surrender. "Your loss." And he moved on through the crowd.

Wishing she could just disappear, Lisa laid her elbow on the seat back behind her and put her fingertips to her forehead. This was pointless. Utterly pointless. The whole idea of bars was to go and meet people and have fun, but she didn't want to meet anyone and the last thing she had time for was fun.

In frustration, she let her arm fall forward where it immediately met up with a brick mildly resembling an arm. "Oh!" Instantly she sat up as she looked across the booth back at the target she had surprise attacked. "I'm sorry." Her eyes widened as the guy sitting there yanked his arm away.

9

"Oh, no. It wasn't you," he said with a visible swallow. "It was me. I wasn't paying attention. I'm sorry."

"It's okay," she said as her senses took in the strong yet quiet features, the black hair clipped neatly over his ears and the gentleness of his blue eyes. She was sure she must be dreaming, and then he smiled, and she knew that in fact she was.

In utter self-defense, she turned back to her table, holding the part of her arm that was now burning from that one single solitary brush with his. She could feel his gaze still on her, and quickly if for no other reason than to quench the fire in her chest, she took a long drink of the ice-cold beer. When she set the bottle down, she wasn't sure if the headache she suddenly had was from the music or the beer or the fact that her eyes were trying desperately to move to the side of her head to get another look at him.

"Come on, Lisa. Get a hold of yourself," she breathed. "He's just like all the rest of them. Snap out of it."

The girls picked that moment to conga line up to her table with what looked like half the bar following them.

"Come on, Lis!" Haley yelled, dancing and laughing, and pulling her sister out of the booth. "Have some fun!"

"Look at you, sitting here all alone," Bridget said as she and Craig followed the conga line back to the table and sat down. The pity in her eyes made Jeff's head fall of its own accord. Softly Bridget laid a hand on his arm. "We've really got to find you someone, Jeffrey. You're making my heart hurt."

Sheepishly he scratched the back of his neck. "It's not so bad." He laid his arm over the booth back behind her, and his gaze followed it to the now empty table beyond. But he shook the sight of the angel-ghost away from his consciousness. "I'm just glad you guys are having fun."

"But you're not having any," Bridget said, frowning. Then she brightened. "How about you dance with me?"

"D-dance?" Every awkward part of his body stood to attention. "Oh, I don't think..."

However, she already had his other hand in hers. "That wasn't a question. You don't mind, do you, Craig?"

Craig smiled at them as Bridget pulled Jeff out of the booth. "Just bring her back. Okay?"

10

Every step was torture for Jeff, all the way to the dance floor. There were things in life that he did well—dancing was not one of them. On the floor he tried to find the beat, but it kept moving on him. Side-to-side not really dancing so much as just moving, he swayed. How did all the other guys make this look normal? It felt utterly foreign to every inch of his body.

At that moment he caught sight of Dustin and Eve slow dancing although the beat was more of a jungle rhythm. He couldn't even dance the way you were supposed to with music like this, and he sure couldn't pull something like that off. No, for all intents and purposes, he was doomed to forever be the awkward one, to forever be the one that the world overlooked.

But that was okay. He didn't need the spotlight. One, true love—if he could just find that, the rest of life would be perfect. As he glanced again at Dustin and Eve, that was his one and only wish.

Lisa's head was swimming by the time they made it back to the table, and in seconds a waitress appeared with a round of shots.

"Oh, no." Lisa waved her hands in front of her. "None for me. Thanks."

"Come on, Lis," Haley said, laughing and begging at the same time, "just one."

It wasn't a good idea. She knew it. "Okay. One."

The glasses were filled, and Chandra raised hers. "To Cory who dang sure better know how lucky he is to be getting Haley!"

"Here, here."

In one motion the other three downed their drinks as Lisa looked at hers knowing how awful this was going to be. She squinted into the on-coming drink, counted to three, and nearly choked when the sharp, stinging liquid assaulted her throat.

"More dancing!" Haley announced, jumping to her feet. The other two followed without question, but Lisa slunk back behind the table so they wouldn't notice her absence. When they were gone, she sat up and coughed again. Peeling her eyes from the back of her eyelids, she shook her head. Work was not going to be fun tomorrow.

"No, no, no," the arm guy from earlier said, sliding into the other booth as he pushed the other two occupants back out to the floor. "That's enough for me. You two go. Dance. Have fun."

Laughing at him, the guy put his arm on the lady's waist, and they disappeared into the crowd. For one moment Lisa folded the edge of her napkin up and then down, fighting not to look over at him. It was crazy. He was just a guy at a bar. One of thousands, and yet... Without her permission, her gaze chanced across the divide between them, and the jolt from the pools of blue looking back at her sent her diving back to her side.

He was looking at her. That wasn't good. No, no. That was not good. Her face went hot. Now he was going to think she was looking at him. Well, she was, but not because she wanted to. She really couldn't help herself. After all, where else are you supposed to look—at the table all night? But still she shouldn't have been looking. That might be an invitation, and she didn't want to be sending out any invitations. Not tonight. Not ever.

Slowly, carefully she wound the strand of hair sliding down her face over her ear. One more furtive glance over the divide between them. This time she was thankful to find only his silhouette. Good. At least he wasn't going to think she was trying to make eye contact or something. Casually she sat up, nodding to herself as she closed her eyes. Her brain coached itself on what to do and what not to do. However, when she opened her eyes, the fact that his arm was again only a foot from her jumped into her consciousness.

Nervously half of her gaze followed the sculptured forearm up past the black sleeve that covered everything from his elbow up to his shoulder. She shut her eyes, trying to block him out, but the second she opened them he was back. However, this time the blue pools were back too. Her gaze locked with his, and she knew he knew she was looking. Quickly she smiled as she wound the errant hair around her ear.

"Nice music," she said.

"Yeah." His smile was better than she had remembered.

She wanted to say something else, but her brain scrambled by the proximity of his arm and the disarming way his gaze fell to the table as if her eyes were too intense to hold on. "You come here a lot?" she asked, wholly reprimanding herself for pursuing when she should be thankful he wasn't.

"No, not really." He shook his head and shifted a little, and this time his smile was less sure. "We're celebrating."

"Oh, really? Us too." With her tone she tried to coax his full gaze back to her although she was only mildly successful. "My little sister's getting married next weekend."

"Oh." This smile was stronger. "Lucky her."

"Yeah, lucky me too." Lisa shook her head and wrinkled her nose. "Bachelorette party. Woohoo."

This time he laughed outright. "Sounds terrible."

"Well, as long as they don't drag me out there, it's not so bad."

He nodded. "I hear you there."

For a moment she sat, gathering her scattering sanity and trying to get her gaze not to notice the gold cross shining atop the solid black shirt at his neck. "So, what're you celebrating?"

However, at that moment her attention snapped to the other edge of his table where two of his friends slid into the booth with him without pretense.

"Man, it's hot out there!" the girl with the nearly-black, wavy hair said, fanning herself with her hand as Lisa self-consciously slunk back into her own world.

"Yeah. I'm sure it's the dance floor," elbow guy said with a laugh as he retreated back to his own table.

"Hey, how would you know?" the guy in the skin-hugging, brown-gold pullover shirt asked. "It's not like you can tell from way over here." He took a drink. "Man, have you seen Ramsey? That guy's insane. He's got like a whole bachelorette party dancing with him."

Lisa's ears tried to peel themselves from the conversation as she slid farther down into the booth.

"Yeah, well, dancing isn't everything," elbow guy said as he laid his forearm on the booth back, causing the remaining sanity in Lisa's head to disperse.

Lunacy. It was the far side of it; however, the alcohol or something had a hold of her because Lisa's brain took a nice little journey to the middle of that hot dance floor with her in his arms, swaying in time with only one another. A low growl of disgust with herself crawled into her gut. Where was her willpower? He was a guy after all. A guy. And that meant only one thing—trouble.

"Lisa-girl! What are you doing sitting over here all by yourself?" Haley asked as she, Bryn, Chandra, and a tall, well-built black man danced up to the table. He had his arms around each of the two girls.

"We found ourselves a fireman!" Bryn said loud enough for the whole bar to hear.

"Hey," the man said with a glance to the table next to them, "well, look what we have here!"

Not one part of Lisa liked the sound of that statement.

"Man, you ladies must have some seriously good compass directions going for you. These are the friends I was telling you about!"

Occupants from both tables looked across in surprise.

"Ramsey, what did you do?" pullover guy asked as though he was reprimanding a two-year-old.

"Two," Ramsey mouthed over the top of the girls' heads as he nodded and smiled.

The darkness under the table was looking very inviting to Lisa at that moment.

Pullover guy waved them over. "Well, what are you standing over there for? Come, join us."

"What do you say, ladies? Join us?" Ramsey's clothesline of a grip around Bryn and Chandra made arguing pointless as he led them over to the other table.

Instantly Haley stood to follow them. "Come on, Lis."

Lisa closed her eyes and exhaled. There was no way this was going to turn out well.

Two

"We're going to be dancing," Bryn said as she stood under Ramsey's arm next to the table, "so why don't you get in first?"

The tips of Lisa's ears flamed, but she didn't want to make a complete scene, so she slid a hand under her straight, light beige skirt and slipped into the booth. Elbow guy slid all the way around until he was sitting by pullover shirt, and in the next instant Lisa was so close to him, she could feel the heat from his shoulder. Carefully she wound the strand of hair around her ear as she smiled over at him sheepishly. At that moment Haley bumped into her and nearly sent her careening right into him.

"So, Rams, are you going to introduce us to your friends?" pullover shirt guy asked.

"Oh, sure," Ramsey said smoothly. "This is Chandra, and Bryn, and the bride-to-be, Haley, and…" His gaze chanced on Lisa and stopped as though he wasn't quite sure where she had come from.

"Lisa," she said so quietly it was drowned out by the music.

Ramsey nodded although she was sure he just wanted to get on with the introductions. "And over here we've got Eve and Dustin and Jeff." He looked around as the name wound right into the middle of Lisa. Jeff. Jeff. It was a nice name. Ordinary. Just like he looked—ordinary in an unbelievably extraordinary way. "Where're Craig and Bridget?"

"Dancing I think," Eve said, looking out to the floor.

"Well, then what are we all sitting here for?" Ramsey asked in annoyance. "Ladies."

One-by-one they slid back out of the booth, and Lisa slid over two inches wishing there was more oxygen in the room. When

Haley was out, she looked back. "Lis?"

It was a trap. Either way, it was a trap. "I think I'll just stay here."

With an annoyed shrug Haley followed the group into the crowd. A second and then two, and suddenly Lisa wished she had followed her sister.

"So, a bachelorette party, huh?" the guy she was pretty sure was Dustin asked.

"Yeah, Haley's getting married next week," Lisa said, clearing her throat to get the whole sentence out.

"Ugh, I remember that," Eve said. "Horrible, horrible, horrendous week." She laid a hand on Dustin's, and he looked down at her. "I'm glad that's over."

"What's over?" a blonde asked as she slid into the booth next to Lisa, and then she stopped for a second when she realized she didn't know who that was.

"The wedding," Eve said theatrically as the guy with the blonde sat down next to her, leaving precious little space between Lisa and Jeff. Why couldn't she even think that name without her heart slamming in her chest? She had to get it together before they all figured out she was an idiot.

"Oh." The blonde glanced at Lisa with curiosity mixed with confusion.

"Guys," Dustin said, "this is... um, Lisa, wasn't it?"

Wishing there was a non-threatening place to put her gaze, Lisa nodded. Instantly the new guy held his hand across the table.

"Craig," he said gallantly, "and this is my wife, Bridget."

Lisa shook the other two hands as her senses wrapped around the fact that although he was inches away from her, Jeff hadn't so much as said a word in ten minutes.

"You know." Bridget looked at her watch. "We really better be getting home. The babysitter's going to fire us."

"Wouldn't want that, would we?" Eve asked sweetly as she huddled closer to Dustin.

"You all take care." Craig extended his hand first to Dustin and then to Jeff, and when Jeff extended his hand, Lisa's senses snapped to a full understanding of the size of his forearm. It made at least two of hers. And it was four shades tanner than hers as well. Then Craig waved at her. "It was nice to meet you, Lisa."

"Yeah, you too," she said, willing rational to come back to her.

16

"Night," the departing two said, and Dustin waved at them.

For a moment the music simply surrounded them, and then Dustin looked down at Eve. "You do realize we're wasting good music here."

"Wouldn't want that, now would we?" she replied. Hand-in-hand they slipped out, and just before they walked off, Dustin turned and pointed at Jeff.

"You behave yourself."

There wasn't a single inch of space anywhere on Lisa's face that wasn't 57 degrees hotter than it should have been. Slowly, hoping he wouldn't notice, she slid an inch and then another away from him. It wasn't the direction she wanted to go, but for her heart's sake if nothing else it was the direction she had to.

A moment and then another, and she was starting to think this would be the longest night of her life. The edge of her finger wrapped around the hair at her temple and pushed it behind her ear as she glanced over at him. He wasn't looking at her—instead his gaze was transfixed on the dance floor. "So, you never said what it is you're celebrating," she said softly, hoping he might actually talk again.

In the next heartbeat his gaze caught hers, and she saw the apprehension in the depths of his eyes.

He smiled kind of. "Oh, we graduated today."

"Graduated? From what?" She laid her temple onto her hand as she looked at him.

"The fire academy," he said, nodding.

"Fire academy?" Then she understood. "Oh, so you're a fireman too."

He nodded as the bottom of his lip disappeared under his teeth.

"All four of you?" she asked to clarify.

"Yeah, but after tonight we're kind of going our separate ways, so..."

She smiled at him with gentle understanding. "That's tough. I guess you get pretty close working together like that."

The glance over at her held only gratefulness. "Yeah." His gaze fell back to the table, and he sat for a moment lost in thought. "It's weird you know. A year ago I didn't even know them, and now it's like saying good-bye to brothers."

"Are they... like leaving for good?"

17

"Ramsey's going to College Station, and Dustin's going to South Houston. I'm not real sure where Craig will get stationed. Probably somewhere around here, but who knows."

The list stopped. She waited, but plans for the fourth person didn't come. "What about you?"

His glance snapped up to her and then drifted back out to the dance floor. "I've got an interview on Monday—downtown."

"Oh really? Huh. I work downtown."

The shift of subject brought his gaze back to her. "Oh? Where do you work?"

Instantly it was her gaze that was running. "Oh, it's just a little office in the Travis Tower."

"What do you do there?"

She hated this part. "Umm, I... well, I own my own..." She cleared her throat. "I'm in advertising."

"Hmm, that sounds cool." Then his face fell in thoughtfulness as he realized where she was headed with her original statement. "You own your own business?"

Slowly she nodded, knowing she should look more proud of that fact than she seemed. "Me and three employees." She shook her head at that statement.

"What?" he asked, zeroing in on her with his gaze making her brain feel like a jammed intersection.

She shook her head. "I don't know. Sometimes I think they're more trouble than they're worth."

"Why's that?"

"Because I just wish I could do it all on my own, then things would get done right the first time, and I wouldn't always be running around after everyone trying to keep things going and redoing everybody's mistakes."

"They don't... I mean they're not trained for that kind of work?"

"Oh, they're trained all right, but that doesn't always mean much."

He seemed to relax a little. "So, what do you come up with? Ads?"

"We're supposed to do it all, but we have to farm the TV and radio production out. I don't have time for that. But I draw up a bunch of the stuff we use."

"Like what?"

18

"Like… well, there's that billboard over on the Eastex Freeway for Zebra Carpets, that's mine."

"The one with all the stripes in the background that has a zebra in the middle if you look real hard?"

Her surprise jumped out. "You've seen it?"

He laughed. "Yeah, I drove by that thing like six hundred times before I ever saw the dang zebra, and now every time I go by, I can't believe I missed it."

"Well, it's kind of hard to see when you're going 70."

"Unless it's five and you're going two," he said with another laugh. It was a nice laugh, hearty but not booming.

"True." She matched his laugh, then shrugged. "Sometimes I wish I could do the stuff I like to do and let somebody else do all the rest."

"Then why own your own agency? Why not just get on with someone else?"

She felt her face corkscrew. "That'd never work."

"Why not?"

"Because I'm too much of a solo player. Teams just hold you back."

The softness of his gaze drifted across her face, and she felt the surface of it go hot. "Sometimes it's teamwork that makes life interesting."

At that moment Haley slid into the booth beside Lisa and bumped into her shoulder. It was quite clear that her sister was having a very good time. "Man, that Ramsey guy is insane! I think my legs are going to fall off."

"That's not good," Lisa said, turning her attention to her sister. "Cory might shoot me if I let something happen to you."

Haley waved her off and looked over to Jeff with a sarcastic shake of her head. "Over-protective maid of honor."

He smiled at Haley and then trained his gaze back on Lisa.

Trying to think of something to do so her head wouldn't spontaneously combust, she looked at her watch. It was nearly one. "What time are we planning on leaving anyway? It's getting kind of late."

"Late?" Haley asked in horror. "It's early!"

"Not when you've got work tomorrow it isn't."

"Work? Come on, Lis. Is that all you ever think about?"

"Well, I'm supposed to pitch that proposal for The Youth

Leadership Conference on Monday, and it's not..."

Haley put both hands in the air and waved at Lisa to get her to stop. "No, no, no. I don't want to hear it. You know what? I want to dance some more." And with that, she slipped back out of the booth.

"But you're my..." Lisa started although Haley was already six deep into the crowd, "...ride." She sighed and shook her head. Nobody understood.

"Looks like you're stranded," Jeff said, and absurdly there was an apology in is tone.

Lisa growled in frustration. "Yeah. Looks that way."

His fingers played with the fraying edge of the paper on his beer bottle. "Well, if you need a ride, I wouldn't mind..."

"Oh, no," she said quickly. "That's okay. I'll just stay until they're ready. It's fine."

He nodded. "Oh, okay. Of course."

Through the crowd Lisa caught sight of Dustin and Eve in a head-to-head, gazes-locked dance on the smoky fringes of the dance floor. "Looks like your friends are having a good time."

He followed her gaze and smiled. "Yeah, those two are always having fun when they're together."

"And they're married?"

"Eight months," he confirmed.

"Ah, newlyweds."

"In every sense of the word." He laughed. "You think they're bad now, you should've seen them that first month. You'd have thought they were joined at the hip."

"They seem like they're really in love."

"Yeah, Eve's great, but she always looks a little incomplete without him by her side." Jeff's whole countenance softened as the thoughts behind his eyes floated away on the wings of a dream. "She comes to the station on her lunch break just so they can be together." He shook his head slowly. "And Dustin's always ready to just get done so he can get back home to her. It's like they are determined to spend every single second they possibly can together."

Lisa heard the wistfulness in his voice, and she turned her head from the dance floor and laid it on her hand to look at him. "What about you?"

Instantly he looked at her as though he hadn't realized he was having a conversation with anyone other than himself. "What about me?"

"You got somebody special in your life? Anyone coming to see you at the fire station?"

"My mom came once. Does that count?"

She laughed. "It's better than nothing."

"Yeah," he said, joining her laugh. "I guess so." Then the smile fell. "It's hard sometimes going out with them. Craig and Bridget are just such a couple, and Dustin and Eve... well..." One of his hands slid down under the table as he straightened from sitting too long in the booth, and he stretched out his jeans. "Ramsey's always got a dozen dates swirling around him. So, I get to sit and hold down the table a lot."

"Oh," she said, nodding. "So that's what you were doing."

"Yeah." His eyes were a mixture of hesitation and thoughtfulness.

"Well, you do a good job of it," she said teasingly, and he looked at her with a question in his eyes. "I mean, look at it." She laid her hands on the tabletop. "It hasn't moved a single inch all night." The hesitation was gone when he smiled at her as she examined the table from top to bottom. "Nope, not a single inch."

"Yeah, well, I've had good help," he said, and his voice faded with the words.

"Oh, you think so, huh? Well, then it's a good thing they brought us along or this here table might have just floated right away."

Amusement danced through his eyes. "So you've got a presentation Monday?"

"Ugh," she said as the lightheartedness collapsed around her. "The Youth Leadership Conference. Don't remind me."

"That bad?"

"They're wanting to do this whole speaker thing and get the all the schools in Houston in on it."

"Sounds great," he said, turning as he laid a casual arm over the booth back, looking much more at ease than he had since she'd first touched his arm two hours before. "What kind of speakers are they going to have?"

"Oh, you know, community leaders, business people, that kind of thing. We're really at the very beginning stages of planning it. It's not supposed to be until the fall, but they want to get going on it now. I'm supposed to have suggestions for speaker names for the meeting on Monday, but at the rate I'm going—I'll be lucky to have them by the time the conference starts."

"The speakers?"

"Yeah, a long list of Houston's most influential business people—the real top dogs, you know. It's just that I've got this dumb Kamden Foods account to worry about because Kurt and Joel can't put a progress report together to save their lives, and we really need to be working on the new campaign for Zebra Carpets—once everyone sees the zebra, that one's kind of pointless." She laughed at her own joke although he didn't seem to catch it.

"Man, you must be going in circles."

"That's what it feels like." She closed her eyes and sighed. "And then I've got Haley's wedding next weekend, so we've got final fittings this week, and she wants me to go shopping with her for her honeymoon stuff, and then the rehearsal and setting up, and I don't really know when I'm going to find time to do all of this." Like she ran into a solid brick wall, she stopped and surveyed him seriously. "You don't know of a way to get more than 24 hours into a day, do you?"

"At the rate you're going, you may need like 75."

The laugh that came from her soul felt very good. "You've got a point."

Movement at the front of the table pulled their gazes over to where Dustin and Eve stood arm-in-arm. "Hey, man, I think we're going to call it a night," Dustin said, and Jeff jerked his arm off the back of the booth.

"So soon?"

"Yeah, we've got to get our stuff boxed up tomorrow. The moving van's going to be there bright and early Monday morning."

"Oh. You needing some help?" Jeff asked as if he might need to go right then to start boxing things up.

Dustin grinned. "Hey, I never turn down a good offer of help."

"What time?"

"Ten… eleven?" Dustin looked at Lisa. "Whatever time you can get there."

"Let's say eleven," Jeff said, and Dustin nodded as he extended his hand, and the two of them knocked fists together.

22

"See ya then."

"Take care." Dustin stepped away from the table and then turned back. "It was nice to meet you, Lisa."

"Yeah," she said as embarrassment crowded on her. "You too."

"Night," Dustin said with a final wave.

When they were gone, Lisa looked at her watch. "Two o'clock." She shook her head. "Good. Now they have to go home."

Jeff nodded as he laid his forearms on the table watching his thumbs bounce back and forth across each other. "So you might get some sleep tonight after all."

At that moment the three girls and Ramsey approached the table, and Jeff and Lisa looked up and straightened.

"Come on, Lis. We're going over to Shane's," Haley said, never really breaking rhythm. "You ready?"

"Shane's? Who's Shane?" Lisa asked as confusion tinged the anger.

"Who's Shane," Haley mocked. "Shane's—the bar, dummy."

"Bar?" Lisa asked in outright dismay. "But…"

"Ramsey says it's excellent," Bryn said, looking up at him in awe.

"But I'm not…" Lisa looked at her watch. "I really need to get home."

The set of Haley's hands on her hips said that Lisa was once again ruining her good time. "So what? You just want to bust up the whole party then? Come on, Lis. It's not that late."

"I could take her," Jeff said from Lisa's side, and Haley shifted her attention to him in the same second that Lisa turned her gaze to him. He shrugged as he looked at her. "I could take you. No big deal."

"Cool," Haley said, accepting for Lisa without so much as consulting her, and instantly Lisa turned and nailed Haley with a would-you-shut-up gaze. Haley returned the look with one that said, what? I want to go.

Lisa turned back to Jeff. "I'd hate to put you out."

"It's not putting me out. I was headed home anyway."

"Great so it's settled then," Haley said, smiling.

"Great," Lisa breathed, wondering when she had stumbled into this nightmare.

23

At the club door Jeff grabbed his jacket and half-followed, half-led Lisa outside. She was as stunning standing up as she was sitting right next to him. With her in that business suit, the slim curve of her waist, and the heels, his already scrambling brain waves were having a hard time keeping up with anything other than her. It felt like walking next to a runway model. As they exited, he swung his denim and brown suede jacket on, sensing how underdressed he looked next to her.

"So, where's your car?" he asked, hoping his voice would hold out long enough to get the sentence out.

"At the office," she said, and he noticed the protective fold of her arms across her chest.

"On Travis?"

She looked over at him, and surprise ran through her eyes. "Yeah."

In slow lockstep they walked to his car, the product of a hundred million hours spent under a hood and on a hard concrete floor—a 1971 black-on-blue Pontiac GTO Convertible.

"Nice," she breathed, running a hand over the shiny paint job when he led her to the passenger side.

"You think so?" he asked, surprised she had even noticed, and even more surprised she didn't turn up her nose at the thought of riding in anything other than the very newest model. He watched her fold herself onto the off-gray seat, not wholly sure if he should take her hand to help her in or if that was just something he'd seen in some old movie. It wasn't like he'd had much practice at this, and suddenly he really wished he had. Careful to make sure that she was securely in, he waited one more second and then slammed the door. When he slipped behind the steering wheel, she was still marveling.

"This is unbelievable. Did you do this yourself?" she asked in awe.

"Me and my dad," he said, not really sure if it was her reaction or the pride he had felt when they had finally finished the project that was filling his chest.

Her smile lit the night around him. "So, is this like a hobby then?"

He started the car as his heart raced ahead of him. Somehow

even sitting next to her in the noisy bar hadn't been this intimidating. "I don't really have the funds for it to be an on-going hobby if that's what you mean."

"But if you did?"

"I love cars." He glanced over at her and then thought better of that move. "Ever since I was like 12. My dad and I would go to all the car shows. Classics, muscle cars, concept cars. It was just a trip to see anything with a motor."

The lights winked across the windshield as they drove down the neon-lit street.

"So why this one?" she asked.

"Well, for one thing it wasn't in perfect condition, so we got it pretty cheap. It really needed a lot of work, but that was cool too because we got to go all around, searching for ones like it to trade out parts. That was half the fun."

"And what was the other half?"

He laughed. "Driving it once it was finished."

She glanced down at the gearshift and wrinkled her nose. "I don't know. I'm more of an automatic girl myself."

"It's not so bad." Expertly he shifted down. "Once you get used to it anyway."

She looked up at the ceiling. "So does the top really go back?"

"Yep, it really does although I don't do that much anymore. I just about ruined it a few years back. I was at school and left it down. About halfway thought a statistics test, it started pouring rain. After that I left it up—just in case."

Her hand glided across the door handle. "Smart."

For an instant when he looked over at her, he wished they could simply drive forever. That would be so much easier than finding the words to get enough information so he could see her again. The question of her phone number slipped into his mind as his hand shifted the gears, but he didn't have a paper or a pen— more than that he didn't have the words to ask. "Okay, I guess you're going to have to give me a little better coordinates than just Travis Street."

"Oh, sorry," she said as her gaze snapped from the car to the street. "Yeah, turn right up here at the light." The shimmer of her red fingernail sparkled in the flash of the streetlight over the windshield. "It's the third building on the right. There's a parking garage next to it."

"Okay." He downshifted again and then spun the wheel to guide them into the darkened parking area.

"I'm on the third level." She settled back into the seat, and when he glanced over at her, he liked how comfortable she looked. At that moment, her gaze chanced across to his, and his heart thudded to a stop. If only there were words...

"Third level, right?" he asked softly.

"Right." Her gaze jumped from his to her window, and reluctantly he turned the car up the second ramp and into the third level. "It's over there—the white Cavalier."

It wasn't hard to spot, there were only a few vehicles left on the whole level. Deftly he spun into a space two over from where her car sat overlooking the street below. Once parked, his brain scrambled for what to do next. The previous minutes had all been so easy, but now what to do or what to say evaporated from around him. Something told him to shut the car off because its noise was reverberating across the concrete. However, the second the car died, the silence around them echoed far louder.

"Well," he said without looking at her, "this is it."

"I guess so," she said, but she didn't move to get out of the car.

Suddenly his brain said, *You idiot, she's waiting for you to open her door.* Not nearly as smoothly as he would've liked, he got out and ran around the back to her side where he reached for the handle. One click and she smiled up at him as she slipped out and waited for him to close the door. His senses didn't miss the red fingernail and the slim finger attached to it as together they pushed the edge of her hair behind her ear. She smiled at him again, but nervous now.

"Well, thanks."

"No problem." Lest he do what his body was screaming at him to do and reach out and touch her, he jammed his hands into his jacket pockets. After a moment she looked over at her car and then turned for it, and although it was only a ten-step walk, he followed her—trying to find some way to make this moment last longer than any one had ever lasted before. "Thanks for helping me hold the table down."

At the door of her car, she turned and her smile held no longer held apprehension. "Thanks for keeping me sane."

"My pleasure."

The muted noise of the cars on the street below was the only sound as they stood there neither really looking at the other. Finally she wound her hair around her ear again as it had somehow become dislodged in the adventure of getting from his car to hers. "I'd better be getting home." One hand produced her keys from some undisclosed place under her suit jacket. She turned, unlocked the door, pulled it open, and then she turned back to him for one more glance. "Take care, okay? And good luck."

With that she slipped into the car as he held the door. *Say something!* his brain screamed. "'Night." *Not that!* He couldn't even get a real smile on his face as he shut her door. Helpless to get what should have been so easy to say said, he stood there and watched as she started the car. One small step at a time, he backed away and then with one little wave she backed out and drove away. At that moment every mistake he'd ever made paled in comparison to that one.

The air jammed into the top of Lisa's throat as she guided the little car to the other end of the parking garage to the down ramp. *Don't look back. Just don't look back.* But her heart wanted one more glimpse, and defiantly it swung her gaze up to the mirror. In it, he still stood there in that jacket that made her skin burn like flames as he watched her drive away.

Go back! her heart begged. *Please! We'll never find him again!*

With a force that felt like it was ripping her soul in half, she refocused her gaze from the mirror to the concrete in front of her. Guys were all the same. It was the way they were wired—nice looking on the outside and total jerks on the inside. Sure, he hadn't tried to maul her like most of them did, but that was only a matter of time, and if she had the resolve to simply drive away, the amount of time he had to disappoint her would vanish just like he would from her mirror.

As she turned first one corner and then the next, it all seemed so easy—just leave him behind, and he would be gone. However, long after she was home and in bed, the will to deny that that last glance was destined to stay with her forever vanished as well. He would be in her heart forever. And, she knew in every part of her that the 'what ifs' dogging her mind would never really fade away.

Three

"So what time did you finally make it home last night?" Dustin asked as he and Jeff sat on crates in Dustin's kitchen carefully wrapping plates in newspaper.

Jeff shrugged. "Three or so."

Dustin's eyebrows arched. "Three or so? Hm. That could be good. So how was..."

"Lisa," Jeff supplied although just saying the name knifed through his heart.

"She was good-looking."

"Yeah."

They wrapped and then wrapped again. After a few seconds Dustin looked at his friend. "So?"

"So, what?"

In exasperation Dustin sighed. "So what happened?"

There were a myriad of reasons that Jeff didn't want to divulge the whole story, and he wasn't at all sure which one was the most relevant. "I took her to her car."

The newspaper in Dustin's hand crunched. "No kidding? Cool."

"Yeah, well, except that I didn't exactly get her number or anything."

A scowl dropped onto Dustin's features. "You didn't? Why not?"

Because I was an idiot. Jeff shrugged. "I don't know if she would've given it to me anyway."

"So you didn't even ask?" Slowly Dustin shook his head as Eve strode through the kitchen and ran her hand over the broad expanse of her husband's shoulders. "You're never going to believe this one."

"What's that?" she asked, spinning her long hair over her shoulder as she turned.

"Romeo here didn't get her number."

Eve dropped her gaze on Jeff. "What? Why not?"

"He didn't think she would give it to him," Dustin said, filling in all the blanks so Jeff wouldn't have to. "That's great, huh?"

"But you talked to her, right?" Eve asked completely into the conversation.

Jeff stumbled on that one. "Well, yeah."

"So then you've got to know something about her. Where she lives, where she works…"

"She owns her own business—an ad agency in the Travis Tower."

"Well, hallelujah," Dustin said with relief. "At least you've got a little bit of a lead."

Focusing his attention on the newspaper and trying not to drop the plate, Jeff shrugged. "Yeah, but what am I going to do? Knock on every office door in the building until I find her?"

"If that's what it takes, yes!" Dustin said. "For Pete's sake Jeff, I've known you for what? Almost a year now, and she's the first girl I've seen you so much as get a 'Hi' out while she was around."

"Well, yeah, but it's not like she really wanted to be there with me. We were just kind of prisoners of the situation."

"Gee, thanks," Dustin said.

"You know what I mean."

"Yeah, but I'm not blind either. I saw how you were looking at her." A small light sparked in the middle of Dustin's eyes as he reached over to Eve and ran a hand down her arm. "It's the same way I look at my baby."

Eve's eyes went soft as she looked down at him, and Jeff's heart turned over. With one tug Eve sat on Dustin's lap, and an anvil of envy dropped into the pit of Jeff's gut. If he just hadn't been so stupid… "You know, if you two keep that up, the movers are going to get to box this stuff up themselves."

With the tip of her nose, Eve rubbed across Dustin's, and Jeff could tell he could have been a wall decoration for as much as they knew he was in the room. Then Dustin looked over at him past the fall of wavy black hair that Eve trailed behind her as she laid her head on her husband's shoulder.

"Find her office," Dustin said seriously. "Trust me, it's worth it."

"I didn't say midnight, I said navy!" Lisa said as she slung the ad board mock-up to the desk in frustration. "No, no, no." She fought to collect herself as Kurt shifted feet on the other side of her desk. "Look, just pull up the color schemes on your computer." Her hand clicked the mouse. "It's the one on Mountain, not the one on Lilac." She handed the ad board back, and Kurt started to leave. "I need that back in ten."

He nodded, and his stringy brown-blond chin-length bob bounced with his head. As his bland-colored, baggy-clothed body exited her doorway, she laid her head on the desk in utter exasperation. Nothing was going right today. Nothing. Exhausted, she wound her wrist around so she could look at her watch as she blew the piece of hair that had fallen across her eyes up. Forty-seven hours, sixteen minutes and counting until her meeting Monday with Cordell. The illusion that she could do this was evaporating before her eyes.

Forcing her head up to the crook of her hand, she snapped the mouse across the screen in aggravation. It would help if her head would quit pounding. She turned and started to type as she blew that straggly piece of hair back out of her eyes.

"Okay, think," she coached. "This isn't that hard. You've done this before. Think, Lisa. 'Great.' What would be great?" Youth Leaders for the Road We Can't Even See Yet, flowed onto the little rectangle on her computer from her fingertips. "Too long." A click to change the font, and she tried again. Making the Leaders of Tomorrow. "Boring. Boring. Boring. Ugh! This is nuts."

"Umm, boss," Sherie said as she ducked into the office hesitantly.

"Yeah?"

"I've got that play thing tonight for Paige... Remember, I told you about it last week?"

None of her ideas were getting any better.

"So, I was just going to take off now. If that's okay?"

Lisa looked up at her in confusion, and then the words actually got through the frustration and into her brain. "Oh, yeah." She waved the secretary out. "Go. Go."

"Great. Thanks. I'll see you Monday."

"Yeah, Monday." Her attention never really lifted from the screen. Minutes after Sherie had disappeared from the front office, a thought suddenly hit Lisa and she jumped up. "Hey, Sherie!" However, when she made it to the outer office, there was no Sherie. "Okay, so I'll just find it myself." She went over to the filing cabinet and opened the first drawer she came to. "Not that one. No."

A little harder than it needed to be, she slammed that drawer causing the pictures and knickknacks on the top of the cabinet to dance. She grabbed the next drawer but didn't get the latch pushed far enough when she tugged. "Oh, come on." She tried again and this time the drawer slid open. Her gaze bounced across the tabs. "Okay, here's something that could work."

"I've got this," Kurt said from behind her.

She turned and nodded. "Put it on my desk." Without really watching him, she looked through the folder in her hands. Finally something she could use.

"I'm going to get on out of here," Kurt said. "I've got a date."

"Okay," Lisa said without really looking up, and before she did, he was gone. For good measure she grabbed the other two folders associated with the one in her hand and walked into her office reading all three simultaneously with each step. At her desk she sat down and pulled forward. That's when she saw the brochure, meted out in one solid sheet of periwinkle. "I said, 'Navy!'" she screamed to the empty room, slamming the folders down onto her desk.

Furiously she jumped to her feet and very nearly twisted her ankle on the little spot in the carpet that was a little softer than all the others. She yanked the door open. "Kurt!" But the call was met with only silence. As usual, she was all alone in this sinking boat.

The distinct feeling of a total life-shift descended on Jeff as he stood at the door of the fire station on Bagby Street Monday morning. If the others could do this, so could he. It was the only thought keeping him from running. With a small push, he entered the station and glanced around. The trucks, red and shiny silver, brought a smile to his face. Yes, he could do this.

Two young men, one Hispanic, the other too grimy to really tell, walked into the large open room.

"Hayes said, 'Change the oil, not wear it,'" the Hispanic man said, laughing.

"Well, if you would've been helping me like he said..." the other man started but stopped when he saw Jeff standing there. Quickly he wiped some of the grime from his hand and extended it. "Hi. Can we help you?"

"I'm... here to see Captain Hayes," Jeff said, pushing every bit of confidence he had to the surface as he shook the man's hand.

The man who had shaken his hand pointed up the metal mesh stairs to one side by the wall. "Up top."

"Thanks," Jeff said with a nod.

"We're going to need the pressure hose to get you cleaned up," the Hispanic man said as Jeff mounted the first three steps.

"Oh, yeah? I'd like to see you try," the other man shot back, and Jeff laughed. At the top of the staircase, he met up with a door marked simply, *Captain*. A knock and then a louder one, and he heard the voice from the other side.

"Come in."

It seemed to take all of his strength to open that door, and once he did, he looked inside fighting the urge to run. "Captain Hayes?"

The man sitting in the chair behind the desk looked more like a statue than a person. He looked up as Jeff entered, and never really meeting his gaze, Jeff stepped over to the desk and extended his hand.

"Jeff Taylor, Sir. We had an appointment."

"Of course, Taylor. Please, have a seat. You're here about the opening."

"Yes, Sir," Jeff said, wishing his head would quit nodding. "I am."

"This is all very nice," Burke Cordell said, laying an old, withered hand across the paperwork Lisa had carefully laid out for him, "but I've been thinking about doing something a little different with this thing."

"Different, Sir?" Lisa cleared her throat. "Um, what did you have in mind?"

"Well, what I'd really like is more of a cooperative effort. I mean we've had these kinds of conferences before, and only the students who are the go-getters come. Then we put up speakers from the various local business firms, and it gets to be more of a recruiting merry-go-round than really teaching anyone anything about leadership."

Feeling like he was attacking every idea she had just put forth, Lisa curled her fingers around the folders in front of her. "I was under the impression that business leaders were what you had in mind."

"It was." The old man's face fell in thought. "But I've been thinking about it, and every conference is for these same two percent of the kids. What about the other 98 percent? How do they determine their roads in life? Why can't we give them some options too?"

"Yes, Sir," Lisa said, faltering for a second. "But this is a leadership conference. Aren't the leaders supposed to be the top two percent?"

After a beat, Tucker Cordell, Burke's grandson who Lisa had no doubt was the exact model of the top two-percent go-getter that the old man was referring to, laid a hand across the table narrowly missing hers. "I think what Grandfather is saying is that he would like to include some more blue-collar types in this conference."

"That's not what I'm saying," Burke shot back, sending Tucker skittering back to his seat. "I'm just saying there are other types of leaders that make this country great—sure business is a component, but it's not the whole enchilada."

Jumbled messages were running into each other in Lisa's brain, not the least of which were the ten thousand not at all liking the unspoken invitation in Tucker's eyes when she looked at him. "How about this?" She tossed her head back. "There's the volunteers that work over at the homeless shelter. Maybe I could get some of them to come and give addresses."

"See, now that's the kind of thinking I like," Burke said, nodding. "What else you got?"

"Well, there's the city engineering department. The ones who keep up the bridges and the parks, they might be interesting." She wrote that thought down on the paper in front of her.

"Keep talking."

"And then there's the road crews... and the police department..."

"And the fire department." Burke pointed at her paper so she would write that down too. "In fact, I've even got a good friend over at the station on Bagby. Anson Hayes. He's a captain over there. I can set something up for you to talk with him if you'd like."

Her brain didn't like the detour that her heart had suddenly taken, but she nodded in spite of herself. "Yeah, that'd be great."

Jeff wasn't sure if they would even have the phone hooked up yet, but he had to tell somebody, so he dialed the number and sat on the sofa in his little apartment. When the other side clicked, the feminine voice said, "Hello?"

He smiled. So they were farther apart, it didn't mean that he'd totally lost his friends. "Hi, Eve. Is Dustin there?"

"Yeah." In the background there was a tremendous crash and a not so subtle string of curse words. "Baby, it's for you."

Without even trying, Jeff heard the curses that followed his friend to the phone. "Yeah?"

"Maybe I should've come and helped you move in too," Jeff said, enjoying ribbing his friend. "Sounds like you could use the help."

"Oh, yeah? You try moving a six-ton box of shoes up a flight of stairs."

"That's what all that weight training in the academy was for. Didn't you read the manual?"

Dustin laughed. "Well, thanks for that. So, to what do I owe the honor of this call?"

"I just figured you'd like to know I'm not going to be homeless."

"Oh, well, that's nice. How do you figure?"

"I went and talked to Hayes this morning over at Bagby." He wasn't a dramatic person, but the pause certainly had the right effect. "I got it."

"All right! Cool! Congratulations." Dustin's voice faded. "He got the job."

And Jeff heard Eve's voice, "Awesome!"

"Eve says, 'Congrats.'"

"Tell her thanks," Jeff said, and his smile shone inside and out. "You start next Monday, right?"

"Yep. We've got a week to find my razor. You?"

"Thursday. I'm going in tomorrow though to get my gear. That kind of thing."

"Fabulous." Dustin said something to Eve who said something back. "Hey, Eve wants to know if you've gone over to Travis yet."

Jeff shifted on the sofa, which was suddenly uncomfortable. "No, I've been working on making sure I can keep eating."

"Okay, I understand that, but don't keep finding excuses or you might just miss your chance."

I already did. "Yeah, maybe I'll go tomorrow."

"Terrific. Oh, and tell me how it goes. We want to know."

"Will do."

The next afternoon after his short appearance at the fire station, Jeff found himself turning right on Travis and staring up at the shiny glass building towering above him. The GTO slowed as it rolled closer to the building, and he wondered if she was in fact in that building at this very moment. He thought about turning into the parking garage just to see if the little white Cavalier might be there, but that was crazy.

Even driving by was crazy. A girl like her, she probably had a million guys after her, and every one of them had more money and more class than he would ever have. Trying not to dwell on that any longer than it took to get him to drive by the garage entrance, he shifted into a higher gear and drove on past. No, Lisa wasn't in his league, and he certainly wasn't in hers. Better to leave it be than risk having to hear that face-to-face. At least this way he had the dreams and the memories. Yes, it was better this way.

"Okay, guys, this is the deal," Lisa said as she sat at the head of the conference desk with her rag tag team Tuesday at four. "We're going in a different direction with this Youth thing, and Cordell wants something solid by Monday. So while I'm working on that,

Kurt I need the new concept sheets for the Zebra Carpet campaign on my desk by Thursday, and I want more than just a few sketches too. I need radio scripts and billboard ideas, and I need the latest ad figures for Chronicle space."

"Got it," Kurt said, and he wrote that down. Lisa wanted to ask if he really did, but there was no time.

"Joel, I need an ad-by-ad breakdown of everything we've done so far on Kamden, and we need to start month-by-month tracking on Kamden sales, too. I don't want last week to happen again. Okay? I want to see those as soon as you round them all up. I also need six or seven more usable concepts for that one on my desk by Monday morning.

"Sherie, I need you to pull up the lists the schools gave us, write the counselors a preliminary letter asking about the viability of a leadership conference for the other 98 percent."

"The other 98 percent?" Sherie asked, stopping the notation.

"Yep, all those future leaders who don't even know they're leaders yet." Lisa's thought train stopped. "Hey, I kind of like that." She jotted it on her notebook. "I want to see the letter before you send it." Her gaze traveled over her crew. "That's it. But I want to be kept apprised of all of this stuff even though I'm not going to be putting in too much face time around here for a week or so. I'm going to be too busy scaring up willing or non-willing souls for this speaking list. Questions?"

None were forthcoming.

"Great. Then let's hit it." They all started to move. "Oh, Sherie, did you get that thing set up with Hayes?"

"Five Thursday," Sherie confirmed.

"Fantastic."

Four

It was like the first day of the rest of Jeff's life, and he felt it. He took one look at himself in the black, HFD T-shirt and smiled. It felt good. He grabbed his keys and his jacket and left the apartment. As he drove through the early morning light down the streets of the city he loved, his mind drifted back through all the turns that had led him to this moment.

A few he smiled at, more than one made his heart pang, but each formed a small brushstroke in the picture he now saw before him. At the station he parked and walked to the door as the phrase, *this is it* tracked through his mind, and with that he pushed in.

"Yeah, well, you already owe me your wife and kids so what's the point of even making that bet?" the Hispanic guy said as he and the other guy worked pulling down a long, grimy cotton hose next to the truck.

"My wife and kids?" The other guy carefully fed the hose off the top. "Just tell me when you're coming to get them, and I'll be sure to have their stuff packed and on the front porch waiting for you."

"You would…" At that moment the door that hadn't fully closed behind Jeff slammed, and both gazes snapped to him. "Hey, it's the new guy."

His friend straightened and extended a hand. "Welcome. Hunter Witkowski."

"Jeff Taylor." Jeff extended his own hand and a smile.

The Hispanic man jumped off the bumper and over the hose, wiped his hand, and extended it. "Dante Ramirez."

"Nice to meet you, Dante," Jeff said with a nod. Not really

knowing what to do next, Jeff looked back to the station behind.
"Come on," Dante said. "I'll show you around."

"These are the ones for the billboard," Kurt said as if he might be
shot at any moment for saying the wrong thing. "And here's the
newest price scale for the Chronicle."

The more she looked, the more Lisa's head hurt. "Wait. On
this billboard, what are you trying to get across anyway? I mean,
this is confusing me, and I'm just sitting here."

"Well, the whole 'We've got every kind of carpet you've ever
even thought about putting down' angle just came to me."

"Just came to you. Like that?" Lisa looked up, feeling defeat
right behind her. "At 70 miles an hour, do you know how many
words people can read?"

Kurt shifted in the chair. "No."

"I'll give you a hint." She looked down and quickly counted
the words. "It's less than 13 plus all this address and the phone
number and the website information. You can't put all of this on
there. It doesn't work like that."

"Well, I just thought they needed contact information…"

"No, this is information overload." She pushed the board
back to him. "Tighten it up. I don't want more than ten words, and
address or whatever is part of that—period."

"Ten? But…"

She cut him off by looking at her watch. "I don't have time to
hold your hand right now. I've got a meeting." Even as she talked,
she stood and straightened her navy suit jacket. "I want the new
one on my desk before you leave tonight." Fixing the knot of her
hair, she stood in front of the tiny mirror off to the side of her
desk before she ran a finger across the edge of her deep red
lipstick.

"But this one took me…"

On her heel she turned. "By the time you leave." With that
she grabbed her black leather notepad, her purse, and her keys and
left Kurt still standing in her office. Quickly she strode past
Sherie's desk. "I'll be back."

"Good luck," Sherie called after her, and Lisa threw a hand in
the air in answer.

Once in the car she checked her watch again, fluffed the bangs on her upsweep and twisted the starter. She needed this one. This one was her ace, around Hayes she was sure she could build the rest of the program.

The first two tasks were learning people's names and getting acquainted with the equipment. This truck was far and away better than the model they had trained on, and Jeff was relieved to note that although he was new, the others had all been together for awhile. At least it wouldn't be a spin the dial to see who shows up kind of program.

Already he felt right at home. Dante and Hunter kept him entertained with their non-stop Abbot and Costello routine, and the best part was that to participate, he really didn't have to say so much as a single word. They were in the middle of refilling air tanks, listening to Dante explain why Levi's come in so many different styles when Jeff saw the flash of the window of the front door swing across the wall behind him.

At first when he looked over to the threshold, he thought it was just his brain creating some kind of mirage in the sunshine. Then the fact that clearly this was all a dream he was having flashed across his consciousness, but not one rational thought was able to erase his heart magnetizing his gaze to that door. To her. The dark hair upswept, the curve of her suit at the slim waist, the heels. It was, and yet it couldn't be. In shock, he ducked behind the truck, busying himself with the first tank that attached itself to his hand.

"Hmm, excuse me," she said, and there wasn't a part of him that still believed he was wrong about who was standing in that doorway.

"Hi," Dante said smoothly as Jeff cowered behind the truck imagining the scene because he couldn't see it. "Something we could help you with?"

"I'm looking for Captain Hayes," she said, and the lilt of her voice tap-danced across Jeff's heart. He closed his eyes feeling every wisp of it.

"Oh, he's up in his office. Come on, I'll show you," Dante said.

Jeff heard the pings of her heels as she climbed the meshed-wire metal stairs across the station from where he stood. Lisa. It was Lisa. She was here. Why was she here? And what on earth should he do next? Dustin would know what to do, but Dustin wasn't here. *Thank goodness.* Jeff peeked out from behind the truck to see the polished navy weave of her skirt back high above him on the landing.

Lest she turn around and see him, he ducked back and flattened himself against the back of the truck. Options rushed over options—all of them viable had he been anybody else. Maybe he could just conveniently be hanging around when she came back down, but how long would she be up there? And what did she want with Hayes? Advertising didn't exactly lend itself to visiting fire stations on a regular basis.

"Hey, Jeff," Hunter said from the top of the truck, "want to help me with this?"

"Oh, sure." Jeff reached for the rung and pulled himself up just as she disappeared into the office. Yes, he could just conveniently be hanging around. That would work, but then what?

He didn't miss the looks back up to the door that Dante made as he returned down the steps and strode to the truck. Two vaults and he joined them up top.

"Now there's a set of chrome I wouldn't mind shining," Dante said, fanning himself as if the fire station had itself just been set ablaze.

"Nice hooks and ladders," Hunter agreed, and the outsides of Jeff's ears went hot.

He crossed his arms. "What did you need?"

"Oh, here." Hunter bent to pick up a piece of supply hose. "Help me with this."

It was nice to have something to do, something to make them stop talking, and something so his heart wouldn't actually pound right out of his chest. As they worked, his own gaze continually traveled up those steps. They were right of course, she was gorgeous, but his memory and his heart said she was far, far more than that.

"Right now I'm putting together a proposal to get the schools interested," Lisa said when Captain Hayes looked at her as if he might throw her out before she got him talked into anything. "We've done the traditional businesses talk to the top kids for hundreds of years, we just wanted to try something new with this thing."

"I thought you were in advertising." The scowl on the Captain's face deepened the wrinkles lining his face.

"I am, but my uncle works for Mr. Cordell, and well... he thought it would be good advertising for their firm, except their corporate agency thought it was just too far out of what they wanted to do, so my uncle suggested me, and here I am."

"And here you are." Hayes crossed his arms. "And you want me to come and speak at this little gathering of yours?"

"Well, yes—unless you want to send someone in your place. Like I said earlier, nothing is really set yet. We're just putting out feelers to see what's possible on this thing."

"I don't know. I don't exactly make a habit of booking speaking engagements."

Lisa's heart fell with her face. Her ace was slipping away.

"However..." Hayes pulled one of his drawers open and slipped a small card out of it. "Here's the number for Vincent Fletcher with the downtown PD. You give him a call. If you can talk Fletch into this thing, I'll consider it."

"Oh, thank you, Sir." She took the card, wondering when she had become so attached to the inner workings of the city of Houston. "I'll give him a call this afternoon."

Hayes smiled with a secret behind his gray eyes, and Lisa's gaze caught on it. Something in his eyes said he'd just won clemency. Before he told her outright that he would jump from the Transco Tower before he'd get up in front of a group of high schoolers, she stood and offered her hand. "Thanks so much for your time."

"Let me know what Fletch says," Hayes said with that smile she didn't like very much.

"I'll let you know."

In the deepest part of his gut, Jeff heard the click of the upstairs door. He had been listening for nothing else during the past half hour. The waiting was enough to make his nerves fray. The instant he heard it, however, his gaze snapped to the figure in navy as it turned and quietly closed the door a story above. Panic gripped him in a tight fist and swung him off the top of the truck and down to the concrete below where his legs barely caught his weight.

"She's back," he heard Dante whisper from above, and instantly Jeff grabbed an air tank and put it into the truck. The heels clicked down the stairs, pinging across his heart like a hammer on spikes. Concrete. She was down, and his breathing stopped.

"Get what you were after?" Dante asked, and all of Jeff's motions stopped.

"Yeah, I did. Thanks," she said, and in his mind he saw the smile that had spent the last five days floating through his dreams.

"See you later?" Dante called.

"Yeah." The door clicked open. "Later." And the door closed along with Jeff's eyes. Ugh. If only he had an ounce of courage, he would run after her. Then again if he had any courage at all, he would've long ago had her number.

"Taylor," Hunter called from the top, and when Jeff looked up, all he saw was a roll of hose dropping on him fast. "Catch."

She's gone. Get back to work, his brain screamed as he fought not to fall over the folds of hose. *She's gone.* The only problem was that his heart was screaming the same thing.

Truth be told Lisa had never been all that attached to fire stations or police departments. No, for way the most part, she had tried to avoid them at all costs; however, as she walked away, she couldn't help but wonder if Jeff had gotten that position he had applied for. A small smile traced across even the doom surrounding her mission. She hoped he had. That soft spot in her heart filled her throat. Jeff somebody in a city of three million. It was a given that she would never see him again, and for all the logic of her head saying that was a good thing, she knew in some deep part of her that his name would trace across the expanse of her heart every time she was lucky enough to pass a fire station.

Long before his car actually got to it, Jeff noticed the Zebra sign as he inched his way up Eastex freeway the next morning after work. He smiled at how intricately she had worked the stripes. It was a work of art—even if it wasn't hanging in some stuffy museum.

Absently his hand shifted gears down, wondering where she was at this moment. At work? Going home? Somewhere on this very highway?

Wherever she was, he knew she would have his heart with her forever.

It was a full 48 hours before Lisa slowed down enough to think about him again. The preceding hours had been a mish-mash of wedding gowns, campaign concepts, and toasts. They were all intertwined so that her brain was having a hard time sorting them all out. However, as she stood at the top step of the church, watching her sister look so in love, her heart drifted back to the sight of his strong arms and those beautiful pools of blue.

In a way she was glad she hadn't pursued anything. He was probably better as a dream anyway. That way he hadn't done anything horrible to ruin her perfect picture of him. Who cared that she had no real chance with him? She didn't anyway. Love in the real world was too messy. There were too many things that could get in the way—like what he was really like and what she was really like.

Knowing that, though, made the dream that much better. She would take the dream of him over the reality of all the guys she had ever actually known in a heartbeat. That understanding only solidified when Luke, Cory's best bud in the whole world, the classy guy her sister's new husband had picked for a best man, chose the moment she had potatoes and brown gravy two inches from her mouth to slide his hand under the table and onto her knee.

A barely muffled gasp jumped from her throat as the potatoes leaped from her fork and landed squarely on the center of her cream skirt with the swirl of vines and pink flowers.

"Lisa," Haley said with concern looking down the head table, "are you okay?"

"Umm, yeah," Lisa said, wishing she could knock Mr. Hand into another wedding party.

"Here, let me help you." Luke's tone dropped as he reached for his napkin.

"I've got it!" Lisa slid backward as anger slashed through the words. "I'm fine. I'll just be in the ladies' room."

"Lis, are you sure?" Haley asked her sister's retreating back.

In the bathroom, Lisa turned the water on full blast, before dabbing and then scrubbing at the gravy. "Great." With no small amount of work, the stain finally looked like it was at least part of the whole general color scheme of the skirt. The only problem was, the water spot didn't. Trying not to think about the logistics of her undertaking, she wiped the side of the sink off, sat down carefully and hit the button on the hand dryer. Yeah, this was exactly where she wanted to spend her evening. If Luke so much as looked at her wrong, he was in for a rude awakening.

It took more time than she wanted, but her skirt finally dried about the time her hatred for all things male reached a boiling point. With a look in the mirror to straighten and perfect, she put her head high, and walked back out to rejoin the festivities. However, she had barely sat down when Luke laid a casual arm across the back of her chair and leaned over to her ear.

"It's almost time for the toast. You want to go first, or should I?" he asked in a whisper that sent puffs of air skittering across her neck.

"Umm, you can go first," she said, fighting to smile.

"Good." His proximity hadn't shifted. "I like to go first."

Her smile faded as he stood, and she choked back a scream. In seconds the crowded hall was laughing at something he had said, and Lisa willed herself to just get through this. When he sat back down, Luke laid that same hand on her, only this time it missed her knee and landed several inches higher. "Your turn."

Putting her head high, she pushed his hand away, pushed away from the table, and stood. She picked up her glass and turned to the happy couple, vowing that if Luke so much as brushed across her backside as she did, she would douse him with the sparkling liquid in her glass.

"Haley," Lisa said, and her sister's gaze made all the bad things slide from her mind, "I wish you luck, and I wish you love. I want you to know I'm here for you always."

A chorus of "Ahh" sounded through the hall.

"And Cory, if you hurt her, I'll kill you," she said, and although there was a measure of levity in her voice, she knew there was just enough seriousness to get her point across. She raised her glass. "To Haley and Cory."

"Haley and Cory!" Rang out around her.

For a full two hours Lisa had managed to stay out of Luke's vicinity; however, when the third dance of the evening arrived, she knew she had run out of time to run.

"You know." Luke pulled her closer even as she strained to push him away. "They say that there are two couples that make it home together on a wedding night—the bride and groom, and the two that stand up for them."

"Oh, really?" Lisa could smell the alcohol on his breath as her brain threatened mutiny if she didn't figure out a way to get away from him soon. "Too bad that's not going to be happening tonight."

"Why not?" His hand tightened around hers as his arm did the same. "I'm free. You're free. We can be free together."

"Because I think you're a jerk," Lisa said as Haley and Cory danced by all smiles.

"Don't get any ideas, Lisa," Haley teased.

"Don't worry!" Lisa called after them, but they were gone.

"You smell so good." Luke leaned into her until the only space that could be counted as hers was that underneath her ribcage. "What's that perfume anyway?"

"Desire," Lisa said, and then immediately wished she had thought to lie.

"Hmm, fitting. Don't you think?"

She wrenched her arm between them for breathing room if nothing else. "I wouldn't know." The music picked that moment to end, and for a half second she thought the torture was over. Unfortunately Luke didn't get the same message. Like a steel trap his arm wrapped around her, and barring pitching him to the floor and running, she didn't see a good way to get away.

The next song started, and he never so much as asked her before she was again fighting against the press of his body. Not one part of her wanted to know how long he was planning to keep this up—or what ingenious designs he had for the remainder of the evening. Not one.

By midnight Lisa wasn't sure if it was the hour or the non-sleep she had gotten the two nights before, but her eyes were in an all out battle just to stay open.

"Well, it's that time." Luke strode over to her and took her hand, which she promptly jerked away from him.

"What time?"

"Time to take the newlyweds to their car of course."

"I thought I'd just stay here and…"

"We're ready," Cory said, his bride's hand tucked in his.

"Great, we are too," Luke said, and before Lisa had a chance to realize what was coming, he spun and caught her shoulders under his arm. "Let's get."

"Where're you going?" Lisa asked in anger when Luke turned in the opposite direction from the hall after they had dropped their passengers off. Her eyelids felt like they might betray her and close permanently at any moment, but she knew the danger of allowing them that luxury. "The hall's that way."

"My place," Luke said, trying to sound smooth. "Just sit back and relax. We'll be there in a second." As if he really thought this was leading somewhere, he reached over and his hand landed across Lisa's knee.

"Umm, no." She pushed his hand away. "We're not. We're going back to the hall."

He looked at her in annoyance. "What is your problem?"

"Guys," she said, irritation searing her tone. "Guys are my problem. Now take me back or you're not going to have to wonder who's got a problem."

Luke's face fell. "Jeez. Cory said you were bad, but he didn't say you were an ice queen."

Ice queen. She folded her arms as she pressed herself against the opposite door. She rather liked that title.

Jeff's first real call came at rush hour on Monday evening. Getting his employment records in line was a far more daunting task than he had thought it would be when he went in that afternoon, and now he was stuck in wall-to-wall traffic. With the window rolled down, he laid his arm through the opening and drummed his fingers to the static-mixed music on the AM radio. It had been a good week—not really exciting, but in his line of work, that was a good thing. The farther he drove up Eastex, however, the slower traffic got. He could just see the zebra painted billboard in the distance, and he smiled at the thoughts it pulled up.

The wedding was over by now, and he wondered how work had gone for her this week. He thought again about Dustin's idea of knocking on every door in her office building, and if it hadn't been so totally not him, he might have considered it. The honking from around him brought him out of his daydream, and he looked around. Cars were everywhere, and although it was always slow going at this time of day, this was more like no going. In fact as he looked ahead, nothing seemed to be moving at all. That's when he saw the people almost a mile ahead of him, standing on the right side of the road in one big knot of humanity.

There was only one thing that brought great crowds of people out of their cars on a rush-hour drive home—tragedy. His first thought was a wreck, his second that emergency vehicles were going to have a terrible time getting up on the freeway and to the injured at this time of day. It was a decision, and yet really there was no decision at all as he angled his car as far off the side of the road as he could get it, parked it, got out and sprinted past the now honking and beeping mess.

The closer he got, the more he knew it had to be bad for that many people to be standing there. When he reached the first straggler of the group, he asked, "What's going on?"

"Somebody's jumping," came the reply, and Jeff's feet shifted up a gear.

On the outskirts of the crowd, he pushed through. "Fire department, excuse me, fire department." He felt the gazes of the people he passed, but he pressed on. This was no time to be shy about his place in the world. "Excuse me, excuse me." When he finally broke through to the other side of the crowd, all the training he had amassed suddenly seemed horribly inconsequential. There, standing on the other side of the concrete railing, was a young man, perhaps a decade younger than he himself or maybe more. His arms were stretched out behind him, holding onto the concrete wall, but with one look Jeff could see the precariousness of that hold. With no time to review any manuals, he stepped past the crowd and approached the scene slowly. It was as though the world around him was in mayhem, and he was in the eye of the storm.

"Hey," Jeff said as if he was walking up to Dustin to say good

47

morning.

The young man, wild-eyed and wary, spun to look at him, and Jeff saw his hold slip. "Stay away. I'm going to jump. I swear I will."

Jeff held up both hands to signal that he wasn't coming any closer. "It's cool, man. I'm staying right here." He took a breath to calm the adrenaline rushing through him. "You know, jumping isn't going to solve anything."

The kid's gaze turned back to the street below. "Yes it will."

A fight was the last thing he wanted to start. "Okay, well, then what's so bad that this is the answer?"

"Everything."

"Everything, huh? Yeah, well,… I'm sorry what was your name?"

The gaze was back with more anger this time. "My name?"

"Yeah, I mean if we're going to have this little conversation, it might be nice if I at least knew your name."

"Oh." The gaze turned back to the wind. "It's… it's Parker."

"Okay, Parker. Well, it's nice to meet you. I'm Jeff." One slow inch at a time he moved closer. "Hey, man, can we talk about this? I mean, come on, you don't want to do this."

"Yes, I do. I'm sick of life."

"Oh really? Tell me one thing that's so bad it's worth this."

A pause as the horns continued to sound from every level around them.

"Why should I tell you? You don't care. You're just like all the rest of them."

"The rest of who?" Jeff heard the wail of a siren blending in with the horns, and he knew help was on the way. However, they were still too far to get here in time if he didn't keep talking. "Tell me who you're talking about, Parker."

"Everyone. Mom, Dad, the kids at school."

"They don't care about you?"

"No, they'll all be glad when I'm gone. Then they can pick on somebody else."

"Pick on somebody? Who? The kids at school?"

Slowly the edges of the light brown hair moved up and down over the dark black glasses frames.

"Oh, I see, so you're going to give them the power to kill you, too?" Jeff asked pointedly, hating every gust of wind that brushed past them.

"What?" Parker turned to Jeff taken aback by the statement.

"Well, they push you around at school, right? What do they do? Make fun of you?" The gaze turned back to the street as the head nodded. "And trash your stuff?" The nodding continued. "And make it so nobody else even wants to be your friend?" Every word was hitting the mark. "And so you're answer to that is to hand them the power to push you off the edge of a bridge. Good plan."

The nodding stopped as Jeff looked up and saw the paramedics running up the shoulder from the other direction. Instinctively, he put his hands up to slow them down. In Parker's state it would take only one surprise to send him plummeting to the asphalt four stories below. One heartbeat and Jeff made eye contact with the first paramedic that broke through the crowd. That one look stopped the young man cold. The paramedic, several inches shorter than Jeff and looking like a cocky jock with his hat turned backward, halted and then approached on soft feet. A silent conversation passed between them, and the paramedic nodded his understanding of the situation.

"You don't understand," Parker said from the edge, and both gazes snapped to him.

"Then help me," Jeff said softly. "Help me understand."

Before he even heard the words, he heard the tears. "I go there every day… and every day, it's the same thing. They hate me so they push me down, and they call me a maggot and a faggot and they say the only thing I'm really good at is being a punching bag."

Jeff looked across at his partner in this rescue, and the ache bled through his eyes as well.

"They pull my shorts down in P.E., and they throw my clothes out the window, and I never did anything to them. I swear I didn't. I tell them to stop, but they just think it's funny, and they make more fun of me. I told one of the teachers, but he said to suck it up and be a man. Well, I'm tired of being a man. I'm tired of hurting all the time. They can just find somebody else to pick on from now on."

"And they will," Jeff said slowly. Instantly his partner looked over at him in fearful shock. For a second, a question ran through his face, and then Jeff knew he understood. "When you're gone tomorrow, they'll find someone else to pick on, and they won't even remember you. Is that really what you want?"

"He's right," the paramedic said, matching his soft tone. Parker's gaze swung around to him as Jeff's heart caught in his throat. "He is. If you jump, you give them the last laugh. Checkmate. They win." The world and Jeff's heart screeched to a halt. "Is that really what you want, man?"

A gust brushed past them, and Jeff held his breath.

"No," Parker finally said like a breath. "I don't. I don't know. I'm just so confused."

"Then this's no time to be making a big decision like this one," Jeff said, sensing the tri-bond that had just formed between them. He took a small step forward. "Come on, Parker. Take my hand and come back across. We can work this out. I promise."

"It's just so hard," Parker said, and Jeff saw the hand on the other side release.

"Parker?" He held his hand out palm up. "Just take my hand. Okay? Just take my hand, and we'll talk about this." One agonizing inch at a time, the hand came across, and finally it touched Jeff's. He could feel the life flowing through that hand—its potential. "Good. Good, man. Okay, careful."

One foot at a time, Parker scaled the concrete wall separating them, and when he was back in the land of the living, Jeff breathed a grateful sigh of relief.

Slowly Parker slid down the concrete to the asphalt as fatigue crowded over his features. Jeff sat on his heels next to the paramedic as the other rescue personnel worked to disperse the crowd. He laid a gentle hand on the bony shoulder of the young teenager. "How you doing? You okay?"

The nod was there but barely.

"Good, these guys are going to take care of you now. Okay?"

Sad, frightened eyes looked up at him. "You're leaving?"

"No," Jeff said without hesitation, "but I don't think you want me checking you out. Doctoring's not really my department."

Two other paramedics broke in as Jeff stood and stepped over to the railing. It was then that he saw the news trucks and the gathering that was now dispersing beneath the bridge. One life. Hardly noticed to this point, and yet when the possibility of it leaving the earth arrived, everyone else stopped to take notice. Why was that? *Why doesn't anyone stop until it's all over?* He breathed out against the air that was blowing in his face.

"He was lucky you were here," the voice said from behind him, and Jeff turned to see that backward turned cap. The paramedic, looking even younger than he had a few moments before, held out a fist, and Jeff hit the top of it.

"I think I was more scared than he was," Jeff admitted.

"Well, you didn't show it." Then the paramedic held out his hand. "A.J. Knight."

"Jeff Taylor." It was amazing the strength of a friendship formed in a crisis.

"You with the department?" A.J. asked in reference to the little yellow letters on Jeff's T-shirt.

"Yeah, I just started last week."

"Cool, we need more like you out here."

"Just trying to help." Then he looked over to Parker, who was now surrounded by the emergency crew but standing again. "I think I'll just go over and see how he's doing."

"I'll go with you." Together they turned and approached the little group.

"Hey, Parker," Jeff said when he got close enough to see the young man. "You good?"

The only thing keeping the tears from falling from the young man's eyes was the knot of men surrounding them. "Yeah."

"I'm glad you made it back, man."

The looks Tucker was giving her sent chills—and not the good kind—up Lisa's spine Tuesday afternoon as she sat across the table for lunch with him and his grandfather.

"It's like this whole kid on the bridge thing," Burke said, chewing on his steak. "That kid's got no home life, no friends, the kids pick on him every day. What do we expect a kid in that situation to do? It's either kill everybody else or kill yourself. Two choices and they're both rotten. That's the kind of kid I want to reach with this thing."

Lisa nodded, fighting to look interested even as her lunch crawled back up into her throat. One Luke a week should be punishment enough, but if she wasn't losing her perceptiveness, another one was sitting right across from her at this very moment.

"So, what did Anson say?" Burke asked, jerking Lisa from her karate fantasy.

"Oh, he gave me the number for Vincent Fletcher. He's like

the police chief or something. I've got a meeting with him in the morning. As soon as I get him on board, I'll go back and talk to Hayes."

"Fletcher's tough," Burke said, twisting his face out of normal. "Anson thought he would help?"

"He thought it was worth a try," Lisa hedged. She wished her gaze would just quit sending alarm signals to her brain. This was no time for that. She pulled herself up to her full height. "Besides I can be pretty tough myself."

"Yeah? Well, I hope so," Burke said unhappily. "Otherwise Fletch just might chew you up and spit you out."

Terrific. The ones she wanted to talk to didn't want to talk to her, and the ones she didn't want to get within fifteen feet of, ogled her like a cat looking at the catch of the day. "I'm not worried. I'm sure I can handle Fletcher. I've handled guys far, far worse." And she smiled sweetly at the cat sitting across the table from her.

Five

"Options," Lisa said as she sat across the desk from Vincent Fletcher Wednesday morning. "It's all about options. We've got kids out there who don't have options. They look around, and all they see is that they don't have the options that the other kids do. It's called learned helplessness." She had read that several years before and had thought it was all a bunch of psychobabble at the time, but if it had a shot at getting through to the human version of Jabba the Hut, sitting cross-armed in front of her, it was worth a shot. "What Cordell Enterprises is trying to do is to show these kids that they have real options, and not just to be some hired hand working for minimum wage in some plant, but real options to lead and to make a difference in the community."

"And why would I want some minimum wage anvil joining my force?" Fletcher asked, clearly unimpressed.

"Because you see, Sir, we're all minimum wage anvils until we decide to be something more. But none of us decides to be more until we really believe that's possible. You think I ever thought about starting my own company when I was 15? No way. That was too far away to think about, but I was lucky enough to have a teacher who showed some interest in me. She helped me with my art. She made my art important, and she helped me see that there were lots of other options with art other than just trying to get it hung in some gallery.

"That's what I'm wanting to give these kids—options. Without them, they're going to end up in here on one side of the desk. I'm just asking that you take a couple hours out of your very busy schedule to show them that the other side of the desk is possible too." She sat, sensing that all the arguments in the world would get her nowhere. "But if you're too busy..."

Slowly Fletcher leaned forward. "Are the schools in yet?"

Exasperation jumped from her. "See, that's the problem, everyone's standing on the sidelines, going, 'Well, I'm not committing until they commit.' And while everyone's standing around waiting for somebody else to make the first move, we've got kids carrying guns to school and jumping off bridges because we're all just too busy to be bothered, or we're too worried about how it will look if we get in and nobody else does. Well, I'll be honest with you, Sir. All the heroics on all the bridges in the whole world aren't going to matter a single ounce if somebody doesn't get in this darn boat and start rowing."

With steely hard eyes Fletcher looked at her. "You're intense, you know that, Ms. Matheson?"

"So, I've been told," she said with no smile whatsoever. "So, what do you say, Sir? You in or out?"

He took one breath, shook his head, and exhaled. "Okay, I'm in."

"Looks like you pulled some overtime," Dante said when Jeff walked into the break room on Thursday morning. He was glad to be back to work. Time off was just one solid sheet of agony.

"Overtime?" Jeff asked as he grabbed a drink from the water fountain. "Is the new schedule out?"

"No, man," Dante said in exasperation. "That whole hero thing on the bridge. I think Hunter's even got it on tape."

"Oh, great."

"No, man, you looked good. It's cool." Dante lowered his eyes with concern. "Isn't it?"

"I was just doing my job." He went to the cabinet and looked inside. "It wasn't a big deal."

"Wrong, man," Dante said as he stood and set his glass in the sink next to Jeff. "Saving a life is a very big deal."

On his heel, Dante turned and walked out as Jeff's head fell on the weight of the statement. He hadn't meant that the way it sounded. The fact that God had placed him on that bridge at that moment was not a responsibility he took lightly, nor one he would've simply passed on, but he just didn't like the five seconds of fame that went with it. It was going to be a long day.

"Hey, Taylor, how's it going?" Hunter asked as he strode into the break room where Jeff was grabbing a drink six hours later.

"Good," Jeff said. "What do we have left?"

"Station clean-up. You can start with the bathrooms and then do the break room," Hunter said, looking around at the tables littered with remnants of meals gone by. "Oh, and don't forget the gunky stuff around this sink. It's looking pretty skanky."

Dante strode in.

"Come on, Dant-man, we've got an appointment with a basketball court," Hunter said, turning Dante around.

"Destroy the skankiness." Jeff looked at the sink when they were gone. "I can do that." He was right earlier. This day was turning out great.

The more they told her it couldn't be done because nobody wanted to do it, the more determined Lisa became to make this work. One way or the other if she had to drag these people up to that podium, she was going to make this happen. Hayes wouldn't be thrilled that Fletcher said yes, of that much she was sure, but what she couldn't quite decide was if he would have the guts to stick to his word anyway. Guys and promises. He was a guy, so it didn't look good going in.

With a shove she pushed through the station's front door at four o'clock, but this time there weren't people swarming across the tops of the trucks. In fact, nobody seemed to be anywhere. She shook her head and peered around the station. "Hello? Anybody here? Hello?" The braid at her back swung around her shoulder as she turned to glance outside. Still no one. The trucks were here, so they couldn't all be gone. "Hello? Anybody here?"

"Sorry. Everybody's out…" The moment froze between them as suddenly the man she had seen only in her dreams for more than two weeks was somehow, beyond comprehension, standing right in front of her. "…back. Lisa?"

Her sanity ran smack into the expanse of muscles protruding from his black T-shirt. "Jeff? Um. What…?" She laughed. "Wow. This is a surprise."

He looked like he wanted to smile for one short moment, then he looked down at the plastic, kitchen-cleaning gloves on his hands. Not too subtly he pulled them off. "Yeah, it is." The gloves were off now, and he looked around for somewhere to put them. Finally he laid them on a table behind the wall. "Umm, are you here to see the captain again?"

"Again?" she asked in surprise.

"I… Oh. Um." He scratched the top of his nose. "Well, the guys said there was a… that a lady came to see him… the other day… We don't get many ladies coming in around here unless they're carrying cotton hoses. I just thought…"

She smiled at his nervousness. "Actually I'm supposed to have an appointment with him in five minutes."

"Oh, well. He was out back with the guys the last I saw him," Jeff said, but even after his words stopped, nobody moved. Her eyebrows went up when she sensed that she might have to figure out where out back was herself. Then the realization lit in his eyes. "Oh, uh. I can show you… if you want."

"That would probably help."

"It's this way." He pointed back in the direction he had come. Wishing they weren't in the middle of a fire station, she nodded and half-following, half-leading, she walked down that hallway to another. At the end of the second hallway, he slipped in front of her and popped the door open as sounds of an in-progress basketball game met her ears. Together they walked to the fence, and she noticed how he kept himself and his gaze well away from her. "Umm, Captain! There's someone here to see you!"

In that instant the game stopped, and eight sets of eyes turned to them.

"We had an appointment?" Lisa pointed to her watch, and in annoyance, Captain Hayes walked off the court and grabbed a towel off the bench.

"We didn't cancel that?" he asked gruffly.

"Uh, no, Sir, we didn't." The heel of her shoe shifted under her weight. Standing there, the gazes of three-quarters of a dozen guys trained on her, she felt like that fish in the market window again. Even that would've been all right except that her senses kept telling her just how close Jeff's arm was to hers, and that alone was enough to send her sanity scattering.

"Oh, well, I thought we had." Hayes ran the towel over his face. "Well, let's get this over with I guess. You're going to have to play without me, boys."

The three of them barely made it back to the door before the game resumed. At the door Jeff opened it, and pushing the strand of hair behind her ear, Lisa entered in front of him. The darkness engulfed her after the brightness of the sunshine, and she willed herself not to trip on some unseen obstacle on her way through the back of the station.

"Umm, if you don't mind, I'm just going to duck in here and get cleaned up a little," Hayes said, stopping at a door.

"Oh, no problem," she said amiably. "I'll just be down here… waiting."

He nodded and disappeared through the door. And just like that, they were alone again. Hesitating with each small movement, she turned and headed back for the front. "So, I guess this means you got that job then?"

Jeff held his hands out palms up. "Yep, this is it."

"Nice." When they reached the break room door, he stopped, and she stopped too. "So, why weren't you out…?"

"New guy on board," he said with a tight smile. "I get to clean, they get to play."

"Ah, low man on the totem pole."

"Basically." Neither gaze could hold the other for more than a few seconds at a time, and his finally fell to the floor between them. "I didn't know we were exactly into advertising the stations. Is business that bad?"

She laughed. "No, not really. I'm just trying to rope Hayes into speaking at the youth thing, but I don't think he's too thrilled about it."

"Yeah, I could kind of tell."

"Was it that obvious?" She leaned closer to him although her arms were safely crossed at her chest. "I think he hates me."

His soft blue eyes caught hers. "Why would he hate you?"

She wrinkled her nose. "Because I didn't just go away."

A breath made it past his throat just as a door snapped down the hallway, and instantly they both looked toward it and backed away from each other. Through the darkened hallway, Hayes emerged.

"I'm ready," he said, and with only one backward glance at Jeff, she left him standing there by the break room, wishing she never had to walk away.

The scum around the sink was gone long before the guys came back in, and it was immediately obvious that her appearance had given them ample fodder for conversation.

"I'm not saying I'm going after her," Hunter said, sliding into one of the break room chairs. "I'm just saying at this moment, I wouldn't mind being in the chief's chair."

"Did you catch a ring on that finger?" Dante asked. "Because I could handle having some of that honey in my hive—if you know what I mean."

In disgust Jeff threw the rag he was finishing up with on to the sink. Bodies. It was all the guys thought of.

"Where're you going?" Hunter asked as Jeff hit the door with one hand.

"I was going out to check the truck. I noticed one of the tires is low." He didn't wait for the shrug Hunter gave him before he pushed out of the room. Quickly he took a look at his watch. Twenty more minutes and he would be sprung from active duty to stand-down.

At the tire he bent and put the tester on it. He was right, it was a little low—not enough to even really notice, but at least he didn't have to hang out in the break room and hear the crude remarks. That had never been his style. In fact, unfortunately he really didn't have any style when it came to women, but if he had, it certainly wouldn't have been that.

Quickly he unwound the air hose, dragged it over to the tire, and attached it. *Just work and forget about all of that.* But for all the coaching, his own thoughts kept going up those stairs and into that chair just across from her.

"Fletch said, 'Yes'?" the captain asked in utter disbelief.

"Yes, he did." Lisa kept her tone level and professional. "So, I just wanted to confirm your position on the schedule as well."

"When is this thing again?"

"Mid-October. We haven't really set a firm date yet, we're trying to get all the available voices in first."

"Well, it's kind of hard to commit to something like that. It's a long time until October."

"Look, Sir, I appreciate that, but in order to have a list to present to the schools, I have to get some solid yeses to go on. Now when I was here last week, I was under the impression that I had your word that if Mr. Fletcher agreed, you would too. Was I mistaken in that impression?"

The wrinkles on the face deepened into a scowl. "And what kind of presentation do I have to do?"

"Some outline to explain the duties of the fire department and the leadership roles available."

"And I have to do it myself?"

Slowly Lisa shrugged as her mind tripped down the stairs. "I guess you could send someone in your place if you absolutely had to, but I really think it would be more effective if you did it. But we can work that out later. Right now I need to know if I can put the Fire Department down with your name as a participant." To bring more pressure, she put the tip of the pen in hand to the notebook. "Will you stand by the police department in helping the kids of our community?"

Yes, she had learned a few things about high-pressure sales tactics.

"Okay, okay. Put me down, but I'd like to be kept apprised of the others who you con into this thing."

She smiled. "Con?"

"Yes, con, Ms. Matheson. You are good at it."

"Why thank you, Sir."

"Hey, Taylor." Hunter strode out into the station at just after five. "You did get groceries, right?"

"Groceries?" Jeff straightened from where he was checking the last tire on the truck. "No. I didn't know we needed them."

"What do you think? That refrigerator's going to restock itself?" Hunter asked with a sarcastic laugh. "Or are you good at cooking with air?"

"C-cooking? I thought Brady and Dante were cooking tonight."

"No, Brady and Dante have a standing date with a poker hand on Thursday night. So, that leaves you. What's it going to be? You going to get groceries, or are you treating everybody tonight?"

Slowly Jeff scratched his ear, having not seen this bend until he was around it. "I guess I could get some pizza or something."

"Oh, come on, we had pizza last week. Get a little creative at least."

Creative. Creative. It was hard to be creative when he'd been working non-stop since just before six-thirty a.m. "Well, there's a little place a few blocks down. I think they do take-out."

"Well then what are you standing around for? Supper's supposed to be served at six."

After taking orders from around the station, Jeff walked down the hallway from the lockers, pulling his coat on as he did. It was time to stop bringing the coat, he thought, swinging it on anyway. Middle of April was far too long to be dragging that thing everywhere. He stepped past the break room on cat feet so as not to call more attention to himself. If Hunter so much as noticed he was in the vicinity, it was a sure bet he would find something new to rag on him about. Trying to keep his spirit and energy from smashing into the ground, he turned from the hallway and nearly crashed right into Lisa coming the other direction.

"Hey," he said as his attention snapped to her. "You get your speaker?"

"Barely," she said with a small smile. "You get your cleaning done?"

"Barely."

A moment and then she started for the door. "I guess I'll see you."

"You want some company?" he asked, wishing there was a way to just stay with her without having to ask all the time. He saw her hesitation. "To your car I mean? The guys want take-out. I'm the designated go-for."

"Oh, sure," she said with an uncertain nod.

He opened the door for her, and together they walked out into the sunshine. His hands found his jacket pockets, and although it was 80 degrees, the safety of his pockets felt very good.

"So, are you going home?" he asked, swinging his feet side-to-side so that the walk to the car had nothing straight associated with it.

"Yeah. Whole bunch of work, a little home." She shrugged. "Not that home's all that great anyway. Little apartment and a television to talk to."

His gaze swung to her. "You sure that's your life you're talking about there? Sounds like you've been spy-camming mine." They ambled into the parking lot, and his heart hurt at the sight of her little car in the visitor spot. He needed something to prolong this. "So, are you hungry? I'm going to get food anyway."

The look she shot his direction sent him back into his own corner. "I'm not really big on dinner."

"Oh," he said softly, but he couldn't let her get away again. "Coffee? You a Starbucks fan?"

"I'm not really into coffee." She shook her head, and he noticed how her gaze traveled out to the traffic, far away from his.

Every logical part of him said she was trying to let him down easy, but in this case there would never be an easy. "Then how about a Coke float?" he asked, and that snapped her gaze back to his.

"A Coke float?"

"Yeah, you know, Coke and ice cream." He shrugged. "A Coke float."

Her eyebrows scrunched together. "And you get this, where?"

"Couple blocks down." He nodded forward as their steps reached the back of her car and stopped. "It's the little cafe I was going to. Nothing fancy, but it's kind of cool." He waited, and when she said nothing, the fact that he was making a huge fool of himself scratched across his soul. "I'm sorry. If you don't want to, that's cool. I just thought…"

She stopped him with one look. "It sounds like fun."

In all the days she had been alive, Lisa thought that she could surely have learned to control herself by now, so where the it-sounds-like-fun had come from, she had no idea. Nonetheless, she found herself sitting in a booth across from him, a tall fountain glass filled with soft serve and Coke in front of her as he waited for the full order he had placed to be finished.

"I can't believe you've never had one of these," Jeff said, in that voice that made her toes curl. "Me and Kit lived on these things when we were growing up."

"Nutritional," Lisa said with a nod.

"Yep, right up there with broccoli and sprouts." He took a drink of his, and then he looked at her with anticipation and a small amount of apprehension. "It won't kill you, I promise."

Slowly she took a sip from the straw, and a reluctant smile crossed her lips.

"Good, huh?" he asked, smiling for her.

She brushed the hair from her face as the fingers on the other hand laid softly on the table. "Pretty good." Admitting any more scared her.

"Told you." He leaned back in the booth and arched his arm over the back of it, pulling the heat to her cheeks. "So, tell me about this youth thing you're working on. Looked like the captain was elated."

She let out an exasperated sigh and shook her head. "You would think it wouldn't be that big of a deal to stand up in front of a bunch of high schoolers and tell them about your job, but it's more like I'm proposing to Chinese water torture them." She leaned back and crossed her arms in a perfect imitation of Hayes and Fletcher. "'Why don't you come back when somebody else says yes, Ms. Matheson? I don't have the guts to be the first one to say yes to this little scheme of yours.' It's so frustrating." Then she glanced around lest one of them might be standing behind her before ducking and taking another sip of her drink. "If I could've just had the businessmen do it, this would've been a snap."

He leaned forward. "So, why didn't you?"

"That's not what the client wants, and the client is always right."

"Ah, the real boss," he said, and she smiled at his grasp of the situation.

"That's what they don't tell you about owning your own business. You don't have one boss, you've got ten clients and each of them think they are the only project you are working on. *Voila*, ten bosses. It's completely annoying."

"I can imagine." The blue of his eyes softened. "But I'm sure you're up to the challenge."

"Sometimes I wonder." Lisa sighed softly. "It just seems like the harder I work, the farther behind I get—like I'm on some kind of hamster wheel going around and around and around, and the only way off is just to get flung into the cage wire." Her finger traced several circles in the air and then pitched off to one side. She shook her head and put her lips to the straw. "Sometimes I wonder if it's even worth it."

He watched her take a sip of the swirled white-brown liquid.

Hopelessness dragged her spirit down. "I just keep thinking maybe there's something else I should be doing—something... more important or something."

"Like what?" he asked, and she felt his gaze although she didn't look up.

"Like what you guys do. Being out there, saving lives. That's something worthwhile. Not just putting some dinky little ads in a newspaper people are going to trash tomorrow."

For a second he watched her. "That's funny," he finally said thoughtfully.

"What's funny?"

He shrugged. "I used to think the same thing back in college." Her forehead furrowed in surprise, and he laughed. "Yeah, college. B.A. General Business. Not for me, for my dad really, but I put in the hours, and it says my name on the diploma. But business wasn't what I really wanted to do. I really wanted this, so after college, I worked for a couple years at a job I hated, and then I decided it was now or never."

"So you chased your dream."

"Yep. But you know, it's funny, I've been telling myself that once I was here, I would feel different. That I would be different, but now I'm here, and it's still me. I mean I look around, and not much has really changed like I thought it would." He looked across at her. "Well, in most things anyway."

"So in some ways life has changed though?"

"Yeah." His gaze went to his finger tracing up and down the glass. "But that's not because of work."

There was a beat in which neither of them said anything.

"Taylor, your order's ready," the cashier called, and Lisa's attention snapped across the little restaurant.

He slid out of the booth with no more words.

She stood with him and swiped four bills from her purse as he held up his hand and reached for his own wallet. "No, hey, this is on me."

Anger and fear flared. "I can pay my own way."

A slow, lop-sided smile slipped onto his face. "I didn't say you couldn't." His hand didn't move when it had the wallet open. "Please. My treat?"

Every particle of her was screaming, *No, don't let him. He'll think you owe him.* However, a hard fist in her chest forced her to nod and pick up her money. "Okay." She was going back to the office after all, back to safety. He wouldn't follow her there. He couldn't.

Quickly he paid first at the table and then at the cashier's for the food. Lisa waited only long enough for him to grab the bags of food before she stepped away from him in case he had any notion of leading her out. On her own push the bells on the door jingled as she strode out into the early Houston evening with him barely catching the door behind her. She was a woman, after all, not a helpless child, and letting him get every door wasn't the best way to show him she had no intention of owing him anything now or ever.

They walked down the sidewalk as the bags of food banged into his leg with every step. Steps and steps they walked until they were standing on a curb side-by-side.

"Have you ever noticed that you can't actually get all the way across a street in this town without the 'Don't Walk' sign flashing?" he asked, and her gaze jumped over to him as she wondered where that observation had come from.

"What?"

"I'm telling you, you can't." There was not even a hint of levity in his tone. "The sign says, 'Walk.' You take two steps into the street, and it starts flashing, 'Don't Walk. Don't Walk.' I mean why don't they just make it say, 'Run' and be done with it?"

Skeptical climbed over her as she fought not to laugh; however, his craziness was too much to withstand. She looked over at him and then shook her head and laughed.

"You don't believe me," he said as he looked out across the intersection. "See, watch. I'll show you." The lights on the intersection flashed green to red, a second and then the sign said: *Walk*. Sure enough she had barely made it three steps into the street before it started flashing, *Don't Walk. Don't Walk.* "Told you."

At the other curb, she stepped up onto the sidewalk. "And how long did this earth-shattering inspiration take you to discover, Einstein?"

"It used to be a game," Jeff said with a shrug. "When Mom would drag us shopping, Kit and I would stand on the curb like we were at a track meet and try to race the walk signs."

"Did you ever win?"

"Not once."

"And your mom let you do that—run across the street?"

"She never knew."

Lisa's eyebrows arched skyward, and he looked at her and smiled.

"Holding hands. That was a big deal with Mom," he said with a sheepish shrug. "You didn't get out of the car that she wasn't going, 'You boys get somebody's hand.' To this day, it feels weird crossing a parking lot by myself."

Lisa laughed outright. "You'll go into a burning building, but you can't cross the street without holding somebody's hand?"

He leaned closer to her. "Don't tell anybody. It might ruin my image."

"Oh, okay. I won't," she said as if they now shared a conspiracy. They reached the next curb. Together but separate they stood waiting. However, the moment the sign changed, she sensed that they were indeed in a race to see if one of them could beat the mythical sign. It didn't work, not even midway across it flashed, *Don't Walk* and Lisa wondered how many times she had crossed a street and never noticed that phenomenon.

Once they reached the other side, their steps fell in sync with each other, and although to an outsider, it might not have been obvious that they were together, to Lisa it felt like they were one in the same. "So, do you work tomorrow?"

"No, all night tonight. The 24-hour shift thing. Then I'm off until Sunday."

"Twenty-four hours? Ugh."

"Yeah. As long as we don't get middle of the night calls, it's okay." They walked a couple of steps as her heart said she hadn't remembered this walk being this short on the way to the soda shop. "You working tomorrow?" He swung his gaze on her for the briefest of seconds.

"Of course, I work all the time. Weekdays, weekends, morning, noon, night, four o'clock in the morning."

"You don't sleep?"

She shook her head. "Too many things to think about most nights to spend time doing something so trivial."

"Four o'clock in the morning, huh?"

Slowly she nodded as they traced their way into the parking lot.

"Well, I guess now I'll be up at four o'clock in the morning half the time, too." He drifted off on thoughts of the nighttime. "It's really a weird time of day if you think about it. I mean it's strange to be up when everyone else is asleep."

Lisa shrugged. "I don't know. It's the nice time of the day for me—nobody calls, I've got the world all to myself. No clients, no employees, just me and work."

"That's funny. The other night I was wondering why in the whole world anyone else would be up at that un-Godly hour. It's nice to know I wasn't the only one." At her car, he leaned back on the Trailblazer next to it. "So, you think I could like, I don't know, get your number or something so I could find out if I'm the only one awake the next time?"

"My... number?" she asked, and her skin jumped away from him. "Oh, I... don't really give out my number."

"Oh." He nodded and halfway smiled. "That's cool. I just thought..."

Stupid, don't do this. The thoughts clawed through her even as she dug into her purse. *Tell him no, Lisa. Leave. Now.* However, her hand produced her business card for her heart, and with her gaze down she offered it to him. "In case you're ever bored a four o'clock in the afternoon."

Gently he smiled at her as he took it. "Like when I need a break from sink cleaning?"

"Yeah, something like that," she agreed with a reluctant smile. Then she turned and looked at her car. "Well, I'd better get back to work otherwise it might be four a.m. before I get to go home."

"Yeah, I'd better get this stuff in before Hunter blows a gasket." He watched her get in the car, and then he stood holding the door and the food. "Drive carefully."

Why was it so hard to just say good-bye? "Don't let Hunter get to you."

"I'll try not to," he said with a laugh.

"I'll see ya."

"Yeah," he said, and very carefully he shut her door.

She started the car, waiting for him to slide out of the space between hers and the Trailblazer. However, when she backed out, he was still standing right at the edge of the car's path, those white bags dangling from his hands next to his knees. Off-handedly she waved as her body traced down everything it liked about how he looked—those pants curved in all the right places, the jacket draped over those arms that she couldn't get out of her head, and that smile, lop-sided and completely amazing. He waved. She did too—kind of. When she got to the street, she looked back. He hadn't moved, and somehow, it was like she was destined to be watching him in that rear view mirror forever.

The next morning Lisa was still on his mind as Jeff went to his locker to grab his coat at 6:30 fully prepared to head out with the rest of the guys. However, Hunter had other ideas. How he accomplished hanging a whole open bag of flour from the locker door without getting it everywhere in the process, Jeff would never know, but the second he opened the locker, the bag ripped and white powder spilled out, hitting the ground at his shoes, and creating a cloud that drifted all the way up his clothes.

With two coughs he waved at the now-white air surrounding him as he looked through it to his cloths. Snickers and giggles erupted from the far side of the lockers.

"Nice," Jeff said with a reluctant smile as Dante and Hunter peered around the end of the gray metal, fighting back the laughter. "Very nice."

"Have fun cleaning that up. I'd hate for the chief to happen by and see it," Hunter said, and he turned Dante toward the door.

A tired sigh escaped as Jeff looked down at the white lava floe still cascading from the locker onto his shoes. Carefully he picked one shoe up and then the other, and he walked over to the sink, knowing he was leaving a lovely white shoe trail behind him.

"Crud, Witkowski baled on me," a short, middle-aged fireman said, coming into the room as Jeff pulled the trashcan over to begin the clean-up. "What am I going to tell Pat?"

"What's the big deal?" the man's colleague, a tall, brownish-blond goateed man about half-a-decade older than Jeff, said in a deep voice that resonated off the concrete walls. "I'm sure she'll understand." However, they stopped in mid-conversation when they turned at the lockers and saw Jeff scooping the flour from the floor and transferring it into the trashcan. "Problems?"

"You could say that," Jeff said, wishing his voice sounded happier about the mess.

The goateed man shook his head in sympathy and turned back

to the conversation. "Pat's cool. I'm sure she'll understand."

"Understand what? That I'm going to miss her birthday again? Like I missed Valentine's Day and Jenny's spring play and our anniversary before that? Yeah, I'm sure she'll understand." The shorter man shook his mostly hairless head. "I just wish I could find somebody else to cover for me on Tuesday. At least it would stave off a divorce for another couple months."

Jeff was listening as he cleaned, and although they would know he was eavesdropping, he straightened and cleared his throat. "I could probably come in on Tuesday if you needed someone."

The older man's attention snapped to Jeff. At first his gaze was hard and cold, then it softened slightly. "I haven't seen you around. You new?"

"Yeah. I just started last week," Jeff said, nodding. The fact that he was still standing in a mound of white flour seemed to escape from his consciousness "But I'm not busy Tuesday. If you need somebody…"

"What's your shift?" the man asked with worry around the edges of the question.

"Oh, no. It's okay. You don't have to switch or anything. It's no big deal. I don't mind covering for you."

"You sure?"

"Yeah. I work Sunday anyway, so Tuesday won't kill me."

The man stood for a moment and then smiled and stuck his hand out. "Wade Fraser."

"Jeff Taylor." He brushed his hand off on his pants, which did no good, and shook first one man's hand and then the other.

"Gabe Teague," the goateed man said.

"So you'll really do this?" Wade asked, rocking backward on the thought.

"Yeah. No problem."

Wade smiled mischievously. "Pat may kiss you."

The tips of Jeff's ears went hot as he shrugged and bent back down to the mess. "Just glad I could help."

When Lisa's gaze chanced on the clock on her computer at 3:55 on Sunday morning, she almost laughed, and had she not been so tired, she would have. It had taken all of Saturday and most of the night to go through Kurt's idea of a ready presentation piece-by-piece and get it acceptable for Monday's meeting.

Why was it that she had hired him again? She couldn't clearly remember anymore. In fact, as her mouse clicked across the screen, anything other than utter exhaustion was getting very little play in her brain. However, every thirty seconds or so her gaze would slip down to that little clock in the corner as her dreams slipped to him.

Her chin rested in her hand as thoughts of him drifted through her. He had said something about Sunday. Was he off on Sunday? Or was that when he went back? She shook her head to clear it of him. However, seconds later he was there again, crowding through her work like a bulldozer. It was because she was so tired, she told herself. Her willpower along with her energy was shot. The mouse slowed as it clicked across her screen.

3:59 glowed back from the ether. Where was he now? At the station? At home in bed asleep? On a call? In the fuzz of sleep invading her brain she hoped it was one of the former and not the later. She was going to have to find out more about his schedule, she thought as the haze finally took over, and she laid her head on the desk. She really was going to have to find out more about him.

Six

"House fire in progress 2545 Arthur Street." The voice cracked over the speaker above the break room table Tuesday night as the alarms sprang to life, and instantly Jeff was on his feet. The whirlwind banked into high gear around him as people scrambled for the trucks. In the next blink six of them were crammed into one, pulling on gear and equipment as they wailed their way to Arthur Street.

The insides of Jeff's stomach flitted in no definite pattern as he pulled on his air tank. This was it. The one he had worked for, trained for, wanted to do, and suddenly the moment was upon him.

Only the streetlights lit the night surrounding them as they sped to their destination where in rapid succession they jumped out. Flames illuminated the night sky, jumping out of the second story of the house and reaching for the roof of the house ten feet over.

"Teague and Jackson cut the utilities," Captain Rainier, the B-shift crew chief said as the truck slid to a stop. "Jameson, you and Taylor get the vent holes cut."

When his feet hit the street, Jeff grabbed the extension ladder and started for the house. In seconds Zack Jameson was there climbing up with the roof ladder and chainsaw in hand. As soon as the saw was whirring, Jeff turned back for the truck, feeding one of the cotton hoses from the top of the truck down to Jackson who had just returned.

The training kicked in. His hands just worked, pulling the hose as it fed off the truck. At that moment a frantic lady dressed only in a thin flowery robe ran smack into the chaos and right up to

Jeff's side.

"Kaleb. Did they get Kaleb out?" she asked, pulling on the edge of Jeff's coat as he fought to extract the last of the hose from the truck. When he turned, those eyes seemed terribly familiar. Fear. Utter, inconsolable terror.

"Who's Kaleb?" he asked even as he worked. The hose hit the end. "That's it!"

"He's the little boy. He's eight. He's about so high with red hair and freckles."

"Where was he supposed to be?" Jeff asked, trying to pay attention to everything at once.

"He was staying home tonight—by himself while his mom and dad went out. They asked me to watch him. I didn't know anything until I heard the…"

"Captain, we've got a problem," Jeff said, striding right up to where Gabe and the captain were strategizing where to go from here.

Rainier looked up. "What's that?"

"There might be a kid inside."

"Might be?"

"I didn't know… he said he was going to bed," the lady said as hysteria invaded her body and soul.

"Where's his room?" Rainier asked.

"It's on the first floor in the back," the lady said. "He just called me thirty minutes ago, and everything was fine."

Jeff looked at the captain who yelled to two other firefighters running by. When they ran up, the captain briefed them, and broke them into two groups. Gabe and Jeff would go around back. The other two would go in the front. Six words of final instructions before Jeff ran to the truck where he grabbed the pry bar as Gabe pulled off an ax. The two of them raced down the darkened side of the house.

At the gate Gabe stopped, rattling the whole fence in his frantic attempt to get in. "It's locked."

"Great." Jeff's brain sped ahead of him like a racecar. "Here." He dumped the metal at Gabe's feet, jumped onto the house's cooling system which stood by the gate. Two short motions and he was over. "Pitch me the stuff." The equipment landed on the other side of the fence in a non-discernible pattern, and his hands moved in rapid succession retrieving all of it just as Gabe joined him on that side of the fence.

They ran for the house, and at the first window, Jeff pounded on the glass. "Hey! Anybody in there? Kaleb? Anybody?"

The only answer was the popping of the flames high above them. At that moment he heard the crash and ran to where Gabe had just hacked through the plate glass back door. He reached in as the smoke poured out of the gaping hole. One click and they were in. The glass crunched under his boot as Jeff stepped through the opening, and the middle of his heart slammed into his chest.

Kaleb. A scared little eight-year-old kid in a two-story maze that he had no map for. Where was that little boy? Jeff pulled on his air mask as the smoke enveloped him. It was blinding, and he bumped into a dining room chair which sent him crashing into the wall. There were so many places a little kid could be. Feeling his way through the darkness list only by the pathetic flashlight he swung this way and that, Jeff slid down the wall until it suddenly broke into a hallway, and he turned into the opening. "Kaleb? Kaleb, buddy? Where are you?"

Nothing was quiet. Voices, water, fire, sirens, windows shattering from the heat trying to find its way out. Then he saw what looked like a white cloth heaped next to the wall. "I found him!" he called to anyone who could hear anything in the mêlée. Gently he picked up the little body, which felt like it weighed nothing at all.

He met Gabe coming from the other direction, and they hit the opening together.

"Get out! Get out!" Gabe yelled as if Jeff had any intention of hanging around for the rest of the show. Snaps and a crack. The fire was eating the second floor away right above them.

It wasn't really running so much as just stepping cautiously as he fought through the smoke to find his way back out into the cool night.

"It's this way." Gabe grabbed his elbow and dragged him back into the dining room. "Hurry!"

Crunch went the glass under his boot as Jeff became part of the smoke pouring out into the backyard. The streetlight beam gave him the first real look at what felt like a rag doll in his arms. Barely eight, the freckles stood out in stark contrast to the pale face. "Oh, God, please."

A wail not wholly like a fire truck sliced through the night.

"Let's get him out front," Gabe said, at the gate which gave way with the first ax hit on the metal.

Jeff's legs were hurrying through the darkness, but he didn't really feel anything as they broke past the trees on the edge of the house and into the swirl of lights flashing across the houses making them look like a fun house gone mad. In a blink he saw the EMTs rushing up the grass. "Over here!" he called, skidding to a stop on the grass and laying the little, limp body in front of him.

"We've got it." One of the EMTs pushed him away, and Jeff backed up enough to let the team take the lead.

"Hey, you okay?" Gabe asked with a clap on his back.

He coughed twice. "Yeah."

"He's breathing!" one of the paramedics said as they all jumped into motion. It was only when the youngest one stood to get the stretcher from the ambulance that Jeff recognized him. That flash and then he was gone.

"Teague, Taylor!" the captain yelled. "We need you guys ready to go in!"

A small look back and Jeff turned. There was more work to be done.

The clock in the locker room read 4:15 when he stumbled back in, his fellow firefighters surrounding him—sooty and grime-covered. They all looked like they had just come home from an all-nighter in hell.

"I hope the kid's going to be okay," Gabe said, pulling off his boots slowly as the sound of the showers hazed out the comment.

"Yeah." Jeff reached into his locker for the little gold cross. He needed it right now. Pulling its strength into his soul, he ran a hand over it and then yanked it on over his head. They weren't supposed to wear things like that at work, but he needed something.

"You did good out there, Taylor," Gabe said as Jeff stood on his way to the showers.

"Just doing my job."

"Well, I'd be happy to help you do it any day of the week."

With a smile Jeff reached out and caught Gabe's hand on the way forward. "Watch what you wish for."

Lisa noticed the picture of the gutted house on the front page of the Chronicle the next morning, and her interest riveted to the story. Midnight on a Tuesday. Sunday flitted through her mind, but after that... Her hand flipped through the paper, but there was nothing about him. Not that she really expected there to be.

It was crazy to even think about him, but the center of her heart hoped fervently that he was at home in bed when that one happened. Of course, she knew even if he was, he wouldn't be forever. Eventually the law of averages would put him in one of those burning buildings. Eventually...

She folded the paper and laid it to the side. Work was what was important now. Work. Jeff and all the other guys in the world would have to take care of themselves. She certainly didn't need to be wasting valuable energy stores on keeping up with them.

"Ten to one the Celtics make it to the finals," Dante said from the top of the truck as Jeff worked below, restocking the first aid kits on Thursday.

"You and the Celtics," Hunter said as a road cone from the top of the truck landed on the concrete behind Jeff. "Why don't you get a real team?"

"Like who? The awesome Nets?" Dante walked past Jeff to the truck door. "Please. They can't even spell basketball, much less play it."

"Oh, yeah, like the Celtics all have Ph.D.'s," Hunter shot back as another road cone hit the ground behind Jeff.

"Hey! Would you quit throwing those down," Dante yelled. "You're going to break something important."

"Like what?" Hunter asked.

"My head for one," Jeff said, looking up at the man standing far above him like a supernatural cowboy.

"No." Dante ducked back out of the truck. "I said, 'Important.'"

Jeff shook his head and buried it into the first aid compartment. Why did he even try?

"Lisa," the voice said at her doorway as she sat in her office Friday evening clicking through the Internet looking for a good picture of a zebra that they could use. She looked up and came to immediate attention.

"Tucker?"

"Yeah, sorry to disturb you." He opened the door wider and stepped in. "Sherie said it was okay."

"Oh." Lisa fought to rebalance her world. "Come in. Have a seat." Her hands went to work straightening her desk. Sherie knew better, but Lisa also knew her secretary had a huge crush on Tucker and his All-American blond good looks. One little please, and Sherie would've dove off a cliff for him. "What can I do for you?"

"I brought over this list of venues." Tucker held them up after he sat down. "Grandpa thought we'd better get something booked before all the space is gone."

"Oh, okay." She reached for them. "Let me see."

However, he pulled them back. "What do you say we do this over some dinner? It's almost six, and you have to eat anyway."

"Dinner? I'm kind of busy right now." She glanced at the zebra on her screen and wished she could join him in that nice green grass. "Can't we just go over them here?"

"I made reservations at La Tour D'Argent."

"D'Argent? Over on the Bayou?" she asked, sensing a trap. "Why would you do that?"

"Because you have to eat, and I have to eat, and we can talk while we eat." He looked at his watch, and all Lisa could think was that she would really like to break that perfectly straight nose of his. "We've got to get though, or we're going to be late."

Late? How about never? Pushing all the protests of her rational side down, she stood. *Let's get this over with so I can get back to work.* Quickly she grabbed her purse and made sure her money was in it. When she got to the door, she felt his hand guide her through it, and every fiber in her body wanted to smack it away.

"Sherie, I'm going to take off." Lisa readjusted her purse on her shoulder, and she didn't miss the dreamy look her secretary wafted over the two of them. "Just lay the calls I need to return on my desk."

"Sure, boss. No problem." And that dreamy gaze followed them right out the door.

At the elevator, Tucker reached past her and pushed the

button. They stepped on, and he pushed two.

"My car's on the third," she said, and when he didn't reach for the button, she did, but he stopped her hand with his.

"Let's just take mine," he said, and she hated that tone. "That way we can talk on the way."

And get this over faster? That would be a blessing. Wishing it wasn't so hard to ignore the slithery way his gaze slid down across her, she stepped out into the parking garage. The second level. It was where she used to park until she hadn't been able to find a space that one day. Now when she pulled into the garage she told herself that parking on the third gave her a reason to take the stairs, which had to qualify for some exercise. However, the real reason was always right there in the shadows of her heart.

They stopped at the new two-tone beige Lexus, and Tucker opened her door first. Smoothly he took her hand as she folded onto the leather seats. As soon as she was in, she pulled her hand from the fingers that felt like they had been soaked in butter for two solid decades. When he shut the door, she sat back, pulling herself straight up as she did. *Professional. Keep this professional, and he won't get any ideas.* Quickly she grabbed the seat belt and wrapped it around herself. One more barrier, one more line of defense.

His smile brought out the alarms in her spirit when he got in on the other side. He backed out, squealed the tires once, and they were off. The whole ride Lisa kept her gaze trained out the window, and her hands wrapped around the edge of her purse. When he turned on the stereo to slow, hold-me-tight music, she tapped her fingers over the purse trying to make time run just a little faster.

At the restaurant, Tucker let the attendant park the car. They were three steps up to the restaurant when Lisa noticed he had no notes in his hands. "I thought we were going to talk business."

He looked at her and smiled in that infuriating way that said she really should stop thinking so much and just let him lead. "We'll talk business later."

Then what are we going to talk about now? But she didn't have time to ask that question as Tucker was already conversing with the maitre d'. Lisa clutched her purse tighter. Why was it that no matter what she said, guys just wouldn't take a hint?

"Right this way," the maitre d' said, leading them up a short set of stairs to a table at the far end of the restaurant overlooking the shimmering blue water of the gulf beyond.

"Perfect," Tucker said, and Lisa saw the bills pass from one hand to the other. Purposefully she sat down, grabbed the menu, and perused it. The only thought going through her head was that this one dinner might bankrupt her entire company. A moment more and Tucker joined her. "I'm surprised you didn't have plans."

"Plans?" she asked. "I was working if that's what you mean."

"No, I mean plans—you know with friends or something."

"I had enough fun last week to last me awhile," she said sourly. "The shrimp looks good."

He wasn't even looking at his menu. Instead he looked like he was trying out for some modeling job for Oscar de la Renta. That suit just screamed, *Do you know how much money I have?* It annoyed her to the nth degree.

"I'm sure glad Grandpa decided to go with your little firm. I just knew this was going to work out so well. In fact, I've been trying to talk the old man into letting me run with this. Well, with your help of course."

"Hmm, that's nice," she said, barely listening. "I wonder if the swordfish is fresh."

"I was really excited about it until he came up with this ridiculous public servant angle. I mean what can kids learn from the blue collar set about leadership? It's almost laughable."

Lisa's gaze jumped to his as a serrated remark crossed her mind; however, the waiter picked that moment to approach their table. They ordered, and Lisa seriously considered grabbing onto the guy's leg and begging him not to leave them alone. However, she discounted that plan because something said that might invite more trouble than it would thwart.

"It's such a beautiful evening," Tucker said, gazing out across the gulf as he took a small sip of water. Then he turned liquid eyes on her. "Almost as beautiful as you are."

Well, that's original. "So, we were going to go over the venues?"

He brushed that idea away with a swipe. "Maybe later. How about we just get to know each other a little better?"

She started to protest, but he didn't give her a chance.

"I bet you didn't know I graduated from Yale," he said, taking the words right out of her mouth. "Second in my class. Did my grandfather mention that?"

"Umm, no, I don't think so."

The waiter returned with two glasses of wine, and as Lisa looked at it, she wondered how fast she would have to drink one glass of wine to make her drunk enough to get through a nightmare like this one.

"Yeah," Tucker continued without even acknowledging the waiter. "And at the rate I'm going, I'll probably take over Cordell Enterprises by the time I'm thirty."

"How nice for you," she said, taking another drink.

"I had offers lined up at the door when I graduated," Tucker said, "but I said, 'No, I want to stay with the family business.' Loyalty you know. People see that, and they know I've got things figured out."

With one solid knock, Lisa's head started pounding. What she wouldn't have given for a loud, chaotic club where conversation was futile. And what she wouldn't give to have the guts to just stand up, call herself a cab, and tell Cordell Enterprises and Tucker himself to go jump off the highest cliff they could find. Instead, she forced a smile, telling herself that if it just got no worse than this, she could deal with it.

When Jeff unlocked his door on Friday evening, he set the two bags of groceries on the little table. His fingers reached into his pocket and pulled out the little card that had spent the last week there. Slowly he turned it over as he slipped the coat off his shoulders. Calling her was crazy. How many ways could a person say, "I'm not interested. Leave me alone"? However, as clear as that was to his head, his heart just wasn't getting the message. Somehow he had hoped she would show up yesterday. Why, he didn't know. It was just that now she and Thursday were somehow intertwined in his head.

Nonetheless, she hadn't, and so here he was. He picked up the phone, held it for a moment, and then dialed his second choice. Maybe if he just talked to somebody who had some sanity left, that would help him forget about her. In a heap he slumped onto the barstool next to the wall. "Dustin? Hey, man."

"Jeffrey! Long time no speak. What's up?"

"Not much," Jeff said as his fingers turned the card over. "How's work?"

"Big station, lots of names. Great fun. You?"

"About the same." Jeff leaned back against the corner of the wall. "How's Eve?"

"Burning supper… again," Dustin said with a laugh.

"Hey!" the voice in the background protested. "I heard that."

"It's okay. I didn't marry her for her cooking skills," Dustin said, and Jeff heard her muffled voice. A twang jumped into his heart as the card flipped over his fingers and onto the counter. "No, she's cool, but she wants to know if you ever got up the guts to go over to Travis."

Air failed. No words would come.

"Hey. Jeff? You still there?" Dustin asked after a moment.

"Yeah. I'm here."

"So, did you go?"

"No. Well, not exactly, but we kind of bumped into each other the other day."

"Fate. Cool. Tell me more."

"Not much to tell. She gave me her card."

"And you called her."

"Well, no…"

"Jeffrey, bud. This bumping into each other thing is cool and all, but you're going to miss this train if you don't get it in gear."

He got the number. Okay, a number. Why wasn't that enough? "I just don't want her to think I'm like…"

"Interested? You are interested. So what's the problem?"

"I don't know." His head hit the wall behind him three times.

"Just call her," Dustin said gently. "I'm sure she'll be happy to hear from you unless she's completely dense. Call her."

Jeff finally sighed and looked down at the little card. "Okay. I'll call her."

Putting her hand on the table was a mistake. Lisa had gotten that message loud and clear. It was like Tucker's buttery hand was a magnet for the top of hers. She had pulled hers back so many times by the time the entrees arrived, she thought she might get a repetitive motion injury.

"And Dad just thinks this's such a wonderful opportunity," Tucker droned on until Lisa's brain had to find something else to think about lest she go insane. "I do too of course. I mean who wouldn't? Great company, fabulous pay…"

The gold cross shining against the black backdrop of muscles and T-shirt floated through her mind, followed in the next heartbeat by that denim-and-suede jacket. It was so low-key, and yet so completely breathtaking. To be honest she wasn't sure if it was the jacket or the layers underneath that intrigued her so much. That arm, exuding strength caught her attention, and she wondered how many hours someone would have to spend in the gym to get arms like that.

"So, how about it?" Tucker asked when the dessert dishes were cleared. "Lisa?"

"Oh, yeah." She shook the dream away from her. "Okay."

It was a good cover until she saw the Colgate smile that was in front of her rather than the lop-sided one in her memories.

"Great, then let's go," Tucker said as he took her hand to help her out of the chair.

Go? Where? the middle of her being asked just as a layer down something said, *Never let them take you to the second crime scene.* She was really going to have to lay off the wine and those deadly fantasies.

"Hi, Lisa," Jeff said, praying his voice would make it through this message. Leaving a message for her at work? Not a good idea, and yet he had made it this far, he wasn't going to turn back now. "This… this is Jeff. From the fire station. Umm, I thought you might still be at work, but I guess not. Well, I just wanted to call and say hi and ask how your week went, but… umm, if you get this sometime, my number is 555-8696. You can call anytime. I guess take care, and maybe I'll try to catch you some other time. 'Bye."

His hand hung up the phone and collapsed head first into the couch. That had to be the worst phone message in the whole history of phone messages. Pushing himself up from the couch, he walked to the back of the apartment to the weight bench sitting in his bedroom. Yanking one barbell laden with weights up from its perch, he sat down on the bench and curved his arm to pull the barbell to him once, twice, three times. She wouldn't call back. That much was for sure. Four, five, six. And why would she? He wouldn't. Ten, eleven, twelve.

In fits his brain showed him pictures that he really didn't want to see. Fourteen, fifteen, sixteen. Why did her smile have to make the top of his chest feel like it might explode at any moment?

Twenty, twenty-one, twenty-two. One look should've told him he
didn't have a chance with her. She was beautiful, gorgeous. The
kind of girl who walks into a room and heads turn. Not like him.
No, when he walked into a room, no one even noticed. Forty-five,
forty-six, forty-seven. Not that he cared whether they noticed or
not. It wasn't them he wanted to notice anyway—just one them,
and he would be happy. At 75, he switched hands.

Dustin could do this. Lisa would've fallen into his arms in a
heartbeat. Craig could've made it work. At least he would've gotten
more than her work number. Thirty-eight, thirty-nine. And
Ramsey, Ramsey would've already forgotten her name by now. He
didn't want to be like that, just a tenth of that. Yeah, a tenth would
be good. Sixty-seven, sixty-eight, sixty-nine. But no, he had to be
Jeff. Good, old, holding-the-table-down Jeff. He put the weight
down as he laughed sarcastically at that thought.

Curling his toes under the bar at the opposite side of the
bench, he let his back lay off of the support, down, down until the
middle of his stomach screamed for mercy. Defiantly he pulled
forward. Lisa was a nice dream, but she wasn't destined for him.
He let himself slowly back down. No, she was destined for
somebody who knew the difference in years and makes of wine.
He pulled up. And how many forks are supposed to go on a table,
and which one to use with what. His body arched down. And the
proper attire to wear for a Sunday luncheon with the mayor. Up.

He had no chance with her. Down. And the sooner he got
that through his head to his heart the better.

"This, umm, this wasn't what I had in mind," Lisa said when
Tucker's car turned up the street to the Bar Houston. "I'm really
not into dancing."

"Just a little." Tucker put his hand a quarter inch from where
hers laid on her lap. "To take the edge off."

"But I need to…"

"Shhh." He laid a finger to her lips, and what she really
wanted to do was bite it off. "I've got a friend who works here. He
said he could get us in no problem."

Funny, she thought as she slumped back into her seat, he had
told everyone about what he obviously thought was a date except
the one person on it with him. Had it not been for Burke and the

account, she would've jumped out of the car—moving or not.

When they pulled up to the club, alarm bells jangled through her spirit. Before he could get around the car, Lisa opened her door and stood. She might not have much choice, but the last thing she was going to do was give him an inch of a chance to think this was going anywhere. At the door, Tucker made a production of summoning his friend, who indeed let them right in. Her brain searched frantically for some way out. However, it kept running right into Burke.

At a booth, Tucker stopped. "How about here?"

Anything but a booth, she thought tiredly, but she shrugged and slid in anyway. It took only seconds to realize what a huge mistake that was when Tucker arched one arm across the back of the booth while the other searched in the darkness under the table for her hand.

"You know," she said in panicked retreat. "I've got to visit the ladies room." She slid out the other side and fled for the back before he had a chance to protest. Once there, a plan formulated in her head, and she checked her watch. Ten-thirty. Terrific. Carefully she sat down by a wall and pulled out her cell phone. Of course there was no one to call, but the other restroom occupants didn't have to know that. "Hi, yeah… Yeah. We just got here. Are you guys coming?"

Soup. Jeff was too depressed to eat anything else. He had already checked the machine six times, and still nothing. Just like he knew there would be—infinitely.

The night was one long, exhausting merry-go-round of trips to the bathroom and fighting Tucker off when he tried to dance with her. Hands. He was all hands. They would slide up and down her back as they danced, and Lisa wondered what the feasibility of simply decking him and being done with it was.

"You know," she finally said, pulling back from him, fighting for air. "I'm getting kind of tired. Why don't we call it a night?"

"Good idea."

You idiot, her brain yelled at her a mere fifteen minutes later. *The office is not this direction.* "This is kind of the long way around, don't you think?" she asked, willing herself not to lose her cool.

"Relax." Tucker flashed that smile that ate away at her gut. "I thought we could have a nightcap at my place."

She closed her eyes, knowing polite was going to get her in the middle of a wrestling match she had been a participant in one too many times. "Look, I'm really tired. I need to go back and get my car."

"Hard to get." He put his hand on her shoulder and dug into the hardened muscles there. "I like that."

"No." She took his hand and put it back on the steering wheel. "Not hard to get. No get. Now, take me back to my car."

He glanced over at her and scowled. "But it's all the way across town."

"So?"

"So, let's just go to my place. You can crash there, and we'll get your car tomorrow."

"No, Tucker. You're not hearing me. I want to go to my car. Now either you take me there, or I'm going to get out and walk." Her gaze chanced out to the freeway speeding by her window.

"Yeah, right," he said with a dismissive laugh. "Like you're going to jump out going 80 on the freeway."

Lisa reached for the door handle. "I'm not kidding, Tucker."

He glanced over at her, and his face fell into a deeper scowl. "But I bought you dinner."

"Money?" She understood his insinuation and dug into her purse. "Is that what you're worried about? Then here. Here's forty. That should cover mine." She pushed the bills into his space as he glanced down at them without moving more than his eyes.

"Put your money back. It was on me."

"No," she said as her patience snapped. "'On me' means you don't expect anything in return. Nothing. Otherwise it's not on you. It's on me. And that's not how this is going to go. So, here, take this." She tried to stuff the bills into his jacket pocket, but he pushed her away.

"We're almost there," Tucker said as his voice darkened. He pulled off the freeway and stopped at an intersection. "Just chill. Okay?"

But she knew all too well where chilling was going to get her.

With no more than a half-second of thought, she reached for the door handle, clicked it, and swung it open as the light turned green ahead of them.

"What are you doing?" he practically screamed.

"What I should've done when you showed up." One hand clicked her seat belt as her first heel hit the pavement. Horns behind them blared to life. Her body out, she slammed the door and stumbled from the middle of the road across three lanes to the other side as the cars played pinball with her path. "Cripes! How do I let myself get into these messes?"

Beep. Honk. Beep. And she made it safely to the other side of the street. "Great. Now what?" She looked around to get her bearings, and then she realized that Tucker might actually have the audacity to come try to find her. That thought jerked her steps down the street. "I truly hate guys," she said into the night air. "I really and truly do. They are nothing but egomaniacal, selfish, inconsiderate jerks, and if I never see another one again, it will be too soon."

Seven

Lisa didn't bother going to work over the weekend. The possibility that Tucker would call or worse--that he would outright show up at her door again make her skin crawl across her veins. How many times had she been so stupid in the past? As she clicked across the zebras on the computer in her living room, she tried not to think about it. However, the thoughts were going nowhere. There was Jay in high school. He had seemed nice enough until they made it to the back row of the movies together.

Then there was Martin, the only prom date she ever had, junior year. Why she had tried to look so perfect for him, she couldn't really tell now. All that had done was send an invitation that had nearly cost her more than the heel of one shoe and half of the top of her dress. Her face set into stone as she clicked across the web. In college it was a whole string of guys—many of which she didn't even want to remember. Culminating with Conner Beale...

In frustration she clicked the mouse twice and shut the computer down. Thinking was a bad idea. She needed something to do so she wouldn't think. Picking up the stereo remote, she flicked the little black box on, found a song that was actually louder than her thoughts, turned it up a notch, and then went into the kitchen where a week's worth of dirty dishes stared back at her. It was better than the alternatives.

The only thing Jeff thought of all weekend was her and the possibility that when he happened by the answering machine, the light would be blinking. However, that little light wasn't cooperating. *She'll call Monday*, he told himself, as he crawled into bed Sunday night. *She has to get the message tomorrow.* Arching an arm behind his head, he gazed up at the ceiling, and let his mind float to the two of them in some distant space in the future. It was all that was keeping him sane.

"Here's the weekend messages," Sherie said Monday morning, laying the small stack on top of the folders piled on Lisa's desk. She took one look at them, and dread traced through her. When Sherie was gone, Lisa reached over and flipped through them— fully intending to trash anything that had the name Tucker on it. However, before she found one so easy to discard, a name jumped out at her. *Jeff.*

Telling herself it made no sense, she stood from her desk and strode out into the front office. "What's this one about Jeff?"

"I don't know," Sherie said. "He just said Jeff, from some fire station. He didn't sound like a client, but I think he knows you."

"Oh." Lisa looked down at the pink slip in her hand. "Okay, I know who it is." She closed the door softly behind her, went around to her desk, and sat down. This was insane. How much clearer message could she have gotten on Friday night? Guys were not to be trusted... ever. Closing her eyes lest her heart see what she was doing, she crunched the little paper up and sent it sailing to the trashcan. It didn't quite make it, but Lisa turned back to her work. *It's the thought that counts.*

That light was getting on his nerves. Jeff checked it twice when he got home from work on Tuesday, but still nothing. "Please, God, I'm asking you here. I just want to see her again. Please."

"I want a full-blown proposal," Burke said on Wednesday when he called. There was no mention of Tucker or Friday, which Lisa was grateful for, but what she really wished was that they would just give up on this whole idea altogether and leave her alone. "If you could put a brochure together to send out to the schools, I think that would put the idea over the top with them."

"A... brochure, Sir?"

"I was thinking. You could get quotes from Fletcher, and Hayes, and that other guy, what's his name at the City Engineering Department. That would put our name out there so the school board and everybody can get behind this thing."

"Oh, yeah," she said. "Great idea. I'll get to work on it right away."

"Great. If you could get those out by the first…"

"The first? But that's only a week away."

"Then I'd better let you get to work."

"Yeah," she said as she hung up the phone. "You'd better."

When Sherie walked past Lisa's door Friday at one on her way back in from lunch, Lisa's attention snapped up. "Sherie, did Hayes call back yet?" She took a bite of the sandwich lying on her desk, hoping that somehow she had simply missed the phone call.

"Nope, nothing," Sherie called back.

"And you called him?"

"I've left all kinds of messages," Sherie said, appearing at the door. "Either he's not getting them or…"

"He doesn't want to talk to me," Lisa finished for her. Furiously she wiped her hands across each other to get the crumbs off. "Okay, if that's the way he wants to play it, then that's the way we'll play."

A whole day of continuing education to relearn CPR after a night of little sleep due to the cornflakes scattered across his short-sheeted mattress was enough to make a minister cuss, and yet Jeff was determined not to let them get to him. They were testing him, and he was going to pass this test as surely as he had passed every other one to get to this point.

However, his eyelids were betraying him the longer the nurse droned on, and when they took a five minute break at 4:20, he stumbled to the break room to grab a cup of coffee, hoping it would get him through the last thirty minutes awake. Cup in hand, he stepped out of the break room and very nearly ran into Lisa coming the other direction. "Oh. Lisa. Hi." His heart did a somersault and two cartwheels as the coffee in his hand nearly jumped from the cup.

"Hi," she said, her tone was harsh and businesslike. "Is Captain Hayes here?"

"Uh. Yeah." He pointed up the wire mesh. "I think he's up in his office."

"Great. Thanks." With no more than that, she turned and her heels clicked across the concrete and up the stairs as Jeff stood, body frozen to the spot, letting his gaze follow her all the way to the door, which she opened barely a half-second after she knocked.

Carefully he bent and took another sip as his gaze traveled up the stairs completely on its own. Whatever he had done, the chief was about to regret it.

"Don't take this the wrong way." Without pretense, Lisa sat in the chair across from a none-too-pleased Captain Hayes who had only to be on-site while his troops took this latest round of classes. "But just because you are a captain, that doesn't give you the right to blow me off like I don't even exist."

"Ms. Matheson, I'm sure I don't know…"

"Messages," she said shortly. "And don't act like you don't know what I'm talking about. I've called—repeatedly. I've left tons of messages, but I guess you were just too busy to pick up the phone and tell me you had no intention of helping so you let the answering machine do it for you. Well, I don't like being ignored, and I am not going to go away. So you can either have the courtesy to tell me to my face to take a long leap into an empty river, or you can start treating me with a little respect."

Slowly his gaze fell from hers to the desk. "I know you're trying, Ms. Matheson, but I really, really wish you would just get somebody else. Speaking is just not my expertise."

"I appreciate that, Sir. I really do, but I'm on a deadline here, and you're what I have to go with—whether either of us likes that or not." She shifted an inch in her chair. "Look, I'm putting this brochure thing together for the schools. They may very well turn tail and run in the other direction over this thing like everyone else has. Who knows at this point? But Burke Cordell wants this project, and I've committed to doing it. So, please. Are you going to help me or not?"

The captain sighed and scratched his head. "Okay, what do you need?"

He really was a nice man, Lisa decided as she shut the captain's door behind her after an impromptu interview which had gleaned exactly what she needed—nice quotes from a very knowledgeable, interesting person. The kids were going to love him if she could ever actually get him up there on stage.

Clutching her black notebook to her chest, she looked down at the steps as she descended them. The fear of catching a heel on the mesh and ending up on the concrete below grabbed her gaze and held it there. However, a thought superseded even that one. She looked at her watch and thanked God above for 24-hour shifts. Although that still put him somewhere in the building, at least if she could make it to the door and out, she wouldn't have to talk to him again.

At the concrete the guys standing around the truck noticed her and half-waved, but none of them was Jeff. She should have been happy about that fact, but something in her just wouldn't let her be. The sunshine outside was definitely getting warmer. The trees were blanketed with tiny pink blossoms, and she breathed in their fragrance as she walked down the sidewalk. One part of her was absurdly sad that she hadn't gotten to see him again. But that was nuts. She should be happy—it would save her the embarrassment of feeling like a love struck teenager again. She hated feeling like that, and she knew anyone who bothered to look could see it every time she was around him.

Barely looking enough to cross the parking lot, she hurried to her car, where her key was halfway to the lock when she first heard the voice. "Lisa!" It stopped her cold for a long split-second, but somehow her brain told her if she just ignored it, it would go away. She fiddled with the keys. "Lisa! Hey!" Jeff said, jogging up past the other cars to hers.

Casually as if she really had just heard him, she pushed a piece of hair behind her ear, telling herself he was just any other guy. "Oh, hi there." But not one thread of her believed that lie, and with one look, the thought scattered like blossoms in the wind. Why did he have to increase her core temperature to scalding with one simple little glance? It was maddening.

"I just..." He glanced back at the station. "Um, we didn't get a chance to talk earlier. I was just wondering how things are going."

Well, they'd be better if I could think straight, her brain said as her gaze, trying to escape from the blue pools, focused instead on his arms. With no jacket covering them and the T-shirt stretched across them, they were making the signals in her brain fire backward. "Oh, fine. It's fine." She tried to unlock her car again, but her hands were shaking so badly, she finally gave that up for fear he would notice.

"You looked kind of upset when you came in." He leaned onto the side of her car and crossed his arms as his gaze held only on her. At this rate she was going to suffer a complete meltdown. "I was hoping nothing was wrong."

"Oh, y-yeah. Well, the captain... I was trying to get in touch with him, and he wasn't returning my calls. So, I was kind of..." Returning calls. Something about that phrase jammed into her other thoughts as her memory snapped to a little pink piece of paper crumpled and lying by a trash can. "I... umm..." This was a disaster. "I got your message the other day."

"You did?" he asked, and his arms uncrossed so his hands could find the pockets of his jeans. "Oh. I figured I must've left it on the wrong machine or something because you know, you never called back."

Nervously she wound the hair over her ear, willing the earth to be kind and swallow her whole. "Yeah. Well, I've been kind of busy."

"Yeah," he said, and with one glance she knew he had gotten the message she was sending. The ache in her heart followed his gaze down to the pavement. Then he looked up and caught her gaze in the depths of his. "Well, I'd better let you get back to work."

"Yeah," she said softly, feeling the middle of her soul rip in half at the hurt in his eyes.

"See ya." He turned and started across the lot as she willed herself to be strong and let him go. However, there was a little, tiny voice that said this time he wouldn't be coming back.

Insanity times two washed over her. "Jeff!" she finally called as he crossed the lot, and she wondered what in the world she was doing as her feet started after him. "Jeff, wait!"

Right in the middle of the driveway, he stopped, turned, and the hurt on his face smashed into her heart. He didn't say anything.

He didn't have to.

"Um, I was just wondering if you're... hungry," she said, battling for words and air. "I mean I only had half a sandwich for lunch, and I'm starving."

A sad hint of that lop-sided smile traced across his face. "I don't want to keep you. I know you've got things to do."

"No. Well, yeah, I do, but I may pass out from malnutrition if I don't get something in my stomach, and we wouldn't want that, would we?"

His smile increased. "No, we wouldn't want that." However, she saw the anxiety wrap around him and lace through his eyes. "So, what? There's a couple of nice places down the block." Then he looked down at his clothes, and she felt the apprehension pouring from him.

"You know what I really want?" she asked, throwing propriety to the wind. "A hot dog."

Disbelief jumped right through his apprehension. "A hot dog?"

"With chili and cheese," she said as her voice gained momentum.

He laughed. "Yeah, right."

"Seriously. That's what I want."

"Okay." He looked past her to the traffic beyond. "Well, there's a place we get lunch for the station sometimes, but it's like ten blocks down, and in this traffic..."

"We could walk," she said, liking that thought more than she knew she should.

"Are you sure?" he asked as his dark eyebrows raised at the thought.

Squaring her shoulders and her chin, she nodded. "Totally. Just point me in the right direction."

She was just being nice, Jeff told himself as they stood at the eighth intersection. He should never have run after her in the parking lot. In fact, he shouldn't have waited for her in the first place. If nothing else, he should've just watched her drive away from the safety of the GTO and been done with it. However, standing next to her at the crosswalk, he had to admit he was glad he hadn't. One more moment with her was worth all the embarrassment in the world.

Just before the lights changed, she looked at him, and he liked the smile in her eyes. "Race you." The Walk sign flashed, and in the next heartbeat she was gone.

"Hey!" In three strides he caught up with her. Heels weren't exactly the best running shoes in the world. Midway to the center, the sign flashed *Don't Walk*. Eight jog strides and they stepped up onto the next curb together. "What are you? Nuts?"

"Just trying to prove your theory wrong," she said with a shrug.

He laughed outright. "Well, I'm thinking next time, you might ought to wear better shoes."

"You don't like my shoes?" She kicked her strapped heels out past the long, straight navy skirt.

"Oh, no. There're fine unless you're racing lights. In which case…"

"You've got a point there," she said, and he couldn't help but think that she gave new meaning to the phrase traffic stopper. She looked over at him quizzically. "So, you're here, but you're not working. What's up with that?"

"CPR classes. Intensive eight-hour day on top of a 24-hour night. Fun. Fun."

When her worried gaze traced over him, he looked away and stifled the yawn. Sleep was now third or fourth priority on the list at least.

"You sure you want to be eating now? You look like you could use a nice warm bed and a soft pillow."

He yawned for real then. "Food first. Sleep later."

Not looking exactly reassured, she nodded. "So, how's work been?"

"Good. We got a call on a fire the other night…"

"Oh," she said quietly, and he saw the smile fall.

Jeff shrugged having not realize the affect that simple admission would have on her. "But as fires go, it wasn't so bad."

"That's good."

They got to the next curb, and mischief danced across his tired heart. "Ten to one we don't make it to the middle before it changes."

"Ten to one? That's a sucker's bet. Hey!" On the breath of the breeze around them, they were running across the asphalt. Two steps beyond the middle, the *Don't Walk* sign flashed. On the other side, she reached out for his back to stop him as she gasped for breath. That touch shot through him like a rocket flash. "Okay, what do I win?"

"Win?" he asked, looking back, and his heart slammed forward as her hand brushed down his back finally landing on her knees as she gasped for breath.

"You said ten to one we wouldn't make it halfway, and we did." When they started back down the walk, her strides weren't nearly as focused as they had been when she'd first strode into the fire station. "So, what do I win?"

He smiled. "I'll have to think about that one."

"Think about it? That's not fair." But before she got that out, he banked to a door on the edge of the sidewalk and opened it. After a moment's hesitation, she crossed in front of him, and into the little dimly lit café. He closed his eyes to memorize the soft fragrance of her as she passed him, and then he jumped back into reality to follow her in.

"Here." His hand brushed across her back as he guided her to a table where he pulled her chair out with one swing. Once she was seated, he carefully sat down across from her and smiled. He couldn't help it. It was what her mere presence did for him.

She tilted her head and gazed at him. "What?"

"I just never pictured you to be a hot dog fan."

"Why not?"

Softly he laughed, wondering why his gaze seemed to lock on her so naturally. "The suits, the heels, you don't exactly look like you've spent much time in dives."

"I've been in my share," she said almost defensively, but still he smiled. "What?"

"Nothing," he said, and for the life of him, he couldn't get that smile off of his face. All of life could have simply stopped, and he knew he would've been perfectly happy to just sit there, looking at her forever.

"So have you heard from Dustin and Eve lately?" Lisa asked as they crossed back into the parking lot two hours later.

"They're good," Jeff said, and even now she noticed how his hands were safely jammed into his jeans pockets. Yes, guiding her to a table, pulling out chairs, opening doors, but beyond that, he seemed wholly content to just be near her. In fact, his hands somehow looked out of place, as though they didn't really know where they were supposed to go. "I think Eve's happy to be close to her folks again."

"I can imagine although I'm surprised she even notices anybody else even occupies the planet besides him."

Jeff laughed. "They're intense, but I guess that's what you get when you really fall for somebody."

"I wouldn't know," she said with a sigh although her heart was saying much different.

"So you don't have some intensity in your life?"

At the moment? her brain asked without her permission. "No time."

"That's too bad," he said softly. "I think everybody should have time for a little intensity now and then."

She slipped up to her car door but still she wasn't ready to just get in and drive off, so she turned and leaned back onto the door. He followed her lead until they were both looking out across the parking lot, shoulder-to-shoulder. "Once I get this dumb brochure thing done, then I'll think about having a life. Until then…"

His gaze fell to the asphalt and then slipped up to her face. "Well, I hope Hayes will cut you some slack."

"What I really wish is that I could just drop the whole dumb idea off a cliff and be done with it. It's causing a lot more trouble than it was ever worth."

Concern wafted over his features. "What kind of trouble?"

She glanced over at him and tried to smile, but it had no strength behind it. Her impromptu trek through the late night Houston streets replayed through her mind, and she closed her eyes and shook her head to block it out. "I'm sure it's just me."

"What is?" he asked, turning as he laid an elbow on the top of her car.

Trying to seem like it didn't matter, she shrugged, but her hand rubbing up and down her other arm not to mention her black notebook held up to shield her from the memories betrayed the shrug. "It's nothing."

She felt his gaze narrow as outright worry across through his face. "What's nothing?"

Suddenly she was right in the middle of intensity, and she had no idea how she had gotten here. "It's just Mr. Cordell's

94

grandson." She shook her head as her gaze tried to look at him, but humiliation pulled it down to their shoes. "Let's just say he doesn't take a hint very well."

The worried scowl looked so out of place in his kind eyes. "Did he hurt you?"

She wanted to laugh at the distress in his tone, but the memories scratching through her wouldn't let her. "No, but not for want of trying."

Concern was banking toward anger on his face. "What does that mean?"

"It means I should've figured out by now that guys are after one thing and one thing only—no matter what other motives they seem to have to start with." The sound of her voice was bitter even to her own ears.

"Not all guys are like that," he said softly.

"Yeah? Well, every one I've ever met has been," she said, and harshness dripped off of every word. Quickly she shook her head. "I've got to go."

"Yeah." He nodded. "I shouldn't have kept you."

That stopped her, and the harshness dropped away when she looked at him, righting himself from her car. "I had a nice time."

He tried to hold her gaze as his hands found his pockets. "I did, too."

She opened her door as her heart begged her not to totally shut the door on him. The improbability was enough to give Einstein a headache, and yet her heart said that if she had indeed found the one nice guy left on the planet, she would be an idiot to make this the final good-bye. "Call me sometime." Rational pulled her up short with a snap, but it was too late.

His gaze jumped to hers in surprise. "Really?"

"Yeah," she said, "and I promise I'll return it this time."

With a grateful smile wafting from the depths of his eyes, Jeff nodded. "I might just do that."

The idea was always there, in the recesses of Jeff's mind, but every time he picked up the phone, his courage evaporated. She didn't really want him to call. Besides she was busy with the whole conference thing, and the last thing she needed was to be wasting time talking to him. Several times during the week her silhouette leaning against that car drifted through his mind, and every time, he saw the defensiveness and the stay-in-your-space stance in her eyes. *Wary*, he thought Wednesday afternoon as the clock wound around to two o'clock. That was a good way to describe how she looked.

"Hey, watch the water thing!" Dante yelled from the opposite side of the truck as the memories drifting through Jeff's head took reality right along with them for a moment too long, causing the water hose in his hands to get a little wilder than he had planned.

"Sorry!" he called over the metal.

"Sure you are," Dante muttered, and Jeff refocused on the task at hand.

With one hand he reached into the bucket teeming with suds as the other held the water hose. The silver across the front of the truck gleamed in the bright sunshine as the sponge worked its way to the other side.

"Think fast!" Dante called over the truck, and Jeff ducked the second he saw the shadow of the object arcing over the top of the truck. The sponge hit the bucket beyond with a splash.

"Nice shot!" Jeff said approvingly.

"Thanks."

He trained the water back to the front tire as his sponge worked across the black rubber.

"Hmm," the voice said behind him, and when he turned, water from both the sponge and the hose splattered across the sidewalk.

"Li... sa?" he asked in surprise as he straightened. He couldn't be totally sure. Her hair cascading down in a brown fall, streaked with just a touch of lighter brown deleted what he had previously thought of as the most gorgeous woman in the world from the disc of his mind. "I didn't... hey... Um, are you here to see the captain?"

Her eyes danced right along with her smile as she brushed a piece of hair that blew into her face back. "Yeah. Is he around?"

"I think he's..." Jeff's gaze ripped from hers into the station. "Yeah, he's right in there." The water followed his attempt to point, and it splashed across the puddles on the driveway as he did.

She looked down at her shoes that had been splattered by the motion.

"Oh, man, I'm sorry," Jeff said as his nerves jumped to the surface. He wasn't at all sure that if he was thinking straight he could've figured out what to do with the hose and the sponge so he could get her dry again, but one thing was for sure, straight was so far away he couldn't even see it.

"It's okay," she said as she backed up. "I've been meaning to take a bath." He laughed hollowly as she glanced into the station. "I'd better go. See you when I get done?"

"I'll be here," he said, and when she stepped away, his heart plummeted out in front of him. Whoa. She was the most beautiful person he'd ever laid eyes on.

"Heads up!" Dante yelled from the top of the truck, and before Jeff had a second to rejoin reality, he turned just as the sponge hit the bucket in front of him, sending suds in a fountain right over the top of him.

"Ugh! Dant!" he yelled furiously. "Crud!"

"Sorry," Dante said with a laugh.

Jeff shook the suds off his arms even as he tried to wipe them off his face. "Sure you are." Then his gaze chanced into the station, and as hard as she was trying not to laugh, Lisa's whole face was lit with laughter. He shook his head at her as his own smile jumped to the surface. *Smooth. Real smooth.* He arched his eyebrows skyward helplessly.

"Oh. You're back again?" Captain Hayes said to her, and Lisa's attention snapped away from Jeff as she stepped into the space vacated by the fireman who had been talking with the captain.

Their conversation faded as Lisa turned her back to the sunshine beyond the garage doors. Jeff tried to keep his mind and his attention on the water and the truck and away from her, but that was like pulling ice molecules apart. No, when she was around, his attention was fused to her, and that was just all there was to it.

The captain pointed up the stairs, and Jeff watched her nod. When she turned, her gaze caught on his for one more second, and a mutual acknowledgement passed between them. She was halfway up the steps when Dante yelled, "Bombs away!"

Instinctively Jeff ducked just as another sponge hit the bucket. Life was so great.

There was only one reason to come and show Hayes the completed brochure, and that reason had nothing to do with

Captain Hayes or the brochure. It had only to do with the fact that her phone hadn't rung in a week. Every single time that thing so much as jingled at work, every piece of her senses jumped out to sit right next to Sherie answering it.

In fact, she had taken to leaving her door open so she could better hear the calls as they came in. However, by Wednesday she could take it no more. So first she called to confirm that the captain was actually on site, and then her feet and heart flew her over until she was sitting across from Hayes acting like a seventh grader handing in her homework as her mind wandered down the stairs and out to the front to the fire truck gleaming in the sunlight.

"Very nice," the captain finally said after reading over the maroon and silver plastic-coated booklet. "And this has gone out to the schools?"

"Umm, yes. Yesterday, Sir," Lisa said, straightening.

"Well, I wish I could say it's horrible and it's never going to work, but if they don't go for it after this, I don't think dynamite would convince them."

"Thank you, Sir," she said sincerely touched by the compliment.

"You mind if I keep this one?" he asked, holding it up.

"Oh, no that would be fine." Furtively she looked at her watch. On to Plan B. "Umm, now that we've got this part taken care of, I was wondering if you knew of any other speakers who might be interested—apart from Mr. Fletcher of course."

As soon as Hayes leaned back thoughtfully, she knew it would be enough to kill a few minutes. Now if Jeff would just hang around if Hayes got on anything resembling a roll, her plan had an actual chance of working.

The trucks were back in the garage, and Jeff was busy rechecking the last of the compartments. Everything seemed to be in place. He slammed that door just as he heard the heels. He was really starting to like that sound. The smile was there before he even turned, and her gaze was on him before he'd so much as said something to get her attention.

"Everything cool?" he asked when she got to the third step from the bottom.

"Almost," she said, looking around hesitantly. "I guess you're on all night again?"

"As always." He held his hands out palms up.

"And you don't have to go get take-out?"

"No, I think Hunter roped me into something last time because he knew he could."

"Oh," she said slowly, seeing her plan disintegrate before her eyes. "So you're stuck here then, huh?"

"Pretty much."

Her gaze and his heart landed on the floor as she pulled her notebook closer to her chest.

"I'm off tomorrow night though," he said slowly, knowing that wasn't what she was after, but hoping it was all the same. "Well, after the CPR test is over at five."

The smile in her eyes flitted across the strings of his heart just as he heard the voices from down the hall.

"I think you're an egg short of a basket, Hunt," Dante said in annoyance. "The whole idea was to… Oh, well. What have we here?"

Instantly Jeff's gaze toppled to his shoes as he backed away from her.

"Well, well." Dante surveyed her slowly, and Jeff felt her back further away from him. "I don't think we've been formally introduced," Dante said smoothly, and Jeff's protective shields came out. However, he was at a distinct disadvantage, and he knew it. "Dante Ramirez."

"Lisa Matheson." She held her hand out to him, and Jeff noted that the formal tone was back in her voice.

"This is my buddy, Hunter Witkowski," Dante said.

"Hunter." Lisa shook his hand as if they were about to sit down for a conference call. The smallest of awkward moments passed before Lisa smiled tightly at all of them in general. "Well, I'd better get back to work. It was nice to meet you all."

"Same here," Hunter said with a small waving. And with that, she put her gaze on the concrete, turned, and walked out.

Had he had the means and the method, Jeff definitely had the motive to kill Hunter and Dante.

"Taylor." Hunter clapped him on the shoulder which brought him back to reality with a crash. "Dante here just nominated you for cooking duty tonight."

His heart lay shredded on the floor as he felt her spirit slip away from him. "Well, I guess I'd better go get to work then."

All day Thursday Lisa batted the suggestion around in her head. Back and forth. Back and forth. Five o'clock. Five o'clock. Showing up without even her normal lame excuses was frightening beyond words. Yet she couldn't get the time or his eyes out of her head. By 4:30 her brain was in an all-out war with her heart. Going was certifiably insane, but not going was going to make her batty too. Finally at 4:45 she gave up and grabbed her purse. He wouldn't be there anymore. At least then she could tell herself that it was fate that had kept them apart and not her.

"Have a good night," she said to Sherie at the door.

Sherie checked her with an odd look as she glanced at her watch. "Yeah, you too."

For the hundred-thousandth time Jeff looked at his watch as the clock wound the around to five 'til five. She wouldn't be out there. He hoped she would, but she wouldn't. Two more pencil marks and he called it good enough.

"Time," the teacher called, and Jeff stood, wanting and yet simultaneously not wanting to get out to the parking lot.

"See ya Tuesday, Taylor," Hunter said with a smile that Jeff didn't like at all.

"Sure, see ya." Knowing what a scene it would make if he went out to the parking lot with them and she was waiting, he hung back, collecting his books and notebook as slowly as possible. When the room had cleared, he exhaled. She wouldn't be there. Getting his hopes up that she would was a one-way ticket to unbelievable heartache.

Once in the parking lot, he surveyed the cars quickly. No little white Cavalier to be seen, and his heart plummeted. He looked at his watch. Maybe she got caught in traffic. Maybe she was running late. Crawling behind the wheel of the GTO, the list of maybes flowed through him. It was only five after. Even college professors got ten minutes.

"This is crazy. What the heck am I doing?" Lisa asked angrily as

100

she turned the car into the fire station parking lot at 5:13. "He's long gone, and I should be working. Not..." But that thought sliced in two when she saw the GTO still sitting at the far end of the parking lot. Panic hit her one second after the relief. "Oh, great. Now what?" The part of her that was happy about the car being there was also the part of her that started traipsing through her chest at the sight of it. Angling her car next to his, she pulled into the space wishing she had a clue what came next.

With every tick of the clock, Jeff had told himself she wasn't coming until all but one lone hold-out believed it. However, the second she pulled in next to him, all of the deserters fell all over themselves thanking the hold-out for keeping them there. In one motion he jumped from the car and ran over to hers as she stood, business mode stretched tightly across her.

"You made it," he said as his hands found his pockets lest they actually reach out and hug her like they wanted to.

"I'm late," she said softly.

He shrugged. "No big deal. The class ran a little over anyway."

For a second he let himself notice the hair falling across the small round arch of her shoulder. It was enough to send his senses flying off the radarscope. "You hungry?"

She looked up, and he was surprised that his feet didn't actually float right off the earth. "What do you have in mind?"

"How about Mexican? I haven't had a good enchilada in forever."

"Sounds good," she said. "I know this little place out in La Porte we could try. A friend of mine said it was pretty good."

"La Porte?" he asked skeptically. "But that's like... 30 miles away."

"Oh, well, if you don't want to... I mean if you're tired..."

"No, I just figured you'd be wanting to get back to work."

"Work will still be there tomorrow," she said, and her voice faded on the words. "So, you want to take your car or mine?"

"Mine's cool if that's okay with you."

"Fine by me."

Being with him was so easy. Alarm bells weren't ringing through her head at every move he made, and there wasn't a piece of her that thought he would so much as suggest something that made her uncomfortable. In fact when they left the Houston traffic behind and the car picked up speed, Lisa couldn't remember ever feeling so free or so safe.

She laid her head back on the headrest and drank in the day around her. If it never got any better than this, she would never complain. When they got to the restaurant, she waited for him to run around and open her door. With him it wasn't about who had the power, and she sensed that it never would be.

In minutes they were seated on a little patio overlooking the beautiful Gulf of Mexico. The breeze blowing in sent her hair skittering across her face, and she tossed it back with a flick of her fingers.

"So, how's work?" Lisa asked after they had ordered.

"It'll be better Monday."

"Oh? What's Monday?"

"The gods finally had mercy on me. They switched me to B Shift."

"And that's better?"

"I was on C, but they just handed out some promotions, and now they're a couple hands short over on B, so I get the lucky draw."

"So, does the captain go with you?" she asked suddenly seeing her one connection to him disintegrate.

"Nope. New shift, new captain. Rainier. But he's pretty cool. I worked that fire under him that night. He seems pretty together."

"And Hayes isn't?"

"Oh, Hayes just has his favorites, and I don't think I'm one of them."

"Why not?"

"There's always a pecking order, but with Hayes, it's a little more visible than usual."

"So you'll be happy with the change then?"

"Yeah. I know a couple of the guys on that shift already, so it's not square one. At least I won't have Dante giving me showers on a regular basis anymore."

She laughed as her gaze drifted over his face. She had kind of like that shower.

All Jeff wanted to do was make the night last forever. When he glanced over at her, relaxed in the passenger seat later, his heart pleaded with him to find a way to make that happen. "Have you ever been out to the Pointe?"

"What's that?" she asked, leaning her head to the side.

"You want to find out?"

"Sure."

It had literally been years since Jeff had put the top down. Up until they parked on the Pointe he hadn't had a really good reason to, but the night was so peaceful, and the stars were so bright, for this one moment he just wanted to experience all of it.

"Where're you going?" she asked when he reached for his door handle.

"Sit tight."

She sat up anyway as he got out and started to work first on one side and then on the other. If they were going to make this a habit, he really needed to put some oil on the latches. The second side finally broke loose, and carefully he pulled the folds of the top back.

"Oh, wow," she breathed, laying back into the seat as she looked up into the velvet-and-diamond night above her. "It's gorgeous."

He got back in, tried to lean back, but he had to rework the position of the seat before he could fully appreciate the world she was looking at. In the short distance ahead, the lap of the waves brushed onto the shore as the soft night wrapped around them. Even breathing felt more real than it ever had before. His gaze chanced over to her, and fascination coupled with awe as she lay back, looking out far beyond the boundaries of the earth.

"I don't think I've ever seen them like this before," she breathed. "It's like they're right there." As if she could in fact touch them, Lisa reached a hand up. "Like Orion. See it, right there."

Training his gaze to where she pointed, he edged his shoulder across the seat and rested his hand on the gearshift between them.

"See, the four stars in a box and then the three together in the middle? That's Orion. Man, Haley would love this. She was always so nuts about this stuff."

"You're not into stars?"

"I never really thought about it. Actually the only ones I've ever really seen were the ones in Haley's books. But this is so awesome." Slowly her hand fell from the sky, and it landed right on top of his. An instant of hesitation, and he felt the decision run across her palm, then she went still.

"You know, I always thought the point of life was to get ahead," she said after several long minutes had slipped by. "But I'm beginning to think I was wrong."

He dropped his gaze over to her, sitting there, still looking up at the stars, and her face was softer than he had ever seen it. Gently he turned his hand over on the gearshift, and when hers came back down to meet his, the mesh was flawless. An inch at a time he shouldered his way across the seat until the rest of her was a breath away. "Does it get any better than this?"

"I wouldn't know how."

By the time they were back in the fire station parking lot, it was after eleven. It was strange because since she'd been in this parking lot the last time, life had become far simpler for Lisa. His hand, her hand, and that was it.

"So, what's up for tomorrow?" he asked, looking across the seat at her.

"Work," she said softly. It seemed so far away. "You?"

"Sleep tonight. Work 'til Saturday morning. Oh, joy."

A pause as the night held them in its embrace.

"And Saturday?"

"A day off for a change. Hallelujah," he said.

"Hmm, a day off. I don't think I even remember what that's like anymore."

He laughed.

"So you're not doing anything Saturday night then?" she asked.

"Saturday night?" He swung his gaze to her suspiciously. "I don't know. What do you have in mind?"

"Mind? Oh. Nothing. I was just asking."

"Oh," he said, and his spirit seemed to dip back to his side.

Her brain said she must be completely nuts for even contemplating asking the question in her head; however, her heart simply wasn't listening anymore. "You ever try rock climbing?"

"Rock climbing?" His eyes widened in surprise. "Uh, we don't exactly live near many rocks."

"No, not real rocks. The fake ones over at the Rock Gym."

"Oh, yeah, Dustin and I went there once. It's pretty cool."

"I've always thought that looked like fun. Maybe we could…" Then she glanced over at him. "But if you don't want to, we could always do something else."

"No, it sounds like fun."

Although he tried to hide it, she saw the yawn. "You really need to get some sleep. You're making me tired."

"Yeah, that CPR stuff is more exhausting than you'd think." A moment more and he smiled, released her hand, got out, went around, and opened her door. Something about that simple act seemed so thoughtful. She got out, and in six steps they were at her car. She knew the night was over; however, in all her years on earth she had never been with a single person she simply did not want to say good-bye to—until now.

"You just want to meet over there?" he asked as she leaned on her car door.

"Okay." The traffic noise descended around them. When she glanced at him, he looked more nervous than her stomach felt. "So, I guess this is good night."

"Yeah, guess so."

A second and then two. She waited, but he never moved. As slowly as she could, she pulled her keys out and opened the door. If he would just reach out, stop her, pull her into his arms, she wouldn't have even protested, but he didn't. The door was open, and she looked back at him, gaze down and hands in his pockets. "Saturday? Six or so?"

With the smallest of smiles, he nodded. Gingerly she folded herself into the seat, and he took hold of the door. "Drive careful."

"You too," she said, and for one split second she thought he might lean in and kiss her; however, as quickly as that thought went through her brain, it was gone as he stepped back and shut the door.

How many times had she wished the guys in her past would just leave her alone? Now that she had one that she wanted to kiss her, he just closed her door. Something about that made no sense.

As she pulled into traffic, he was still standing there, watching her drive away.

Eight

"Have a good evening," Lisa said, Saturday afternoon at 4:30 as she strode through the outer office, her hair in a ponytail and sweats gracing her frame.

Sherie's face dropped in surprise. "Where are you going?"

"Rock climbing," Lisa said as excitement pulled a smile to her face. "See ya." And she left her secretary open mouthed, staring after her.

By the time he yanked the electric blue pullover and black jeans on Saturday at five, there were so many emotions swirling around in Jeff's body, brain, and heart that he couldn't catch even one of them long enough to analyze it. Excitement was there, but so was dread, and fear, and the certainty that somehow he would find a way to mess this up.

This wasn't really a date, he told himself. Well, it kind of was, but if he thought about the implications of that too long, he was sure his brain would completely short circuit. Running a quick comb through his short, black hair, he pulled the chain from the dresser, put it on, and looked down at the cross. "You're going to have to help me with this one, God. 'Cause I have no idea what I'm doing."

"Do you know how insane this is?" Lisa asked as she stood, strapped to a hard nylon cable at the bottom of a jutted beige-brown structure, curving its way up a side wall that loomed two stories above them. That wall looked much taller than it had in the brochure she had picked up months before, and the music blaring on the speakers sounded like a night club gone mad.

"Hey. This was your idea," Jeff said, sliding the spotter's harness around his waist.

As she readjusted her own harness, Lisa's gaze snapped to the glint of the gold chain at his neck. Between that cross and the electric blue shirt curving right along with his muscles, she knew the wall was going to have a hard time holding her attention.

"Well, next time, talk me out of it," she breathed, wondering what part of her said this was a good idea.

One more cinch and he grabbed the rope between them. "Okay, I'm ready."

Her gaze traveled up the rock, and then she shook her head. "I'm not. Let's go home." She turned from the wall although she was still strapped to it.

However, she hadn't taken even a step when he grabbed her shoulders to stop her. "Hey, now. No chickening out." Laughing softly, he turned her back to the wall. "Now, get up there."

Exhaling slowly, she took a step forward, reached up for the first handhold and laid a foot on one lower. One pull and she was up six inches from the ground. That wasn't so bad. She reached for the next one, and wound her foot around beneath her to find a support. Up.

"Cool," he said from behind her, and she felt the slack go out of the rope. "Looking good."

At that moment, it entered her mind what he was actually looking at and still holding on, she glanced back at him. "Hey, now, keep your mind on the rocks."

"It was." Then he laughed. "Well, mostly."

She reached up. Two more movements, and she was a full four feet off the ground. "Would now be a bad time to tell you I'm afraid of heights?"

His laugh jumped to her ears. "I think you should've thought of that before now." The laughter faded. "Just don't look down."

"Don't look down," she said to herself. "That ought to be easy enough." A hand, a foot, a hand, a foot, and she reached the first big jut. "So, how does popcorn and a movie sound?"

"For tomorrow?"

"No. For right now." Her body was climbing even as her mind tried to find something else to think about.

"Have you ever heard the term concentration?" he asked as the slack disappeared from the rope. "You might want to try it sometime."

"Have you ever heard the term scared to death?" One hand reached up to the little rock she could barely get to as her knee arched onto the jut. The only good thing was that if her own body failed her, she knew his wouldn't. The only bad thing was, what her body really wanted to do was turn around and look at his holding her there.

"You're doing good. Don't stop now."

"How tall do you think this thing is anyway?"

"I don't know. Forty-fifty feet?"

"Really?" She started to look at him, but her hand didn't quite have hold, and it slipped off, sending her crashing into the hard surface. "Ow."

"You okay?"

"Crud," she said, holding on with one hand as she shook her other hand and examined her nails. "I broke a nail."

"You want to come down?"

She looked up and then down. Halfway. There was no halfway in her vocabulary. "No. I made it this far. I'm not quitting now." With renewed determination, she reached up and grabbed a support. "Do you have any idea how sore I'm going to be in the morning?"

"A little?"

"Yeah, a little," she said as her foot found another hold, and her gaze slipped up the side of the rock that now angled just enough backward to make her stomach turn. Pushing that away, she willed her arms not to fail her. One grab, two. She could see the top now, it was only a few hand holds up. The pull on her arm muscles was unbelievable. It felt like 5 G's of torque stretching every fiber.

"Who's dumb idea was this anyway?" she asked the ceiling above her. There was only one more hold to the ceiling. She could see it, but her body was already stretched to its limit. As she clung there like Spiderman, she looked around trying to see a way to get to that last one without having the ability to fly. Her arms were screaming at her to just go back down, but that one more hold taunted her. *Just one more.*

"What's wrong?" he called from far below her.

109

"I'm just not…" As she stretched for the last hold, her foot slipped away from its mooring, and her body spun away from the wall dangerously. "Ahh!" A hand, a foot, and suddenly the only part of her attached to the wall was one hand stretched far above her.

"It's okay! I've got you!"

The rope around her tightened as her body screamed in fright. Frantically she lurched for the hold above her as panic shrieked that she was going to fall if she didn't get a hold of something.

"Lisa! It's okay. I've got you. Let go."

Her heart dropped right through the center of her chest. How far had he said she was above the ground? It felt like miles. Finally her hand found the other hold. She grabbed onto it, but when she forced her other arm to retake the other hold, tears sprang to her eyes. There was no strength left in it.

"Listen to me," he called from below, concern bleeding through the words. "Just let go. I've got you. Lisa, let go."

And then what? I crash to the ground? No way. She reached up to grab the support again, but sharp pain screeched down her arm with the effort. How many handholds were there on the way back down?

"Hello, am I going to have to come up there and get you?" he asked. "Because I will, you know."

Humiliation crowded through her. If her arm just didn't hurt so badly, she could make it back to the ground on her own.

"Lisa, let go." This time it was a command, not a request. Then his voice softened. "I promise I won't let you fall."

Squeezing her eyes against what would happen next, she released first one foot, and then the other slipped from its hold. For one small moment the rope jerked, and her heart jumped into her throat. But in the next heartbeat she was floating downward as peacefully as if she was on a cloud. Small jerks and only that as she slowly drifted to the ground. The closer her feet got, the more her shoulder hurt, and she reached up and rubbed it gingerly as tears stung her eyes.

Two seconds after her feet hit the mat, he was next to her. "Are you okay?"

"Yeah," she said furiously as she beat the tears back. "But I didn't make the top."

"Well, you got back down in one piece. That's what counts."

110

Annoyance with herself seeped through her as she looked at him. "I think I'll just go grab something from the snack bar. You can find somebody to spot you." Her hands were working to unlock the harness at her waist and chest, but her right arm hurt every time she so much as moved it.

"That's okay." With no hesitation, he reached over to help her, and in two clicks she was free. "I'm not really in the mood to go up tonight anyway."

"But…"

Quickly he let his own harness down to the floor. "What do you say? How does a hot dog sound?"

An instant of embarrassment, and reluctant gratefulness washed over her. "Wonderful."

Seated across from her in the little booth, Jeff looked over at her—exhausted and clearly in pain when she moved—he couldn't quite figure out why she had suggested the outing in the first place. On top of that, he wasn't at all sure he should ask. "How's the fingernail?"

She pulled one hand up to display the jagged white over red index nail. "It's been better."

"How's the shoulder?"

Her gaze fell to the table as her opposite hand reached up for it. "Sore."

The question tracked across the middle of his forehead. "You know, we could've just gone to the movies or something."

"I figured you'd be bored at the movies."

"Bored? I love the movies. Besides it's better than you getting hurt."

Slowly she shrugged. "I just thought this looked like fun, but I either never had time, or I never had anyone to go with."

He swirled the water in his glass. "Your friends didn't want to go?"

"What friends?" she asked, and the admission in that question pulled her gaze down.

"Your friends," he said as he leveled a questioning gaze on her. "You know the people you hang out with."

"The people I hang out with are the three people who work for me, and I don't think they'd consider me a friend."

"But surely you have... I don't know... college friends, high school friends—something?"

Back and forth her head moved, and his heart fell at the sad look on her face.

"I've had a few friends, here and there, but I guess I never made the time to really hang on to them. Most of them I don't even know where they are now."

"But you go out surely?"

"On business," she said, and he saw the cringe. "Or with Haley once in awhile, but that won't be happening much anymore." He watched as she leaned over next to the wall, her ponytail swinging gently over her shoulder. "I wanted to get ahead, so I put all my energy into making the company a success." She laughed. "Bad thing is, it's still a disaster, and what do I have to show for it?"

If he could've put his arms around her, he would have.

"Number 76," the speaker above them said, and Jeff looked up.

"I'll be right back." With a swipe he collected their food from the front counter, and angled his way back over to the table where he set her hot dog and fries in front of her. "You need ketchup or mustard?"

Without looking up she nodded, and he turned back for the condiments. When he came back, he could see by her face that it was time to talk about something else. "Have you ever dropped mustard on carpet?"

She glanced up at him as if he'd just dropped there from Mars.

"No, seriously." He worked putting ketchup on his plate before holding up the little bag he had just opened. "You want some?"

Slowly she nodded.

"I was making a sandwich at my apartment one time, and I dropped a whole jar of mustard, and now there's this horrible yellow stain right under one of the bar stools. I've tried everything, but I think that thing is part of the carpet now."

"Did you try vinegar?" Lisa asked, taking one fry out of the basket.

"No."

"You should've just put some vinegar on it and laid a towel over it."

112

"That works?"

"It's supposed to. I read that somewhere. I always thought it was a good thing to know, but I think you have to do it right away before it sets."

"So, it wouldn't work now?"

She shrugged and winced with the movement. "You could try it. What's it going to hurt?"

His glance chanced down to her uneaten food. "You not hungry?"

"Oh." She looked at the hot dog with chili still lying whole in the basket. "I'm not sure how to pick it up."

He thought for a second. "Sit tight." Quickly he jumped up and went to the counter where he retrieved a small plastic fork. When he returned, he slid her basket over and cut the hot dog into eight portions. Then he slid the basket back and laid the fork with it. "There. That ought to help."

She reached in not bothering with the fork, grabbed one small bite from the end, and popped it into her mouth.

"Better?"

Her eyes danced with gratefulness. "Much."

Later as she lay between the cool sheets and took the heating pad off her shoulder, Lisa smiled as the memory of him waltzed through her head. He still hadn't kissed her, but in reality he had touched her far more deeply than anyone who ever had. As she closed her eyes, the feeling of floating, supported by the anchor of him drifted over her. It was a feeling she could get used to.

Although she really wanted to just chunk work, it was piling up, so Sunday when he called, she had to tell him no. Monday was the same story although he was on shift anyway. By Tuesday, however, Lisa was starting to worry that he might just stop calling altogether—although she had done her level best not to give him that impression on the phone.

As she sat in her office on Tuesday evening, she glanced at the clock and concern traced through her. He hadn't called, and as normal as that should've felt, it didn't feel normal at all. The questions flowed through her. Had he been called in? Was there some big fire she hadn't heard about? Hoping it would see nothing, her gaze traveled up from her paperwork and back over her shoulder to the bits of the sky she could see beyond the windows. No billows of smoke that she could see, and yet there was so much she couldn't see. "Stop thinking about that, you're going to make yourself crazy."

"Lisa," Sherie said at the door.

"Yeah?"

"I'm going to take off."

"Okay."

However, Sherie didn't move. "Umm, and there's someone here to see you."

Tucker. The name slammed into Lisa's consciousness on the dreamy sound of Sherie's voice. Gently Lisa reached up and rubbed her still-tender shoulder as she prayed for the strength to fight him off. Knowing that letting him into her office would be a huge mistake, she stood and righted her suit jacket as Sherie turned back for the front office. Lisa's stride held determination and dignity as she rounded the desk and followed her secretary out and into the reception area.

"Sherie, did you find those..." However, the instant Lisa stepped into the outer office, the sentence stopped. There, in the middle of it, stood a dream she hadn't even allowed herself to have. Black jeans, white T-shirt, denim cover shirt, that gold cross—the beauty of the single pink rose he was holding paled in comparison to him. "Jeff."

"Hi," he said, but his gaze couldn't quite hold hers. "Umm, I thought I'd stop by and bring you this." Awkwardly he held it out to her, and her left hand reached over to accept it.

"Th-thanks." The petals looked like soft velvet, and Lisa couldn't help but put it to her nose and breathe in its sweet, soft fragrance. Air flowing into her lungs felt so good that she took another long smell, and the top of her brain started swimming from all the oxygen.

"I'll just..." Sherie said quietly gathering her things and pointing to the door. Lisa didn't have the presence of mind to say good-bye.

Seconds flowed past each other like water over river rocks as in Sherie's absence the silence of the office engulfed them. Finally Lisa's sanity cracked back into place. "Um. Come... come on in."

114

"You sure?" he asked as his hands found the pockets of his jeans.

"Yeah, maybe your brain will work better than mine seems to be." In an I-can't-believe-he's-here haze, Lisa walked back into her office, feeling his presence fill the room around her the second he stepped through that door. At first she laid the rose on her desk, but the desk was such a mess, she picked it up again and laid it on the top of the computer monitor. In rapid succession her hands flitted over the desktop, trying to clear it off enough so she wouldn't look so chaotic, and so she could actually see him when she sat down. Suddenly she noticed that he was still standing in front of the desk. "Oh, please, have a seat."

Slowly he slid into one of the chairs, and his gaze on her yanked up her nerves in fistfuls. "So, this is where the magic happens."

"Well, this is where something happens, but I'm not sure it could be called magic." In her hands was a stack of files, and she looked around for a good place to put them. Finally in desperation, she stacked them on the floor next to the wall, careful to let her left arm do most of the moving. "I'm sorry. If I would've known you were coming…"

"Hey, you don't have to clean on my account. I work in a fire station. Remember?"

Why that made a difference, she couldn't quite tell but still she appreciated the effort. Seeing the utter futility of her cleaning efforts, she finally sat down and folded her hands on her desk. "So, what's up?"

As if it took real effort, he shrugged as he shifted slightly in the chair. "I was just driving by, and I figured you've seen where I work, so…"

She wished she'd had a week to get the office presentable. That's why she usually used the conference room for one-on-one meetings. That way nobody saw how jumbled her life really was. Her gaze chanced around the office even now wanting to find a way to keep him from seeing the mess. "Did you want to go get something to eat or something?"

"No. I just… I'm sorry." He started to stand. "This was a bad idea. You're working. I shouldn't have come."

"No!" The word jumped from her throat and her heart simultaneously. "I mean you don't have to leave or anything. I just thought, I mean, sitting in an office all night isn't exactly the greatest date experience."

"Yeah, well, we all know how wonderful the last one of those we had turned out." That lop-sided smile played through her brain as half-standing, half-sitting he looked right at her. "How's your shoulder anyway?"

"As long as I don't get it past... there." She raised it midway to shoulder level and winced in pain. "It's great besides that."

"See, maybe we'd be safer just hanging out doing..." He sat back down. "What is it you were doing again?"

Stress blindsided her, and she sighed heavily. "Kamden Foods. I've got to find a workable concept tonight, and nothing sounds right."

Skeptically he looked across her desk at the scattered mock-ups. "Well, what have you come up with so far?"

She fingered one paper, wondering how he was suddenly sitting across from her asking to see her work. A moment of decision and she stacked the papers together and handed them across the desk. "They're not very good."

His gaze held hers for one second before she dropped the papers into his hands. Slowly he pulled himself up in the chair with his elbows. Then he grew still, and her heart stopped. Trying to find something else to think about or at least look at, she refocused her attention on her computer. Being graded, she hated that.

"This one's pretty good," he said after her nerves had crawled all the way outside her skin.

She looked over, and her eyebrows arched in revulsion. "That one?"

"Yeah, I like the fade thing on the edges." He glanced at her. "What? You don't like it?"

"That's like the worst one of all of them."

"Cool," he said as his eyes danced. "If that's the worst one, then there's got to be something we can use." He picked up a cotton candy pink one. "How about this?"

The laugh jumped to her throat as she shook her head. "You're kidding, right?"

"Not the color, but I like the line, 'Where Houston Shops.' Nice, short, catchy."

"It's not too bad," she admitted with a small smile. Her hand reached over and clicked the mouse across her computer as she pulled that one back up and cut out the tag before placing it on a new sheet.

"Now I like this one—the whole display falling over on the guy. Funny."

From the fringes of her eyelashes she looked over at him, and her heart said that not one of her employees had ever put even a tenth of this much heart into any project they had ever worked on.

"Here, look at this." He pulled himself forward to her desk. "You take the tag from this one, and the color off of this one, and the concept from this one…" His gaze snagged on hers. "What?"

Lisa couldn't have stopped the smile had she tried. "You."

"Me?"

"Yes, you." Had she tried to explain it, she couldn't have, so she ducked her head. "Show me what you're thinking."

Three hours later they had mock-ups for the billboards, the newspapers, and the store circulars. Outside there was nothing but faded sunlight twining through the buildings beyond. Jeff watched her stand from her desk and stretch in that deep navy suit.

"So, how long have you been in that chair?" he asked as she got ready to go.

"How long have you been alive?" she asked, grabbing a few more things before she picked up her keys and the rose.

"You really need to get out more."

"Uh-huh." She followed him out and locked the door behind them. "We tried that, remember? I think I'm safer behind my desk."

"Well, we don't have to go that extreme." He waited for her to lock the hallway door. "Maybe for you we should start with something small and safe—like flying kites."

She turned a skeptical gaze on him. "Kites?"

He shrugged. "So long as we anchor you to the ground, I don't think you could hurt yourself too badly."

"Gee, thanks."

"Then we can work our way up to say bowling or something."

"Oh, great." Lisa pushed through the door to the stairwell and started climbing to the third level.

"By the way, what's up with parking on the third level anyway?" he asked from behind her as they climbed. "Wouldn't it be easier to park on the floor you work on?"

"Exercise," she said as she opened the door and stepped out into the parking garage. To the far right sat her car, right next to it sat the dark muscle car with the top pulled down. "How'd you find me anyway?"

"Car. Building. Directory. Lisa." He shrugged as his hands found his pockets. "It wasn't hard." The logistics weren't bad, it was convincing his brain that this was all a good idea that had been the difficult part. "How about we go for some supper?"

"Hot dogs?" she asked.

"Your call."

Talking with him, being with him was so unbelievably easy. The whole when-is-this-going-to-turn-into-a-wrestling-match thing was simply a non-issue with him. At the little café, he sat on one side of the booth, she on the other. No questions, no pressure.

In fact, he didn't so much as even reach out to take her hand, and by the time they were speeding back through the Houston night to her car, the need to just touch him was overwhelming. So when he laid his hand on the gearshift, hers slipped over his and caught there. She smiled over at him as the night floated past them.

"You know, you're going to have to teach me to drive this thing some time," she said, brushing a wind-kissed strand of hair from her eyes.

His gaze jumped to hers in surprise. "You got a day in mind?"

"Friday, Saturday, Sunday?" It didn't matter, to her heart any day, any minute that she could spend with him was the only one she wanted to be living.

Nine

Jeans. Lisa hadn't worn a pair of them since junior year in college. That was the year the course of her life had been set in stone. Professional. It was how you dressed if you wanted anyone to take you seriously.

She gazed into the mirror at the ponytail holding her hair Saturday morning. Until that moment the one and only focus of her life had been to show the whole world that she was serious, that she was for real, that she was more than just some pretty face who had cotton candy for brains. Ponytails and jeans were for teenagers.

The knock on her door jolted her from the thoughts, and she had to beat down the pounding of her heart. On legs she forced to be steady, she went to her door; however, the sight of him on the other side of that threshold sent her heart into an all-out spasm.

"Hi," she said as the softness of the gray jersey-shirt and the glint of the gold chain shining just beneath it at the edge of his throat stopped the breath in her chest.

"Hi." His hands jammed into his pockets as his gaze fell from hers, and her brain waves scrambled. "I think I'm a little early."

"That's okay. Just let me grab my shoes." She sat down on the couch, pulling the hard denim of her jeans down when they didn't stretch with her. "So, where are we going?"

"I thought we could go over to Memorial Park. It'll probably be jammed, but surely we can whittle out a few square inches."

She stood, grabbed her purse, thought better of that move, and pulled money out to put in her pocket. "Ready."

There had always been something about flying kites that had fascinated Jeff. It had ever since he was little when he and Kit would finally beg enough so their mom would take them to the little park near their home. After catching a nice breeze, the triangle, dragon kite sailed up, up, and away from him, and Jeff stepped back, watching it soar higher and higher.

"Impressive," Lisa said from the blanket ten feet away.

"Yeah, I noticed you're not over here helping," he called in her direction teasingly.

"Watching. That's much safer."

"Oh, come on. I promise, I won't let you fly away." He stepped over to her, careful to keep the kite in the air as he reached down for her hand. One second of hesitation, and her slim, smooth hand latched onto his. She stood, and he didn't miss the brush she did to the backside of her jeans. Gently he pulled her farther away from the tree, and out into the open field where he transferred control of the kite to her. "It's not hard."

However, the second she took control, her face set as if she was working on a micro-chemical component in a laboratory that might explode at any moment. His gaze chanced over her.

"Hey, this is supposed to be fun, remember?" he asked, but with only inches separating them, even he was having trouble remembering that.

"I'm not very good at fun," she said, and he noticed how her whole body set to alert at the very word.

"Well, then we need to work on that." Carefully he reached around her, and although the curve of her arm was only a breath from his, he managed to keep just that much distance between them. "Roll some out." His hand helped hers without touching it.

"Aren't you worried about highline wires?" she asked.

He laughed. "Look around you, do you see any highline wires?"

She brushed the hair out of her face from the breeze. "Well, no."

"Here, let's sit." He folded himself onto the grass.

Her gaze jumped down to him nervously. "What?"

Reaching up, he took her hand, and his brain instantly said that highline wires weren't the only electricity conductors in the area. "It's okay." He pulled her down next to him. However, she sat like a rod, and the inches she put between them felt like miles.

"Here. Man, you're using way too much energy." Gently he took her shoulders and pulled her back until her head was resting on the top of his thigh. "Now relax."

"Relax," she said as though she was having to tell herself how to do that.

"You don't do this much, do you?"

"What? Fly kites?"

"Not work." The middle of his chest filled as he looked down at her, the breeze blowing the loose strands of hair across her face. Softly he reached down, caught them, and wound them back around her ear.

"No," she said, and her eyes turned liquid when her gaze caught his. After a moment, her gaze traveled back up to the kite. "No time."

"There's always time for the things that are really important."

She squirmed. "Work is important."

"So is this."

He leaned back onto this elbows, and the kite soaring high above them didn't seem all that different from his heart. How many nights had he wished for this very moment? And how many times had he simply decided that this was too far out of his reach to even attempt? Now, inexplicably, here he was, with her. "God," he breathed to himself, "if I'm dreaming, I don't ever want to wake up."

Lisa really wanted to shoot whoever had come up with the concept of weekend shifts. Didn't they know how hard it was to get to this place to begin with? However, because he had to get back to be ready for work the next morning, it seemed like mere minutes that she was back at her door saying good-bye. With those hands in his pockets, Jeff said his good-bye, smiled, and turned for the stairs taking her heart right along with him.

"Take care tomorrow," she called softly as the bottom of sanity dropped out from under her.

He nodded, waved, and turned the corner. She didn't move as she closed her eyes. "Dear God, please keep him safe." At that moment he slapped the wall next to the staircase, and she jumped.

"What do you say? Monday? Your office? Five-thirty or so?"

The smile flashed through her. "I'll be waiting."

"So, do you want to try it?" Jeff asked Monday evening when they had left North Houston in the rear view mirror.

"Try what?" she asked fearfully.

"Driving."

"Me?"

"Sure why not?"

Lisa could think of a hundred-thousand why nots, but before she could voice one of them, he pulled onto an exit. "I don't know about this."

"You said you wanted to learn." The car stopped, and Jeff got out to run around.

After only a moment's hesitation, Lisa gingerly crawled across the gearshift and half fell into the driver's seat. The wheel seemed much bigger from this vantage point, and she laid her hands on either side of it as he got in on the passenger side and slammed the door. When her gaze slipped over to the cross at his neck, she couldn't help but think they were going to need every ounce of help it could give them.

"Okay," he said. "First, you mash the clutch."

"The clutch?" she asked, looking around for something that could pass as a clutch.

He pointed past her. "On the floorboard. The one next to the brake."

"Oh." Carefully she put her foot on the clutch and pressed.

"Now, you have to put it in first."

In fear she looked down at the gearshift, knowing this was a terrible idea.

"It's easy. First." His hand moved the gearshift slightly. "Second. Third. Fourth."

Memorizing, even as half of her brain made a point of telling her how strong his hand looked, she nodded. "Got it."

"Good. Now, mash the clutch." She did. "Put it in first. Now let go of the clutch... gently." The car jerked forward with a lurch. "Gas." And they were left sitting in silence.

"What happened?"

"Too much gas. Hit the clutch. Try it again."

She gripped the steering wheel and pressed the clutch as he put the car back in neutral and restarted it.

"Put it in first and give it a little gas."

All the rest of the world dropped away from her consciousness as she worked to coordinate her body in time with the car. It lurched forward but kept rolling this time. She looked down at the foot pedals in fright. "Ahhh!"

"It's okay. Just get a little speed up. Now, mash the clutch and shift."

"Oh, yeah, no problem there." Determination fell over her as she gripped the gearshift in a stranglehold. "Mash the... Ahh! Which way is second?"

"Down."

A small click and she was in second. Slowly they drove to the stop sign.

"Now you have to go backward through the gears. Clutch, and back down."

Somehow she got all of that done and got the car stopped too, but she had no idea how. "I think that's a long enough lesson."

"Come on, you're getting it. One more time, just to the next on ramp."

In frustration she exhaled. "Okay, clutch, shift, let out the clutch, gas." They rolled through the intersection. "Clutch, shift, let out the clutch, gas." The car picked up speed.

"You've got it."

"Don't throw a party yet," she warned, yanking all of her attention to her. She had been driving for more than a decade, and yet this was nothing like any driving she had ever done.

"Let's go to third."

Lisa pursed her lips together. "Clutch, shift, let go, gas." Her whole body breathed in relief.

"See, it's not so hard," he said, and his hand dropped on top of hers on the gearshift.

Suddenly there weren't enough brain waves left for everything.

Minutes had never flown by so fast. Where they had all gone, Jeff couldn't quite figure out because in what felt like a blink he was standing on her apartment threshold saying goodnight. This was the part of the date he hated the most. Awkward uncertainty leaped through his chest like an out-of-control circus. If his body would just take a rest for a minute, walking away would be so much easier, but it was locked on telling him what an idiot he was for not kissing her already.

After all how long had they known each other? Kissing her should've been a no-brainer by this point, as easy as taking a breath, and yet every time they got to this moment, alarms started ringing through his head—simultaneously telling him to just go for it and telling him if he messed this up, he'd never get a second chance.

"Well, I'd better go," he said, backing away from her as his hands slipped into his pockets. "All nighters on top of 24's isn't the best way to make a good first impression."

The sight of her leaning against the doorpost threatened to pitch him down the stairs. He had to keep talking, or he might actually do what his heart was begging him to do. "How about Wednesday night at your office?"

"Or we could meet over here," she said, and the softness in her eyes wasn't making leaving one bit easier. "If you want."

"Six?"

"Sounds good."

He stepped over to the stairs. "Take care."

"K. You too," she said as hazy dreaminess fell across her eyes.

With a nod he started down the stairs, but the need for just one more glimpse brought him back to the top, where he slapped the side of the wall and ducked back around. The sight of her slammed into him, and for a moment he forgot what his excuse for coming back was going to be. "You need me to bring something?"

She smiled. "Yourself."

"Myself." He nodded. "I can do that."

The stairs were merely a formality as he floated down them and back out to the street to the car.

All night she was with him, in every dream in every thought so that by the next morning when Jeff pulled into the station parking lot, he was surprised that her car wasn't actually sitting there. However, when he parked, the fact that no one was leaving crashed him back to reality, and with one motion he locked the car and ran to the station door. The trucks were gone.

In a blink she was gone, not because he wanted her to be, but because to get back to her in one piece, he needed every resource he had available. Yanking one set of cloths off and the other set on, he pulled the chain from around his neck and threw it into the locker.

"It's a wreck." Gabe strode through the locker room in full gear. "Pile up on Southwest. Sounds like a mess. You ready?"

Grabbing his helmet, Jeff stood. "Ready."

Chaos flashed over chaos as they snaked their way up to the scene. People were everywhere, some obviously hurt, some simply trying to do whatever they could to help. The police directed their little truck to the smattering of emergency vehicles surrounding the twisted multi-colored metal that had once been cars and trucks.

"We've got more jaws coming," Captain Hayes said as Jeff's small company ran up.

"What's going on?" Gabe asked for the group.

"We've got people trapped all over in that pile," Hayes said, and Jeff looked over to the area where workers were swarming like bees. "There're probably some we haven't even gotten to yet. That gas truck is leaking all over everything, and the whole thing's a tinderbox that could go up any second. They're trying to spray it down, but…"

"What can we do?"

Chief Hayes eyed them. "I need you guys to make sure everyone's out from the last car forward."

"Got it," Gabe said with a nod, and they turned and ran for the back of the line of smashed and twisted vehicles. How many there were was impossible to know. "I'll get this one."

"Is everybody out?" Jeff asked, swinging the first door open. The acrid smell of the used airbag slid into his nostrils. Nobody. He ran past the one Gabe was working on, and yanked on another door, knowing the next ones were going to get progressively harder to open. "Anybody in here?"

Over and over again, down the line he went, and then the doors would no longer open as the cars became pancaked together. "Gabe! There's somebody in this one!" Jeff called as he yanked on the door that didn't budge. "Get the hammer. Are you okay in there?" Carefully he knocked on the spidered glass. Movement. "Hang on. We'll get you out. Gabe, hurry up." Gabe ran up with the hammer. "Careful."

A crack, two and the glass gave way. Gabe yanked it back out and away from the driver. When there was a clear shot into the car, Jeff looked through the shards to the middle-aged woman still strapped to the seat. Blood streamed down the side of her face, and her moans wrenched across Jeff's heart. "Hang on. Okay? We'll get you out." Furiously he scraped the forearm of his coat across the window ledge to dislodge the glass. He reached across her and unsnapped the seatbelt. "We're going to have to pull her out."

Wails pierced the air coming from every direction imaginable.

"That steering wheel's going to be a problem," Gabe said with a shake of his head. "It's too close. We're going to have to wait for a ram."

A moan, and Jeff knew they didn't have time to wait. "Give me the hammer."

With concern Gabe handed it over, and Jeff vaulted over the crumpled hood of the car to the other side. Trying to put enough force into his swing to get in quickly and yet not enough to go all the way through to her, he whacked at the passenger's window. However, when the glass gave way, he knew that he and his gear would never make it into that car as one. Quickly he shed the coat and wound his way through the window, carefully brushing the glass away as he did. "I'll see if I can get her far enough out," he called, "so you can pull her out."

"I'm telling you, you might as well wait for that ram," Gabe said.

Gabe was right. The steering wheel smacked Jeff on the head on his way down past the dashboard for her feet. "Ow. Crud." Undaunted, he slid one hand down into the shallow space at the floorboard and wrapped it around her ankle. A tug and her ankle slid from its perch. "One more." The second one with only a bit more work, wedged out of the tiny space. "Okay, Gabe. She's free. Grab her shoulders. Count of three. One, two, three." The woman's body slid up through the opening, and suddenly Jeff was the only passenger in the car.

Moving like lightning, he extricated himself, yanked on his coat, and glanced through the early morning light where he caught sight of A.J. running up with his kit to Gabe's side. There were more to get out, and she was in good hands, so Jeff ran for the next car that didn't have people swarming it. "Hey, anybody in there?" A gash in the passenger's side window afforded him a view into the confines of the interior, and opposite it laid the body of a man, arched over the steering wheel. His glazed, dead eyes stared at Jeff blankly. With a gasp Jeff pulled back in hideous revulsion, closed his eyes, and said a quick prayer. "God, take his soul to You."

"I can still hear her, but she's panicking," someone closer to the front called.

Jeff's steps carried him past three vehicles that were so mangled, telling what they had been half-an-hour before was all but pointless. "You've got somebody?"

"Yeah," the firefighter who Jeff only then recognized as Hunter said, "but she's so far down there, the fumes are going to kill her before we can get her out."

"Can we get her some air?"

"It's too tight. I can't get to her."

"Do we have some air?" Jeff asked again.

"Yeah." Dante raced up with a bottle and a mask. "But I don't think…"

It was too late, Jeff already had the bottle and the mask in hand. "How long 'til more jaws get here?"

"They're on their way," Hunter said, pushing back from the wreck.

The hard asphalt met his knees as Jeff dropped to the ground next to the garbled steel of the car that had somehow gone head over heels in the melee. "What's her name?"

"I don't know," Hunter said.

More questions of Hunter would have to wait. "Hey! Hello? Can you hear me?"

"Yes!" Two choked coughs. "Help me! Please!" Through the coughing, he heard the panic and the tears.

"Okay. I'm going to. What's your name?" Jeff's hands went to work unwinding the hose from the bottle.

Another cough. "Reagan. Reagan Cooper."

"Okay, Reagan. Can you see any light from where you are?"

"Umm, yeah, a little." More coughing and he heard the sniffling too.

"Where?"

"To my… to my left."

"Great. Good. You're doing great."

Her voice floated out to him, sounding hollow and weak.

"Something's on my shoulder. I can feel it."

"Okay, we'll have to deal with that in a minute. For right now, I'm going to pass this little mask through this hole. Can you still see light?"

"Umm, yeah, no. Yeah, but not where it was."

"Good. I'm going to work this thing in to you. Tell me when you get it. Okay?" He laid down on the black top and wedged himself into the small angle of sheered metal.

"It's so dark in here, and I can't feel my leg."

"One step at a time, Reagan. Stay with me, girl. Can you see the hose?"

"Everything's just so dark."

"Dear God, please," Jeff breathed, pushing his arm as far into the hole as it could possibly go. The fumes of the ruptured gasoline tanks threatened to take his own oxygen, but he fought off that thought.

"Here. Here it is."

"Thank You, God. Good. Now put the mask on, and we'll give you some air." He motioned for Dante to turn on the air. "You getting anything?" Soft words but he couldn't make them out. "Reagan?"

"I can feel the blood," she said, and the panic had returned although the haze surrounding the voice nearly melted it out.

"They're here," Dante said, and Jeff looked back as three more fire trucks made it to the scene.

"Thank God. Hang on, Reagan. We'll have you out of there…"

"What's your name?" the soft voice drifted out to him.

"Jeff."

Silence. And then a small gasp. "Jeff, can you tell my parents… Jim and Mary Cooper… can you tell them that I love them?"

"Reagan? Now you listen to me. You hang on, girl, the guys are here to get you out."

"Tell them for me, okay?"

"Don't give up on me now. They're here. They're right here."

"Please, Jeff… Please, tell them for me."

He breathed, feeling the very life in that car slip away. "Yeah. Okay. I'll tell them."

"Promise?"

"I promise."

"Jeff," Dante said, laying a hand on his shoulder.

"You're going to have to move," a firefighter said as he and a partner came up with a cutter. "You're going to have to move."

How he didn't know, but Jeff stood and backed away. They were too late. Reagan was already gone.

"Ramirez! Taylor! We need you over here. This fuel's got trouble written all over it."

With one glance at the small opening he had just vacated, Jeff turned. "Coming."

Exhaustion—emotional, physical, mental—crowded over him as he sat on the little bench in the locker room so many hours later, he couldn't count them all. He was vaguely sure that five o'clock rush hour would soon take over the scene they had worked all day, but even that was just a hazy thought mixed with all the others. Slowly he pulled the chain out of the locker and looked at it.

"Good job out there," Gabe said as he stopped at his locker next to Jeff's.

"Yeah." Needing something, Jeff yanked the chain over his head and let out a long breath.

"I kind of lost you after we pulled that one out." Knowingly Gabe sat down next to Jeff. "You go help up the front?"

Jeff nodded. "Yeah. We weren't so lucky up there."

Slowly Gabe's head moved up and down. "That's the breaks of this job. You aren't going to get them all out."

Breathing hurt. Living hurt. "Does it ever get any easier?"

"Wish I could tell you it does, but I've been doing this for almost eight years, and every time you lose somebody it's like ripping your heart out and stomping all over it."

"Great. Something to look forward to."

Gabe smiled softly. "Hang on to the ones you get out. They're what makes this worth it."

"Think I'm going to head up and catch a few winks. Unless somebody needs something else."

Gabe smiled sympathetically. "Go on. Get some rest."

The next morning when Jeff stepped out into the sunshine, the sirens were still blaring through his brain. The newness of the morning permeated every piece of air so that it felt soft as it brushed past him. He got in his car and gripped the wheel. How much time had Reagan had to react? A blink? Less? Those thoughts dogged every step he had taken since he'd walked away from that car, and still they hounded him.

He reached down and started the car, trying not to think, trying not to replay the sound of her soft voice and the sight of the horrible, bloody mess they had finally pulled out of that wreck. He was sure she was beautiful. A carefree college student on her way to morning class. His car picked up speed as he merged onto the freeway. The tears blurred the cars around him. If they just could've gotten to her sooner, if somehow he could've gotten in there to stop the bleeding, then maybe things would've been different. Then maybe…

Hard, his hand hit the steering wheel. "I needed your help, God. Cripes! Reagan needed you. Where were You? Huh? Where?"

Ten

All day Wednesday Jeff tried to sleep, but every time he closed his eyes, the scene was right there. Finally at three in the afternoon he got up, got dressed, grabbed a phone book, and went out to his car. He had made a promise, and if nothing else, he kept the promises he had any control over keeping.

Knowing that his eyes were a mix of sadness and exhaustion, he put on his sunglasses in defense against the sun. He drove, the address imprinted on his heart. Just before he reached the neighborhood turn, he saw the little flower shop, and his hands said they would really like to have something to hold when he got there.

After the short stop, he turned the GTO onto the little street and around several turns. When the car rounded the last turn, he knew exactly which house it was—the one with the myriad of cars parked out front. His promise pulled him forward as he parked and walked up to the door. If it could've been any other way… The front door opened, and suddenly Jeff had no idea what he was supposed to say to the lady standing there. "Hi. Umm, I'm Jeff Taylor. I'm with the fire department." His hand swiped off the sunglasses. "I just wanted to come by and give my condolences."

The skepticism in the lady's tearstained eyes gave way to gratefulness. She pushed the door wider. "Please, come on in."

As they crossed into the living room, Jeff had no doubt which one was Reagan's mother. She sat in one corner, surrounded by people and yet not at all in reality.

"Mary," the lady said, leading Jeff over, "this young man is from the fire department."

With grief-stricken eyes the lady in the chair, looking far older than he knew she was, looked up at him, and the words in his head evaporated.

"Ma'am," he said slowly willing himself to find the words he did not want to deliver, and then he held the small white rose out to her, "I wanted to come by and tell you about your daughter." Carefully he sat on the footstool in front of her because his legs felt like they might give way at any moment. "Umm, I got to talk to her right before…" Pain surged through him, but he pushed that down. "Reagan wanted me to tell you that she loved you—you and her dad." His gaze dropped from the woman's face as the knowledge of how completely insignificant this was now crashed over him. "I'm very sorry for your loss, but I thought you should know she was thinking of you."

Tears, gallons of them, buckets of them, lined up at the back of his head, but he was a firefighter and he was on a mission. Tears had no place here.

"You… you talked to my Reagan?" the lady asked weakly.

"Yes, Ma'am, I did. She was very brave."

"And she said she loved me?"

"Yes, Ma'am, she did."

The hand reached from the center of her chair to grip his. "Thank you. Thank you so much for coming."

Jeff didn't want to be thanked. No, he wanted to give back every thanks in the whole world so that mother could have her daughter back. Grief poured over him as he drove to Lisa's without even bothering to think about where he was going. She didn't want to see him like this, he was sure of that, but he needed somebody to hold onto for fear that he would fall right into the pit that threatened to suck him into it once again.

At her apartment he realized he was almost 45 minutes early, so rather than go up and wait in a dark hallway, he sat down by the little tree in the courtyard directly below her apartment. Worn out, he leaned back onto the tiny circle of the trunk, closed his eyes, and relaxed. Somehow he had always focused on those he could get out, those he could save. Somehow those he wouldn't had never really entered his mind. Standing up and going forward after losing one would take more strength than simply carrying 100 pounds of gear. This strength required far more, and he wondered if he had what it would take.

"What? Are you holding up trees now too?" her voice cut through the still air around him, and as Jeff looked up into her angelic face, his heart turned over. The smile fell from her face. "What's wrong?"

Awkwardly he stumbled to his feet. "You're early."

"Yeah, and you look like you just got hit by a truck." It was supposed to be a joke, but it ran right over his spirit.

His gaze dropped to the grass. "Can we talk... upstairs?"

Worry slipped over her features. "Yeah."

All of her thoughts for a wonderful romantic meal went right out of Lisa's head the second she saw him. So when they got into her apartment, she threw a handful of spaghetti in some water and dumped a jar of sauce into another pan. Then she went into the living room where he sat, head down on the couch, and carefully she folded herself next to him. "The wreck?"

He nodded.

Oh, Lord, help. What do I do now? "It was bad."

Even slower he nodded. When he looked at her, the anguish in his eyes cut her to the core. Softly she reached over and put both arms around him as he collapsed into her.

The whole evening he was so quiet, a few words, a small smile, but the melancholy followed him with every step he took. At the door later Lisa noticed how his hands didn't even have the energy to get to his pockets. Gently her hand bridged the gap between them and took his. "You going to be okay?"

He tried to smile, but the liquid in his eyes gave him away. "Yeah."

Slowly she laid her head on the doorpost, knowing if she didn't know he had made it home, she would never sleep. "Call me when you get home, okay?"

"Call?"

"So I know you made it."

A half-inch at a time he nodded, and then he turned and ambled to the steps. Down. Down, and she could see him no longer. She waited but no hand slapped the wall, and after several

133

long moments she heard the door at the bottom snap open. Her head fell forward. If she only knew what to say to take the sadness away…

Without turning any lights on in the apartment, Jeff threw his keys onto the table and collapsed in a heap on the couch. His hands swiped over his face, and he sniffed. *Call her.*

Her. The tether keeping him from falling right through the void in his heart. He reached over, picked up the phone, and dialed.

"Hello?"

The middle of his heart bounced softly. "I made it."

"Good. You going to be able to sleep?"

"I think so."

"Well, if it gets to be four and you need someone to talk to, you know how to reach me."

His chest filled with the invitation. "I may have to keep that in mind."

It wasn't four in the morning, it was three the next afternoon when exercising and watching television had used up their ability to keep his mind occupied. He really needed to talk to somebody, but she was working, and although she was great about him showing up to help, he knew he couldn't make a habit out of it. So instead he picked up the phone and called the other name on his short list.

"Knox residence."

"Dustin, man, how's it going?"

"Jeffrey, hey. Just the man I was going to call later."

"Uh-oh."

"No, this is good."

"Bigger uh-oh."

"Listen, the station's softball team's playing this weekend, and we've got people dropping out like flies."

"What did you do to them?"

"Me? Jeffrey, I'm hurt."

"Sure you are."

"We need a left fielder for Saturday. Noon. You up for it?"

He needed something. "Sure."

Jeff hadn't bothered to tell Dustin he would be bringing a friend. The questions that would raise sent the hairs on the back of his neck reaching for the stratosphere. No, a better idea would be to just show up with her. Dustin would be smart enough to keep his comments to a minimum while Lisa was around—of that much Jeff was sure.

Asking her wasn't all that difficult, even calling her was getting easier, and when he picked her up, the feeling of the world being right again descended on him. In fact it wasn't until they pulled into the little softball field lot that he really started to get nervous. He parked, hoping Dustin would be too busy to notice they had arrived until Lisa was safely in the stands.

"Jeffrey!" the voice called from behind him as they stood at the car's trunk, pulling out the little cooler, Jeff's equipment, and the sunscreen. In the next heartbeat Dustin was there, hand raised in greeting. Jeff reached up and slapped the hand. "Cool. I was wondering if you got lost—my wonderful directions and all." It was then that Dustin stopped in mini-reunion. With one hand at her eyes to block the sun, Lisa smiled up at him. "Well, now, Mr. Taylor, I wasn't aware you were bringing the cheerleaders."

Jeff wanted to deck him. If Dustin said something to mess this up...

"It's Lisa, right?" Dustin asked, extending a hand and a smile.

"Yeah." She shook his hand. "I thought you might be able to use an extra fan."

"Always room in our stands for a fan like you."

Together the three of them walked over to the bleachers. Lisa slid her stuff up onto the fourth one up, and when she stepped up to the first riser, Jeff took her hand and helped her the rest of the way up. "You going to be okay here?"

"I'm great," she said, sitting down with her hands in her lap, smiling.

"Eve should be here before long," Dustin said. "She can keep you company."

"Knox! Hey, you going to warm up or what?" one of the players called from the fence.

"You ready?" Dustin asked Jeff.

"Yeah, I'll be there."

135

Thankfully Dustin took the hint and faded from the conversation over to the dugout.

"You sure this is cool?" Jeff asked, realizing she was going to be sitting in a whole bleacherful of people that she didn't know.

"I'm fine. Go have fun."

And he didn't miss the way she said that word.

Bases, innings, bats, balls—Lisa wasn't much of a sports fan and even less of a baseball fan, so she listened to the fans behind her and cheered when they cheered. When the guys took the field, position-by-position she surveyed them until finally she picked Jeff out in the far open grassy area straight ahead of her.

"Let's go, Fire Department!" she yelled, mimicking her fellow fans, and she clapped for emphasis. "Strike him out." Whatever that meant. A pitch and everybody cheered. She clapped, having no idea why. It didn't matter. She was too enthralled with the guy standing out in the middle of nowhere waiting—just in case the ball happened to come his way.

He looked happier today. At least the light was back in his eyes.

A crack and the ball sailed out, right to him. She stood, following the ball in its arc and right into his glove. "Yea!" He had such good hands.

Down 5-4 in the top of the last inning, Jeff grabbed a bat and swung it over his shoulders to loosen them up. "Come on, Dustin. Just a hit, man. That's all we need."

At the plate Dustin set his stance and waited for the pitch. Over the plate and right into the catcher's glove the pitch sailed.

"Strike," the ump called, and the fans behind Jeff groaned.

"That's okay. That's okay. Shake it off. Now you know where he throws."

Another pitch, in the air, and it dropped right past Dustin's bat. Instantly Jeff saw the frustration crawl across Dustin's face.

"Hey, man. No big deal. All you need is one." For a second, Jeff looked across the field at his lone cheerleader and his heart jumped. "Just one."

With a breath Dustin refocused on the pitcher, and the next

136

pitch connected with the center of his bat.

"Yes!" Before the centerfielder even got to the ball, Dustin was around first. However, the guy's arm was amazing, and Dustin had to pull up on second.

"That's what we needed!" Jeff said with a nod. Then he put on his game face, hit each of his shoes with the bat, and stepped to the plate.

"Hey, it's Lisa, isn't it?" the lovely lady with the olive-toned skin and wavy black hair that streamed halfway down her back said at Lisa's knee as Lisa clapped for Dustin's hit.

"Hey, Eve. You missed it. Dustin just sailed one."

Eve ducked under the railing and climbed up into the stands without bothering with the steps.

"Jeff's up," Lisa said, clapping. "Come on, Jeff! You can do this!"

The ball went up and down across the plate. "Strike."

"It's okay," she said, clapping again. "It's okay."

Softly he hit the bat twice on home plate, swung it once slowly, and looked out to the pitcher. Every piece of attention that was hers was focused solely on him. On his bat. On his hands. On his arms. Focused so it was she who saw the ball arch toward him. Focused so that like watching a dancer in perfect time, she saw the bat swing around his body and meet the ball coming the other way with a solid crack.

"Yes!" She was on her feet, following as the ball sailed over the outfielders who were all running for it, following even as it dropped right over the ad on the right field fence. The crowd around her screamed in delight, jumping and celebrating even as she did her own little celebration dance. "Yes! Go, Jeff! Woohoo! Yes!"

As he rounded third base on the way to home plate where Dustin stood waiting for him, Lisa thought she saw him glance up into the stands at her, and she raised both hands in the air to make sure he saw her applauding. At the plate he simply stepped on home and caught both of Dustin's raised hands in the air. Together they swung down and clapped at the bottom of the arc.

Happiness for him scattered through her. What he really needed now was his friends—and a reason to celebrate. She was glad he had Dustin, someone who understood. His statement about taking the time for the really important things drifted through her, and when he turned for the dugout and his gaze caught hers, she had the impression that she had never occupied a moment that was more important than that very one.

After a few more moments the celebration died down and play resumed.

"Man, it's a good thing I decided to come on over," Eve said, sitting down next to Lisa. "That was some hit."

"No kidding."

The next batter took up his position.

"So I guess this means Jeff finally got up the nerve to make that phone call," Eve said with a sly smile as she looked over at Lisa.

Lisa's eyebrows arched questioningly.

Eve shook her long locks as she leaned back on the bench behind her with her elbows. "Jeff's such a great guy, but he's so dang shy nobody knows he's around half the time."

"So, you've known him awhile then?" Lisa asked treading through the conversation carefully.

"Almost a year." Slowly Eve shook her head. "And six words is still a stretch." She laughed. "We tried to set him up once—double date with us and Dustin's cousin. Boy, was that a disaster."

"Why? What was so bad about it?"

Eve laughed as though the question itself was funny. "I don't think he got a full sentence out that entire night, and he was so jumpy, I was afraid he might actually have a heart attack on us right there. Dustin tried. Man, did he try, but there was no salvaging that wreck. It's just so weird because when Jeff's with just us, he's shy but he's not *that* shy. I mean he'll actually laugh and joke around a little, but bring a girl around—Oh, Disaster City."

Protectiveness for him slipped into Lisa's heart as she looked out to the field where they were retaking their positions. So he was quiet. That wasn't such a bad thing. In fact, she could think of things far worse.

"I thought Dustin was going to have to come find you himself," Eve said softly, and Lisa's heart jumped as she looked over into the beautiful almond eyes.

"He… they talked about me?"

"Of course they talked about you." Eve laughed as she sat

forward. "Dustin thought Jeff should go knocking on all the office doors in your building to find you, but Jeff... well, let's just say I'm glad whatever he did worked."

Yeah, Lisa thought as she gazed out into left field. It had definitely worked.

The players for the second game of the day were on the field warming up as the four of them stood at the fence talking. It was then that Lisa really realized how Jeff naturally stayed a foot away from her. She had noticed it before, but now there was some semblance of a reason behind it. More than that, she now knew it wasn't her he was staying away from. The hesitancy, the tentativeness in his stance and in his eyes weren't her doing. It wasn't her so much as the whole idea of her. Standing there, it was clear how ill at ease he was with the whole situation.

The more she watched him, how far they had come together slipped through her. If what Eve said was true, then Lisa knew she was privileged beyond measure by the risks he had taken to get even this far, and that understanding pulled her that much closer to him.

"You can't leave already," Dustin said in dismay when Jeff looked at his watch and said they should probably getting back. "How about we watch this next one? At least a couple of innings. Of course it won't be as good as ours, but..."

"Hey, Mr. Wonderful," Eve said, in her normal position right in the crook of Dustin's arm, "you might want to remember who the real hero of that game was. Nice hit, Jeff."

Instantly Jeff's gaze dropped to his shoes, and Lisa could see the reluctance flash though him like a laser beam. Slowly she reached over to him and put a hand on his back. "That was some hit," she said, and his gaze jumped to hers in surprise. The tenderness in her heart transferred to her smile, then through her smile to his eyes and then into his smile.

"I think it had something to do with the cheerleaders," he said as their gazes locked. The world jerked to a halt, and suddenly she wanted nothing more than for him to kiss her. A breath and she had to shake out of that crazy idea.

"You know, they might make us play this next one too if we keep standing here," Dustin said as two team members crossed past them to the gate. "Let's go grab some seats."

When they turned for the bleachers, Lisa didn't wait for Jeff to take her hand. Hers simply slid down his rock hard arm and twisted into the crooks at the bottom. His fingers entwined in hers as if they were made to fit that way, and had she tried to keep it from her heart, the smile would've come anyway.

"I got moved to B shift first of May," Jeff said as he and Dustin sat behind the girls in the stands. He was fighting not to notice how Lisa's hair kept brushing across his knees with every gust of wind. He liked her hair down, and he really liked those jeans. She just looked so much more relaxed and… happy.

"They switched you already?" Dustin asked, raking his fingers through Eve's hair casually. "That's a pain and a half."

"Yeah, well, they had a whole shuffle at the top, so the bottom got reshuffled too." Wanting only to get closer to her, Jeff rested his elbow on the knee that was right next to Lisa's shoulder. After a moment all his hand wanted to do was touch the glinting strands flickering across his sweatpants. Gently he laid his hand down on his knee and twirled one strand of her hair across his knuckle. Strange what that did to the insides of him.

"Isn't it a pain, Lis?" Eve asked, leaning back into Dustin's knees. "Having him gone all the time?"

However, when Lisa looked up at him, softness was all he saw. "I work all the time anyway so it's not that big a deal."

Dustin tilted his head to look at her. "You're not working today."

"Yeah, well," she said as she smiled up at Jeff, "sometimes you have to make time for the really important things."

Had they been anywhere else, all the nervousness about kissing her would've made no difference whatsoever. Unfortunately they were in the middle of a ballpark full of people, and that wasn't the most romantic place in the world to kiss somebody for the first time. The breeze picked that moment to whisk her hair across her face, and softly his finger traced across her forehead to corral it. Gently he tucked it over her ear.

Gazing into her eyes, he knew she was thinking the same thing that was screaming through his soul. Slowly she leaned back against his knee. At that moment the stands around them erupted into cheers, but all the noise in the world didn't have a chance of breaking through the spell that had snatched them from reality.

Without warning, she reached up and wound her hand over his. That touch, that hand. Never had he felt anything like it. He knew she didn't want to be watching a game, but if they didn't want to end up under the bleachers in the next five seconds, the moment had to be broken.

Mischievousness spread through him as he leaned down to her ear. "You're not watching the game."

A laugh jumped right onto her face as she gazed up at him. "You're not either."

His laugh matched hers even as his gaze reluctantly traced back out to the field. She turned back out to the field as well, but her body never really left his knee or his hand behind. When his glance chanced over to Dustin minutes later, there was a smile on his friend's face that he had never seen before. He had to admit, Dustin was right. This was more than worth it.

Eleven

"Thanks for going with me today," Jeff said when they were standing at her door, their hands meshed between them as they had been since the baseball diamond.

Safe. It all felt so safe to Lisa, and she had almost forgotten how that even felt before he showed up. "I had fun."

"Fun?" he asked as one side of his smile came up. "I thought that word was taboo."

She laughed. "It used to be."

His gaze dropped between them and then twisted back up to find hers. "So what's changed?"

The laugh faded from her as she looked into his eyes feeling every single thing she had felt since the first time she had surprise attacked his arm. "You."

"Oh," he said softly. "I could've sworn it was you." His free hand slipped up to her neck and traced through her hair.

Fight was the last thing going through her mind as he closed the space between them. Joy was so much closer. The first brush of his lips across hers sent a gasp through her body that threatened to take her knees right out from under her. Not one single atom escaped the heat that surged through her with that touch. Rock-solid and yet intoxicating, his arms wrapped around her, pulling her closer until she could've melted right into him. His lips found hers again, and haze clouded through her mind. Suddenly in all her world there was only him, and that was perfectly fine with her.

A heartbeat and then two and his lips left hers, but his arms had gone nowhere. Her body slipped into the protection of his, and the world was absolutely perfect for one single moment.

"I've got to get home. Work tomorrow you know," he said after several long moments of simply holding her. Still he didn't let go. Instead, his lips brushed across her hair.

Tenderly her fingernail traced its way across his chest. "Can't you call in sick or something?"

He laughed as pulled her back and leveled his gaze at her. "Oh, yeah. I've heard bosses love that."

She wrinkled her nose at him. "Yeah, they're thrilled."

"No." He pulled her back into the circle of his arms and tightened his grip. "I've got to go, but I'll be back."

"Promise?"

His smile was filled with only peace. "Promise."

Life had never been so right in Jeff's world. For two weeks they had been together at every available moment. When he was off and she gave up on work, they ate at her place. If she didn't, it was becoming increasingly easy to rationalize a trip to her office. He could help her lock up. She shouldn't be there so late by herself anyway. The excuse didn't matter. What mattered was that he could be with her, and that for one more moment reality couldn't get in.

It was Thursday, the fifth of June when reality took its first real swing at them again. Two days earlier Lisa had gotten word that the school district had finally okayed the youth conference idea, and she had been working on it nonstop ever since. Jeff had even resorted to bringing supper to the office the night before. She hadn't really eaten so much as inhaled the food, but he was glad he could make sure she was eating just the same. Because she needed to talk to Hayes, they met in the fire station parking lot Thursday afternoon, planning to enjoy a long evening together. With him, days off seemed few and far between, so they had to squeeze them in when they could.

"How's work?" he asked, catching her hand two seconds after she stood from her car.

"Work. Joel and Kurt are having a contest to see who can come up with the dumbest campaign."

"Who's winning?"

"Not me." At the station door, he stepped in front of her and swung the door open.

"' Course I got mine," Dante said, rolling a tire back to the workbench from the truck where Hunter stood. "Didn't you get yours?"

"Yeah, Tracy saw it, too," Hunter said. "I just don't get what it is about women and formal dances. You'd think the prom would be enough to keep them happy for..." He stopped when he looked over to the door. "Oh, hi."

"Hi," Lisa said not sounding wholly comfortable.

"Come on." Between them Jeff took her hand. They walked over to where Hunter still stood, and Dante stepped back to join them. "Guys, you remember Lisa? Lisa, this is Dante and Hunter."

"Nice to see you again," she said, and the relaxed tone from moments before was gone. It was all business now. After the introductions she stood for one awkward moment. "Umm, is Captain Hayes....?" She pointed up the stairs.

"No, he was in the break room last I saw him," Hunter said, recovering before his partner.

"Oh, okay. Thanks." She turned from them, and when Jeff snagged her gaze, he couldn't quite read everything that was written there.

When she disappeared around the corner, Dante was the first to move. "Are you seriously kidding me?"

"What?" Jeff asked.

"What? How did someone like you end up with someone like her?"

A hard ball of revulsion smashed into Jeff's chest at the implication. However, voices from behind them yanked his gaze that direction. Lisa, locked in conversation with Hayes, walked out from the dim hallway.

"We're confirmed on Oct. 16th and 17th. I was wondering if you could think of anyone else I could..."

A blare so loud it lifted Jeff right off the floor blasted above them, and simultaneously all five of them looked up. "A 10-7 in progress on 3836 Silver Street. Repeat 10-7 in progress 3836 Silver Street. All units respond."

"Crud! Not today," Hayes said in frustration. Then he looked over to the little knot of firefighters. "Taylor? We're two guys short, you mind giving us a hand?"

"Sure thing," Jeff said, and quickly he ran past her and the captain on the way to the lockers. "Give me two minutes. I'll be ready."

It was like a whole sleeping system snapped awake around her. People she had no idea where they had come from were suddenly running in every direction at once.

"Sorry, Ms. Matheson, we're going to have to do this some other time," Captain Hayes said, but she was too stunned to do more than nod.

Men, gear, boots, equipment, and then just as the truck roared to life, the last fireman in full gear flashed by her and jumped into the back door. All the air vanished from the earth itself when he slammed that door closed. The blaring continued above her, but she hardly heard it as her eyes blurred against the sight. Slowly the truck pulled out into the street, leaving her standing alone in the empty station house.

"Oh, God, please, let him be all right."

Smoke streamed from the orange flames jutting out of the roof of the little house until the whole thing was engulfed by it. Jeff ran back for the truck after cutting the power to the house with Dante. It was truly amazing to him how close together people built houses in this city. The other little wooden structures, barely standing the way it was, could light at any moment.

"Get some more water over to the side," Hunter commanded, and Jeff grabbed the hose Dante was unwinding. "If that side collapses, that next house will be toast."

The heat from the blaze, now licking into the early evening sky, was like a broiler, but still Jeff pressed closer to it. They couldn't get between the houses, which was where they really needed to be to forestall a collapse.

"More water!" Jeff called. "We need more over here!" From the middle of the roof to the back, the whole structure wobbled unsteadily. "Get some water on that next house or we're going to lose it, too!"

To his right another set of firefighters appeared, hoses pumping gallons onto the conflagration.

"More on that roof!"

The heat from the front was dying down, and Jeff yanked on

the hose, which Dante immediately pulled behind him. They had to get closer.

The office was dark save for the light from Lisa's computer screen. She'd watched the early news, but there was no report. What was a 10-7 anyway? Somebody choking on something? No, they had called out several units. That was worse. Another wreck? Or a fire maybe?

Under her blouse, her skin itched with the thought, and slowly her nails went up and down the silky cloth. If she just knew he was okay, just had some way to contact him and make sure. She looked over to the phone, willing it to ring so she would know everything was all right. Her eyes closed with the knowledge that it could very well be morning or after before she heard anything. The sinking thought of what that news could be seeped through her. "Dear God, I'm asking You. Please, keep Jeff safe out there." Her heart had never meant a prayer more.

Although charred, the second house had withstood the fire's onslaught. Of course the first house hadn't been so lucky. The whole right side sagged sadly down to the ground over its own blackened remains. But the fire was out, and for this time the crisis was over.

Back at the station, Jeff glanced at the clock. 11:30. She was probably asleep already—no need to wake her. Yet the fear in her eyes said waking her would probably be merciful. He of all people knew about lying there, staring up at the ceiling, wondering... Technically he could have gone home, but the truth was they might need him again tonight, and he wasn't going to abandon them.

Trying not to think about it, he picked up the phone and dialed her number. It rang and rang, and then her voice via the answering machine came on to greet him. He loved that voice.

"Hey, Lisa, where are you?" he asked, spinning the phone under his chin. "Well, just wanted to tell you I'm fine. I was hoping we could get together tomorrow. I'll be home in the morning. Call me." He hung up the phone, but he didn't move. A beat and he picked it up again as a thought traced through him. The phone on the other end had barely gotten through the first ring when it

146

snapped in his ear.

"Hello?" There was nothing but anxiety in that voice.

"Hi, Lis."

"Jeff? Oh, thank God. Are you okay?"

He smiled although the fact that he had made her worry at all bled through him. "Yeah, I'm fine. It was a residential."

"A fire?" And he heard the soft gasp.

"Yeah, just a little one though."

"But you're okay?"

"I can stop by your office in the morning so you can see for yourself."

A laugh. He liked that laugh.

"I'd like that."

Since he had driven away the night before, Lisa had gotten absolutely no work done. Even after he called, she couldn't shake the nagging thought of what happened after they hung up. Was there another call? Another call meant more danger. And more danger meant…

"Knock, knock," Jeff said, softly rapping on her office door at seven a.m., and when Lisa looked up, she had never seen a more wonderful sight. Black hair, shower-shined, black shirt over blue jeans, that cross and that smile.

Tears sprung to her eyes as her thoughts said simultaneously, *He's alive, and thank You, God for keeping him that way.* Office or no office, she jumped from her desk and met him halfway around it. Those arms. His arms. So strong and steady around her, righted the wreck that had been her world for 16 hours.

"Man, I'm glad to see you," she breathed.

"Not half as glad as I am to see you," he replied, and she felt the breath pull into his chest. It was the epitome of remembering how to live.

By the time he left, promising they would go do something on Sunday when he was off again, work was the very last thing Lisa wanted to be doing. Why was she here? She should be with him every second of every moment that she could. A picture of Eve and Dustin sitting in the booth that first night traced through her, and suddenly she understood far more than she ever thought she could.

One moment. It was all anyone was guaranteed, and yet how many had slipped by without her ever even noticing? That, she swore to herself right there, would never happen again.

"I want to drive," Lisa said on Sunday as they drove out of North Houston to fly kites. Her kite was now tucked safely in the trunk next to his.

"You sure?" Jeff asked, looking over at her, and those sunglasses did nothing but yank her alarm system to its knees.

"Yes, I'm sure. What? You think, I forgot how already?"

He didn't bother to answer, just pulled onto the exit, stopped the car, got out, and ran around as she dove into the driver's seat. The size of that steering wheel never ceased to amaze her. She looked over at him playfully. "Better buckle up."

With a laugh, he complied. Slowly she exhaled, put her hand on the gearshift, one foot on the brake, and one on the clutch, marveling at how easy he made this look. She looked out the windshield, put the car into gear, and looked behind her. "Let the clutch out," she said softly. "Gas." The car jerked forward but didn't die.

"Very nice," he said appreciatively.

"First gear," she replied. "It's a start."

Monday night when she heard the two soft knocks on her office door, Lisa's breath caught. He wasn't supposed to come, but she wasn't surprised.

"Still working?" Jeff asked with half a smile. "Man, you work more than anybody I know."

"Besides you of course," she said.

He shrugged. "Of course." He held up a bag. "You hungry?"

"Starving."

"I thought so." He went to work clearing a corner of her desk. Opening the bag of food, he nodded to her computer. "What are you working on?"

"Speaker schedule for the youth conference. I've still got all these holes, and I'm at the bottom of who else to ask."

Carefully he pulled one Styrofoam plate of food out and

148

handed it over to her. "Who do you have so far?"

"Hayes, who I'm praying doesn't no-show on me; Fletcher with the police department who's not a whole lot more excited about the deal; Doug Parsons from the city engineering department; a couple guys from the drilling rig off of Galveston; some volunteers from the homeless shelter; and then… not much." She picked up a fork and dipped it into the mashed potatoes as he sat down in the chair across from her. "Man, these are good. Where'd you get this?"

Sheepishly he looked up. "I thought it might be nice to eat something other than take-out for a change."

Her eyebrows reached for the ceiling. "You… made this?"

He shrugged. "No big deal."

"You cook like this, and I've been cooking for you? Ugh. Now I'm embarrassed." However, embarrassment didn't trump hunger as she dug into the pile of roast which fell apart across her fork.

"It's food."

Her gaze drifted over him. "You cook, you clean, you save poor stranded souls from the top of rock climbing walls. Is there anything you don't do well?"

Part of the smile faded from his face. "A few." He didn't look up for a moment. "Hey, how about the health care field? That would be interesting."

She nearly dropped her fork to get to her pen. "Now that was way too obvious."

"I even know a guy on one of the EMT squads in town. Well, I kind of know him. I could see if he'd be interested—if that would help."

"Help? Are you kidding?" She wrote that down. "What else you got?"

They had rounded out the list with people in landscaping, construction, mechanicking, banking, and travel. In addition to the main list they had even compiled a just-in-case one, so that by the time they were walking to the cars, Jeff should've been ready to call it a night. However, the last thing he wanted to do was go back to his empty apartment alone.

"You going to be okay getting home?" his heart asked for him, noting the slow droop of her eyelids.

"I've never had any trouble before," she said slowly. "But you never know."

"Well, I could follow you… if you want."

"If I want? Now there's a trick question."

He held up his hands, dragging one of hers with his. "No tricks. Promise." Pushing her eyes open, she nodded. At her car, he helped her in and shut her door. The GTO roared to life underneath him moments later, and for the first time she wasn't driving away from him. As he followed her through the streets, his brain said this was silly. She was dead tired, and he wasn't much better. Home made far more sense—except sense didn't have anything to do with this.

When they pulled up to her apartment complex, he was at her car door before she even got it open. There was something about opening that door for her that felt so right. One heeled foot at a time she slid out, and he shut her door. The night, soft and hazy, enveloped them as he took her hand and led her across the parking lot. He glanced over at her, and the lids of her eyes were closed even as they walked.

"You look wiped out," he said softly.

"I'm trying not to," she said, but her eyes never really opened.

They crossed into the grass. "I should let you get some sleep."

"You don't have to."

Gently he smiled as under one of the little trees he stopped. "You didn't have to put up with me tonight either." His arms pulled her to him, and he noticed how the curve at the waist of her gray skirt fitted neatly into the palm of his hand. He knew she wanted to say something, but she yawned instead. He pulled back to look at her. Eyes still closed as though she was literally sleeping standing up, she was the essence of beautiful. Without asking him if it was okay, his other hand slipped up and brushed across the white fall of her neck. "You know, I think I finally understand that whole kissing a sleeping princess thing."

The reference pulled a laugh from her as her nose wrinkled. "Ugh. I always thought you had to be terribly desperate to kiss a dumb princess."

"You saying I'm desperate?"

She laughed outright at that. "Your call."

The words evaporated into the air around them as his lips

found hers. For all the solid information in his brain, he could very well have been dreaming that moment. Life opened up around them as his lips left hers, and he pulled her to him again. "Go get some sleep. Tomorrow's another day."

"Promise?" she asked softly.

"Promise."

With the speakers being contacted, and the other two campaigns on solid legs, Lisa decided they could take a night off from the office. So, when Jeff called on Tuesday, her curiosity won out.

"You know those potatoes were so good," she said as she leaned back in her office chair. Her shoes were kicked off under the desk and the phone cord was wrapped around her arm as she gazed out the window at the buildings and street beyond.

"Is that a hint?" he asked.

"Well, if I'm cooking, you're going to get canned spaghetti and year-old noodles."

"The first hint was plenty," he said with a laugh. "What do you want me to do? Make something and bring it over to your place?"

"Actually, I was thinking. You've seen my place, but I haven't seen yours yet."

"There's not much to see. A tiny place with a big mustard stain on the carpet."

"Can't be much worse than mine."

"Okay, I guess I can throw the junk behind the couch or something."

"Hey, don't clean on my account," Lisa said, and then her gaze snapped over to Sherie standing in the doorway. Her chair crashed back to straight up. "Listen, Jeff, I've got to go."

A slight pause. "Umm, if you're coming over here, don't you need directions?"

As her attention zeroed in on Sherie watching every movement, Lisa grabbed for a pen. "Yeah, I guess that would help."

Quickly he gave her the directions as she scribbled an incomprehensible map onto the edge of a paper she hoped wasn't important.

"What time you taking off?"

"Midnight if I don't get going," she said.

"Great. Everything should be nice and burnt by then."

Despite the interested gaze of her secretary, Lisa laughed. "Seven?"

"I'll be waiting."

When she hung up, Lisa took one breath and smiled at her secretary. "What's up?"

"Mr. Cordell's here to see you," Sherie said.

"Mr. Cordell?" Lisa asked. The smile slid from her face as she grabbed for her shoes and her jacket. "We didn't have anything scheduled today, did we?" Then she caught a glimpse into the front office. Tucker. Terrific. She pursed her lips together. "Tell him I'll be with him in a few minutes."

Sherie nodded and closed the door quietly behind her. Lisa's hands went to her forehead as she tried to squeeze back into business mode. She stood and nearly turned an ankle on the heel of one shoe. Quickly she went over to the little mirror and whipped the back of hair up, twisting it around and around before jamming three hair clips in. Then she readjusted the shirt under the dark jacket before smoothing everything out over her stomach. With a breath, she opened the door and strode out with the fakest smile she'd ever mustered on her face. She extended her hand to him as he stood, feathering one hand through his ash-blond locks as he did so.

"Tucker."

"Lisa, you're looking well."

"So are you," she said, and the words and the smile threatened to choke her on the spot. "What brings you by?"

"I brought over some of the recommendations from our board of directors. Grandpa thought we could go over them before you start formally contacting the speakers."

Too late, but she smiled anyway. "Let's go to the conference room. I'll just grab my notes." She raced back into her office, grabbed her black notebook, and ran a finger around the back of her heel. Why had she never realized how much those things hurt? Pulling herself to her full stature, she strode back out and indicated the door on the other side of the office. "Please."

Slow strings, a piano, and then the rest of the band joined in on the stereo in the living room as the lemon pepper steak surrounded by small potatoes and carrots slid into the oven. With his other hand, Jeff reached up and wound the timer, knowing every tick brought her that much closer to him. That much closer. He smiled at the thought.

A slide step across the kitchen in perfect time to the string-crescendo brought him over to the cabinet where he picked up a can of green beans, tossed it in the air, and conga danced his way back to the stove. As the can opener hummed, he sang. His body melting to the beat. With a click, he released the can even as his voice blended into the harmony. Dumping the can of beans into the little pan, he pulled out the minced onion from above the stove and spun around on his feet before using the jar for an impromptu mic. He sprinkled the onions into the green beans and put the little container back.

Smoothly he slid over to the sink where he grabbed two wooden utensils and banged them across and down the wall, and then right over the sink as he did his best to imitate the short drum solo. It wasn't perfect, but it sure felt good. He put the bowl end of the spoon to his mouth, singing into it as if he was standing on the middle of a stage. Slowly his feet twirled him around. At the sink he let one dish slide into the water, and the scrubbing matched the beat. He stopped and turned dramatically as the music did the same. Then he continued scrubbing.

How many times he had heard that song before, he did not know, but this was the first time he ever realized he had heard it. He loved that song.

Lisa checked her watch, not liking how many minutes this was eating up. "I've already contacted these people, so..."

"But you didn't run this by us," Tucker said with a glower.

"I wasn't aware that I was supposed to. The last I heard, Mr. Cordell said I could put whoever I wanted to in there, or at least get them contacted before he finalized the list."

Tucker's gaze slid over her and right into the bottom of the v of her beige blouse. She wanted to squirm, to cover that up, or to outright knock him through the window—none of which were options, so she straightened further. "At least that was my impression. Did I misunderstand?"

"That's kind of been going around lately," Tucker said as his elbow suddenly let his hand go, allowing it to land within inches of hers.

She cleared her throat. "I don't think I'm following."

"You know," he said as his tone softened, "I've been thinking we never really finished what we started the other night." His fingers slipped closer to hers. "I mean, I'd hate for there to be any bad feelings between us. Grandpa really wants this to work out."

Revulsion spun through her. "Could we please stick to the subject?"

Soft doe eyes met her request as his fingers crawled closer to hers. "Come on, Lisa. What are you so afraid of?"

"I'm not *afraid* of anything. This is a business venture. Period. I don't know why you keep thinking I'm interested in anything else. I'm not." She slammed the notebook closed, nearly catching the tips of his fingers in it. "When you're ready to deal with me like a professional, you know where I'll be. Until then, I don't think we have anything else to discuss." She stomped her way to the door, which she opened, realizing with a start that Sherie was already gone.

"It doesn't have to be like this, Lisa," Tucker said, his voice becoming snake oil soft. "Think about it. We could be so good together."

Lisa turned and leveled her gaze at him. "Listen carefully because I'm only going to say this once and then I'm going to call security. I am not now, nor have I ever been interested in pursuing anything personal with you. In fact, if I could just deal with your grandfather and leave you totally out of this altogether, that would be peachy with me. However, it seems that I'm stuck with you, so in the future when you come for a meeting, I'd appreciate it if you'd stick to the topic and leave your comments and innuendo at the curb. Now, if you don't mind, I have plans this evening."

She knew better than to simply walk out. He would follow her, and in her office, with him at the door, there would be no last-ditch escape route. Still, when he stepped past her in a huff, Lisa's skin did a rolling earthquake move down her back. Then at the outer door he stopped, turned, and the look in his eyes was pure evil. "I'll be sure to give Grandpa an update." And then he was gone.

Hate seeped through her. On the wave of her anger, she hurled her notebook at the door. With a deep growl, she stomped over to the door and locked it—just in case. Pulling her sanity back with a yank, she jerked the notebook off the floor and tracked her way back into her office. Another hour gone, and nothing to show for it.

Her gaze checked her watch although she barely saw it. 6:45. She really needed to sit down and do some more work, but at the same time she knew she would get nothing done. In frustration she snapped off the computer and grabbed her purse. The feeling that Tucker might be waiting when she opened that door slipped into her consciousness. Defiantly she straightened her clothes, put her chin in the air, and walked slowly to the door. The empty office would be the only one who would ever know how thoroughly Tucker Cordell had rattled her.

There were no candles. By the time Jeff thought about them, it was too possible that she would show up and he wouldn't be there. However, everything else was ready when her knock sounded on his door at 7:15. He swung the door open, and his arm slipped up the side of it at the sight of her. "Hi."

"Hi," she said, her gaze bouncing up and down but never really landing on him.

He noticed the hair, knotted tightly at the back of her head, the curve of her dark gray suit, and the strapped heels at her feet. She looked so much like she had that first night that his mind traced back there unbidden. "Come in."

"Thanks." As she stepped past him, she wound one stray strand of hair over her ear. However, once she was in, she didn't move.

"Oh, here." Trying to breathe, Jeff guided her into the living room and to the black couch. "Here. Have a seat." Awkwardly he grabbed the remote to turn down the music but dropped it halfway up. It clattered to the floor. Frustration poured over him as he bent to retrieve it and snapped the volume button. Then he glanced at her, seated on his couch, in his apartment, and logic scrambled. "Uh, can I get you something? Water? Tea? I made some Sangria, but I didn't know if…"

"That sounds good," she said, but he heard the hesitation and the harshness.

"If you want something else, I could…"

"No." She laughed softly as if forcing herself not to attack or run. "That sounds fine."

He hated that tone. It screamed her unease. However, not wanting to argue, he went into the kitchen and filled two drinking glasses, willing himself to keep them upright until he could get one into her hands. When he crossed back into the living room, the 45-degree angle her knees made as she sat perfectly straight on the couch caught his attention. "Sorry. I don't have wine glasses."

"That's okay." She accepted the drink from his hand without really looking at him and took a sip. The smile didn't make it all the way to her lips. "Hmm, that's good. You made this?"

"It wasn't hard." Carefully he slipped onto the opposite end of the couch, fighting to be cool about it, but not really succeeding. "So, how was work?" Aversion scratched across her face, and he was sorry he had asked. "Bad subject?"

"You could say that."

"But I thought things were going good when I called."

"They were."

His mind traced through the possibilities as concern laced through him. "So what changed?"

The top of her gaze landed on his coffee table and didn't move for a long moment. Then the index fingernail that wasn't quite as long as the others slid across the bottom of her nose. "It's a trap, you know."

He sat forward so he could see her better. "What is?"

"Thinking that they think I can do this job with the rest of them."

True concern invaded his spirit. "Lisa, what are you talking about? You're great at what you do."

Slowly she shook her head so that one strand of hair fell from her ear. "That's what they want me to think so they can get close enough so I can't say no."

"Can't say... okay, now you're scaring me." He set his glass on the coffee table and followed it so he was sitting right in front of her.

Her gaze traced up to his, and she smiled weakly. "You wouldn't understand."

However, he latched onto her gaze and refused to let go. "Try me."

He saw the unshed tears glinting behind her eyes just before she looked away. "At first I thought it was how I dressed that made them think… that I was interested in playing that game. So I changed that. Power suits. The most intimidating ones I could find. I even wore reading glasses for a while in college. Not that I needed them, just so maybe they would distract them from the rest of me." She sighed. "But they were such a pain. I finally figured if I just turned every guy down who asked me, that would fix the problem. Become an ice queen and they'd leave me alone. Then they got smart."

The story stopped, and his protective side jumped out. "What do you mean—smart?"

For a moment he thought she might simply stand and walk out. It was a lovely evening and all that, but then her head shook slowly.

"When I was in college, I was on the debate team. I did everything I could to be prepared for every single competition whether it was just a classroom thing or more. I guess I needed to prove that I wasn't just a nice body with a pretty face. And I guess I was okay at it because they finally picked me for one of the competitions. I got paired up with Conner Beale. He was a senior. I was a junior. All the other girls were crazy over him. He was okay, but I was so excited about the whole being chosen thing, I never really bothered to notice what a jerk he was."

She didn't want to go on. He could tell by the way she sat in thought, spinning her glass around and around in her hands. Her glance up at him was only that before it fell back to her glass.

"One night we were working real late at the library. I think we had a debate the next morning or something. He thought we should go over to his place because the library was going to close and we weren't near done." She laughed softly. "Stupid me, I thought that was a good idea." The spinning liquid in her glass slowed. "You know, I honestly thought he liked me because of what I brought to the team—when what he really liked was what he thought I could bring to his bed."

The words, spoken so softly, felt like a sucker punch to Jeff's gut. If he could have flattened the guy, this Conner Beale, he gladly would have in that moment.

"It wasn't long after we got to his apartment that I figured out what an idiot I'd been to come in the first place. I didn't want to. I wanted to tell him no, but I knew if I did, he'd find a way to get me thrown off the team. We ended up sleeping together—if you could call it that." She nodded as the tears came in earnest then. "It didn't matter. I was off the team in two weeks anyway."

Horror clawed through him. "You got thrown off the team?"

Softly she laughed, and then she looked right at him. "No, I took myself off the team. It was too humiliating to face him sitting at that table every day. And I knew if I gave him another chance, it wouldn't be any different the second time around. In three days I was replaced, and no one ever really knew the truth."

The suits, the hair, the stay-in-your-space-or-else stance—they were starting to make way too much sense.

"It's funny," she said sadly. "I keep thinking one of these days guys are going to get the hint, but I'm beginning to think that isn't going to happen."

"The guy," he said, putting the last piece into place. "The one with the leadership thing..."

Her gaze traced the other way across the room as she nodded, and his heart plummeted.

"Either way, I lose," she said softly, and the hollowness of her voice slid him back to the couch next to her where he put a tender arm around her shoulders. Her eyes fell closed as she slipped into his arms.

If he could just hold her here forever, make all the bad vanish... If he could erase her pain, and show her that she had far more to be proud of than how her body looked to the outside world... If he could prove that having fun and letting your guard down didn't automatically mean you were a target for hurt and humiliation... If he could just do that, then the rest of life could take care of itself.

"Hey, you know what?" he asked, bending his head to look at her. "Dustin called this morning. Seems they're a man short on the basketball court for next Saturday."

She laughed as she ran a finger under her nose. "I think Dustin's always a man short for something. Are you sure that's not just an excuse?"

"No," he said with a smile, "but it sounds like fun anyway. What do you say?"

"I say..." She pulled herself up from his arms and sniffed the air. "...something smells like it's burning."

"Supper!" In a breath he was off the couch racing for the

kitchen. The clattering he made as he pulled the now-burnt store-bought pie out of the oven made far too much noise for his jangled nerves. He threw it onto the stove burners. "Dang it." It was then that he felt her presence behind him. "Well, so much for the cherry pie."

Slowly she stepped over to where he stood and surveyed the charred crust. "You got a knife?"

"You're going to eat that?" he asked, arching both eyebrows at her.

"Just get me a knife."

Without further protest, he pulled the drawer open next to her, and she reached in and grabbed a butter knife. Potholder in one hand and pie in the other, she took it to the sink and angled it carefully.

"I don't have a garbage disposal," he said with concern as he stepped up a heartbeat away from her.

"Won't need one." Her hand moved the knife back and forth over the top of the pastry, sending blackened flakes raining into the sink. "Apparently you didn't graduate from the Lisa Matheson School of Cooking."

"No, I think I missed that one," he said, thinking that it sounded like a course he'd be more than interested in taking. "What's this lesson called?"

"It's call, 'Oh, my gosh, I forgot I put something in the oven!'"

He shook his head and laughed. "You're something else. You know that?"

"So I've been told." She held up the pie. "How's that?"

"Marvelous. Let's eat."

"You really don't have to worry about those," he said when the meal was over, and Lisa stood to carry the dishes over to the sink. "I can get them in the morning."

"You cooked. I can clean." Carefully she removed her jacket, laid it on the side counter, and rolled up her beige-colored sleeves. "Where's your soap?"

He stood from the table, bringing another handful of dishes with him. "To the left, bottom shelf."

The water splattered up as it hit the bottom of the sink, and she put some soap in over it. She wound a piece of hair behind her ear and pulled the sponge from the back of the sink as he stopped right behind her. The voltage from his proximity to her snatched the breath from her chest. "You can just set those there," she said, indicating the side of the sink. The edge of the royal blue jersey brushed her arm, and she almost dropped the dish in her hand. "So, where'd you learn to cook like that anyway?"

"What burnt store-bought pies?"

Her gaze leveled at him. "No, ding-dong, the three course meal before that."

"Oh, that." He shrugged. "I got tired of peanut butter and jelly sandwiches."

She laughed. "Take-out?"

"Too expensive." Two more dishes slid to the cabinet next to her.

"I'd probably die if there wasn't take-out." The sponge went around the dish, and she set it into the next sink for him to rinse. "By the way, did you ever call that guy? The one you said you know? The EMT guy?"

"Oh, crud. I completely forgot about that." He reached over to the edge of the sink, grabbed a pen, and made a quick note to himself. "I'll do that tomorrow."

"I thought I was the disorganized one."

He looked at her, and his smile melted through her soul. "You must be rubbing off on me."

The next afternoon when he picked up the station phone to make the call, Jeff's mind drifted back to the feeling of her arm, a half-an-inch from his own. It was a feeling he could get used to. "Yes, this is Jeff Taylor with the Houston fire department, and I'm trying to track down one of your paramedics. His name is A.J. Knight, but I don't know exactly what his shift is or his truck number." It took a few minutes, but the receptionist finally paired the name with a phone number, which he dialed and went through the whole spiel again. This call produced yet another phone number. He felt like he was traveling through a maze, looking for a single piece of cheese. "Yes, this is Jeff Taylor with the Fire Department, I'm trying to get in touch with A.J. Knight."

"Just a second," the voice said, and he heard the, "A.J.! It's for you."

A beat and then, "This is A.J."

For a single moment Jeff's tongue twisted. "Umm, A.J. Hi. This is Jeff Taylor with the fire department. You probably don't remember me. I was the one on the bridge that day with that kid— the jumper."

"Jeff!" A.J. said as though he was some long, lost friend. "I saw you at the wreck that day. Didn't get a chance to talk though. What's up?"

"Umm, well, listen, I know you're probably way busy and everything, but I've got this friend who's working on putting a student conference together for the fall. She's looking for people in the service fields to come and talk at the workshops. I thought you might be interested." Man, that sounded lame. "But if you don't want to…"

"No, that sounds cool," A.J. said slowly. "I've never done that kind of thing, but how hard could it be, right?"

"Well, if you'd like to meet her to get a better feel for the project, I can give you her number."

"Just a sec, let me grab a pen."

Jeff waited until A.J. came back. Then he transferred the name and number. "I'm sure she'd really appreciate any help you can give her—even if it's just to give her somebody else's name."

"I'll give her a call."

"Thanks, A.J. I'd appreciate it."

"Call on line one," Sherie's voice jumped over the intercom.

"Matheson," Lisa said, laying the phone on her shoulder absently.

"Hi, this is… A.J. Knight. I'm with the EMT. Jeff Taylor asked me to call you."

Her pen dropped to the desk as her heart jumped at the name. "A.J. Oh, good. I was hoping you'd call."

Twelve

Jeff was working. That much she knew when she hung up with A.J. Had there been a good way to call and be assured that Jeff would answer, she would've ventured out and called him. However, there wasn't so instead she sent up a small prayer so that God would keep him safe long enough for her to adequately thank him at some future moment.

"Thanks for coming," Lisa said the next afternoon when she sat down across from A.J. at the conference table. "I know this is a little formal and all, but…"

"No, hey, it's cool," A.J. said, looking rather out of place in his black, backward baseball cap and over-sized jersey-shirt. Then he remembered the cap and quickly yanked it from his head as he smoothed out his light brown hair. "Jeff didn't say to dress up or anything…"

"Oh, don't worry about it. We're not the fashion police around here."

"I'm really glad Jeff called me," A.J. said, and she could hear the nerves in his voice. "I mean I was surprised and all. I figured he'd have a hundred people he could call before me for something like this."

Lisa's eyes narrowed inquisitively as she opened the folder ready to make her presentation. "Oh, yeah? Why's that?"

A.J. shrugged and pulled himself up in the chair on his elbows. "He's just so… I mean everybody has such respect for him and everything."

Now she was really intrigued. "Well, I have respect for all you guys. I never realized how tough your jobs are—getting in there, risking your life to save others, that's pretty awesome."

"Yeah, that's what I mean… about Jeff and all. That guy's fearless, you know? Jumping into cars that could explode at any minute, walking into smoke pouring out the other direction, crawling into spaces that no human should be able to fit into. I'm telling you, that day on the bridge would've been enough for me."

"It was bad, huh?" she asked, just to keep him talking. Every piece of information she could glean was one more that held the keys to who Jeff really was.

"To this minute I can't believe that kid didn't jump." A.J. shook his head as Lisa fought not to question the statement. Apparently A.J. thought she knew all of this, and she wasn't going to let him in on the fact that she hadn't heard a single word. "He was so shaky, you'd have thought he was on crack or something, but Jeff, man, he never backed down, never gave that kid the slightest reason to think he wasn't completely serious about how much he wanted him to come back across. I was just glad Jeff was there, or Parker would've been a goner."

Her body absorbed the story as her mind fought to slide it into the right pigeonhole. Of course she had heard about the kid, Parker, but never had she known… "I guess the wreck the other week was pretty bad," she said as if she had heard most of that story too.

"Yeah, they don't get much worse," A.J. said softly as he folded the hat in his hands tighter, a move Lisa took to mean he didn't want to talk about it. However, after a heartbeat, he continued. "Mangled metal, blood and bodies everywhere, and that gas smell…" He stopped and looked at her with soft, golden-bronze eyes. "I try not to think about it much. It can get to me sometimes."

Tenderness for him—for them—seeped through her. "I'm sure." The more she looked at him, the more she understood. "It's hard to care that much and never have a guaranteed outcome."

"It's hard to care that much. Period." He took a breath and exhaled. "But if it means somebody's life, I guess that's a trade I'm willing to make. I'm just glad I've got people like Jeff out there to watch my back. I'm telling you, he's the definition of a hero in my book."

"Yeah," she said softly. "Mine too."

As soon as A.J. left, Lisa picked the phone up and dialed Jeff's number. "Have I told you how wonderful you are lately?" she asked when he said hello.

"Now that's one I don't think I've ever heard before," he said with a laugh.

"Too bad. Somebody's been falling down on the job then," she said. "I just talked to A.J. He's exactly what I needed."

"I'm glad."

She twirled the phone cord around her finger. "So, you got any dishes that need washed?"

"That's a trick question."

"Just asking," she said innocently.

"Seven?"

"Let's make it six."

"Six it is."

The music wafted softly into the kitchen from the living room speakers as Lisa, heels kicked under the table and hair flowing down over her shoulders stepped up behind Jeff as he put the finishing touches on a homemade potpie he'd just taken out of the oven. Letting her eyes fall closed, she put her arms around him, leaned against his back, and swayed with the music.

"Hey, now," he said over his shoulder. "That could get you in trouble."

"Oh, yeah?" Her hands slid up to his shoulders and then drifted down across the jet black of his T-shirt and onto his biceps. "How about this?"

"Yeah. That too."

At the moment she didn't care, she just wanted to feel him close to her. It felt like forever since she'd seen him. "Hmm." She heard his eyes close as a sway at a time, he turned to her and laid one arm on either side of her. Greedily she snuggled closer to him as her spirit floated away. Together they simply held each other in time with the strings and the words which hardly made any difference anymore. "Hey, I thought you didn't dance."

He smiled at her. "Yeah, so did I."

"So, are you going to the Ball?" Gabe asked as he replaced the blankets in the truck the next morning.

Jeff stuck his head around the side of the engine where he was rechecking the ladder's rigging in preparation for their training run later. "The Ball? What am I? Prince Charming?"

"Hardly," Gabe retorted. "No, the Ball. You know, the big fireman thing at the end of the month."

"Well, let's see, last weekend of the month, B shift, night, dancing. I'm thinking no." He went back to work.

"Oh. And Lisa's okay with that?" Gabe asked.

Instantly Jeff looked around the side again. "Lisa?"

"Yes, Lisa. You know. She's about so high, nice long hair, body that should be on a runway somewhere... Hello."

"Oh, well, yeah, Lisa. Of course. But what does she have to do with the ball thing?"

Gabe stopped what he was doing to look over at Jeff. "Okay, did I totally miss something here? You're going out with her, right?"

Defensively Jeff ducked back into the safety of the engine. "We've gone out."

"Uh-huh, and that whole can't take your eyes off of her thing?"

Okay there was no explanation for that.

"You should ask Wade since he's on C Shift now," Gabe continued. "Besides, he owes you."

"I didn't do that so he would owe me."

Gabe shrugged. "Doesn't matter. He still owes you. Besides Pat won't let him go anyway. Not after that year she had to take him home in the back of their truck because he was going to ruin the upholstery up front."

"I'm sure Wade's got better things to do than to fill in for me."

"Well, I'm supposed to help him study for his final driving test Sunday night. I could ask him for you."

Why did people think he couldn't handle arranging his own life? "Thanks, but I don't think the Fireman's Ball is exactly our... I mean, my style."

However, Gabe's face implied that the idea wasn't dead. Jeff's only hope was that he would somehow forget the whole dumb thing. The thought of accidentally dropping something off the top of the truck occurred to him, but it wasn't worth that—almost.

It had been the longest 24 hours of Lisa's life, and when the clock wound around to 4:30 on Friday evening, she could take being away from him no longer. Grabbing her purse and the inch thick leadership folder, she strode out. "I'm going to take off."

"Late meeting?" Sherie asked, looking up.

"Yeah, something like that."

The first thing Jeff noticed when the truck pulled back to the station on Friday at five was the little white Cavalier sitting at the edge of the parking lot, and his heart jumped at the sight as he struggled out of the last of his turnout gear. "Come on, Taylor, it's just a car." But the fact that it could be her car twisted through him. That was ridiculous. What would she be doing here on a Friday evening? If nothing else, she knew he was working. They'd talked about it the night before. True, neither of them were really focused on work at the time, but still that white Cavalier held out the hope of seeing her again.

When they pulled into the station, it took only seconds to spot the car's owner, tucked securely between Captain Hayes, Dante and Hunter whose hazmat class had just adjourned for the evening. Something in the middle of Jeff didn't like the arrangement at all. Telling himself it would be ready in case of a call, Jeff left his gear in the truck and jumped to the ground.

"Jeffrey!" Dante said by way of greeting when Jeff started over to them. "Have you seen this production Lisa's putting together?"

A slow step at a time, Jeff approached the group as his hands found the pockets of his pants.

"They're going to have like 500 kids at this thing," Dante said. "Man, I would've killed to go to something like this when I was in high school. Then maybe I wouldn't have wasted six years changing majors."

Jeff's gaze caught hers, and he smiled slightly as Hayes looked at his watch. "Well, boys, looks like that's a day. Thanks for bringing that by, Lisa. It's looking good."

"You're welcome," she said, nodding. "I'll let you know how

the registration goes in August."

"Good enough." And Hayes turned from the group and made his way out the front door.

"So, Lisa." Dante swung an arm over her shoulder, which Jeff immediately wanted to knock off. "Save me a dance at the Fireman's Ball? Okay?"

"The... Fireman's Ball?" she stumbled as she wound a piece of hair over her ear.

"Yeah," Dante said. "You're coming with my man here, right?" Dante's other arm dropped over Jeff's shoulder.

"Oh, yeah," Lisa said, recovering. "Yeah. I'll save you one."

"Cool." He smiled and backed away. "Come on, Wit, I've got a date tonight."

"Lucky you," Hunter said unenthusiastically. "See ya, Lisa."

"Yeah, see ya," she said softly. Neither she nor Jeff moved until Bip and Bop had vacated the room and closed the door behind them. "Fun guys."

"You think?" Then he really looked over at her. "This is a surprise."

Her gaze bounced to the floor. "Yeah, well, I needed to show the captain our latest schedule. He said I could meet him here."

"Oh," Jeff nodded. "Mind if I look?" His hand came up expectantly.

A hesitant inch at a time, she pulled the folder away from her chest and handed it to him. He took it, but quickly realized that holding it, reading it, and keeping the pages corralled while standing in the middle of the station was a feat too arduous for his stumbling brain. "Mind if we sit?" he asked, indicating the mesh steps.

She shrugged and followed him over. He waited for her to choose a step before he took the one immediately down from her. Slowly he thumbed through the papers. "So you got in touch with the construction guys?"

"Confirmed this morning," she said.

"And the travel agency?"

"I'm meeting with the owner on Monday, but she sounded excited about it."

He examined the paper with the master schedule and one entry dropped a lead ball into his stomach. "What's this computer one?"

"Oh, that's something the Cordell board of directors came up with. I figured it was a good addition."

"Sounds good." Wishing he could brush his feelings away as easily, he slipped that paper away to read the letter she had sent to the superintendent and principals. Top notch, as always. "Hayes sounded impressed."

"Yeah, at gunpoint," she said with a laugh. "Your friends didn't exactly give him room to sound anything less than enthusiastic."

Sliding to the side, he leaned against the wall even as he continued down through the file. "You know who would be good?"

"Who's that?"

"That guy, the one that owns all the dry cleaners in town."

"Dry cleaners?"

"Yeah, he was in the paper last week. Came here from Vietnam or Japan or something. Didn't have a dime, and now he owns like three-quarters of the dry cleaners in Houston. It was an amazing story."

"Do you remember his name?"

"Ummm." Jeff leaned his head back against the wall as if he was trying to read it out of the air. At that moment his attention snapped to Gabe who had just come into the room. "Hey, Gabe, what's that guy... the one with all the dry cleaners?"

"Takashi?"

"Yeah, that's him Takashi Suni. You should call him."

Gabe strode to the stairs and started up them. "Excuse me. Got some people to check on."

Simultaneously Jeff and Lisa slid their feet out of the walkway. When Gabe was gone, Lisa leaned down to Jeff's ear. "I think I'd better go."

"Go?" he asked in surprise. "Why?"

"You're supposed to be working."

"I am working," he said seriously. "I'm helping you put the best face on the fire department's newest ad campaign."

"This isn't the fire department's ad campaign."

Half his smile went up, and he raised his eyebrows. "Close enough. Come on, at least let me get through the rest of this."

She sat, still fidgeting behind him.

"Now, I like this one." He held one of the flyers up as if she hadn't had the opportunity to see it yet.

The fidgeting stopped. "You would," she said in mock horror, and when he leaned back onto her legs, she didn't move them. In fact, she draped one arm over the shoulder next to the wall. "That one looks just like you. It's a little on the loopy side."

"Loopy?" he asked, looking up at her as if he was offended, but the light in her eyes was enough to make his spirit float right off the earth. "I'm hurt."

"Why? Loopy can be a good thing." Quickly she bent and pecked the top of his forehead. Then she sat back, looked at him sheepishly, and started laughing. "Oops."

"What oops?"

She bit her bottom lip to keep from laughing as she looked at his forehead. "I forgot to put my kissable lipstick on today."

"Oh, great. You're going to have to think about these things," he said, wiping his forehead, which he was sure now sported a nice off-red set of lips.

"Just kidding," she said mischievously as she fought back the smile.

Instantly he stopped wiping. "Okay, now that was just cruel."

"But it was funny, wasn't it?" Reaching to the edge of his ribs, she worked her fingers into his side. "Admit it, that was a good one."

"Hey, cut that out. I'm supposed to be working, remember?"

"You were the one who wanted me to stay."

"How very loopy of me," he said with a laugh as he twisted away from her fingers. "Remind me not to say that again."

"Back down," Gabe said, suddenly appearing at the top of the stairs behind them with an armful of boxes. Instantly their laughter stopped, and they slid away from the railing in embarrassment as Gabe stepped past them. "Sorry."

When he was gone, Lisa smoothed her skirt and pulled herself up. "I really should be going."

As she stepped past Jeff to the next step down, he carefully folded the pages into their home and handed the stack back to her pulling himself up as well. "I'll see you tomorrow?"

"My place or yours?"

"Better make it yours, my frig is empty."

"Mine it is then," she said. With a quick check to make sure they were alone, she tiptoed back up to him and caught his lips with hers. Then she backed up with a wink. "Take care."

"You too," he said, feeling her slipping away as she went down the bottom three steps. "Oh, Lisa." He leaned on the railing as she turned. "Spaghetti's fine."

A small smile, a nod, and she left. If it weren't for the leaving thing, his life would've been perfect.

The wail of the alarm jerked Jeff's attention up from the television fifteen minutes into the ten o'clock show the next Friday night, and he was on his feet.

"Time to go to work," Gabe said, swinging out of his chair and following Jeff to the truck.

When the truck screamed around the last corner, it was a relief to not see flames or smoke. However, Jeff wondered at the exact nature of this call as he and Gabe jumped from the door and ran up the sidewalk. The door opened before they knocked, and a frightened young woman barely more than 20 stood there in near hysteria. "It's the baby. It's the baby. I can't get her out."

"Okay, calm down, Ma'am," Gabe said slowly. "Where is she?"

"Upstairs. In the bathroom."

Jeff pushed into the house, fighting to get his bearings just as a cry from up the stairs met his ears. Six strides and his legs were carrying him up the stairs. "How long has she been in there?"

"I don't know. Thirty, forty-five minutes? I tried to get it open, but I can't find the key, and she's been screaming and screaming." The mother followed them up to the second floor where Jeff banked and met up with the door from which the screams were emanating. Carefully he laid his hand on the door, willing the knob to just turn, but it didn't. He bent down and examined the knob.

"I didn't think she could lock it," the mother said.

"What kind of lock is it?" Jeff asked.

"It's one of those turn kind. Where the inside of the knob turns. I didn't think she knew how to work it."

"Was there any water running?" Gabe asked as Jeff inspected the knob.

"No, I'd almost started it when the phone rang. I knew you

170

weren't supposed to run water with babies." Hysteria was taking over her voice.

"How old is she?" Gabe asked.

Helpless tears streamed down the mother's face. "Almost two."

"What's her name?" Jeff asked as the terrified screaming on the other side hit a crescendo.

"Alicia."

"Hey, Alicia," Jeff said in a soothing voice as he stood and knocked softly on the door. "Hey there, my name's Jeff, and we're going to get you out. Okay, sweetheart? But, listen; you're going to have to be a little patient with us. This might take a minute or two."

The volume of the screams decreased a notch.

"You must be a big girl to do something like this," he continued as his hand jiggled the knob, but it held fast. "How are you at picking locks?" he asked Gabe who stood behind him.

"It's not my specialty."

Jeff exhaled as the little screams escalated again. "I'm going to need a screwdriver or something flat like that." Gabe turned to leave. "You might bring a hammer too just in case." He heard the gasp, and he looked over at the mother. "It's okay. We can get in without hurting her." Gabe left. "How big is the bathroom?"

"Umm, there's a sink right by the door, and then the toilet and the bathtub."

"And there's no water in the tub?"

"No."

He nodded and bent back by the door. "Alicia, sweetheart. How you doing in there?"

Sobs of fear but the screams had dissipated.

"Yeah, I hear you, I'm not big on tight places either," he said. "Listen, I'm going to need you to do something for me. Can you?" He waited, pleading with God to do His part on the other side of that door. "I need you to go over by the bathtub. Okay? Can you go over to the bathtub for me?" It was difficult to tell, but he thought the sobs moved.

"Here you go," Gabe said, holding out the screwdriver and the hammer.

Jeff chose the screwdriver. "Alicia, hang on, sweetheart. We'll have you out of there." He bent down to the door. "Let's hope this works." Carefully he fitted the end of the screwdriver into the notch on the knob, but with little light to guide his hand it slipped off and cracked into the door.

Fear from the noise jumped out from the other side of the door out at him. "It's okay, Alicia. It's okay. It's still just me. Hey, do you know how to count to five? Tell you what, why don't you count with me? One, two." Fitting the screwdriver back into the notch, he turned it slowly, willing it to work the lock. "Three, four, five." The door sprung open. "Hallelujah."

He stood and stepped back, knowing that a man in black boots and full fire gear wouldn't exactly be a calming sight for the frightened little girl. In half-a-heartbeat the mother had the little girl in her arms and was kissing the top of her head and sobbing. Alicia, frightened and wary, stuck her thumb in her mouth as big teardrops shone in her tiny eyes framed by a plethora of blonde curls.

"Hey, kiddo." Jeff cocked his head so he could look at her as he reached over and ruffled the soft locks. "You had us pretty worried there, you know that?"

Through her tears the mother smiled as she bounced the little girl in her arms. "Tell, the nice fireman thank you. Can you tell him thank you?"

The fear never left the little eyes.

"That's okay," Jeff said with a quick wink at the child. "That's what we're here for."

Although she was fighting the tears, it was clear they were winning as the mother looked at him. "Thank you so much."

He smiled. "No problem. Glad we could help."

"You know," Gabe said as he swung into a chair next to the one Jeff occupied when they were back at the station, "I'm curious."

"'Bout what?"

Gabe looked at him for a long moment as if deciding if he should really ask the question. "I've been watching you, and I can't really explain it, but you always seem to know exactly what to do, exactly how to calm people down. Why is that?"

Jeff shrugged. "Never really thought about it."

The intensity of Gabe's gaze narrowed on him, and Jeff felt it to the core. "It's like you know what they're thinking—it's like...

it's like you've been where they are. How do you do that?"

"I don't know. I guess I just think how would I feel if I was them."

Slowly Gabe shook his head. "It's more than that. It's like they can sense that you know, like they trust you completely the minute you start talking to them."

"I didn't know that was a bad thing," Jeff said, laughing even as his insides curled into a tight ball.

"I didn't say it was a bad thing," Gabe said. "I just wish I knew how you did it— that's all."

"If I knew, I'd tell you." The words barely made it from his heart.

"Yeah." Gabe nodded and stood. "Well if you ever figure it out..."

Thirteen

"Seventeen." Dustin dribbled to the center of the court Saturday afternoon as Lisa sat on the bench watching and clapping absently.

The sunshine pouring down on her felt heavenly. Shorts and a tank top were hardly her style, but they sure felt good today. She leaned back, resting her elbows on the hard wood behind her. On the court Dustin drove around one side and passed the ball off to Jeff at the last second. Instantly Jeff drove in underneath the flailing arms and flipped the ball up to the net. It rolled around and back out again. Six bodies went up for the ball, crashing together in one twisted knot.

It was nice he had this Saturday off, but she was already dreading next Saturday when all she could do was sit and watch the clock, ticking off seconds until he was safe again. She hated those Saturdays and those Mondays and those...

"Foul!" Jeff yelled as he tried for another shot and got hammered by an opposing player coming the other direction.

Panting, they stood under the basket, and Jeff took the ball. The shot bounced off the front of the rim with a clang, and three guys dove for it. Had Lisa tried that, she would have been bruises from head-to-toe, but they seemed to be thoroughly enjoying getting bashed to pieces by the other guys on the court.

"Well, Lisa-Lisa. Dustin said you were coming," Eve said, swinging up next to Lisa without so much as a hi. "So you got conned into the wide world of sports again, huh?"

"Basketball, softball... I'm becoming a regular Howard Cosell."

Eve laughed. "Wait 'til it's time for skiing."

"Oh, Lord, I don't want to know!"

As the body-smashing game continued on the court, Lisa's gaze slipped back to it. Something about Jeff with no shirt on riveted her gaze to him so that she had to think it wasn't humanly fair to do that to a person.

"So, how are things up north?" Eve asked. "Is Jeff behaving himself?"

Lisa laughed at that. "Always. Me on the other hand..."

Eve's gaze joined Lisa's on the court. "Basketball's so much better than softball."

"I'm not arguing."

From the top of the key, Dustin pulled up into a jump shot, and the ball swished through the net. "Twenty-one! Woohoo!"

The two women clapped on cue.

"What do you say?" Dustin asked as the five others stood with their hands on their hips, fighting for more oxygen. "Best of three?"

"You're on," his opponent said, grabbing the ball.

When Jeff shook his head in exhausted exasperation, Lisa laughed. He wasn't going to back down, but though the spirit was willing, the body was hardly awake enough to compete for hours on end with five guys who hadn't been on call and awake the whole night before. From what she could tell, he was liking the new shift better, but she knew he was still adjusting to life at the fire station—if, in fact, someone could ever fully adjust to that life.

"It's nice to see Jeff getting out," Eve said although her gaze never left the court. "All Dustin had to do this time was ask. Usually it's begging, 'Please, Jeff. Please, please. We promise won't try to find somebody there who'd be perfect for you.'" She laughed. "He's such a hermit."

"I think the station's probably helped that," Lisa said, brushing the hair from her eyes.

Eve looked over at her and smiled. "Yeah, the station."

It didn't take a brain surgeon to catch the implication. "So, how's Dustin doing at his station these days?"

"Oh, great." Eve's gaze traveled back out to the game and then dropped to the bleachers.

Concern jumped to Lisa's heart. "He doesn't like it?"

"He likes it fine," Eve said softly, and then she looked over at Lisa with pensive eyes. "It's not such a joy ride for me though."

Sympathy flooded through her. "I hear you there. I mean we're not even married or anything and every time Jeff's on shift, it's all I can do to keep myself in one piece."

The smile Eve trained on her said she understood implicitly. Then she exhaled. "They had a fire the other night over at the college. Real bad one. Me and God got to know each other real well over those 12 hours."

"Have you told him?" Lisa asked as much to get her own life in line as to know about Eve's. "Have you talked to him about how you feel?"

Slowly Eve shook her head. "It wouldn't do any good. I don't like to fight with him." She laughed softly. "Besides, that's part of the deal. If you love him, the job comes with it. That don't make it any easier, but that's the way it is."

Lisa nodded, knowing in her heart how true that statement was. "So, does he talk about it—the fires and stuff—when he comes home?"

"No," Eve said and the word was short. "That's honor code or something. The fires stay at the fire." She fell silent for a moment and then brushed the wavy strand of black hair that caught on the breeze away. "That's why I was glad Jeff could come today. Dustin's been pretty down."

"Yeah, it's nice when somebody understands."

A smile lit Eve's eyes when she looked at Lisa. "Yeah, it is."

The steaks sizzled on the grill three feet away as Jeff sat, head back, in the soft lawn chair soaking up the afternoon sun. It felt so good, he was afraid he might actually go to sleep although he knew that wasn't exactly what Dustin had in mind when he'd invited them.

"How about a cold one?" Dustin asked, breaking into the quasi-dream Jeff was having.

When he opened his eyes, the beer was already being offered. "Sure."

Transfer made, Dustin took a drink of his own and stepped over to the grill.

"So," Jeff said, pulling himself to an upright position, "you guys going to the ball next weekend?"

Without turning, Dustin looked over his shoulder. "Probably. Eve wants to anyway."

"And you don't?" Jeff asked, concerned by the tone in his friend's voice. "I didn't think you ever passed up a party."

Dustin sniffed, turned one steak, and took a drink. "I just think it'd be nice to stay home for a night. I mean I see those guys all the time, do I really want to go see them on my night off too?"

Slowly Jeff stood and stepped over to the grill as orange flames shot into the air. With a flick Dustin grabbed a spray bottle and tamed them.

"I hear you there. Sometimes I think I'm going to go completely nuts if I have to spend one more minute at that station."

The spraying slowed as did the sphere of reality around Dustin. "But you wouldn't trade it. Right?" His gaze trained on Jeff as if his friend suddenly possessed some miracle potion that could make all the bad disappear.

"No, I wouldn't trade it," Jeff said softly, "but that doesn't mean it's easy." He watched as Dustin set the bottle down, picked up the brush, and put the barbeque sauce on. Dustin wasn't going to say it, but Jeff could see it in his friend's eyes. He shifted his weight slightly to get a better view. "I read about the college."

Dustin didn't look up. He didn't have to. "We had three guys that almost didn't make it out."

"And you?"

"I was back up. I was headed in right as the thing got totally out of control." There was hardly breath behind the words. "They were lucky to get out." The look in Dustin's eyes froze Jeff's blood solid. "I just kept thinking about Eve. You know? How if things had been just a little different she'd be here all by herself right now. Of course her parents would be here, but…" Slowly Dustin shook his head, unable to get more words to come.

"Do they have someone at the station you can talk to?"

"I did." He rubbed the edge of his nose. "I don't know how much it helped though."

"I think it always helps to talk about it," Jeff said, kicking the memories out of his mind even as he said the words.

Softly Dustin smiled. "I know this has."

"Yeah," Jeff said, comprehending far more than he could ever put into words. "For me, too."

Honor code. That phrase was on a repeating loop in Lisa's brain as they drove back into the thick of the city hours later. She knew it. She understood it. She had lived it. Yet something about it still snagged in the spider web of her mind.

"You're awful quiet tonight," Jeff said as the darkness sped by them. Gently he reached over and laid his hand on hers. "Want to talk about it?"

"Why didn't you tell me about the wreck?" Lisa asked so softly the night almost swallowed the words.

"The wreck?" His hand stiffened but didn't move. "I did tell you about it."

"No, you said it was bad, but you never really told me what happened."

"Oh. Well, there was this semi that jack-knifed, and a car…"

"No, I don't mean how it happened. I mean what happened… after you got there."

His hand slid off of hers and traced back over to his side although his gaze stayed firmly outside the windshield. "I think it's better if that stuff stays at work."

"Why?" she asked, pursuing him even though she knew he didn't want her to.

One brief glance and his gaze returned outside. "Because you don't need that to deal with, and the less I think about it, the better."

Her new reality was beginning to sink in. "So you're never going to tell me what happens out there? Just that it's bad, or kind of bad, or really bad, and I'm supposed to decipher the whole story from that."

His gaze jerked over to her face, but it couldn't hold. "There are things… Look, things happen out there that…" He exhaled. "You wouldn't understand."

The words crawled through her. "Is that what this is about? That I won't understand? Then help me understand. I want to know, Jeff."

Although he was supposed to be watching the road, it seemed that his gaze was anywhere but there. After several long moments he looked over at her, and his eyes were a mix of pain and pleading. "Could we talk about something else? Please."

She knew how badly he didn't want to talk about it. What he couldn't know was how badly she did. Irritation dropped over her as she crossed her arms and slumped back in the seat. "Sure. What do you want to talk about? The Ball?"

As if grasping for the last thread before he fell off a cliff, Jeff lunged for that one. "It starts at seven on Saturday. I thought maybe I could pick you up six or six-thirty."

Her eyes fell closed as she stepped through the emotional door that slammed shut behind her. "Fabulous."

"I need a huge favor," Jeff said Monday morning as he and Gabe went through the checklist of safety equipment.

"What's that?"

"You remember you said you'd talk to Wade if I wanted you to?"

"Yeah."

"Well, I guess I want you to."

Gabe's eyebrows arched. "You guess?"

For a second Jeff thought about it, and then he exhaled. "I'm prepared to beg, and I'll go as far as groveling if necessary."

The skeptical look didn't leave Gabe's face. "Why the sudden change of heart?"

Jeff shrugged. "It was the least worse of two options."

The goatee on Gabe's chin moved back and forth. "Then I'd hate to hear the other option."

"But you'll do it? You'll talk to him?"

"You'd better find yourself a tuxedo."

"We're all set," Jeff said over the phone Tuesday evening, his voice sounding breathless. He didn't know if it was her or the ball or the thought that she might bring up the wreck again that was holding his chest in a clench like a pipe wrench trying to break a seal.

"For what?" Lisa asked, sounding wholly distracted, and he knew he was off the hook. Work. Blessed work. For once, he couldn't have been more thankful for it.

"The Ball, silly." Then a horrible thought hit him, and his head dropped on the weight of it. "That is if you still want to go."

"I thought you had to work."

"I called in a favor."

"I thought you didn't dance."

"I don't," he said as his heart fell, "but maybe we can find a table that needs holding down."

For a moment he thought she might actually turn him down flat, and the middle of him screamed for a way to go back and do everything over again so they wouldn't end up at this juncture. Then through the fear, he heard her sigh.

"Six-thirty?" she finally asked.

"Make it six," he said, knowing the very next moment wouldn't be soon enough.

"I'll be ready."

Fourteen

Nervous didn't even begin to describe it. No, all-out terror came much, much closer. Until Jeff stood in front of his mirror on Saturday evening, adjusting and then readjusting the black bow tie at his neck, he had never really put into words why he had begged off the prom, the Harvest Festival, his cousin's wedding, the Sweetheart Dance...

Now he had the words. Thousands of them jamming through his head. They had to do with a certainty that this night could end in no good way and how foolish he was to think otherwise. They had to do with the fact that he had two left feet that couldn't communicate with each other enough to even fake dancing. And they had to do with the fact that somehow something was bound to go wrong and smash any chances he had of this relationship going forward.

Okay, so it had been on all-but pause for the last four days anyway, but until that moment he had succeeded in convincing himself that that was because of work—his work, her work. Work. Not the tremulous way they had left things when he had walked away from her door the Saturday before with barely a kiss. She was angry, hurt. He knew that, but still his best instincts said that she didn't really want to know. She thought she did, but she really didn't.

With a frustrated sigh over the perpetual tilt of his tie as well as the perpetually negative track of his thought processes, he shook his head and stepped away from the mirror. Good enough was going to have to be good enough. There was no more he could do.

One set of fingers wound over the black satin bodice ensnaring Lisa's chest. She pulled upward, knowing the motion was pointless but trying anyway. This dress had been in her closet for three years—ever since the last fiasco of the formal dinner party she had been invited to. She remembered buying it, at the behest of Haley who had thought she looked just gorgeous in it. The only problem was gorgeous had nothing to do with comfort.

Even pressed business suits, cinching in all the wrong places were more comfortable. At least those she couldn't fall out of. True, the dress sported a sequined jacket that did a passing job of concealing most of the strapless top, but that didn't make it any more comfortable. All week she had thought about going to get something else—something other than this nightmare. However, in the back of her mind she had thought this moment would never really arrive anyway. That he would talk himself out of it, that she would come to her senses and call off tonight, that the whole idea would simply blow over.

Instead it blew right to her doorstep. The knock, soft yet undeniably there sounded, and she took a treacherous breath in as she yanked the jacket on. She hadn't seen him since Saturday, and over the course of the week, tucked neatly behind her stacks of work, she had tried repeatedly to convince herself that he wasn't as wonderful as she had originally thought he was. No, he couldn't be as handsome or as sweet or as thoughtful or as...

The nanosecond after she opened the door, however, those thoughts splintered into a hundred-million non-discernible letters for standing there, on the other side of her threshold, gaze down, he looked more incredible than any human being had a right to. Muscles concealed by the black material spread across his shoulders—strong even hiding beneath propriety. As she fought to catch her breath from the sight of him, his gaze bounced sheepishly to the wall and then up to hers as the pink rose in his hand trembled.

"Hi," he said when his gaze caught hers although the syllable floated just beneath the air.

A smile, gentle and soft, drifted over her as all her doubts receded. "Hi."

Traveling a half-inch at a time, he held the rose out to her as his gaze bounced to the floor and then back up to hers. "For you."

"Thanks," she said, mesmerized by the denim blue of his eyes. The white shirt made the depths of them seem positively endless. "Come... come on in."

As he followed her forward, he looked at his watch hesitantly. "I'm a little early."

"I'm not complaining." She smiled as she set the rose in a glass in the kitchen. "Let me just grab my purse, and we can get going."

He nodded although she noticed how stiffly he stood, how formally, how awkwardly, and she wondered if that was because of the tuxedo, the night, or something else. With one more check in the hall mirror, she arched her shoulders backward and walked out to meet him. "Shall we?"

That lop-sided, shy smile sent her senses reeling away from her. "We shall."

Every moment was fraught with possible perils. At the car it was the second he opened the door and her dress didn't get all the way in. Should he say something, help it in himself? Then she reached down and pulled it in, and relief flooded through him. Making conversation in the car was equally risky. He didn't want to say anything to remind her of their last conversation if she had indeed forgotten, yet what do you talk about when even work is a dangerous subject?

He settled on cars. His car. This car. It was a relatively safe topic although not very interesting. She didn't seem to mind, and he had to admit even though he was one push from going over the edge that he liked how perfectly she fit in the passenger's seat—no matter what they happened to be talking about.

At the hotel his nerves kicked into overdrive, so much so that when the lady at the sign-in table asked for his name, his memory lapsed just long enough for Lisa to have to take his arm and save him.

"Jeff Taylor and Lisa Matheson," she said confidently, and his breath snagged on the sound of her voice.

"Ah, here it is," the lady said with a smile. She checked their names off. "Have a nice time."

"Thanks," Lisa said with no trouble at all. Gently she laced her arm through his and steered him away from the table. They walked in slow lock step across the gathering. "Are Dustin and Eve coming?"

"He mentioned it, but I'm not sure," Jeff said, crawling carefully back to the surface of life. He looked at her, but that did nothing more than tie his tongue as tight as the bow at his neck. Somehow he had to calm the rush of anxiety flowing through him before he completely humiliated himself.

"Hey, isn't that Dante?" Lisa asked, pointing across the room.

Jeff glanced over to where she was pointing. "Yeah."

"Quick, hide me," she said, sliding around and ducking behind him.

He arched an eyebrow at her. "You don't like Dante?"

"He might ask me to dance," she said, and Jeff wasn't sure how much of the fear was pretend and how much was real.

"Well, at least he won't ask me to."

The smile in her eyes when she looked at him lifted his spirits. "Now that would be scary."

"So you made it after all," Hunter said from behind Jeff, and simultaneously he and Lisa turned.

"In one piece and everything," Jeff said, extending his hand.

"Lisa," Hunter said, nodding to her. "It's nice to see you again."

She nodded at him.

"Well, have fun, you two," he said and turned back to cross the dance floor.

The second he was gone Jeff breathed an audible sigh of relief.

"What?" Lisa asked as she stepped up to the food table.

"With him around I never quite know what to expect."

"Why not?"

"Cornflakes in my bed, flour in my locker. He's a regular laugh-a-minute."

As she slowly filled her plate, Lisa looked over at him, and her face scrunched. "Cornflakes? Maybe you should've applied for hazard pay."

"With Dante and Hunter, that was a definite possibility." He put a radish on his plate and three carrots. "I wonder if Hayes is going to be here tonight."

She licked the dressing that had gotten a little carried away off her finger. "If he sees me, he'll probably run for the exits."

Jeff stole a glance down the side of the black satin that streamed to the ground. "Not looking like that he won't."

Her eyes narrowed. "What's that supposed to mean?"

Mischievously he leaned closer to her. "It means, I don't think I told you how gorgeous you look tonight." The statement brought her gaze to his, and sincerity flooded through him. "What a horrible oversight on my part."

For one glorious moment the world around them ceased to exist, and for him living in that moment forever would have been more than enough.

"Taylor?" the voice asked behind him, and reluctantly Jeff turned to it and found Craig and Bridget, standing, plates in hand, at the edge of the carpet.

"Craig. Hey, man." Jeff transferred his plate to the other hand so he could extend one to Craig. "It's been awhile."

"We were just going to find a place," Bridget said. "Want to join us?"

"Lead on." Jeff picked up a glass of tea from the end of the table. The foursome wound their way around to the tables and picked one midway from the back.

"So, I guess the fact that you're here means you actually found a job," Craig said when they were seated.

"Downtown," Jeff said, nodding. "You?"

"Galena Park."

"How are the kids?" Jeff asked as he set the napkin on his knee, willing it to be kind and stay there.

"Growing," Bridget said in exasperation. "Cari starts school in August."

"Ugh. That doesn't even seem possible." Jeff picked up his fork. Then he realized Lisa was being left out of the conversation, and he leaned over to her as he cut into the salad. "Cari was the cutest little kid—all blonde curls. She was fascinated with the pump controls. Man, she could sit up there for hours on that thing playing supervisor."

Bridget laughed. "She hasn't grown out of that one either."

"So, have you heard from Ramsey?" Craig asked.

"No, we've been down to see Dustin and Eve a couple times, but haven't heard from Ramsey."

"Oh? How are they doing?" Bridget asked.

"Good. Good," Jeff said, nodding. "They might be here

tonight."

"Well, speak of the devil," Craig said as his attention snapped up behind Jeff who turned to see their conversation topics approach the table.

"Well, well, what have we here?" Dustin asked, sounding far less melancholy than he had the previous weekend. "I didn't know you guys cleaned up so good."

"Yeah, and I didn't know you had such good eyesight either," Craig taunted back. "Have a seat."

"I believe we will."

The evening, so similar and yet so very different from the first time Lisa had shared a table with these people, seemed to stream by on fast forward. Conversation and laughter flowed from every quarter until it occurred to her that this was easily the most fun she had ever had.

At nine the band started playing, and someone turned down the lights so that their little table, which had been at least partially lit, was now all-but black.

"I do believe it's time to dance," Dustin said, turning to Eve formally. "Mrs. Knox?"

Eve smiled at him, and Lisa smiled at them. There was nothing but love in the look they exchanged. Slowly Eve stood and accepted Dustin's hand, and the two of them slipped out to the dance floor as a slow song enveloped them.

"Sounds like a plan to me," Craig said, standing and helping Bridget out of her chair. They followed the first couple to the floor as Lisa sat watching them.

She laid her chin in her hand as dreaminess overtook her. "Craig and Bridget are nice," she finally said to fill the void the foursome had left.

"Yeah." Uneasily Jeff slid his hands under the table to straighten his pants.

A minute. Two, and Lisa's gaze slid from the dance floor to him. "I'm glad Dustin and Eve made it. I think they needed a night out."

He turned a confused look on her. "Why would you say that?"

She shrugged as trepidation tiptoed across her heart, and her gaze traveled back out. "She was pretty worried about him last week. Not that I blame her, he looked pretty bummed."

"Yeah, he was." Absently Jeff's finger tapped on the table. "I guess it's as hard on the wives as it is on the guys sometimes."

Sometimes? her mind screamed, but she let it slide. "Hey, Kamden liked the proposal for the new ads—you know the ones with the displays falling over on the guy."

His gaze snapped to hers. "No kidding?"

"Sick, twisted sense of humor," she said with a playful shrug. "Must be a guy thing."

"Gee, thanks," he said, and there was a hint of that smile again.

"Jeff, my man." The voice came from behind Lisa, and she jumped at the sound of it. Dante. She knew it without even looking up. Head bent, she watched the two shake hands. "And is this…?" He put his hand on her back and wound his body around to get a good look at her. Pulling rational to her, Lisa looked at him and forced herself to smile. "It is. Lisa!" Smoothly Dante swung the chair next to her around and sat down. "Now, you know, I could be wrong about this, but did you or did you not promise me a dance for this evening?"

If there had been any way out of it, Lisa would have found it, but from where she sat, she could see none. Dante stood and offered her his hand. "You don't mind, do you, Jeff?"

Stricken. It was the best word to describe the look on Jeff's face when Lisa looked to him for an excuse out of this. "No. 'Course, I don't mind."

Twice on her way to the floor, with Dante's arm securely around her waist, she looked back at the table, and the only thing she could think was how incredibly alone Jeff looked, sitting there watching her leave. The middle of her heart twisted at the sight. When they got to the dance floor, Dante took her in his arms, and Lisa pulled herself up straight. Formal. *Don't give an inch. Don't let him think that I'm at all interested.*

They moved together for a few minutes without so much as looking at each other. Then something in her said it was rude to not even look at the guy. Hesitantly she glanced up at him and smiled. He caught the gaze and held it.

"You know I have to tell you, Taylor is one lucky guy," Dante said, and although she fully expected him to be smooth and oily, his voice was anything but. Curiously her head turned as the fear she had felt in his presence prior to this moment slipped away. In his eyes was only softness and sincerity. "I still can't believe he had the guts to make a move on you. I mean I didn't even have the nerve to do that—although I wanted to."

She knew the fear should be creeping up on her. She waited for it, but there wasn't a shred of it anywhere.

"Jeff's a pretty good guy though, so if it couldn't be me, I'm glad it's him," Dante said with a soft smile.

Tears sprang to her eyes although she wasn't exactly sure why.

"We gave him a pretty hard time when he first got there," Dante continued, wholly taking over the conversation so she didn't need to so much as nod to keep it going. "But I've got to tell you, that guy is one of the gutsiest people I've ever known."

"I think all of you are pretty gutsy," she said finally corralling her voice.

"Not like Taylor. He's a fireman's fireman." Then Dante smiled. "Well, he will be in a few years when he lives down the whole rookie thing. But I've got a lot of respect for him—rookie or not."

The song ended, and they stood for one more moment. Then Dante's hold on her broke so that his hand went just to the small of her back. "Better get you back to your boyfriend. He's probably itching to dance with you himself."

Lisa smiled as they wound their way through the tables to where Jeff still sat all alone. She slid into the chair next to him as Dante extended his hand. "Thanks man. You've got quite a woman there."

"I know," Jeff said as his gaze landed on her in lock-time with his arm which draped across the back of her chair. With a small wave Dante disappeared into the crowd. When he was gone, Jeff leaned in to her. "Sorry about that."

"No," she said softly, still trying to get used to the idea. "Dante's cool."

In confusion Jeff looked at her just as Dustin and Eve stumbled through the tables and collapsed into their chairs.

"They really should have this thing in December when it's less than 90 degrees outside," Eve said, fanning herself theatrically. She picked up the fall of wavy black hair and fanned her neck. "It's not healthy to get this hot."

"I don't think outside's the problem," Jeff said with a laugh.

"Oh, yeah?" Eve shot back as she let her hair go. "How would you know? I haven't seen you out there shaking your booty yet."

"And you won't either," Jeff said seriously.

Dustin shook his head in exasperation. "Lisa, how in the world did you get stuck with someone so dead set against having fun?"

With a long look of love at him, Lisa slid her hand down the length of Jeff's thigh. "I'm not complaining."

He looked at her in surprise, and a second later gratefulness slipped into his eyes.

"Ugh," Eve said still fanning. "You two make me sick."

"Why? You jealous?" Jeff asked although his gaze never left Lisa's face.

"Remind me," Eve said to Dustin dramatically. "Isn't that what you always said to him?"

"You know, I think you're right," Dustin said with teasing around the edges. "When did he suddenly get all lovey-dovey on us?"

"I don't know. I think it had something to do with a bachelorette party as I recall," Eve said. "And the way it looks now, we may be headed for another one real soon."

That remark slammed Jeff's eyelids down as he laughed. He pulled Lisa's shoulder under his arm and turned to his friends. "You two sure make it hard to be romantic. You know that?"

"Romantic?" Eve asked in horror. "Oh, my gosh. Did that word just come out of your mouth? Lisa, what have you done to our sweet, little, innocent Jeff?"

Lisa shook her head as her hand caught his under the table. "It wasn't me. I was just sitting in a booth minding my own business."

"Now I know that's a lie," Dustin said, laughing, "because Jeff wouldn't know a move if it jumped up and bit him."

Jeff settled in next to Lisa as he shook his head. "You have such little faith in me."

"I know you. Remember?" Dustin asked as the next song started. He sat for four beats and then looked across at Lisa. "Well, Lisa, since I know Romeo here's not going to ask you, I guess it's up to me. Would you do me the honor?" He stood and held a hand out to her.

Embarrassment heated its way across her face as she laid her hand in his. "Sure." She stood and then looked back at Jeff. "You don't mind, do you?"

He looked first at Lisa and then at Dustin as lightheartedness danced across his face. "Would it matter if I did?"

"No," Dustin said quickly pulling Lisa forward, and she laughed.

"Yeah! That's what I thought!" Jeff called after them as he sank back into his seat. He couldn't be mad. He loved them all too much, and it was too obvious that against every probability, they all liked each other. The music floated around him as his heart filled with gratefulness.

"Well, if you're not going to ask, then I am," Eve said suddenly standing. "Let's dance."

Fear slammed into him as he looked up. "Dance?"

"Sure," she said quickly grabbing his hand. "I'd love to."

Dustin was a good six inches taller than Jeff, and Lisa wondered how Eve's arm didn't go completely numb by the end of the night from laying it on his shoulder. Dancing with him wasn't difficult though. He had such a commanding presence about him. It wasn't demanding. It was simply powerful in a comforting kind of way. The only one she could think that came close to it was Jeff, but Jeff's version of presence was far less conspicuous than Dustin's. It was only on display for a precious few.

"I'm sure glad my plans didn't work out," Dustin said, leaning closer to her after they had danced halfway around the floor.

"Oh? What plans were those?" she asked, arching her neck so she could look at him.

"All those plans to set Jeff up with someone I thought would be perfect for him." Dustin raised his eyebrows in quick succession, causing the good-natured side of her to vault forward.

"Oh, yeah? And just how many someones are we talking about here?"

"Countless," Dustin said with an exasperated sigh. "I'd just about given up on that boy. He was so hopeless."

"Hopeless? It was that bad?"

Slowly Dustin's face fell into a pained expression. "My cousin thought he had xenophobia or something."

"Ah, the illustrious cousin."

"And she wasn't even the worst of them. There was the secretary at Eve's office, and the cute blonde from the fast food place, and Bridget's friend, and my hairdresser..."

The incredulousness poured over her. "He went out with all of them?"

"Well, that depends on your definition of 'going out.' The hairdresser never even got picked up, he chickened out on the way to go get her. Bridget's friend... Well, let's just say Catalina Salad Dressing doesn't exactly go well with black heels and white velvet." He shook his head. "Trust me, it wasn't pretty."

"But they did go out?"

"Once," Dustin said. "Then it would've taken a United Nations conference to get either one to so much as talk about the idea again. I thought we were going to have to call in Cyrano de Bergerac before any girl would have a chance to get close enough to decide he was worth a second date." In two perfect circles Dustin spun her before catching her again. "But I'm very happy to see that Providence stepped in."

"Providence, huh?"

Teasingly he looked at her. "What would you call it?"

The best thing that ever happened to me, her mind said happily.

"Oh, no, don't look now," Dustin said, turning her so she couldn't see the rest of the dance floor.

"What?" she asked, trying to turn despite his efforts to keep her from looking.

"I said, 'Don't look.' This could forever alter your perception of his romantic possibilities."

Confused, Lisa yanked Dustin around and surveyed the dance floor until her gaze landed on them. Jeff and Eve moving together although it couldn't really be called together, and it really couldn't be called dancing either as he was looking only at his feet which were not in any kind of sync with the beat or with Eve's. Instantly protective compassion for him slid over her.

"My sympathies," Dustin said, glancing down at her.

A peaceful sigh whispered from her lungs. "I wouldn't want him any other way."

Dustin's gaze snapped to her questioningly, and she looked up at him with perfect peace.

"Otherwise he wouldn't be Jeff."

Understanding flowed over his features as he spun her again with the end of the song. Instead of guiding her back to the table, however, he angled their trajectory over to where Jeff and Eve stood. The first thing Lisa noticed was that not a scintilla of Jeff's stance was at ease. Fidgety and awkward. Out-of-place and embarrassed. Those were all much closer. The next song started.

"Thank you for keeping her warm for me," Dustin said, nudging Lisa next to Jeff as he took Eve's hand.

"Yeah, no problem," Jeff said, but he never really looked up.

"See ya," Dustin said, and they danced off.

Uneasily Jeff's gaze followed them even as Lisa's tried not to. However, even trying not to, she caught the silent conversation that passed between the two men, with Dustin shooing Jeff forward even as Jeff seemed to shrink back.

"We could go sit down if you want," Lisa said, searching for some way to diffuse the panic permeating Jeff's expression.

A moment and he nodded, and she turned back for the tables.

"Or we could... dance."

Her feet stopped, and when she turned back to him, his gaze was on the floor.

"If you want," he said as his eyes slipped up to meet hers.

A soft smile accompanied her silent nod. Slowly she stepped over to him, and when her arm slipped up to his shoulder, she couldn't help but feel how perfectly they fit together. Forever, she could dance with him, and her arm would never go to sleep. The first sideways step wasn't smooth, but neither of them tripped either. The second one to the other side was better—hesitant but better. By the third, her mind had stopped worrying about her feet and had started tracing the track of the points of his body that were touching hers.

Arm-under-arm, his supported hers like a breath. On her back the web of his hand pressed firmly, holding her, guiding her—solid and safe. The lights winked around them as after several steps, he turned her other hand around to hold it to his chest. Funny how much more natural that felt. As she swayed, the appreciation that she wasn't dancing to show off to anyone slid over her. This wasn't about anyone other than the two of them.

When she glanced at him, her heart slammed to a stop when she found him gazing at her. He didn't have to say a thing, only to smile, and any doubts she had left melted into the strength of him. Slowly her hand slid forward, dropping over the solid muscle of his neck and chest so that when it stopped only her elbow was still on his shoulder.

His chest, strong and true, called her to it, and softly she laid her cheek on the scratchy black material. It gave new meaning to breathing for simultaneously she felt energized and completely lightheaded drifting on the fragrance of his cologne. She hadn't noticed it before. How it had escaped her, she couldn't quite tell because the part of her in charge of deciphering little things like how she had even gotten to this point seemed no longer to be in service.

The only thing she could feel, the only thing she ever wanted to feel again, was him holding her, swaying to a beat that she didn't even hear. In her ears rang only the faint sound of his heartbeat far beneath the layers, blending with hers in a harmony so perfect it should have been reserved for Heaven itself.

How long they had been dancing Jeff wasn't really sure. It seemed like forever, and yet it seemed like mere seconds. Holding her, moving with her had nothing to do with where his feet were or where his hands were supposed to be. She was here, in his arms, everything else was academic.

"Hey, you two," Dustin said, his voice breaking through the knot of contentment that had settled over them. Blearily they pulled apart but never really let go of one another. "We're going to take off."

Jeff's movement slowed to a halt. He knew that Dustin never left a party early, and his leaving could only mean that the time for them to leave as well was upon them. "Already?"

"Already? It's after one," Dustin said with a check of his watch. "I've got work tomorrow."

"Oh, yeah. Of course." Still caught in the haze of her, Jeff extended his hand. "Take care out there."

"Yeah, you too," Dustin said with a smile that said that comment didn't just mean work. "Call me."

Jeff nodded, and his friends stepped away from them. Regretting that he had to, he looked at Lisa, who was more beautiful now than she had been seven hours before. "Well, I guess it's time to call it a night."

For a second he wasn't sure she had even heard the comment. Then a gentle pleading look traced through her eyes. "One more dance?"

Like a thousand racehorses at the gun, his heart leaped forward as he smiled. "But I don't dance."

Her smile held no irony. "I know."

Once again she was in his arms, and his only wish was that she would be forever.

At her apartment door Lisa wondered when she had stumbled into this unbelievable dream. Life swirled around her—arching in no definite patterns so that she felt like she might fall right off of it at any moment. The one and only thing keeping her upright was his arm, tucked securely around her waist, holding her lest she fall.

"So, you going to be hungry tomorrow night?" he asked softly as his other arm slid around her to join its partner at her back.

His heartbeat drifted over her again.

"Yeah, and the next night, and the next night, and the night after that," she said, floating away on the words as his lips found hers. It was by far the most amazing moment she had ever occupied.

"I tried to call you last night," Dustin said when they were six sentences into the conversation on Tuesday afternoon. "What'd you do, go AWOL on me?"

In a heap Jeff sat down on the couch and propped his feet on the coffee table. "No, I was at Lisa's trying to find a way to make office supplies sound interesting."

"Office supplies?"

"Yeah, she got a new account on Monday. She was kind of freaking out."

"Only about Monday?" Dustin asked.

One foot slipped off and the other followed as Jeff sat up. "What's that supposed to mean?"

Dustin laughed softly. "Like you don't know. Oh, by the way, Eve's wondering if we should plan on a winter wedding or late summer. She needs some new shoes."

"Ha. Ha."

"No, I don't think she was kidding."

Jeff shook his head. It never ended. They were never satisfied. "Well, I think she's going to have to ask someone other than me."

"Oh? Who's that?"

"I don't know, whoever decided I could handle all this in the first place." He sighed and ran a hand through his hair. "Lisa is so great, and I'm so..."

"Hopeless?"

"Thank you very much."

"You're welcome," Dustin said with no trace of laughter. "But, listen, I've got to be honest with you, I really don't think she cares how hopeless you are."

"I don't know why not." The statement vaulted Jeff off the couch, and he took two steps one way and reversed course. "Every other one has."

"Okay," Dustin said slowly, "maybe you haven't noticed this, but she's not like every other one."

"But why not? What makes her so different?" Jeff asked in frustration as he collapsed onto a barstool.

"Well, for one thing, she's in love with you."

"In... love?" The word smashed through him as his head snapped up. "Oh, I don't..."

"And you're in love with her," Dustin continued gently. "Trust me on this one, Jeffrey, when that gets right, everything else is moot." There was a pause as Dustin let that sink in, and Jeff frantically searched for a way to refute it. "So, have you told your mom about her yet?"

That question exploded through the middle of all the others as Jeff closed his eyes to squeeze it out. "No."

"Why not?"

There were ten thousand why nots lined up at the mere question. "Well, for one thing, I haven't talked to her since November..."

"She'd want to know," Dustin said. "She still cares about you, Jeff. She wouldn't have come that day if she didn't."

Slowly Jeff sighed. "I wouldn't even know what to say to her anymore... not that I ever did."

"So your solution is to not say anything at all?"

Yes! screamed through him. Definitely yes. Life would be

much safer that way. "She doesn't want to hear from me. I can't put her through that again."

"And one day when a building does fall on you, and you're taken away too—you think she won't hurt just the same?"

The top of the counter pulled Jeff's head down to it, and he knocked it three times on the hard Formica. "I don't know. I don't know what to do."

"Whether you believe it or not, you deserve to have her in your life. Maybe this time she'll come around."

His hand pressed hard against his forehead, pushing to get the very thought out of his head. "And what if you're wrong?"
A pause and only that. "What if I'm not?"

Fifteen

For two solid weeks, Jeff tiptoed around the wisdom of his friend's words. Thankfully Lisa hadn't been privy to that conversation. It was enough that he could hear the deeper questions she didn't ask every time they talked about his work. If she knew the rest of the story... He pushed that away as he arched his body up off of the weight bench and let it down again.

How could he explain the unexplainable? Like the incomprehensible fact that it had been he who was left when the smoke had cleared, or that the one person he had never been able to connect with would be the only one left in his small, small world. How could he explain all the nights spent listening for any hint of trouble, a door squeak, a faraway wail, a crack, a pop, the slightest off-kilter sound? How could he tell her about all the nights he had gotten up three and four times to check the hot water heater when he thought he'd smelled something strange in the air?

No, no one knew about those nights. And no one ever would. It was his silent vigil, the one he had signed on for the moment he hadn't thought past where he'd thrown those rags...

"Stop it, Taylor," he commanded himself as he pulled the barbell off the floor. "You're going to make yourself crazy." Once, twice, he pulled the weight up. "It's in the past. Let it stay there." Numbers flowed over numbers until he lost count of them all. "It has nothing to do with now. Nothing. Don't let it start again. Please, don't let it start again."

When the clock wound around to seven and he hadn't called, Lisa's worry system jumped to attention. Trying not to think about the reasons he wouldn't have called, she dialed the phone and tapped the pencil twelve times before her panic was assuaged.

"Hello?"

"Well, I was afraid you'd dropped off the edge," she said, laughing at her own melodramatic imagination.

"Nope, not quite. Just doing some reps. I've been slacking too much recently."

"Bringing supper to poor, malnourished souls instead of working out? What were you thinking?" She leaned back in her chair and kicked her shoes off under the desk, liking the fact that she had the whole office to herself. "You really need to get your priorities straight, you know that?"

It was at that moment that she heard the unmistakable snap of the front door. Strange, she thought sitting up, Sherie usually locked that on her way out.

"You make it hard to keep anything straight," Jeff said lightly although Lisa barely heard the statement over the pounding of her heart.

"Yeah," she said, breathing the word as she strained to hear into the outer office. The first rap on her door sent a gasp right through her as she scrambled for her shoes and her jacket simultaneously.

"Lisa?" the voice said on the other side of the door. "Are you here?"

"Umm, yeah, just a minute," she called, pulling, buttoning, and fixing as fast as her shaking hands would possibly move.

"What's wrong?" Jeff asked in her ear.

"Somebody's here," Lisa said as the door creaked open, and the black hole of helplessness opened up at her feet. "Tucker. Hi."

"I thought that was your light," Tucker said smoothly as he stood right in the middle of her one and only way out.

"Tucker? What's he doing there?" Jeff asked. "It's almost seven o'clock."

"Listen," she said into the phone, forcing her voice to remain calm. "I have to go. I'll call you later."

"Are you...?"

"I've got to go. Bye." And she hung up.

It took Jeff less than two seconds to make the decision, grab a shirt and his keys, and be out the door. The fact that he was still in his sweats didn't register. Tucker Cordell didn't take no for an answer, and sooner or later she was going to run out of excuses to put him off. Unless… "God, I'm going to need some wings here."

Lisa cleared her throat and sat up straighter as she worked the last button closed on her jacket. "Our office closed at five," she said, "and Sherie didn't mention you were coming."

"Sherie didn't know," Tucker said, closing the door behind him.

"Oh," Lisa said, fighting to decide if he was indeed here for the reason that kept creeping through her mind or if his visit was somehow innocuous, and overreacting would do nothing more than humiliate her.

"You mind if I…?" Tucker indicated the chair.

She barely nodded as she folded her hands on the desk. "Is there… Is there something I can help you with?"

"I thought you should know that Grandfather's not doing well," Tucker said, ducking his head on the statement. "He had a slight heart attack last night."

The understanding that she was in fact the stupidest person on the earth cascaded on her. "Oh, I'm sorry. Is he… Is everything all right?"

"They think he's going to be all right, but while he's recuperating, the board has decided that the officers are going to have to take a more active role in running the business."

"That sounds reasonable."

"Yeah, well, I was put in charge of this whole conference idea," Tucker said, and the tone in his voice shifted slightly. "Look, I'll be straight with you: I was never a big fan of the plan in the first place. I mean a leadership conference for non-leaders? Doesn't make much sense to me. You know?"

The world stopped as Lisa forced air into her lungs. "I thought it made a lot of sense."

"Well, unfortunately what you think doesn't matter all that much."

Fear snaked through her. "What are you saying?"

Tucker shrugged as though the whole question was of no consequence to him. "Just that I don't see the point of committing valuable time and resources to a project that I don't think is in the best interest of the company to begin with."

"Valuable...?" Rationality was scattering. "But I waved all but a small deposit to get this account, and I've put hours and hours into this thing already..."

"I know. It's unfortunate timing, but some things just can't be helped."

Breath and sanity failed her. "You can't be serious."

"I can, and I am. So unless you can say something to change my mind..." The sentence drifted into nothingness as she tried to force words that weren't screaming obscenities to get all the way to her lips. Finally Tucker nodded. "That's what I thought. I think I've heard all I needed to hear." He swung up and out of the chair.

"Is this because I won't go out with you?" she finally asked, searching the injustice surrounding her for the answer she already knew.

Tucker turned back and shrugged as if the whole thing meant nothing to him. "You made a decision," he said, and his voice was as cold as ice. "And now I'm making mine."

"And if I would've gone along with your little idea? That would've made a difference?"

His gaze slid through her like the serpent in the garden. "Everything makes a difference, Lisa. Don't you know that by now?"

Before she really heard the first sound, Jeff was standing in the middle of her doorway, gasping and panting. "Oh, man. I'm sorry I'm so late. Those stairs are a killer."

The surprise in her eyes was no match for that in Tucker's.

"I got caught in traffic. You know, I really hate downtown sometimes," Jeff said in one continuous stream of words. He recovered with remarkable speed. Then he seemed to notice Tucker whose smooth exterior had shattered with the astonishment. "Oh, I'm sorry. I don't think we've met. Jeff Taylor."

Gaping, Tucker shook Jeff's hand. "Tucker Cordell."

"It's nice to meet you, Tucker. Lisa's so excited about that whole leadership thing. It's all she talks about. Morning, noon, and night." Somehow Jeff managed to wind his way past Tucker and around to her side of the desk. In the next heartbeat his arm was around her shoulders. "Isn't that right, Sweetheart?"

"Umm, oh, uh, yeah," she said, her own gaze registering the thought that he must have fallen and hit his head on something very hard. "All the time."

"Well, Tucker," Jeff continued, unabated. "I hate to break this up, but Lisa and I have a date with a couple of hot dogs."

"H...ot dogs?" Tucker asked as if he'd never heard of such a thing.

"Extra mustard," Lisa said, finally catching hold of her sanity long enough to get her bearings. She scrunched her nose. "It's a fireman thing."

"Oh, so you're with the department?" Tucker asked slowly.

Jeff nodded. "Yeah, it gets kind of old sometimes, lugging those hundred pound hoses up and down all those extension ladders, but it's a paycheck, you know?"

Lisa didn't miss the slide Tucker's gaze did across the expanse of Jeff's mostly uncovered chest muscles, and it was clear the message hit dead center of its mark.

"I can imagine." Tucker was backing away, away from the desk, away from her. She could feel it. "Umm, well, I'd better let you get to your... hot dogs then."

"Yeah, you'd better," Lisa said barely stifling the laugh that jumped to the middle of her.

Clearly shaken, Tucker walked to the door and then stopped. When he turned, there was only regret and understanding in his eyes. "I'll call you tomorrow, Lisa. We'll talk. I'm sure we can work something out."

She smiled sweetly. "I look forward to it."

With the slightest of nods, he opened the door and walked out. It wasn't until the outside door clicked closed that Lisa started breathing again. However, she held up her hand to keep Jeff from saying a single word. Quickly she went out to the front office and threw the lock herself as Jeff, wild-eyed, stepped from her door.

"What was that about?" Jeff asked.

"*That* was one of those really bad ones," she said simply. "I hope you're buying because I'm starved."

"You should've told me, I would've worn my running shoes," Lisa said when they had reached street level.

"I didn't know you owned running shoes," Jeff said, liking how her hand felt in his, but still not beyond the overwhelming adrenaline rush of the flight to her office.

Lisa scrutinized his profile carefully. "By the way, I thought you were working out tonight."

He shrugged as half his smile slipped onto his face. "Some things are more important than working out."

The gaze she leveled on him was a mix of teasing and mischief. "Oh, yeah? Like what?"

"Like trying to prove these lights can be beaten." He looked up at the sign and then over at her. Love. In one breath, he knew that was undeniably what he felt.

"Go!" she yelled, and when she bounded from the curb, she took not only his hand but his heart with her as well.

Jeff knew he had to find a way to say it or he would go stark raving mad. As he and Gabe sat watching the late comedy show that neither of them was really paying attention to on Saturday night, he knew he needed some advice. The only problem was he wasn't sure that advice could even help where this was concerned.

"So, you're married?" Jeff asked like he hadn't been rehearsing this conversation in his mind for four days. The stand-ups babbled on screen, completely forgotten.

"Six years." Gabe reached for the remote and turned the television down.

"Must be hard, being married and being with the department and all."

Gabe shrugged. "Neither was an option for me, so I wouldn't know."

That Jeff understood. "She must be pretty special, your wife."

"Ashley? Yeah, she's the best."

"And she doesn't mind all the long hours and stuff?"

"I wouldn't say that she doesn't mind. She's just accepted that this is what I want to do, and the rest... well, we figure we'll let God take care of that."

Jeff sat, searching for a way to phrase the next question. "So, how'd you know she was the one?"

"Ah," Gabe said, lifting his goateed chin knowingly. "I see where this is going."

"Where?"

"I knew when you and Lisa went to the Fireman's Ball this would be coming sooner or later."

"What…? I didn't say…"

However, the end of that statement was cut in half by the blare of the station alarm. "Mutual assistance requested at 1601 Richland Avenue."

"Oops, hang on to that thought," Gabe said as they both jumped to their feet and headed for the pole. "Duty calls."

The scene was semi-organized chaos when their truck joined the others already surrounding the apartment complex that loomed in the night sky over them. Firefighters, police, and paramedics rushed in all directions at once around the base of the building. Tanks on and masks in hand, they each left their ID tag on the dash as they jumped out. A rumble sounded above them accompanied in the next second by the sound of shattering glass. Running even as he looked up, Jeff saw the flames shoot out ten or so stories up. The tinkling of the glass clinked down against the sidewalk around him.

"Bagby Station reporting," Gabe said for the six of them as they approached the command center.

"We need more hoses up on twelve. Go up the right wing stairs. We've got to get that smoke contained if we're going to get anyone above that thing out."

"Got it," Gabe said before leading the charge back to the truck where they each grabbed several lengths of hose.

"Go! Go! Go!" someone yelled from one side as people from the building raced out past them.

Through the commotion Jeff heard the distinct sound of a hand slapping the side of a nearby ambulance, which sprang to life and began picking its way through the emergency vehicles choking the street. How many people had already gotten out? More importantly, how many were still above those flames? "God, please be with us. We're going to need all the help You can give us with this one."

From the first floor to the tenth, they had to fight traffic.

People, some holding small children, some old, some young—all with that look of bewildered panic etched on their faces filed down the stairs to the left. *Stay right, and keep climbing,* Jeff told himself, wishing he could calm the terror in every eye he passed. However, at the tenth floor the mass of people slowed and then stopped altogether.

Jeff hoped the other stairwell was jam-packed to overflowing with people coming down from above because not a single, solitary soul was coming down this one. The smoke, gray and menacing, caused them to have to stop on the tenth to put on their masks. Then through the growing smoke they proceeded up, and for the first time Jeff noticed the slippery stairs. At least the sprinklers were going to give them some help. However, the smoke pouring out of the eleventh floor door was like a blinding blanket that only got worse the higher they went. Anyone that ventured into it without a mask and air would surely succumb before they got below it.

"Baker and Stevens, you set up at the front, Miller and Jameson start left and get anybody out you find. Jeff, you're with me," Gabe yelled through his mask. "Let's go!"

When Gabe opened the door, it was like running headlong into a broiler. Even through the fire suit Jeff felt the flames heating their way into his skin. They entered a hallway pock-marked with blazing carpet as pieces of flaming ceiling dropped like rain from above. It was then that Jeff noticed the absence of water accompanying the downpour. He looked up, and the fact that the sprinklers were dryer than the carpet swept fear right over the top of him.

He didn't have time for fear though, so he picked his way behind Gabe through the flames to the wall on the far end of the hallway, leaving the others to their tasks.

Fourteen minutes and counting before the air ran out.

At their end of the hall a flaming set of boxes stood on either side of the exit. Whoever had been carrying them down wouldn't have to worry about coming to get the rest, but for those trying to get out, they closed off one more route to safety. That thought made his hands work that much faster when they found the wall water supply valve.

Gabe threw the hose onto the floor and grabbed one end. "I'll get it hooked up, get some water on that mess."

Without question, Jeff grabbed the other end, stretched it as straight as he could and then turned to aim the water at the flames shooting up from the boxes. The wait for water seemed interminable to the point that he almost dropped the hose to go see what was wrong. However, just before he did, he heard the screams from the other side of the door where he stood. Turning to it, he glanced down the hallway to the nearest good escape, but all he could see were fire-blurred figures moving like ghosts. It was true. These people hadn't gotten out. They were trapped, and they would die unless...

The water gushed out of the hose, knocking him a step backward, and immediately he aimed it at the carpet in front of the door as Gabe appeared at his side.

"No, at the exit!" Gabe yelled.

"There's someone in there!" Jeff yelled back, knowing how much smoke was already choking through that apartment. "Get them out first!"

The two feet in front of the door cleared, and Gabe rushed past Jeff. It took one shoulder for the door to give way for Gabe, and Jeff saw only the figures, huddled next to the ground just before a section of the ceiling behind them crashed down. A scream jumped to his ears. "Get them out! I'll get this!" He saw Gabe's hesitation. "I'm all right. Just get them out! I'll get this exit cleared!"

Determination coupled with training surged on him as he proceeded back down the hall, aiming the water across the heat pulsating at him from the now-unrecognizable heap of boxes. If he could just get that passageway open, they would have a chance.

As the flames engulfing the boxes surged upward crumbling what was left of the cardboard, Jeff heard the crack above him. Instinctively he jumped sideways as three sheets of ceiling tile crashed to the carpet behind him. Flames tore through the unburned carpet reaching for the ceiling as he fought to keep his balance and his sanity. "Don't think about that. Just get this one open."

More water and the flames on the boxes subsided and then died. Quickly he spun around and doused the ceiling and then the floor down the other direction, creating a semi-safe passage. In the next breath he reached over and tried the door to his left. It swung open. "Anybody in here? Hey!"

No answer. He wanted to go in and check, but there wasn't time. The fire lining the hallway was gaining ground although the hose was doing all it could to keep it at bay. Forcing the water to clear the path in front of him, he snaked to the right. With a foot he kicked at the door as a small beeping penetrated the other sounds around him. Air was running out, as was time. "Anybody in here?" Again no answer although the fact that most of that apartment was already orange with flames as more of the ceiling dropped into it didn't escape his consciousness. He prayed that whoever had been in there had made it out. That thought pulled him forward as the beeping in his ear became more persistent. With a kick he opened the next door.

"Jeff!" a blurry ghost said, stepping out of the flames like a nightmare come true. "Company 3 can take it. We've got air in the stairwell."

He didn't want to release the hose, but the beeping could not be ignored. Carefully he handed the hose off, and then fairly running alongside Gabe, they raced back to the far stairwell as Jeff's brain ticked off the number of doors still not open. By the time he was at the exit, his brain had stopped counting for fear that he would completely give up hope. Down one flight and then the next they ran as his lungs began to scream as loud as the tank on his back. On the eighth floor they met up with both air bottles and another team of fully geared figures who were preparing to brave the inferno above. The last one was just donning his mask as Jeff yanked his off, gasping in the air. "Dustin?"

"You going back up?" Dustin asked even as Jeff changed the bottles on his back.

"Twelve," Jeff said as he clicked the hoses together, grabbed his mask, and pulled it back on.

"Then I guess I'm following you," Dustin said, and in tandem the four of them started back up the stairs.

This time there were a few people coming down the other way with firefighters for escorts, but not enough. Not nearly enough.

Hell could've been no worse, Jeff thought when they reentered the firestorm eating its way through floor 12. Other firefighters had raced past them on the stairs, up to the other unseen floors. He didn't want to think about how many floors were above them or what state those other floors were in. This one was horror enough.

Waves of heat made the movement of the other teams resemble mere mirages. Back across the burning carpet, over the mounds of fallen ceiling, they stepped, picking their way back to their replacements.

"Go get some air!" Gabe yelled at the one he grabbed the hose from.

For the first time hope surged through Jeff. The other exit door was now open as were more of the apartment doors. That had to be a good sign. It had to be. One door, two, he opened, walking into them far enough to satisfy the dread in him that someone wasn't still in there trapped.

Seven, eight more doors and this floor would be cleared. He banged through the next door calling his familiar, "Anybody in here?" ahead of him. However, an eerie silence met him, and he stopped. Listened. He felt the sound more than he heard it before he ducked back into the hallway. "This one might have someone!"

Stepping across the threshold, he followed the pounding of his heart into the darkened apartment. Strange, after all the others that the flames hadn't touched this one. Back, back, into the black of the apartment until he found a door. He twisted the knob and pushed, but it gave only a fraction of an inch. It wasn't locked, but still it didn't open. "Fire department! Open up!"

"Just a second!" came the whimper from the other side. A pause and the door swung open to reveal a bent, frightened, gray-headed woman and two small children. The bathroom looked much like any other would in the middle of the night—nothing like the tomb it would've been had he not come to check.

"Hang on!" Jeff said, and he raced back to the hallway. "I need help over here!"

"You got somebody?" Dustin asked, stepping over the mound of flames on the hallway floor from the door he had just come out of.

"Three." Together they raced through the apartment to the bathroom. When they got back to the door, one of the children sent up a helpless scream. It was a sound destined to be etched in the center of Jeff's soul forever. "No. No. Sweetheart. It's okay. We're going to get you out." Knowing the nightmares she would now have forever about this very moment, he picked her up and watched Dustin stand to hand him the boy.

"Get them out. I'll get her," Dustin commanded.

A nod, and Jeff was running through the apartment. He had made it just out of the apartment's front door when a sickening crack sounded behind him. *Run!* was his only thought. How heavy the two figures clutching him were, he couldn't tell, but it was as though they weighed nothing for his feet could have moved no faster. To the stairwell and down he raced as heavy smoke rose all around him. Somewhere around the fourth flight down, he realized that both children were crying. "Hang on. I'll get you out. Just hang on to me."

The instruction wasn't necessary. They could've held on no tighter had they tried. He was nearing the bottom when finally he ran into a group of firefighters just as the beeping began in his ears.

"Could somebody take these two down?" he asked, handing them off. "I need a bottle." It was in his hand in an instant, and without bothering with conversation, he started back up the stairs. It was crazy to make the change in the smoke. However, he wanted to get as high as he could before he had to switch them out. Higher, higher, and then as the smoke again increased around him, a thought hit him. He should've already met Dustin on the way down. Snap, snap went the hoses on his back as terror took over his motions. With a clank he set the old bottle next to the wall, changed it out with the new one, grabbed the handrail, and sprinted back up the stairs into hell.

The hallway was clearer now, but the apartments weren't so lucky.

"Where's Dustin?" Jeff asked Gabe who still manned the hose.

"I need someone to take this," Gabe said.

"Where's Dustin?" Jeff asked again as Gabe thrust the hose into his hands.

"Who's Dustin?" Gabe asked, and then his attention snapped back to his tank. "I've got to go." And he started down the hallway as Jeff's heart screamed after him. Pandemonium reigned around him from firefighters, hoses snaking across each other, mounds of smoldering debris, and the crackling of the falling ceilings emitting from every door.

Another firefighter scrambled up close enough for Jeff to call to him. "Hey! Can you take this?"

The air thing. They all knew about it, so without question the man took over the hose. Instantly Jeff turned down the hall. Which one was it again? Rushing into apartment after apartment, he checked each one, looking for the one that looked familiar. Three down, he pushed into one that was lit in a spectacular ball of orange and red. Logically he couldn't have explained it, but just below logic was the undeniable knowledge that this was the one he was looking for.

Two steps in, he suddenly understood the crack he had heard on his exit. The ceiling or what was left of it hung from the rafters in flaming shreds. Unlike its companions in the other apartments, a whole section had decided to come down in one fell swoop rather than a piece at a time. However, like its companions it had given no warning of its collapse.

At that moment he heard it—the unmistakable chirping beep of a PASS. Worst case scenario. Firefighter down. Praying he wouldn't need the help, but taking the precaution anyway, Jeff ducked back into the hallway. "Firefighter down! Firefighter down!"

No more time to summon help. Praying even as the flames shot up from the upholstery in the living room, he stepped through them in the direction of the bathroom and the beeping. "Please, God, where is he?"

By the window the carpet ignited a curtain sending it up in a whoosh that took Jeff's breath right out of him. It was in that flash that he saw the boot, lying sideways under a pile of flaming ceiling tile. "Oh, God, no!" Grabbing the first piece he came to, he slung it off of the immobile figure. "Hang on, Dustin, buddy. I'm coming." A piece. Another. Across the room a second curtain flamed to life. The fire on the tile in his hand seeped its way through the cracks forming in his gloves, searing the skin it found there. "You're almost out! I've almost got you! Hang on, Buddy!"

Two more pieces and the blackened peeling remains of the fire suit emerged to reveal Dustin lying face down like all the horrible outlines they draw around murder victims. Frantically Jeff reached for the shoulders and rolled the body over and off of the heap underneath that only then he realized was the woman. His senses reeled to the edge of overwhelm. The mask on Dustin's face was askew, exposing the skin beneath, and making him appear like some crumpled robot destined for the recycling heap.

"Just a second I've got to get some help," Jeff told his friend, and he jumped up and ran to the door. "I've got a downed firefighter and a victim here! I need help! Hey! Somebody! I need help!"

A figure and then another ran up as the beginning of the beeping started in Jeff's ears. Step-for-step they followed him into the apartment, where one of the men picked up the woman and started out. Jeff grabbed Dustin's shoulders and arched them up enough for the other firefighter to get an arm under them. The beeping was now coming from all directions at once drowned out only by the pounding of Jeff's heart. "Let's get him out."

The big black boots dragged the ground as they angled around the flames. The head, limp and lifeless, bobbed with each labored step. The screaming of Dustin's PASS and Jeff's own dwindling tank of air was making Jeff's head swim. When they got to the exit, they met up with a knot of men coming fresh from replenishing their tanks. Jeff's steps had begun to sway under the emotional and physical strain so that the only thing keeping him standing was sheer determination.

"We need help over here!" the man on Dustin's left yelled at the men.

Only when his replacement edged him out of the way did Jeff realize who it was.

"Get yourself down," Gabe yelled at him. "We'll get him."

No nightmare had ever seemed so surreal. No moment so bizarre. On feet that he couldn't figure out how they were moving, Jeff descended through the smoke, following something that he vaguely remembered he was supposed to. The beeping in his ears was an all-out scream now, and still one foot followed the other down. "Please, God. Let him be okay." They were the only thoughts getting through the haze.

Finally they broke through to the base of the cloud of smoke, and immediately they met up with a cluster of firefighters preparing to go up.

"We need help!" he heard someone yell. "He needs air, and this one's bad."

The mask jerked off Jeff's face, and air like none he had ever tasted slid into his lungs.

"Man, you should've quit while you were ahead," the figure said, kneeling next to him although Jeff didn't fully understand the comment. His gaze, now clearer from the oxygen, slipped forward as the two figures and the seared black plastic rounded the bottom corner and disappeared from sight.

"No! Wait!" he felt himself yell. Instead he choked on the air those words would've taken to utter. It didn't matter. They had Dustin, and he had to get down there. Pulling himself up from the floor where he had somehow fallen, he forced strength into his legs and started descending even as his makeshift nurse reached for him.

"Hey! Where're you going?"

With barely a wave backward, he pushed through the men on the landing and around the corner. Down. Down. Going faster with each passing step until he wouldn't have been at all surprised to find himself in China at the end of that staircase. However, their task had slowed his quarry, and just as they pushed out of the front doors of the building, he caught them.

A swell of people engulfed them as Jeff pushed his feet through them. The two men on either side of the dragging boots were practically on the curb before they stopped and lowered their fallen comrade to the ground.

"Medic!" Gabe yelled, ripping the mask from Dustin's face. "We need a medic!"

"Dustin!" Jeff's heart carried him right to his friend's side where he grabbed Dustin's hand as all medical training he'd had failed him. "Dustin! Man, don't leave me! Come on! Don't leave me!"

He heard the feet on the concrete behind him, but the sound didn't register as he looked into the eyes that were no longer open. "Dustin, man! Can you hear me? Come on! Fight! You've gotta fight!"

On the other side a paramedic appeared, kneeling, checking. "He's breathing. Get a stretcher."

"There isn't one," someone behind Jeff said.

"Then find one!" the first paramedic yelled. "Sir, you're going to have to give us some room. Sir!"

But nothing was making any sense anymore. Only those closed eyes, and memories he couldn't fully remember.

"Jeff." A hand cupped over his shoulder. "Jeff, they need to work."

It made sense that he should stand. The only problem was he couldn't. He simply couldn't back up and leave his friend. "Dustin, man! Please say something! Come on! Please!"

"Jeff!" Fingers on both sides of him pulled him backward. "Jeff, come on. Let them work."

As he was pulled away, he felt Dustin's hand drop from his to the hard concrete, and his whole being screamed in a gut-wrenching howl. "No! Dustin!" He fought them off, trying to get back to that hand. "No! Please! Let me go! He needs me!"

"Hey!" the paramedic standing only inches from Jeff's struggling frame said, and only then did Jeff recognize him. A.J. "Listen to me. We'll take care of him. We'll do everything we can, but you've *got* to back off."

An entire conversation, quick but spirit-squelching passed between them, and then Jeff nodded.

"I promise we'll do everything we can," A.J. said, gazing right through Jeff. "I promise."

One set of hands dropped from him as Jeff watched A.J. turn and kneel over the charred heap on the sidewalk.

"It's going to be okay," Gabe said slowly.

Dry tears slid down Jeff's face. He could feel them although no one else could see them. They felt like they had been there forever. The haze slid over him as he reached up to his cheek to wipe them away.

"Good, Lord, what did you do to your hands?" Gabe asked in shock.

Jeff could see nothing. Nothing was making any sense.

"Hey! Could I get an EMT over here?" Gabe yelled, dragging Jeff from the spot and over to an ambulance. "We've got a burn!"

"What's the problem?" a young lady asked, jumping from the back of one ambulance. Gabe turned Jeff's hands over. The EMT recoiled. "Jeez. Don't you know those gloves aren't foolproof? Here, let me get the stuff."

Gently Gabe sat Jeff down on the ambulance bumper, clearly afraid his friend might end up on the asphalt if he didn't. "God, man, don't you know when to quit?"

"I think we're going to have to cut the gloves off," the EMT said, jumping out and landing right at Jeff's side. "I'll patch you up as best I can, but I think you need to go the hospital to get these taken care of."

"The ambulance?" Gabe asked.

She shook her head as she pulled out a monstrous pair of scissors. "Badly injured only."

"Could he ride up front with someone going?"

"If you can talk them into it," she said with a shrug.

"Hang on. Okay?" Gabe said, clapping a hand on Jeff's shoulder. "I'll get you a ride."

Sixteen

The wailing barely registered above Jeff's head as the ambulance swung around first one corner and then another. At least it felt like swinging to his perilous hold on reality. Every turn sent his shoulder crashing into the door, but it wasn't the recklessness of the driver so much as the weakness in his body that was betraying his balance. What little strength was left, he was fighting to will through the metal partition and into the back. Dustin needed the strength far more than he did. With that thought, others he didn't want to think flooded over him, and he squeezed his eyes shut to block them out.

Finally they screeched to a stop under the emergency room canopy, and the driver jumped out. Even the pain didn't make it all the way through his swirling thoughts as Jeff reached down, popped the door handle, and all-but fell out of the cab. Like a drunk on Saturday night, his steps threaded around the front of the vehicle to the other side where blinding light cut right through his brain.

Six green-clad medical personnel already surrounded the single white gurney indented with two solid black boots, and in seconds they had slipped through the sliding glass doors. He wanted to follow them, but his spirit was the only thing still moving.

"He's as okay as he can be right now," A.J. said, striding up to Jeff from the back of the ambulance. "And he's in good hands. Come on, let's get you taken care of."

When the phone by her bed rang, Lisa rolled over and squinted at the clock. 4:22. Gingerly she sat up and scratched the side of her head. She cleared her throat and retrieved the receiver. "Hello?"

"Lisa?"

"Yeah?"

"This is A.J. A.J. Knight."

The name sounded familiar. Where had she heard that name again?

"Listen, I thought you should know, Jeff's in the emergency room."

Sleep's shackles shattered as her whole body wrenched up off the pillows. "What?"

"I don't have time to go into the details, but he's at Ben Taub General. Tell them you're family. They'll let you back. Sorry, I've got to go, but Lisa?"

"Yeah."

"Come, okay? He needs somebody."

The middle of her hurt like it had never hurt before. Somewhere in the middle of the phone call her heart had stopped and with it her breathing. "Please, please, please, God, please, let him be all right."

When the white Cavalier rounded the last corner, even that prayer stopped. She counted four ambulances all with their lights on lined up next to the curb, and she knew it was bad. No, it was really bad. Really, really bad. Those words put wind under her feet as she jumped from the car and raced through the doors to the information desk.

"May I help you?" the receptionist asked.

"Yes, there was a firefighter brought in earlier. I'm his..." She looked down at her naked hand and carefully slid it under her other arm. "...fiancée."

"Name?"

"Umm, Jeff. Jeff Taylor."

A pause as the computer worked on locating him. "Yes, he's in emergency. Bay 14."

"And emergency is?"

"Through these doors and to the right."

"Thank you," Lisa said, fighting for breath as her steps picked up speed. The rubber of her tennis shoes thumped against the hard floor. At the doors she pushed through them with one hand and entered a world of smattered commands and frightened weeping. Forcing resolve into the void in her heart, she half-walked, half-ran all the way to the sign reading: "Admissions."

Chaos. People, carts, medical equipment everywhere, and voices raking right over the top of them. She considered stopping to ask for directions, but there wasn't an unoccupied hospital employee anywhere. Instead she turned her steps to the curtains on the side that read: "1," "2," "3" above them. Never before would she have been so bold, but there was no thinking involved in this decision.

At 14 she took one breath and pulled the curtain back slightly. Just enough to look inside, and her soul shifted beneath her. In the next heartbeat she was in the cubicle and at his side as he lay on the bed, gaze melded to the ceiling. On soft feet, she stepped over to the bed, aware that he hadn't seen her although he was clearly awake. One gentle hand reached over and brushed the hair from across the grime-stained forehead. "Jeff?"

Uncomprehendingly he looked at her and blinked. "Lisa?"

"Yeah," she said, trying desperately to squelch the tears.

His chest heaved as anguish filled his face. "Lisa?"

"I'm here."

He reached for her seemingly oblivious to the blood-red bandages covering both his hands. Her mind pushed that away from her. He was alive—all else they could handle.

She held him, fighting to breathe through the horror crowding her heart.

"I don't think Dustin made it," he said, and her mind collapsed around the statement.

"What?" She pulled back from him. "Dustin? But…"

"They called in all units," Jeff said as he released her and lay back into the plastic pillow. "We were trying to get some people out…"

"Shh!" she said, realizing that if he freaked out, she might not be able to calm him back down. "Shhh! Just relax. I'll go ask. Okay?"

His eyes dipped back into the haze as he nodded and slipped further into the pillow. The gaze drifted back up to the ceiling as her spirit fell within her. Struggling to stay stoic in the face of an incomprehensible situation, she stepped out of the bay, sniffed once, and squared her shoulders for the admissions desk. "Yes, I need to know the status of a firefighter. Dustin Knox."

"I'm sorry, Ma'am, I can't…"

"Don't tell me you can't," she said as emotions crashed onto her from every side. "He and his wife are close personal friends of ours, and if he's here and as bad as my fiancé thinks he is, then his wife needs to be notified."

The young man sighed. "What's your fiancé's name?"

"Jeff Taylor," she said, doing that hide-the-left-hand maneuver again. "He's in Bay 14. Burned hands." Charred seemed to be a better word, but her heart couldn't take being that honest.

"And the other name?"

"Dustin Knox."

Her breath snagged at the top of her throat just below the prayers for Eve, for Dustin, for all of them.

A pause, and then: "According to my records, Mr. Knox is in CCU. The critical care burn unit on the sixth floor, but he's not allowed any visitors at this time."

"O…" The syllable stopped as her world reeled on the news. "Okay. Thanks."

He nodded as her grief and shock reflected in his eyes. Carefully she turned back. She wished she knew more, and yet one part of her was glad she didn't. At the curtain she stopped and called for God Himself to help her with her next task. Quietly she slipped back into the cubicle and over to the bed. That never-blinking stare unnerved her to the very core. She couldn't lie so her hand, that bare-naked left one, slipped up to his arm as the tears stung her skull. "He's in CCU. They didn't know anymore."

For one moment Jeff's gaze turned to hers, which he searched to the depths of. Then he nodded, turned his head, and regained his silent conversation with the ceiling. She had never felt more helpless in all of her life.

"Umm, do you have… I mean do you know Eve's number? I think we should call her," she finally said.

His gaze snapped downward to the sheet at his leg, and she wished there was a way around asking.

"I didn't have the new one memorized yet." His voice sounded weaker with every word.

"Is it at your apartment?"

The nod wasn't even really there. "My keys are in my locker at the station. It's number 24 on the bottom. The book's in my top drawer next to the sink."

She didn't want to leave him—not like this, but want and need were two very different things. Slowly his gaze slid down from the ceiling and landed on hers. "I'll be all right. Eve needs to know."

Emotion took over then as she leaned down to him and pulled the warmth of his kiss into her. Fighting the grief, she pulled away from him, and his gaze narrowed on hers seriously. "Drive careful. Okay?"

Never had she taken an admonition more to heart. He couldn't afford to lose someone else tonight. Rational gained the upper hand as the white Cavalier banked into the station parking lot. She had a job to do, and she was going to do it. Her friends were counting on her whether any of them knew it or not. With long strides she entered the vacant fire station.

"Visitor!" she called, presumably for the benefit of the spiders in the corners because no one else heard it. "Lockers." Steeling her nerve, she walked down the hallway to the door beyond the break room where she knocked solidly. Nothing. Carefully she opened the door. "Knock. Knock." Still nothing. She stepped into the room, past the benches, to the lockers. "24. 24."

When she found it, her shaking fingers touched the cold metal and slid it upward. His locker. Somehow she never thought she would see it. Staring into it, she couldn't help but feel his spirit wrap around her. Pushing the thought of Eve down, she grabbed the keys off the top shelf and then caught sight of the cross. In a split-second it was in her hand, and she was off to the next step in this nightmare of a plan.

It was like the world had forgotten him. Jeff could hear it—over the curtain, under the curtain, all around him. He could hear the pleas for help, the cries of pain, the ache of humanity just beyond that thin veil, and for all his heart, he wished that he would never again have to rejoin it.

Lisa placed the first call from his apartment and was surprised to only get the answering machine. She left a vague message saying she would try back again. That wasn't the kind of news one delivers via answering machines. The second call she placed from the pay phone in the hospital lobby. In the rush to get to him, she had forgotten her cell phone. This time when she got the answering machine, she wondered if Eve was already here. Maybe someone had already gotten in touch with her. That thought lifted the pallor around her heart.

Willing her steps to be steady beneath her, Lisa walked down the hallway, through the doors, past the admissions desk, and right to Bay 14. When she peeked into the curtain, her heart fell. He hadn't moved during the last hour—not a single inch.

"I got you something," she said, approaching the bed slowly as the tiny bag of clothes she had procured from his place banged on her leg.

Vacantly he looked at her, and with a soft, hopeful smile, she held up the gold chain and cross, letting it dangle at the bottom of her fingertips. In the next instant grief flooded across his features as he looked first at it, then at her.

"You want me to put it on you?" she asked, and the imperceptible nod was unnecessary.

Except to con a pitcher of water from a nurse once, Lisa left his side only to place her every-fifteen-minutes phone call. By the time morning washed across a sky they couldn't see, Bay 14 had become their temporary home. She did everything she knew to do to make him more comfortable, which wasn't difficult. He was hazed out, barely acknowledging that the rest of the planet even existed. At seven-fifty she looked at her watch. Presumably they would get to him eventually, but his injuries didn't make it as high on the scale of life or death as too many of the other emergency room occupants had that night. Worse, even on a good night, she had heard of eight to ten-hour horror-story waits. It wasn't difficult to see they were a mere three hours into theirs.

Sunday morning. The first one that she had really thought about church in years. Now, her mind wondered: if she had just gone the week before, would it have made any difference? Would Jeff not be lying here? Would Dustin be at home enjoying the breakfast Eve had waiting? Slowly Lisa shook her head. She didn't understand any of this, and something told her she never would.

There was a bed shortage in the area hospitals. The scene the night before told Jeff that much. So after the doctor appeared sometime around eleven, did what he could with the blistering skin that covered Jeff's palms, and then asked if he wouldn't be more comfortable at home, Jeff understood enough to say of course he would. Really it didn't matter, he wasn't leaving anyway.

With slow movements, he slipped out of the ash-covered shirt he had spent the night in, laid it on the bed, and picked up the one Lisa had put across the chair for him before she had quietly slipped out. A sleeve at a time he worked the fabric over the bandages and onto his body. The fact that he couldn't have worked the buttons if he tried never occurred to him until the blue plaid was draped across his shoulders. Overwhelming helplessness in the face of all he had been through washed over him when he tried to take hold of the first button and his knees went weak beneath him.

"All better?" her voice asked at the curtain, and he looked up as pain slashed through him.

"I can't get this thing buttoned," he said, and the words broke with the weight of the unshed tears.

With a gentleness he had never experienced, she stepped over to him, took the top button in her fingers, and slid it into its rightful place. Down. One button at a time until they were all exactly where they were supposed to be. Then she took the bottom edge of the shirt and carefully worked it under the waistband of his jeans. When she was finished, her gaze locked on his. "Better?"

"Much."

She turned and began picking up the heavy fire suit from the floor.

"Umm, if it's not too much trouble," he said, and when she looked at him, he held up both sleeves to reveal the cuff buttons dangling loose. She looked at it, questioning what she could do about that because it was obvious they were not going to close around the bandages. "You could roll them up," he suggested softly.

Her skepticism slid into a smile, and she dropped her former task in a heap. A roll at a time, she turned the sleeves until both stopped just at his biceps. Then she stepped back. "Anything else?"

Short of going back 24 hours and changing everything, he could think of nothing. "I guess that's it."

Together they crossed out of Bay 14 and back into life.

After a quick check with her buddy at the admissions desk to make sure Dustin's condition hadn't changed, they went for breakfast which Lisa had to insist that Jeff eat bite-by-bite until at least half of it was gone. The hands were going to be a problem, but she did her best to make sure they didn't interfere and remind him anymore than they had to.

When they went back to the hospital and up to the sixth floor, she stayed close to his side. Steady could hardly describe him. His steps swayed just as precariously as his spirit seemed to be.

"Excuse me, we're wanting to find out about Dustin Knox," Lisa said at the nurse's station as determination echoed in her voice. "He's a firefighter that was brought in last night."

The lady behind the desk looked at Lisa doubtfully.

"He's a friend of mine," Jeff said, pulling the lady's gaze to him. The next second slid by and then just as she looked about to tell them to go away, the lady glanced down and caught sight of the bandages on his hands.

"Are you...?" She nodded. "Let me check." Her fingers clicked over the keys. "Mr. Knox is in critical condition. Only close family every two hours for ten minutes."

"When is the next visit time?" Lisa asked.

"Twenty minutes," the nurse said, checking the clock.

"Have you gotten in touch with his family yet?" Lisa asked, holding her breath for the answer.

"No, Ma'am. The department's been overwhelmed with this thing. I'm surprised we even know his name."

It wasn't what Lisa wanted to hear, but she smiled anyway. "Okay." She looked around. "Where do we wait?"

"Through those doors. There's chairs. Coffee too although I wouldn't recommend it."

Lisa nodded. "Thank you." What she wanted to do was take his hand, instead she wound her arm under his and guided him across the lobby. "You know, Eve's machine is going to get tired of hearing from me."

"I just wish I knew where she was," he said softly.
"Yeah, so do I."

Ever since he had seen that boot in the burst of flames, Jeff had tried to prepare himself for this moment, lining up the words in his head just in case he ever got the chance to say them. Now was his chance, but the tears choking out the air wouldn't let the words come as he stepped over to the unmoving figure on the bed. Dustin lay face down on the white sheets, and Jeff's own hands were no match for the strips of charred and crimson flesh rippling up and down Dustin's back. Jeff tried not to look too closely for fear that his composure would collapse completely.

"Hey, Dustin, man. What's up?" How many times had he said those words? Half a million? But they had never, ever felt like this. Defiantly he pushed that away as he pulled a chair over to the bed. Dustin's arm, bent at the elbow, wound up next to the short brown hair so that his hand lay right next to his still closed eyes. "Boy, this really stinks, huh?" Jeff blew the air out of his lungs slowly. "Listen, we're trying to get in touch with Eve. Lisa's on perpetual vigil by the phone. We'll get her here though. Don't worry. We will. I know she wants to be here with you. I know she would be if she knew…"

He sniffed back the tears and ran his cheek down the plaid sleeve. "You know I know if you can, you're going to come back to us. So, don't take this like I'm writing you off or anything, but there's some things I think you should know. I didn't get to say them last time, and…" He closed his eyes to stop the words. The breath out was harder to control this time. "I want you to know how much I appreciated all those hours we spent together. I know you had Eve, and you didn't have to make time to include me, but you did. I appreciate that…" Pulling the tears back to him, he sniffed. "…more than you'll ever know.

"You should also know that I'd never have made it through the academy without you. Back in November… Oh, man, every time I needed someone, you were always there although I think you talked more than you listened." A small laugh jumped through the center of the tears. "When didn't you, huh? But I needed that. I really did. There wasn't a second all the way through the academy that I wasn't glad to have you by my side." The tears came again.

"Not one single second."

The words stopped, held by the invisible grip of grief. "Look, we both know this thing's bad. Yeah, we do. But if God thinks you've got some more to do here, then you've got to know that I'll be right by your side every step of the way no matter what."

A sound at the door and Jeff looked over to where a nurse slipped in. When she saw him, she stopped, unsure of what to do next. "Oh, I'm sorry. I didn't know anyone…"

"That's okay," Jeff said, swiping at the tears with his own bandages. "I'd better let him get some sleep." He looked at the closed eyes one more time, said a silent good-bye, and stepped away from the bed. At the door, he could hardly catch his breath for the tears, and it was at that moment that the nurse laid a soft, comforting hand on his shoulder.

"We'll do everything we can," she said gently.

He knew that of course, but as he stepped out into the bright room beyond, he couldn't help but think their best wouldn't be enough.

Shoulder-to-shoulder they sat in the little waiting room as the seconds turned to minutes and the minutes turned to hours. At five-thirty Lisa tried to talk him into going home to get some sleep, but she knew even saying the words was pointless. No, he needed to be here, and so she did too.

They had managed to get in touch with Dustin's fire station, but between the two shifts that fought the fire, there weren't enough men to spare one at the hospital. At seven Jeff had willed his way to the phone and called his own department. No one he knew was there, but they took a message anyway.

"I think I'll go try Eve again," Lisa said just before eight when the waiting began to grate across her nerves. At the pay phone she deposited her dwindling supply of quarters and listened to the phone ring. However, the fourth ring never made it across the wires.

"Hello?" The voice sounded fragile and frightened.

"Eve?"

"Yeah?"

"Eve, this is Lisa."

"Lisa? I just got home. What in the world is going on?"

"Umm, can you get down to Ben Taub General right away?" Lisa asked, forcing her voice to sound urgent but not dire. "We're on the sixth floor."

"How's Dustin?"

"We'll talk when you get here," Lisa said, feeling Eve's knees go weak in her own. "And Eve? Drive careful. Okay?"

"O... okay."

Breathing down the tears, Lisa walked back into the waiting area. "She's coming."

His gaze grabbed hers. "You got a hold of her?"

"She'll be here," Lisa said.

Jeff looked up at the clock. "It's eight. I'd better go give Dustin the good news."

Lisa nodded. "Yeah, I'll wait for Eve."

"Good news, buddy," Jeff said when he pulled the chair over. "We finally got in touch with Eve. She's on her way. You know, if I didn't know better, I'd think you were looking forward to having her for your nurse for awhile... Yeah, don't deny it." He smiled half-heartedly at his own lame joke. "I'm going to try to talk them into letting her come in as soon as she gets here—even though it won't be visiting hours anymore. I know how much you want to see her... and how much she'll want to see you..."

The machine behind him screeched to life, and the bottom of Jeff's heart dropped through his feet as he turned to look at it. In two seconds a host of green-clad workers were rushing into the room.

"...Code blue... Code blue... respiratory failure..."

For the second time in what seemed only moments Jeff felt himself being pulled backward. "We need to get in here, Sir. Please."

In disbelieving horror, his body backed away although not a single other piece of him did.

The small jerks of the body on the bed sent fist-hard punches right through Jeff's gut.

"We're losing him... His blood pressure's dropping..."

Time and space floated away from Jeff's consciousness as he stood there in the corner, watching the scene but never moving. Dustin was leaving, and somehow he had to find it within himself

224

to let him go. "It's okay, buddy," he whispered so that only the spirit now floating above them could hear. "I'll take care of Eve for you. I will. You do what you have to." A solid beeeeep permeated the air around him. "I'll take care of her. I promise."

At the door to the waiting area Jeff's steps slowed until he couldn't even be sure he was still moving. However, the moment he emerged through the door, Lisa was there, worried and confused. "What happened? All the alarms went off and..."

Words wouldn't come as Jeff looked into her eyes, and the message was received in the next second. "Oh, my God. No." She covered her mouth to stop the words. "Oh, Jeff, no. I'm so sorry." Her hand reached over to his shoulder, and for that moment he needed to be in someone's arms more than he ever had before. Warm, tender, and alive, she surrounded him in her embrace, and just stood there, holding him as though she would never again let him go. And with that, life and death met in a silent embrace.

The warmth of the windows as the sun dipped below the horizon at their backs did nothing to thaw Lisa's dead-cold spirit. Dustin was gone. Eve would be here any minute. Jeff looked like he might pass out any second, and somehow she had to find the courage to help them all even though what she really wanted to do was curl up in a dark corner and cry her eyes out.

When the elevator dinged, they both looked over to it. With a quiet whoosh the doors slid open, and Eve rushed out, wild-eyed with panic as she looked around for what to do next. A moment too long Lisa hesitated, and in her place, Jeff stood—looking far too steady for the shifting her world felt like it was doing.

"Jeff, what happened? Where is he?" Eve asked, rushing toward them, her feet going as fast as her words.

Lisa saw the breath he took and the square of his shoulders when he faced Eve and put out his arms to soften the blow.

"He didn't make it," Jeff said softly.

"Oh, no!" Eve said as her hand went to her mouth, and her knees buckled. "No! No!"

Jeff seemed not even to notice the bandages as his hands and arms caught her on the way down. Gently he took her to a chair and sat her down. The torment in her eyes when she looked up at him tore Lisa's heart right out of her chest. She could never have found the words to continue; however, carefully as Jeff sat on his heels in front of the woman who had suddenly become a widow, he looked unnervingly calm.

"Dustin said that he loves you. He wanted you to know that," Jeff said quietly. "Okay? He did. He loved you so much, Eve." And when Eve leaned forward into Jeff's arms, there was no way anyone would've questioned that the feeling was mutual.

Seventeen

His car was still at the station, but although outwardly Jeff looked better than it made any sense to, Lisa knew that him driving in that state was not a good idea. So after Eve's parents arrived and their usefulness waned, Lisa suggested that they get him home for some much needed rest. Of course, he didn't want to go, but her focus was increasingly on how he was dealing with this, and he was really beginning to worry her.

"There's nothing else we can do here," Lisa said emphatically even as she fought to keep her voice under control. However, the glance from Eve across the room told her it hadn't worked as well as she would have liked.

Slowly Eve got up and walked over to where they stood by the now-dark window. "Lisa's right," Eve said, and her voice was stronger than Lisa's would have been. "She is. You should go home and get some sleep."

"But…" His eyes were glassy with pain and lost sleep.

"No. Now you listen to me, we have a long couple of days ahead of us, and you need some rest." Softly she laid a hand on his arm. "Please. For me."

At those words his gaze snapped up to hers, and in his eyes Lisa saw the tumult of emotions just before he nodded and his gaze fell.

"Good," Eve said, and when she pulled him into her arms, neither could comfort the other's grief. Finally Eve stepped back and wiped her eyes. "You take care of yourself. I'll call you tomorrow." Then she turned and looked at Lisa, and her tears became harder to contain. "Take care of him for me. Okay?"

In an instant they grabbed for each other like the only line that could pull them up from the side of a crumbling precipice. "If you need anything," Lisa said as tears streamed down her face. Eve nodded her acknowledgement of the statement. When they backed away from each other, both had to wipe their eyes.

"Now go home and get some sleep. Both of you."

Home. Somehow it had never felt so empty. The world seemed to be spinning without him. Sense had ceased to exist, drowned in the haze of tears and fear and shock. Still somehow Jeff kept walking as though if he just kept going, at some point, he would walk right out of this nightmare or right off the edge of the earth, and either would have been welcome.

"I'll throw something together," Lisa said after she had turned the key and let him in. "How does sandwiches sound?"

He shrugged having not really heard the question. His feet carried him over to the couch where he sat, looking at the room and trying to remember why it was he was here. A sound, a small whir, and a voice filled the air.

"Jeff, man, where are you? This is Gabe. They said you checked out of the hospital. Call me when you get in, please." Jeff's mind couldn't focus on the number Gabe left. It couldn't focus on anything.

Through the sounds of the dishes, he heard her voice, but only dimly. "Yeah, he's okay... his hands... I don't know... I think so... Yeah. It was bad... No, we finally got in touch with Eve... his wife... No. Okay, I'll tell him. Thanks, Gabe... I will... 'Bye." A plastic-on-plastic knock, and the voice went silent.

He should be moving. Some part of him said he should move, and yet nothing would.

"Here you go." Lisa came striding into the living room a few minutes later with a plate which she set on the coffee table in front of him. "I'll get you some water."

Bewildered at the sight of a simple sandwich, Jeff could only blink at it, and in seconds she was back. Carefully she sat next to him on the couch.

"You're going to have to eat," she said after a moment. "Here, I'll break it in half." Then for good measure she broke it into quarters. "There, that should be easier."

Still he looked at it. The messages in his brain were no longer making it all the way to his body. Finally she picked one quarter up and slid it between the tips of his fingers. "Eat."

His gaze fell to the sandwich, and then blinking off the action he put it to his lips. The middle of his stomach threatened revolt. It hurt to chew. Every piece of his whole body hurt—ached under the strain of keeping him alive even one more second. A piece at a time she handed him the sandwich and then watched to make sure he ate it. When it was gone, she took the plate away and was back before he knew she left.

"See, that wasn't so hard. Here's a painkiller. The last one will be wearing off any minute now." She gave him the pill and watched as he swallowed it. "Good. Now, I think you've got a date with a pillow and a mattress. What do you say?"

No words would come. There simply weren't any more in his brain.

"Come on." She coaxed him up off the couch. "I'll tuck you in."

Lisa didn't have the heart to pull him back out of the bed when he collapsed into it the second they stepped into the bedroom. There were more important things than clean sheets. "Better?" she asked, pulling the top cover up and around his shoulders, but when his gaze caught hers, she wondered if things would ever be better again.

"Will you lay with me?" he asked, the words barely a whisper.

The pleading in his eyes was more than her heart could bear. She smiled, turned out the light, and walked to the other side. Carefully she lay down and slid over to him, flipping her hair back so she could hear his heartbeat when she laid her head on his chest. She needed to be close to him, and if he needed to be close to her, there wasn't a no anywhere in her body.

"How is he?" Gabe asked late the next morning from the phone that Lisa had caught in the middle of the first ring.

"Sleeping for now, which is good," she said, keeping her voice quiet in the softness of the kitchen. "What're we supposed to do about work? Does he need to come in sometime?"

"I talked to Rainier, and it'll be okay for him to come back when he's ready—you know this week or early next. The sooner the better so Rainier can set up his leave status and all that, but get him through the funeral first. We can deal with the other stuff later."

Funeral. She hated that word. "So, is there somebody down there that he can talk to... when he's ready? You know, about what happened?"

"We've had a counselor on-call since Saturday night. If he needs it, all he has to do is ask."

"Okay. Thanks, Gabe."

"Sure thing," Gabe said quietly. "And Lisa?"

"Yeah?"

"We're all sorry for your loss."

"Yeah," she said, but the syllable broke in two. "Thanks." When she hung up the phone, she knew there was one more call she had to make. It was a call she had never made even once in her life. On the other end the receiver clicked. "Sherie, this is Lisa. Yeah, I'm fine, but I'm not going to be in for a while. I... We... Umm, there was a death in the family, and I've got some things to take care of here. I probably won't be in until at least Thursday. Yes, I know it's Monday. Tell the guys to get whatever they can done, handle what you can, and I'll deal with the rest when I get back... Yeah... Okay... Thanks. Talk to you later."

Her hand hung up the phone as every other part of her said it just wanted to go in to work. Not because of work but because somehow then she could make believe this wasn't what it was. In the middle of that thought a tremendous crash sounded from the bedroom, and she dropped the plate she was holding to the cabinet and ran.

"Jeff? What's wrong? What happened?" she asked, bursting into the room only to find him seated, head down on the edge of the bed.

With lifeless eyes, he looked up at her. "I just wanted a drink." It was then that she saw the shattered glass sprawled across the solid black base of the weight bench. "I guess it slipped." As she watched, he slowly bent to try to retrieve the pieces.

"No!" she yelled, jerking toward him. "Don't! I'll get it." Every instinct in her said that her job now was protection and prevention, and she took that job very seriously. "I'll get you some water, and I'll get that cleaned up when I get back. Don't move."

Sitting on the bed, looking at her with that vacant stare, she knew the glass wasn't the only thing broken. If she could've wrapped him in tissue and put him high on the top shelf, she would have. Anything so she would never have to see that frightening helplessness around him again.

"I know what this is asking," Eve said slowly. The soft gray of her fitted suit dress picked up the silver flecks in her dark eyes as she sat in the sunlight of her parents' living room Monday afternoon. "And, believe me, I wouldn't ask if it wasn't important."

A full night and half-the-day's rest had cleared enough of the fog surrounding Jeff's senses so that the fact that she was tiptoeing around him wound all the way to the place in his brain that could perceive the information. Regardless of the fact that half the neighborhood was milling about, watching the scene, his focus was on only her. "Anything, Eve. Name it, and it's yours."

"You are—umm, were—his best friend." Her gaze fell, and she took a shaky breath. "I'd like you to give the eulogy."

With a screech the world stopped around him. "Me?"

"I think he would've been honored for you to give it," she said with a tight smile, "and I know it would make me feel better. Please, Jeff. I swear, you know I wouldn't ask if…"

A breath of a decision. He had made a promise. He nodded. "Okay. I will."

"You will?" she asked in surprise.

"Yeah, I will."

"What are you going to say?" Lisa asked, not wanting to pry but wanting to know all the same. They had been by Eve's side all day and half the evening, and there hadn't been an opportunity to ask until they were alone in her car headed back to his place.

"I don't know," he said, his voice wistful and faraway. "I wish I did."

Her gaze went before her hand which touched the side of his arm. "You're a good friend. You know that?" But his gaze just sank into the black oblivion at his feet and stayed there. "Whatever you say, it will be just what Dustin would've wanted."

For as long as Lisa could remember, she had wanted to ride in a limo, but somehow this scenario had never entered her mind. Across from them sat Eve, flanked by her parents, the dark glasses hiding nothing. The private memorial at the little funeral home was enough to make a stone weep, and to this minute Lisa's brain was having a hard time comprehending that the man now lying in that coffin had been her dance partner less than two weeks before.

Laughing, joking about his "hopeless" friend, and now that friend was preparing to give the speech of his lifetime. She hoped Dustin wasn't far away because Jeff was going to need all the help he could get today. More than that, if anyone tried to convince Dustin what his friend was about to do, he would never in a trillion years have believed them unless he saw it for himself.

She looked around at her fellow passengers. There were two at the center of the grief in that car. The others were there to help them get through it.

Dark, navy blue. It was that color that would be with Lisa forever when she thought about how walking down that aisle alongside Jeff, a heartbeat behind Eve, felt. She could almost smell the polish on the shoes, feel the scratchy wool from every uniform that turned to watch the entrance of that flag-draped coffin in front of them. The walk to the front of the church could have been no longer. It was like walking the wrong way on a moving carpet. She walked, and she walked, and still she got no closer to the front.

Not until the six men with hands on the rails of the coffin stopped, checked it, and stepped back did the reality of what they were about to do hit her. With a breath she grabbed onto Jeff's arm with both hands. One bandaged hand came up to meet her hand, but he never looked at her. Somehow she had to pull it together. He didn't need to be holding her up right now. No, he had other far more important tasks to concentrate on, and she needed to be there for him—even if it killed her not to break down into hysterics right there.

When the preacher signaled Jeff's cue, his legs stood and he felt her hand slide from his arm. Courage was a pitiful thing in the face of that moment. Absolutely pitiful. At the podium he turned to the audience, which gazed up at him like he knew something that would make this whole horrible situation go away, but he knew nothing.

"For three days I've tried to sit down and put some words on paper," he began, and each word was a fight to get out. "There were a couple of problems with that though. One, the pen was kind of hard to hold." He held up one bandaged hand, and there was a small ripple of choked laughter. "Two, I'm not very good with words." A smaller ripple from those who really knew him he was sure. "And three, what do you say at a time like this?" He sniffed back the tears, laid his bandaged hands on the podium, and ducked his head. It was only with great difficulty that he raised it again. "So, I didn't write anything down. Instead I thought I'd tell you a few things I know about Dustin Knox, and for that I don't need ink anyway."

His gaze found the second row where Lisa sat, holding him up on the softness of her gaze. He tried to smile at her in assurance that he could handle this. He tried, but it didn't quite make it that far.

"During our time together at the academy I learned some things about Dustin that I'm sure some of you don't know. He was really into football for one. He loved the Cincinnati Bengals— although he really could've picked a team that wins a little more. I'm sure his wallet would've been appreciative." Smatterings of laughter sounded in the midst of the sniffs of tears. "He made a mean bologna sandwich, and he always carried a comb in his wallet and one in his car—just in case." More laughter, this time louder. "He was always on time. Well, except for his own wedding, but that really wasn't his fault." The nod and smile from Eve told him he was on the right track. "Dustin Knox never knew a stranger. He could walk right up and strike up a conversation with Attila the Hun, and you would never have known they hadn't been best friends forever.

"And he was always the first to help out when someone needed it. Studying, working, cleaning. It didn't matter. If someone needed help, Dustin was there. Always with a smile and never making you feel like he'd planned anything else for that moment. There wasn't a guy at the academy that he didn't help over at least one or two rough patches. His own rough patches, you rarely saw. Others were always more important to Dustin. Always."

The breaths were getting shallower, but Jeff pressed forward despite them. "Here's something else I know about Dustin Knox... there was a certain young lady that took his breath away, and there wasn't a moment that he didn't want to spend with her. Not one. Dustin and Eve weren't two halves that made a whole. They were one. So much so that it was hard to tell where one ended and the other began, and that was exactly the way they liked it."

Jeff sniffed the tears back into his skull and pounded a bandaged knuckle on the podium lightly. He would get through this. For Eve if not even for Dustin. "I can't tell you why this happened. I don't have any grand answers. I wish I did. All I can tell you is that Dustin Knox lived every moment of his life to the fullest. He didn't waste a single one. It's a standard I think each of us should strive for because we never know..." The tears came then as haunting flames ripped through him. "We never know." He sniffed, but the tears were overtaking him. "Dustin, buddy, we're all going to miss you." There was no escaping from the cold salty droplets as they slid down his face. "May you rest in peace."

And quietly he stepped away from the podium.

With everything he had, Jeff wished he was the one in the coffin that the pallbearers set over the open grave. It had to be easier than the reality he was now standing in, the one that seemed intent on breaking them all in half. The pressure of Lisa's fingers grasped his arm gently as the preacher read:

"Even though I walk through the valley of the shadow of death, I fear no evil for Thou art with me; Thy rod and Thy staff, they comfort me. Thou dost prepare a table before me in the presence of my enemies; Thou hast anointed my head with oil; My cup overflows. Surely goodness and kindness shall follow me all the days of my life, and I will dwell in the house of the Lord forever... May we pray."

A beat of silence as Jeff prayed only that he would wake up any minute now, that this nightmare would stop, that time would stop and he could somehow just get off.

"Lord, in your infinite love, we know you are with us now as always," the preacher said. "Please use our grief a means to purify these lives we must now lead. Bless especially Eve and all the men and women who serve unselfishly to protect us all. And take Dustin now to the special place You have prepared for him with You in Heaven. In Your Holy Name we pray."

"Amen," whispered across the crowd spread across the breeze swept grass.

The preacher signaled to the two uniformed firefighters who snapped forward and slowly lifted the flag from over the coffin. In its place someone slid a bouquet of red, white, and blue flowers as the other two wrapped the cloth until no red or white could be seen. One of them slid the last of it into place, took it to Eve, and presented it to her. Jeff squeezed his eyes closed to stop the tears but forced them opened because he couldn't be weak the moment Eve had to be strong.

"From dust we came," the preacher intoned, holding a hand over the coffin, now stripped bare of the flag, which Eve clutched to her chest like a long lost teddy bear, "and to dust we shall return. Father, we commend our brother, Dustin, into Your hands. May he rest in peace."

"Amen."

The first one through the line was the preacher who shook Eve's hand, said a few words, and moved on to her parents. When he stepped up to Jeff, the pain in the center of Jeff's chest fought to get to the surface even as he pushed it back down.

"Thank you, Reverend," Jeff said, struggling to keep his grief in check.

"You did a good job, Son," the preacher said. "I know that was tough."

"Yeah, well, some things you have to do."

"If you ever need to talk, I'm here."

"Thank you," Jeff said, wishing it didn't hurt so badly to smile.

As the preacher walked on, many, many more mourners took his place. Most didn't know what to say, some hugged him, some didn't. All said how sorry they were, and what was left of his sanity thanked each of them for coming.

When Ramsey stepped up in front of him, it didn't even register who it was at first. The dress blues. No smile. He wasn't sure why, but it just didn't look like Ramsey. "You did good, man. Nobody could've done it better."

"You heard?" Jeff asked, wondering how the news had reached Ramsey.

"Everyone in Texas has heard by now."

Everyone in Texas. Somehow that was fitting.

"Thanks for coming," Jeff said.

"I wouldn't have missed it."

Three people further down, and Bridget stepped up. With no words, she wrapped Jeff in her arms. Jeff felt the clap on his back from Craig as he held on to Bridget, fearing he might fall right through the earth if she let go.

"I can't believe he's gone," Jeff breathed.

"I know," Bridget said, nodding as the tears slid down between them. "I know."

Six more people down, and gaze glued to the ground, hands in pockets, A.J. stepped up. "I'm sorry, man," A.J. said quietly. "I wish we could've done more."

Jeff shook his head as he extended half a smile. "You did everything you could."

For one moment A.J. stood stock-still and then he put his arms around Jeff. The breath out felt like a car shifting down without the benefit of a clutch. "Thanks for coming." One more second before with barely a nod, A.J. stepped back and then walked on. The nightmares, the questions, the regrets would now live with them all. One look in A.J.'s eyes told Jeff that much.

Willing the haze to take over his brain, Jeff greeted the next mourner. *Just don't think, and you'll get through this.* But on the other side of this, he could see only the abyss that they were all headed for. It was coming, he could feel it rushing toward them, intent on swallowing them whole, and he couldn't be sure he had the strength to fight it off this time.

Sometime in the middle of the line it occurred to him that if that line just went on forever, they would never have to leave, never have to walk away, never have to say that final good-bye. So it was with an ache in his heart that he saw the members of his own station as they inched their way forward, the line dwindling behind them. People were talking again. The service was over, and life was going on—whether that made any sense to him or not.

"Taylor," Hunter said, stepping up to him.

"Thanks for coming," Jeff said, holding out a hand wrapped in white.

Instead of taking it, however, Hunter threw his arms around his colleague, and the bear hug slammed tears into Jeff's skull. "Get better. Okay? We need you back."

Jeff nodded. As soon as Hunter let him go, Dante grabbed him. If he could just hold onto someone, it felt like maybe he could stay standing, if not…

"You know, Knox must've been one smart guy to have you for a friend. I don't think they come any better," Dante said. He pulled back with his hands on Jeff's shoulders. "Hurry back. Okay?"

Again Jeff nodded and was passed off to Gabe.

"I've been worried about you," Gabe said, leveling his gaze at Jeff seriously. "You know that you don't have to handle this alone, right? We're all here for you. Every one of us. Don't forget that. Okay?"

His head was nodding for no other reason than it hadn't gotten the signal to quit. Slowly Gabe nodded too. "Take care of yourself." When Gabe stepped over to Lisa, emptiness washed over Jeff. There was no one else. Cars were leaving. People were walking away. Blankly he looked over to Eve who stood by the coffin with one hand slowly rubbing across the top of it.

With a heavy heart he walked over to her and laid a hand on her waist. Her gaze slid up to his, and the anguish in his heart was no match for the agony in her eyes. She laid her head on his shoulder, and the tears came for both of them.

Long after the last car was gone and they had sent Eve in the limo with the assurance that they would just get a cab, Lisa sat next to him in the empty graveyard. He was so alone. She could see it in his eyes. His heart was shattered into ten thousand pieces, and she had no idea how to pick up even a single one. In fact, her presence seemed not to even mark the blank slate of his consciousness.

"I should have said he liked trees," Jeff said softly, and Lisa's gaze went to his face. "Pine trees were his favorites. Pines and firs. Something about their needles." He squinted into the thought. "I don't really remember why."

"You did all you could," she said gently. "I'm sure he was

totally amazed you got up there at all."

"I didn't want to." It was the first time he had admitted that. "I thought I was going to lose it there for a minute. Man, that was hard."

"But you did it."

"I just wish I could go back and do it all again," Jeff said. "I think we missed so much."

"No," she said with a soft smile, "I think you got all the important stuff done."

His gaze swung to her face. "You think?"

"Yeah, I do."

Under her hand the bandages lifted, carrying her hand right up with them to his lips which he laid softly on the smooth skin. "I couldn't have gotten through this without you."

Gently she laughed. "Yes, you could have, but I'm glad you didn't have to."

Their hands dropped back into his lap as he took a ragged breath in. "Well, I guess it's time to go."

"Whenever you're ready."

When he looked at her, she knew the words before he spoke them. "I'll never be ready."

"Me either."

In the next second she was in his arms, and for as safe as that should've felt, in this place, it felt anything but. For here, there was no denying that one day instead of holding him, she could be the one left holding only a flag and pleading with God for just one more chance to hold him again. It was the most sobering space she had ever occupied in her life.

Eighteen

He was lucky. That's what the doctor said when Jeff went in on Thursday. Five weeks and he could be back on active duty—good as new. Another week and he would be able to go back on light duty. And although the doctor went on to explain how easily the damage to his hands could have been much worse, Jeff still didn't feel all that lucky. Numb was a better word for it. Tired and numb. When he crawled behind the wheel of the GTO, a thousand memories were there waiting for him. None of them were good, and none of them understood that he just wanted to be left alone.

As he drove down the streets, he thought about going by to see her, but he knew how overwhelmed she must be with all the work that would've piled up in her absence. That was part of it. The other part of it was that he hated the pity in her eyes. He hated when she hesitated, trying to find the right words so he wouldn't be reminded. It didn't matter. The reminders were everywhere. In fact, they were attached to his own body. How much more reminder did he need?

Thoughts swirled inside him until he was surprised his brain didn't just shut down from the overload. He needed something. Someone to talk to. Angling his car off the freeway, he turned up the station's street. Days and shifts crisscrossed in his brain so that he had no idea who would be there when he walked in. Anyone. Anyone who understood would be a blessing. The trucks sat on the driveway pad, the water dripping along the sides as Jeff walked up the sidewalk toward them.

"Heads up!" the voice yelled from the other side of the truck, and Jeff smiled as the sponge hit the bucket of suds, sending a fountain of them into the air.

"You know, you're going to have to show me how you do that sometime," Jeff called.

Instantly Dante's head appeared at the top of the truck. "Jeff? What in the world are you doing here?"

Jeff shrugged. "Where else am I supposed to be?"

With one leap Dante was on the ground. "You're injured, boy. Injured. That means you can stay at home and watch soap operas all day and eat bon-bons if you want to."

"Bon-bons, huh? Are they any good?"

"I wouldn't know. I've never gotten the chance to try them. You on the other hand have a perfectly good excuse, and what do you do? Come here. Now tell me in what realm does that make sense?"

"Taylor?" Captain Hayes said, emerging from the dark station. "What brings you by?"

Jeff held out his hand, which the captain shook very carefully. "I was hoping Captain Rainier would be in. I wasn't sure what shift it was today."

"C-shift today, but Rainier's upstairs anyway. Paperwork, you know. Come on."

The clock couldn't go fast enough for Lisa. At 4:42, she could've sworn it had actually stopped. It wasn't until she watched it for a full two minutes before she decided it hadn't.

"The Chronicle ads came out today," Sherie said, walking in as Lisa stared at the clock. "They turned out pretty good." She laid them on the desk.

"Huh, did you know that if you look at it real closely that clock hand looks like it's bent?"

"B...bent?" Sherie asked, glancing back at the clock. "No, can't say I've ever noticed that."

"And that little peggy thing in the middle, how do they get it so that it holds the hands where they're supposed to be but still lets them move?"

"I wouldn't know."

"Hmm, somebody should look into that. Surely there's a grant out there for something like that. Wouldn't you think?" Sherie's blank look and utter silence brought Lisa back. "What?"

"Nothing." Sherie stood there for one more moment and then pointed at the desk in front of Lisa. "The Chronicle."

Lisa nodded and looked down dutifully although she never saw anything. Life itself was a blur of worry and fear. When she looked up again, Sherie was gone, and Lisa thought it was probably for the best. She couldn't hit rational with a two-foot pitch. The clock tugged her gaze back to it, and she stood in surrender. He would need supper.

Taking a shower with only elbows was one of the hardest things Jeff had ever tried to do. How he had managed to accomplish it prior to this he was sure was a question only the haze surrounding him at that time could answer. The plastic bags and rubber bands covering his hands helped, but not nearly enough. His fingers felt like immovable sticks, and pressure on the palms felt like a million tiny needles jabbing into every nerve ending. He couldn't hold the soap. It ended up on the floor, and the little bit of shampoo he managed to get out seemed to go everywhere other than his hair. It was the epitome of frustration.

Finally he leaned an elbow against the faucet to shut off the water. That would have to be good enough. Another week in these infuriating bandages would be a real test of his aggravation tolerance. He pulled on sweatpants over his boxers. Jeans were out. A T-shirt would have to work too. Buttons and zippers were enough to make a monk curse.

When he stepped to the bathroom mirror and worked the sink drawer open carefully, the top edges of his fingers delicately worked the comb upward. This had always seemed so easy before. Everything had seemed so easy before. Halfway to his head, the comb slipped from his grasp and bounced across the floor. With a frustrated kick he sent it crashing into the cabinet. What had he done to deserve this? Any of this?

He heard the knock out front, but it like the phone would have to get itself. Doorknobs were now the bane of his existence. "Come in," he called angrily as he trekked through the living room.

Three brown bags of groceries in hand, Lisa walked in. "Don't ever go grocery shopping at five o'clock. It's a madhouse."

"When should you go?" he asked, bewildered by her entrance.

"Midnight. It's much saner." She set the bags on the counter and started unloading them.

Watching her, he leaned on the cabinet. "I didn't know you were coming tonight."

Incredulously she looked at him. "Of course I was coming. Didn't I tell you that?"

"Not that I remember."

"Well, who did you think was going to change your bandages?"

He glanced down at his hands now free of the plastic bags. "I hadn't really thought about it."

"Well, it's a good thing one of us did. We don't want those things around any longer than they have to be." She put three things in the cabinets. "So, what'd the doctor say?"

"Oh, he said I was lucky. Next week I can go back to light duty," Jeff said as if that was the most natural news in the world.

The whirlwind of action around her slowed. "Next week?"

"It's a good thing, too," he continued, oblivious to her unspoken concern. "Sitting around here is going to make me nuts in like ten seconds." Her motion resumed although not nearly as fast as it was before. "I went to the station today. Dante was washing the truck. He's insane."

Barely moving she put the cheese in the refrigerator. "I didn't know you were going back in today."

He shrugged. "I didn't have anywhere else to go." For a moment there was only the sound of the last two things in the bag being put away as he struggled to find a topic. "So, how was work?"

"It was there. Problems and more problems. Same old thing. Liver?" she asked, holding up a small plastic container.

"Whatever. I think I'm going to sit on the couch and put my hands up a little. The doctor said I'm supposed to."

"Okay," she said, nodding.

When Jeff walked out of the kitchen, it was all Lisa could do to keep the exhale quiet. He didn't need to know how hard this was for her, how her stomach turned when she worked to redress the swollen, red and purple wounds, how every small gasp of pain he sucked in went right through her like a knife, how tired she was from sleepless nights spent worrying about him and about Eve. She had tried to call Eve earlier in the day, but she wasn't home.

Lisa wished she knew the number for Eve's parents. Somehow she thought after the funeral Eve would've ceased the campout at her parents' house, but apparently that hadn't happened yet. Not that Lisa blamed her. She just would've liked to know Eve was okay.

Trying not to think about what the raw liver looked like, she used a dishtowel to cover it while she cut it into thin strips. Meat. Good red meat. Food to make him strong again. Food to help his body to heal. She only wished there was a food that could make the slices in her soul heal as easily.

Jeff noticed the small chunks of meat in the gravy. He noticed that even he could pick them up. The plastic glass she had put his water in had ridges in all the right places so it wouldn't slip from the bandages. He wondered how much she had thought about those things and how many were mere coincidences, but he didn't ask. Asking would ensure a conversation that he wasn't ready to have. So what little they talked, he focused on telling her about all the things the guys were doing at the station during his visit and how he couldn't wait to get back there—back to life.

A life that didn't involve sitting around with his hands above his head for hours. A life where he didn't even think about the difficulty of picking up a comb or a simple glass of water. A life where he could choose what to eat by what he was hungry for rather than by what he could conceivably get out without making a total mess.

"This is really good," he said as the food on his plate disappeared.

Her fork pushed one mound of liver around. "You sound surprised."

"No, not surprised really." Then he caught himself. "Well, a little. I thought take-out was more your style."

She shook her head. "Too much grease. You don't need that… right now." Her face beat that comment back. "So, what'd you do for lunch today?"

He pushed his plate over so she could put more liver-gravy on it. "Some little TV dinner thing I found in the back of the freezer. It was Chinese food I think."

"You...?" she asked, stopping in mid-scoop and not even being able to get to the last word out. She took a breath. "I'll make you something tonight— for breakfast tomorrow and lunch. What would you like?"

"For breakfast?"

"Yeah."

He raised his eyebrows. "How would I know that now?"

"Because I'm going to make something for you now, and making it without knowing what I'm making is going to be rather difficult. So, what do you want for breakfast?"

He wished he knew— if for no other reason than to calm the frustration in her voice. "How about a bacon sandwich?"

"Good. Then I'll make a bacon sandwich."

They were like two robots getting through one task just to get to the next. After supper Lisa did the dishes, made his bacon sandwich, and put the leftovers from supper on a plate draped with plastic. The fewer fine motor skills he had to use, the better. Then she walked into the living room. "You ready to change those?"

"Do I have a choice?" he asked, not fully kidding.

"No, but I thought I'd ask anyway." She walked over to the couch. "Come on. Let's get this over with."

That night as he lay in bed alone, looking up at the ceiling, his thoughts drifted over her. For one brief moment in time she had let the business side of her down to reveal the woman underneath. Now the business side was back in full force. Even when she kissed him goodnight, it was more about her duty than her desire. He felt it, and he wondered if she did too.

On Friday Murphy's Law kicked into full force in Lisa's life. There were the ads that said, "Kamen" instead of "Kamden." There was the whole "I think my computer's got a virus" thing from Sherie which took a full two hours to fix. Then there was the call from Tucker, who Lisa simply didn't have the patience to deal with anymore.

"Why do you keep calling me?" she asked furiously as the end of her rope sailed away somewhere high above her. "I thought you had decided…"

"I told you I'd call back," Tucker said uncomprehendingly. "That we'd talk. Don't you remember?"

She couldn't remember anything before she'd heard the words: "Jeff is in the hospital." Everything before and since was a solid blur.

"I tried to call, but Sherie kept saying you were out. I thought you were avoiding me."

The sigh escaped her before she knew it was there. "I was out of the office the first part of the week."

"Out? On vacation?"

"Funeral," she said levelly.

"Oh. I'm sorry."

Like water seeping from a barely opened drain, she felt the energy ooze from her body.

"So, you haven't done any more on the leadership conference then?"

"No." It was all she could muster.

"Good because I talked to Grandpa, and we've decided we want to include some of our own factory workers and supervisors. You know, get them in the game too."

In the game. She had never felt more out-of-the-game.

"I can give you their names if you want," Tucker said.

"I don't have time to meet with you."

"No, I mean now. You got a pen?"

Somehow she took down the names, but it would be a miracle if any of them were right or even legible. When Tucker finished the list, he signed off, and Lisa was left holding the phone. Tired pulled on her eyelids. Slowly the desk took her head, and she was asleep before her body could protest.

Except for the ache in the muscles of his forearms, Jeff was beginning to get used to the hassle of using everything other than his hands to do things. He had learned to open cabinet doors with his elbows, to open chip bags with his teeth, and that feet were good for a lot of things he'd never noticed they would be useful for. However, when he tried to start supper, the limits of his improvisational abilities ran out.

By the time he gave up, a jar of pickles lay in pieces on the floor by the refrigerator, and half the carton of milk was spilled all over the counter. The tuna can was open but upside down under the can opener, and every time he stepped, he trod on another fork or spoon he had dropped. A few he had managed to get back up to the cabinet with his toes, but the others were now one interminable web of stainless steel booby traps.

"Hi!" Lisa called when Jeff was in his room doing sit-ups next to the bed. If he couldn't be useful, he could at least work off his frustration. "Jeff?"

"Yeah," he called. "I'm back here." Eighty-one. Eighty-two.

"What's up with the kitchen?" she asked, surveying him carefully when she made it to the door of his room.

"Tuna sandwiches and soup," he said, pulling himself forward. "I thought that sounded good for supper."

"Uh-huh," she said with a nod. Then she shrugged and arched her neck one way, squeezing her eyes closed at the pain that caused. "Okay. Well, I'll be in here when you're finished."

"Okay," he said. Ninety-three. Ninety-four. When she turned down the hall, it occurred to him how slow her steps had become, and a vague concern for her traced through him. At one hundred and ten, he pulled the towel off the weight bench and threw it over his shoulder before walking to the kitchen. He found her bent over the shards of glass at the refrigerator.

"Those pickles had a mind of their own," he said timidly.

"Yeah, it looks that way."

He waited a beat. "How was work?"

"Work," she said, dumping a handful of glass into the trashcan.

"Have they come up with the office supply ads yet?"

"I don't know. I was working on other things."

"Like what?"

"Like… I don't know. Other things."

"Oh," he said quietly. He paused a beat trying to decide if he should venture into the next subject that came to mind. "Gabe came by today."

"That's nice." With the little hand sweeper she worked to corral the last little green shards cowering under the counter.

"He said they've got a new truck coming in next week. A brand new one. They're going to trade the old one down to one of the suburbs."

"That's nice."

"I wonder how different this new truck is going to be. You know— if we're going to have to retrain for it or anything."

With a clang and three thumps on the trashcan with the dustpan, Lisa stood and wiped her hands. She closed the trashcan, put it back in the corner, and stepped over to the counter where she ran water on a dishrag and started wiping up the milk.

"Hayes must have some pull though to get a new truck. That other one's only eight or ten years old."

The milk clean, she stepped over to the other cabinet and picked up the tuna can. "How about tuna casserole, seeing's how we don't have any more pickles."

He shrugged. "Okay by me." Gently he wiped his forehead with the towel. "I really can't wait to get these bandages off next week. This itching thing is starting make me nuts."

"Your hands?" she asked with concern.

"No, everything else. Do you know how hard it is to itch your nose with these things?" He held both hands up in testimony. "It's annoying."

"I can imagine," she said softly as she dumped the contents of first one can and then another into the pan.

His nose slipped from his consciousness as he really looked at her. "Are you okay?"

"I called Eve today," Lisa said although her back was to him.

"You did?"

"To make sure she's okay."

"Is she?" Guilt slid over him for not thinking to make that call himself.

"She's trying to be," Lisa said, but her voice didn't make it all the way through the statement. Gently he walked over to her and laid a hand on her shoulder. In the next heartbeat she spun into him and crushed her eyelids into his chest. "I can't imagine what she's going through right now. I can't even imagine it…"

Something told him as he held her that she could come closer to imagining it that most of the other people on the planet.

On Saturday they went to see Eve. Lisa drove although they took his car, so talking on the way was out. She needed too much brainpower to work the car. That was good, though. In her books the less they talked right now the better. At the little townhouse, Lisa tried not to imagine them moving in, decorating, dancing in the kitchen—but it was difficult. Everywhere she looked, she saw not only Eve but Dustin too. Jeff was right. They were inseparable.

"So, how are you doing?" Jeff asked when they sat down in the living room which opened high above them into the bedrooms upstairs.

"Surviving," Eve said softly. "How about you?"

"I've been better."

"How are the hands?"

"Bandages come off in a week."

"And then…?"

"Light duty only for four weeks," he said with a nod. "At least that will give me something to do."

Next to him, Lisa shifted on the couch, reaching for a change of subject. "How are your parents?"

"Adjusting. I think if they could, they'd put me in this little box and bubble wrap me. You know? But I'm just trying to get to the next minute in one piece."

"Has the station called?" Jeff asked.

"They've been great. Really supportive. One of the guys even brought… the things over so I wouldn't have to go down there."

For that, Lisa was thankful. Standing by Jeff's locker traced through her, but she pushed that away. "So, do you think you're going to stay here then?"

Eve, thinner even than Lisa remembered, sat wordless for a long moment. "I don't know. I haven't thought that far ahead yet. I go back to work on Monday, and then I guess I'll see where life takes me from there. Right now, there's no big plan." Eve's gaze fell to her hands. "Not anymore anyway." The fight against the tears was obvious in her voice, and when she looked up, they were glittering on her lashes. "I'm sorry."

Lisa's own resolve buckled as she watched Jeff stand and cross the two feet to envelop Eve in his arms.

"Hey, hey. Don't ever apologize to us," he said as he held her. "If you need to cry, then that's what you need to do, and that's okay."

Eve sniffed. "It's just that we always knew this was a possibility. You know? We always did. I just... somehow never thought it would be us."

"No one does," Jeff said as he held her. "No one does."

She sniffed again. "I feel like such a burden on everyone. Like they all have to stop what they're doing to take care of me."

"Hey, you're not a burden. Besides that's the point of this life—being there for each other. If we didn't have that, what would there be to live for?" He hugged her and then pulled away to look at her face. "This thing is on your time table. As long as it takes we'll be here. Okay?"

Slowly she nodded.

"Don't ever forget that."

The whole next week Lisa tried to keep that comment in her heart. As long as it took—that's how long she wanted to be there for him, and she was determined not to let him forget it. So, when they were seated at the table over pasta the next Friday it was all she could do to squelch the terror when he made his announcement.

"I'm going to start hazmat classes in September," he said as if he was telling her he'd picked up the dry cleaning.

The noodle slipped down the wrong pipe in her throat, and Lisa choked on it. "Hazmat?"

"Yeah, hazardous materials. I didn't get my certification when I got out because it was going to take too long, but I really think it would be a step in the right direction now. Besides if I take it in September, I can take aircraft rescue in October, and be fully certified by November."

She swallowed the protests with the drink she took. "But your hands...?"

"The doctor said it shouldn't be any problem by September. Besides if I get these two certs, then I can start working my way up the ladder to driver and then to lieutenant."

Her gaze wouldn't leave the table. "I didn't know you wanted to work up the ladder."

"Of course I do," he said with a small laugh. "Doesn't everybody?"

"Well, yeah, I guess. When do you start?" They were the hardest four words she'd ever spoken, followed instantly by the two hardest she had ever heard.

"September second."

Lisa couldn't get that date out of her head. While she redressed the wounds that were looking far too good for her sanity, while she sat next to him on the couch watching some movie she didn't really care about, while she stood on his threshold, saying goodnight and wondering how many more "good nights" they would have.

In her dreams Eve was there constantly saying how she had never thought it would be them, and Jeff was there, sitting next to her in that graveyard, and she was there, clutching a flag and screaming at God above for one more moment with him. In the daylight she held her world together by the barest of threads, hoping against hope that he would change his mind and end her nightmares. It was this side of impossible to hear him sound excited about going back to work. She hated that job, the station, and everything associated with it. If she could just find a way to tell him that, make him see that it was killing her to think of him walking into another fire, that her heart seared at the center just thinking about it. If she could just do that, then her world could get back to normal. If she couldn't, she was vaguely aware that nothing would ever be right again.

Nineteen

Jeff was glad to be back at work even though he took some ribbing for the whole "light duty" thing. He knew that the comments were meant to make a bad situation a little better. As long as he took the painkillers religiously and watched out for that one sore spot in the web between his thumb and finger on his right hand, he was okay. In fact, he thought as he worked a metal maintenance kit across the floor with his foot, he had found ways his body could help that he had never realized were there.

"I need that torque wrench," Gabe called from the front of the truck as he worked on the motor in mid-August.

"At your service," Jeff said, handing the tool over. "New truck. You would've thought the thing would run for more than a couple of weeks."

"Takes awhile to break them in," Gabe said. "Kind of like women."

Jeff laughed a little at that. "How's Ashley anyway?"

"Thrilled. We got an offer to go to New Orleans with her parents over Labor Day weekend."

"That's good."

"No, it's not. The flight leaves Thursday. We're on shift Friday."

"Oh, great."

"Yeah, that's what Ash said, except with more colorful language." The wrench clicked on the metal. "So, how's Lisa?"

Jeff shrugged. "Good, I guess."

The clicking stopped, and Gabe looked over at him. "You guess?"

For all he was worth, Jeff wished he could hold Gabe's gaze. "This month's been kind of tough on her."

Gabe's working slowed. "I can imagine."

"She doesn't talk about it much," Jeff said, squinting through the middle of that thought.

"How about you?"

"What about me?"

"Do you talk about it much?" Gabe handed the wrench back.

"What's to talk about? I'm okay." He held his hands which now sported only a couple of band-aids up for inspection. "Getting better every day."

Gabe bent back over the fender. "I didn't mean your hands."

"She's having enough trouble as it is. She doesn't need my sob story to add to that."

"How about someone to lean on?" Gabe asked. "Does she need that?"

"She leans on me," Jeff said defensively.

When Gabe looked at him, Jeff got the feeling that he could see all the way through him. "That's good because I know Ashley. She'll drive herself into the ground to take care of things for me—if I let her."

"Yeah, well, I think Lisa's hanging in there," Jeff said although his certainty at the statement waned the moment it was out of his mouth.

Gabe nodded. "I'm sure she is."

No matter where he ran, Jeff couldn't get those words to leave him alone. How much had Lisa taken care of for him in the last four weeks? And he had let her, leaned on her for strength and sanity the whole time. Like a rock she had stood there, unbending, unbreaking. Yet until that moment, he hadn't really even noticed. Tuesday afternoon when he woke up, the fact that it was repayment time swelled within him. He owed her, and now it was time to start paying her back.

When Jeff stepped into her front office at 4:30, a bag of take-out hot dogs in hand, he put a finger to his lips so that Sherie wouldn't alert Lisa that he was here. Quietly he stepped to her office door as Sherie stood to stop him, but he put up a hand to warn her off and to shush her protest. The second her gaze dropped to his hand; however, he saw the step she took backward, and he tried to smile at her to assure her he was fine. Her look said she knew better.

Without a sound, he turned the knob and cracked the door to Lisa's office.

"What? You think this is, a joke?" Lisa asked furiously as the phone cord dangled around the back of her chair to the receiver. "Trust me, I'm not in the mood to be coming up with jokes at the moment. Now, if you would be so kind as to check your records, I'm sure our payment will be documented in your accounts receivable. We sent it on the tenth of June. I don't care if it's not showing up on your computer! I'm telling you, we sent it. I've got the cancelled check right…"

Her chair spun around, and Jeff's breath caught. She looked at him, and her eyes tilted across the fury. Her hair stuck out in all directions, the circles under her eyes were hard gray lines, and the edges of her skin were sallow and sunken. When had all of that happened? And why hadn't he noticed?

Quickly she bent her head and swiped across her desk. "…here. It's number 1715, for $1,241.19, made out to Corporate Printing on the tenth of June. It even says what it's for down here: Leadership Brochures… Yeah, I can fax it. Would that help? Fine. I'll have it there in two minutes. What's the number?"

In a scrawl that looked far too pointy and slanted for her handwriting, she transferred the number to the yellow pad which couldn't have been staying on the top of the stack by more than an eighth of an inch. "Yeah, I got it. Okay." The phone hit the cradle, and she stood without so much as acknowledging him. She ripped the paper out of the notebook and the check off the top of her desk and stomped out to the front office. "Fax this to Corporate Printing… now." On her heel, she turned and stalked back into her office and around her desk where she started sorting through the top layer stacked there. "I didn't know you were coming."

"I didn't either," he said softly. "Is this a bad time?"

Her face was hard. "It's always a bad time these days." Then she seemed to remember who she was talking to, and she closed her eyes and took in a long, slow breath. When she opened them again, it took a moment for her to look up from the papers. "I'm sorry." Her face had softened in the span of seconds, and even the circles had lightened. "Did you need something? I was going to pick up some groceries before I came tonight. I figured you were probably out of milk if you ate cereal this morning."

Watching her, his heart asked how he could have been so

blind. "No, I didn't need groceries. I just wanted to see you. It's been awhile since I've been over here."

"Oh," she said, the act sliding away from her. "Well, you should've called. I would've..." Her hands dropped to the desk as they moved folders back and forth, fighting to make her world look less chaotic.

Slowly he set the bag in the chair, stepped around the desk, and took her in his arms. "I'm so sorry." Even in his arms, he could feel the rigidity of her body. Stiff like iron.

Unsettled, she barely returned the hug before backing away from him and swiping at her eyes. "That's okay. I just had the Office Supply place call about their radio spots, and I can't find the Kamden report to save my life, and... damn it!" Her hands slammed the folder they traced across down. "I can't do anything right anymore!" She reached up to lay a finger on the top of her nose to stop the tears.

"How can I help?" he asked, as helplessness washed over him.

The composed look that she finally leveled at him chilled him to the bone. "I think this is one I should handle on my own."

He felt himself back up. "Are... are you sure?"

"Yeah," she said softly. "Don't worry about it." Pulling sanity to her she shook her head to push the emotion down. "I'm sure I can dig out from under this mess somehow."

"I could..."

"No, Jeff," she said, the iron just under the softness in her voice. "I can do it."

"O... okay." His feet backed him around the desk. "You going to come to my place tonight?"

Slowly she nodded. "Yeah, I'll be there."

"I thought a small can would be enough," Lisa said as she stood at his stove, stirring the meat sauce. "It's always so hard to tell."

Had he not seen the before and after picture, he never would've guessed, he thought as he leaned against the counter and watched her. Never. Hair perfect, eyes tired but circles gone. No, he never would've guessed how out-of-control she looked when she wasn't in his company. Somehow he knew that wasn't a compliment.

"These companies. They think we don't notice how much

they're skimping on the contents of their product." She lifted the can. "See 14 ½ ounces. It used to be 16. I did a paper on that in college." She set the can back on the counter. "So, how was the station?"

"Busy. That new truck's giving us problems."

"Already?" Her hand reached down and spun the knob to lower the fire as she continued to stir. "Didn't you just get that thing?"

Jeff shrugged. "Gabe thinks it's a timing problem."

"Huh, sounds logical," she said although he wondered if she had any idea what the term even meant. Somehow he hadn't noticed how few in-depth questions she asked about the station. A few here and there to keep the conversation going, but nothing beyond that. It was like she didn't want to know anymore.

"This stuff is like paste." She picked up the spoon and turned it over. The red sauce glopped back into the pan. Quickly she opened a cabinet and pulled out a measuring cup he didn't remember having. "Could you get me some water?"

"Sure," he said, taking the cup from her. He filled it and returned it to the cabinet beside her. It was the first time he had been so close to her in what felt like years. Gently he put his arms on either side of her arms. "You smell good."

"Yeah, like over done meat sauce."

One push at a time he swayed to one side and then the other. Why had he ever been so reluctant to dance with her? He must've been insane.

"What are you doing?" she asked, and he heard the annoyance.

"Dancing," he whispered in her ear.

"You don't dance. Remember?"

With one arm he spun her around. "Oh, yeah. I forgot." He tried to bury his head into her shoulder, but she wouldn't stay still long enough for him to accomplish that.

"Hey!" She pushed him back. "Hello, I was cooking."

"What? You don't want to dance with me?" he asked, and the hurt in his chest screamed through his voice.

Her eyes closed on the accusation. "I'm sorry. Of course I want to dance with you."

As he took her in his arms, he knew something had changed. Their timing was off. Their rhythm was off. They were off. "Want to talk about it?" he finally asked, when the space she put between them punched through his heart.

"You don't want to," she said, shaking her head miserably.

"How do you know that?"

She looked at him, and bright tears glinted across her lashes. "The fire stays at the fire. Remember?" Her gaze dropped from his. "I'm trying to."

His heart broke for the pain he had seen in her eyes. "Come here." With just enough hold on rational, he reached over and snapped the fire off from under the meal. Then he led her to the couch, sat her down, and laid an arm around her shoulders. "I know this has been tough on you. The burns, and keeping me together, and Dustin…"

The breath she took in seemed to steady her as she sat up and put her elbows on her knees. "That's part of it," she said, nodding as though she was telling herself this lecture. "If you're with a fireman, that's part of it. You just have to learn to deal with it, and go on. Dwelling on it doesn't help. Worrying will make you crazy. So you deal with it—however you have to."

"That's what you've been doing? Huh? Dealing with it?"

"I don't have a choice. I love you, so there isn't another option."

With that word, his world slammed to a stop. "What did you say?"

She looked back at him, but her face was laden with sadness. As she straightened her head and her shoulders, sorrowful determination slipped into her eyes. "Love isn't about when it's easy. That's what Mom used to tell me, but I never really understood that until… well, until recently. I watched her, my mom…" Lisa nodded at the memory. "When Dad was late for supper and she'd get upset about it but try to act like she wasn't… Yeah, she'd just keep going like it wasn't a problem. And the nights he'd come home too tired to help with us, Mom would feed us supper, help with the homework, run the baths, read the stories, and put us all to bed. I asked her about it once, and she said, 'Lisa, that's just what you do when you love someone. When you really love someone, you can't think about yourself anymore.'

"I'd never found anyone that meant enough for me to do that before you. Fact, I guess I'd decided it'd just be easier if I didn't. Families, relationships, they just complicate life too much. At least that's what I used to think before…"

"You went to a bar and made the mistake of finding someone."

"Something like that," she agreed. "At first I thought Mom was wrong because I felt like it wasn't nearly as hard as she always made it look… I don't know." Lisa sighed softly. "All I know is I want what's best for you, and I'll do whatever I can to make that happen."

"And what about you?"

Slowly she shrugged. "I just have to figure out a way to live with it."

He slid over beside her. "But I don't want you to have to do that. I don't want you to have to live with it. I want you to be happy too."

Her fingers crisscrossed over themselves. "Well, from where I'm at, I don't see how both of us can be happy. You want one thing, I want another, and for you to get what you want, I don't get what I want…" The track she was on slid from under his feet. "…and if I get what I want, you'll be miserable."

"What do you want?"

The question stopped the thread of her words. After a moment it was with permeating acceptance that she looked at him. "Something I could never ask you to do." She shook her head. "Don't worry about it. Okay? It's just the adjustment. I mean I was a free spirit. I could come and go as I pleased, do whatever I wanted whenever I wanted, and now… now I feel like I'm tied to something that I really want to be tied to, but it's taking awhile to get my life rearranged around it."

Although he should've been happy about what she was saying, he couldn't quite get there. She was giving up her life because of him, and somehow, he thought that wasn't how it was supposed to work. Suddenly she stood and straightened her jacket.

"I've got to finish supper, or it'll be midnight before we eat."

He watched the back of her navy skirt walk into the kitchen and around the corner, and never in his life had he wanted to talk to Dustin more. Some rational advice from a friend who really understood would've been really nice right about then because one thing was for sure, he himself had nothing resembling rational running around anywhere in his brain.

Twenty

For two weeks Jeff spent his time either at work or tiptoeing around Lisa. She was better, from what he could tell. On Friday night they went to the movies and had a nice time. He held her hand; she kissed him goodnight. Once or twice she had even laughed, but the melancholy in her eyes was never far away.

By the next Tuesday, however, when she was making supper, she surprised him with a joke Sherie had told her. Slowly the light was coming back into her face and into her spirit. They talked about the weather, and how annoying the city could be. They talked about who was going to pick up groceries and whose night it was to cook. But venturing any deeper than that? Neither one was willing to take that leap. It was easier to push that aside, to pretend that if neither acknowledged its presence, it didn't really exist.

"Well, well, I guess this means you're sprung," Gabe said August 25th when he entered the back room of the station at 6:30 in the morning and found Jeff elbow deep in a washtub full of water.

"I told Hunter we'd get this," Jeff said, indicating the cotton hose he was washing. "They just got back from a residential."

Gabe nodded. "Let me grab some coffee so I can get my eyes open, and I'll help."

"Like I'm going to turn that down," Jeff said with a laugh, very much liking how it felt to no longer be on the injured reserve list.

"Hey, Mr. Taylor," Captain Hayes said, coming through the door. "I thought you were banned from the water thing."

"Good as new," Jeff said, holding up his hands for inspection and then laughing when he realized they were covered in white suds.

Hayes smiled. "Glad to hear it." He stepped past the tub and then turned. "Say, have you heard from Lisa lately? I saw her at the funeral, but I had to get back to the station before we could talk."

"Uh, yeah," Jeff said slowly. "I see her all the time. Why?"

"Oh, well, I was just wondering how that conference is coming together," Hayes said. "She hasn't been by in awhile."

Jeff's heart sank on the statement. "Yeah. I'll probably see her tomorrow if you want me to ask her for you."

"If you think about it," Hayes said with a shrug. "Well, a bed and some breakfast is sounding mighty good about now. Tell Lisa I'll be here in the afternoons all week if she wants to come by."

"I'll tell her," Jeff said as the words choked into his throat. When Hayes walked out, Jeff sank his hands deep into the water wishing the signals going to his hands could crowd out all those in his head.

"So, you couldn't come up with some excuse to keep you on light, huh?" Gabe asked as he walked up, a coffee cup steaming in his hand.

"Why would I do that?"

"I don't know because it's umm… *easier.*"

"Depends on your definition of easier."

"Well, it's not washing cotton hoses out when you don't have to," Gabe said, indicating the emerging stained-white hose as it was transferred into the other sink.

"It's called getting on with your life," Jeff said, heaving one part of the hose out of the water.

"Oh, really? And what else do you have planned for this 'getting on with your life' idea?" Gabe asked teasingly.

"Hazmat classes for one. I start next week. Then I'm going to do the aircraft thing in October. Get that out of the way, too."

"Ah. Gunning for my job, are you?"

"Just trying to do what makes sense," Jeff said defensively.

Gabe leaned on the water tank next to the tub as he narrowed his gaze at Jeff. "And where does Lisa fit into all of this?"

Jeff's work slowed. "Right where she is now—by my side."

"So, you're going to be doing hazmat, aircraft, and planning a wedding all at the same time? That's industrious."

"Hey, now, who said anything about a wedding?"

"You did. You said she was going to be right by your side, and don't go flaking out on me here. You're in love with her, right?"

For a long moment there was no answer. "Right?"

"Right," Jeff finally said softly.

"And she loves you. Right?"

"Right," Jeff said more solidly.

"Then what in the world are you waiting for—an engraved sign to appear in the sky?"

In all the time he had spent with her, this thought had never occurred to Jeff. Why he didn't know because it seemed so obvious. She was beautiful, gorgeous, fun, hardworking, and dedicated. And she loved him. She had told him so point blank. What more could a man want? No more, he decided as he transferred the hose to the rinsing tank. No more.

Everything had to be perfect, Jeff thought as he set the two wine glasses on the table which was set with the tablecloth he had spent half an hour choosing. There were three more in the back closet on standby if this one hadn't worked. Candles just so. Plates—the non-chipped ones, were on the table. Silverware, all but one matching, lay next to the plates. It was as perfect as it was going to get. Carefully he turned down the lights and traced into the living room where he turned on the CD that always made him think of her.

Yes, tonight was going to be perfect... even if he had to knock himself out to get it that way.

Work, as usual, was one thick mess of trouble. Lisa exhaled as she pulled into his apartment parking lot and saw the GTO. He was here. She sighed at the thought. She hadn't had time to call him to find out how his shift had gone the day before although that was all she had thought about for 36 hours. Every beep on her intercom made her jump, every ring of the phone made her heart pound. At lunch she had spilled her coffee all over the table when a siren wailed through a close intersection. Her nerves were on the very edge of disintegration, and it was taking everything she had to hold them together.

When she opened his apartment with the key she had finally just taken, it was a moment before she realized that anyone was even there. That's when she saw it— the table set, the candles, the wine, and her breath jumped to her throat. "Jeff? Hey, are you…"

However, 'here' never made it to her voice because suddenly he slipped around the corner and leaned there looking at her. White shirt, blue cover shirt, black jeans, that cross, and half of the lopsided smile, and she knew whatever was up, it was big.

"Hello," he said softly. "You made it."

"I… did." She nodded, frozen to the spot at the door. "You didn't tell me you were cooking tonight."

"I wanted to surprise you."

"Well, that worked." Her gaze chanced to the table as he pushed away from the wall.

"Here, you look like you could use a little TLC." He took her arm and led her into the living room which had even less light. At the sofa, he sat her down. "How about a neck massage?" Carefully he sat down beside her and turned her shoulders.

"Oh, I don't think—hello." His fingers worked into the grooves of tension in her shoulders, and their pressure sent waves of exhaustion undulating through her body. Slowly she relaxed into the motion. "That feels good."

"It's supposed to," he said right in her ear. She felt his fingers as they left her shoulder to trace across the side of her hair. Helpfully she reached up and snapped the clip so that her hair tumbled onto her shoulders. "Better?" he asked.

"Much." Her eyes closed of their own accord as her body and spirit moved in time with his fingers and the beat on the stereo. "Did you go to masseuse school while I wasn't looking?"

"Nope, first massage I've ever given."

"Huh, you ought to open up shop, you could make good money." One finger hit an extra-sore spot, and she jumped forward. "Ow."

"Sorry," he said as his fingers continued but lighter now. "Nope, these are just for you."

"Hmmm, then I'm not telling anybody." If she could've gone to sleep right there, she would have.

"Would you like some wine?" he asked after time no longer held any meaning.

"Do you have to stop to get it?"

"I think so. I'm good, but I'm not that good."

"Then, no, I don't want any wine."

He laughed as he pulled her back to him on the couch.

"You're too easy."

"You're too good." Muscles she had forgotten she had relaxed all the way down the length of her body. She took a deep, long breath. This was something she could definitely get used to. Drifting. That's what it felt like. Forgetting everything else in this one moment. She never wanted to join reality again.

"I made your favorite," he whispered in her ear.

"What's that?"

"Lemon pepper steak, carrots, potatoes, and unburned cherry pie."

"Sounds delicious."

"But it's going to be hard to eat from in here," he said.

Her body relaxed into his. "It's called osmosis."

"How about we call it eating?"

As much as her body would let her, she laughed.

"Come on," he said, helping her up. "It's going to get cold."

"Wouldn't want that."

By the time he served the pie, she had forgotten her surprise at the sight of the table. It was like remembering she was alive as they debated the merits of cherry versus apple pie. Cherry getting points for pulling off tart and sweet. Apple garnering its own share for the addition of cinnamon.

"You finished?" Jeff asked when Lisa laid her fork down by her half-eaten pie and sat back.

"Yeah, I think that would be a good word for it." She sat for one more second, sighed, and then pulled herself up to pick up the dishes.

"No," Jeff said, stopping her with a hand. "I'll get these… later." His hand turned and caught hers. "Let's go relax for awhile."

She arched an eyebrow skeptically. "If I relax any more, I'll go to sleep."

"Oh, don't do that," he said, taking her in his arms in the center of the living room. "You might miss something." Slowly he swayed back and forth as her arms over his shoulders pulled him closer.

"Oh, yeah? Like what?"

A second of a pause and he slipped to the floor on one knee.

Still holding her hand, he looked up at her. The room spun around her as her head said this was not really happening.

"Lisa, I can't imagine living the rest of my life without you. Will you marry me?"

"M... marry?" Lisa asked, blinking through the shock. "I... I'm... What?"

With a snap he opened the little box in his hand as her mind said how many hours she had spent worrying about the very hands that now held that box. Inside the box was a thin gold band supporting a small sparkling stone. "I know it's not much, but..."

"Jeff," she said as her heart pushed tears in front of the words. "Oh, I love it. It's perfect." And indeed it was. Gentle and subtle. The perfect reflection of him in her heart.

"So?" he asked, still on his knee gazing up at her.

She closed her eyes to imprint the moment on her memory. To say no was to deny who she really was, and who she really was at that moment was a woman who loved the man kneeling in front of her with all of her heart. "Yes."

With a smile he stood and gathered her into his arms. Her eyes squeezed closed as he stood simply holding her as though he might do just that forever.

"I didn't think it was possible to be this happy," he finally said softly.

"You didn't? What about me?" Her heart burst inside her. "I hated guys. Remember? All guys, and now I'm getting married?" She squealed on the words. "Oh, my gosh, Haley is never going to believe this! Haley, heck. I don't believe this! Oh, man, Sherie's going to go nuts!"

He laughed. "I thought you didn't want to be married."

"Did I say that?" she asked innocently.

"Yeah, I think so."

"Well, I must've been delirious, or maybe I'm delirious now. I don't know... I'm just so excited!"

"Is it me or the ring?" he asked jokingly.

"It's you of course, you dope," she said, and she laid her lips on his, pushing into him so that he took a step backward.

When she broke free, he looked at her with a smile. "Oh, good. Then I'll just take this back..." He started to put the case in his pocket.

"Oh, no you don't," she said, pulling his hand free of his

pocket. "Your ring goes on my finger, buster."

He extracted the ring from the case and tossed the case onto the couch. "And only on your finger." Gently he took her hand and slipped the ring onto her finger. However, it took more than a simple push to get it on, and once on, she turned it and winced.

Jeff exhaled hard. "Oh, crud. I got the wrong size. I knew I was going to do that. I guessed, and…"

"No," she said softly. "It's perfect." Her hand went up into the side of his hair, and she gazed into his eyes. "Just like you."

"Okay, now I know it's wrong," he said with a laugh. He took her hand from the side of his head and pulled it down in front of them. "It's not a big deal. I'll just take it in and get it resized. I kind of figured I'd have to."

"But I don't want to give it to you," she said, pouting as she pulled her hand to her chest. "I just got it."

"And when you get it back, it'll be right," he said, pulling her hand away gently. He tugged on the ring, but it didn't move.

Reluctantly Lisa sighed. "Okay, but only if you promise to take good care of it." She twisted the ring off her finger and held it out to him.

"I promise."

"You're never going to believe this in a million years," Lisa said to a half-asleep Haley over the phone the minute after she arrived home.

"Oh, no. What now?"

"I'm getting married!"

"Married?" Haley's voice came awake even as it dropped into incredulousness. "I thought you said you'd walk a mile on burning hot coals before you'd ever tie yourself to some idiot guy." Haley's words stopped for a moment. "Wait. This isn't that fireman you were seeing, is it?"

"Yes. What's wrong with a fireman?"

"Well, for one thing, their pay is lousy. They've got long hours and scary work—doesn't exactly sound like your kind of guy— whatever that is."

Lisa didn't want to think of Jeff as the job he held. He was the man she loved—strong, steady, dependable, and gentle. He was exactly the guy she hadn't been looking for. "Being a fireman also means he cares about others, he puts people before a pay check, and he's got more courage in one little finger than most guys have in their whole testosterone-filled bodies."

"Whoa. Okay, I get it," Haley said slowly. "So, when's the big day?"

"I don't know," Lisa said, looking at her left hand and smiling at the memory of the ring. "We haven't set it yet."

"Uh-huh."

"But as soon as we do, I'm going to need a matron of honor."

"Matron? Ugh. That sounds so old."

"Okay, how about the lady who's been married six months but still wants to be called maid of honor?"

"Much better."

Gabe was thrilled. In fact, Jeff got toasted with coffee by the whole station. Even Hayes congratulated him saying that now Lisa would have no time to make that trip over because of all the wedding plans. Jeff's memory crumpled over Hayes' previous invitation.

"Oh, man, I forgot to give her your message."

Hayes smiled. "I think you've had a few more important things on your mind."

"A few," Jeff agreed.

"Just tell her to stop by any time," Hayes said. "I'm sure I'll be around. This paperwork has overtime written all over it."

"I'll try to remember, Sir," Jeff said.

"Did you get my ring back?" Lisa asked the moment she opened his door the next evening.

"No." He accepted her kiss as he stood at the stove. "It's going to take a week."

"A week? It's one little ring."

"That's the problem," he said with a smile. "This is ready. You hungry?"

"Starving," she said, unbuttoning the front of her jacket and pulling the clip from her hair. "I think that energy bar I ate for lunch ran out some time around three."

"Energy bar? That's nutritional."

"It's better than nothing." She reached past him into the

cabinet for the plates, and when her body brushed his, he glanced down the side of her.

"That could get you in trouble."

Setting the plates on the counter, she opened the silverware drawer. "Oh, yeah? What kind of trouble?" Before she grabbed a breath from saying those words, she was pinned against the refrigerator, a spoon in one dangling hand.

"This kind," he said, pressing next to her. His lips found the top of her blouse, and life shifted. Lower, lower his lips went, tracing zigzag lines across her neck. "You really should learn to behave yourself."

"I was just setting the table," she said breathlessly.

"Yeah, uh-huh. That's what you say." The pressure of his lips slid down her throat.

"I swear, officer. I didn't mean to cause any trouble."

"I may have to take you in anyway. We've had a rash of heart stealers running around recently." He backed up and looked right at her with the intensity of a laser. "You wouldn't know anything about that? Would you?"

Lost in the middle of his eyes, she shook her head without moving it. "I wouldn't have a clue."

When his lips found hers, she was glad for the refrigerator. There was no way her knees would ever have been able to keep her standing. At that moment the timer on the stove dinged, and his kiss slowed and then stopped.

"Hold that thought," he said and stepped over to take the casserole out of the oven.

Slowly she slid away from the refrigerator, having never realized how warm one could get. "Man, it's hot in here. The humidity outside must be creeping up again today."

He looked at her with a hazy light in his eyes. "I don't think it's the humidity."

A memory dropped between them, and the lightness dissipated. He swung the dish over to the table, and she followed, picking up the plates from the cabinet on her way.

"Oh, I forgot to tell you," Jeff said as he sat down. "Hayes wants to see you."

"Yeah, right."

"No, really, he told me yesterday, but you make it hard to remember anything." He smiled at her as she sat down, and in case she didn't understand what he meant, he leaned over and kissed the top of her head. "He said he's free any night this week. He'll be in the office around four or so if you want to come in."

"Oh," she said softly. The thought of going to the station exploded through the peaceful dream she had been diligently building in her head. "Maybe I'll come tomorrow if I get time."

Jeff dug into the casserole that now sat in the middle of the table. "If you do, watch out. They may throw you a parade."

"A parade?" she asked skeptically.

"I've never been congratulated so many times in my life, and that includes three separate graduations." He laughed. "That's just a friendly warning."

She nodded, getting lost in thought until her senses picked up that he was looking at her with a questioning concern in his eyes. Quickly she looked at him and smiled. "I'll keep that in mind."

"So, is Lisa coming today?" Gabe asked in that deep bass that had become so familiar to Jeff over the last few months.

"I told her about Hayes, but I don't know, she didn't sound too keen on the idea," Jeff said, rethreading the hose up to Gabe at the top of the engine as their practice run ended.

"You should call her," Gabe said. "Tell her we'll even make her supper if she'll come."

"Is that a bribe or a threat?"

"Miller's cooking. You be the judge."

"Bribery. Definite bribery."

Although Gabe laughed, Jeff's spirit curled around the plan. Something told him her turning him down cold was a real possibility, and even it being just a small possibility ripped his heart out.

Friday afternoon. All day long Lisa had been fighting the thought of going to the station. Truth be told, she had been fighting it longer than that. Just the thought of the station, of what it meant for him, for her, was enough to send her spirit crashing through the depression. No, if she just stayed away, pretended it didn't exist, somehow came up with a way to convince herself that it wasn't a part of their reality, then life felt almost normal. It was only when she thought about the station, and more to the point him at the station, that breathing became like running a jagged knife through her heart and soul.

"I forgot to tell you," Sherie said, standing in Lisa's doorway at four when Lisa had all-but succeeded in solidifying the excuse that there was no way she could go for all the work stacked on her desk. "Jeff called while you were out for lunch." The perceptive smile her secretary slid onto her face was unnecessary. "He said if you'll come around five, Gabe said you can have supper with them at the station tonight."

Lisa buried her gaze in the paperwork on her desk. "Oh, okay. Thanks."

Sherie nodded knowingly and shut the door. Lisa closed her eyes. This was horrible. No escape. No excuse. No way out. Her worst nightmare come true.

"That hose couldn't have been any more trouble if it had tried," Bob Miller said as Lisa sat in the break room, surrounded by ten of Houston's finest. Of course, the finest one of all was sitting right beside her with one arm slung around her chair and that lopsided grin spread across his face. Her heart danced as she looked at his profile, remembering why she had fallen for him in the first place.

Sitting around the tables, they really were very much like a little family—kidding and teasing but very much caring about the others seated there.

"It got snagged on the top and then on the bumper," Zack Jameson said, laughing. "It was a good thing it was only a practice run because whatever was burning would've been toast by the time we got that hose over there."

"Rainier was thrilled," Gabe said before taking a drink of water. "I think I got like five demerits for that one run."

"Yeah, but who knew they tied the thing down," Jeff said, sliding into the conversation easily. "I mean who ties a hose down? That's like saying it's here but you can't use it."

"I'll tell you what though," Bob said with a laugh. "I would've given a mint to have a video of you up top trying to untie that thing. It's loose. No it's not. It's loose. No it's not. I thought, 'Uh, boy, what has the academy sent us this time?'"

"I'm sure," Jeff said with a laugh. "I'm just glad I'd been here for awhile. That would've been a great first impression." He smiled at Lisa who remembered her first impression of him, and her gaze fell to the table.

"So, Lisa, when are you going to hog-tie our boy here and make it official?" Bob asked, clapping Jeff on the shoulder.

"Hog-tie?" Lisa asked skeptically, and then she shrugged as embarrassment descended on her. "Whenever he has four days off in a row I guess."

"Ah, a very politically correct answer there," Zack said, nodding. "Smart woman. She knows which side of her bread the butter's on."

"Just trying to make sure Hayes doesn't permanently ban me," she said seriously. "He loves me so much."

"That's okay," Zack said. "I'm sure one of us could manage to sneak you in the back if we had to."

"There's a hole in the roof too. Well, there was," Bob offered. "We used to crawl out at night and go down to the donut shop."

"It looks like it," Gabe taunted, looking at Bob's rounded belly. "I think first thing on my list is patching that hole."

"Too late. Rainier caught us. Hole's gone now," Bob said mournfully.

"Pitiful thing to have to live in a place with weights but no donuts," Zack said, shaking his head. "Just pitiful…"

The laugh that started in Lisa's throat slammed into the alarm that blared to life around them, and simultaneously every gaze at the table looked up.

"Well, party's over," Gabe said, pushing out of the chair as sheer panic seized Lisa.

Unsteadily she stood as Jeff jumped to his feet, leaned over, and kissed the edge of her cheek. "Got to go." He squeezed her hand once and followed the others out the door.

Stunned to the core, she stood there watching him go, and she couldn't even feel fear— just complete numbness. Slowly she walked to the break room door and laid a hand on it as three men rushed down the hallway past the glass. Her hands pushed through the door although in reality she felt like it was someone else moving and she was just watching life from their eyes.

"Everybody in?" someone yelled from the truck. A bang on the side of the engine, and the huge metal monster rolled forward out of the opening in the wall, blasting a horn and blaring the siren as it did so.

The sounds were ear splitting, but more than that, they were soul splitting. Her last glimpse as it bumped into the street was of the three men in the back, pulling on their suits. She now knew how heavy those suits were, and yet how horribly inconsequential they could be in the face of...

Trying to push those thoughts out of her mind, she turned back for the break room. The last thing they needed to be doing when they got back was dishes. It wasn't much, but it was something she could do, and at that moment she had to do something to help or she would go insane with the bottled up grief, anger, and concern so overwhelming she felt like she had fallen into a deep, dark well with no light and no way to get to the top. "Oh, God, please..."

"Taylor and Miller, cut the vents; Jameson, set the vent fan," Gabe ticked off the assignments as they swung around one corner.

Jeff nodded as his stomach knotted inside of him. That look. He hated the look she had given him. It said all the things that he didn't want to face and more. When they screeched up to the house which had billows of smoke rising from one side window, the six of them jumped from the truck, and as Jeff laid his ID tag on the front dash, his mind flashed back to the last time he had done that. With a blink he banished that thought. Concentration was paramount here. Concentration would be what would get him back to reclaim that tag.

He grabbed the roof ladder and half of the extension from the truck side and started up the lawn. Forty hours of ladder classes. He should know how to do this in his sleep. Click went the extension until it was positioned on the eve of the roof. One step, two, he climbed. At the top he angled his way onto the roof and closer to the peek where carefully he hooked the top of the roof ladder on and then attached himself to it.

"You got it?" Bob asked from the extension where he held the chainsaw.

"Done." The chainsaw changed hands, and duty took over. He was here to do a job, a job that could mean someone's life. That's why he had started this in the first place, and now it was a part of him. The chainsaw in his hand roared to life. One life at a time. Just save one life at a time, and someday surely he would be able to out-run the ghosts that were gathering at his heels.

The dishes were all done. Lisa had even convinced herself that they would come back if she just put them all away. However, the dishes were away, and they still weren't back. She knew she should leave, go home. There was no one here, no reason to stay, and yet something in her just had to know he was all right. She wished she'd had the sanity to decipher the message when it had come in, maybe then she would at least know where he was, and what kind of call it was.

As it stood, she had no idea. Pushing through the break room door to the station beyond, she walked out as fear and helplessness fought for control inside her. One wire mesh step at a time she climbed until eight up, she stopped and slid down against the wall, praying like she had never prayed before. It wasn't fair to ask him to do this, she told God. He had as much right to this life as anyone else—more than some. He was a good guy. He didn't deserve to die out there fighting to save someone else's life.

It was then that she thought about Dustin. How had his final call come in? Much like that one had? A simple call out, and he never made it back to the station. She wondered how it had happened. Maybe he was fighting the fire and he fell into something he couldn't get out of. Or had someone made a horrible mistake, miscalculated how long a mission would take and he was caught without air. Was he alone when it happened? Or was someone there fighting to get him out immediately but it took too long? The scenarios, each one worse than the one before played and replayed through her head.

Had he known it was the end before it was? Had he felt it? In that last moment who had he thought about? Eve, to be sure. Jeff, maybe. But who else? Or was it too quick to think about anything or anyone? One split-second and it was over. How many one split seconds was Jeff facing right now? She tried to breathe for him, tried to force the air from her lungs into his—one more breath so that he might get to the next.

Exhausted by the non-stop battle she had been fighting since she'd first gotten that call in the middle of the night, she let her head fall back against the hard wall. She didn't want to picture the scene he was living right now, and yet it was all she could focus on. Men racing around, trying to beat back a furious dragon bent on taking them down with it. And it could. It had. Her mind traced to Eve standing by that coffin, and Lisa's heart twisted. Eve had loved Dustin, but what difference had that made? He was gone now. *From dust we came and to dust we shall return.* He was dust now. Cold and dead. What power had love wielded in the face of that moment when death took him? None.

Death took one look at love and laughed. It had swept Dustin into its arms and flown down into the pits of darkness. Love never fails? Who had been dumb enough to write that? From where she sat, it looked like love never triumphed. Even her mother's love, that soul-sapping love she had professed to have, had died. It said so down at the county courthouse on the divorce decree.

Eve's love was lying in a graveyard. Dead. Over and over Lisa had watched girlfriends, clients, employees. One minute they were so in love they were practically hysterical. The next minute they hated the other person. She had to be kidding herself if she thought that love could ever triumph in the end. It was ludicrous. What made her think that their love could last when so many others had perished before them? What made her think that they would be the lucky ones? What made her think that one day that truck wouldn't pull back into this station, one rider short for all eternity?

And she would be the one left standing, holding a flag in some cold, gray graveyard, and love would again have lost. What was love anyway? It was a feeling, and feelings change. How many times had she said that to Haley when Haley had first come home talking about this wonderful guy she had just met? Walk a mile across burning coals... Lisa laughed softly at the thought. It wasn't far from what she was doing right now. The searing pain shooting through her at that moment couldn't have been that different.

Then his face drifted into her consciousness. Jeff holding her. Jeff smiling. Jeff sitting there gaze down that first night in the booth. "Ugh." Her breath released with one whoosh as she banged her head against the wall, and then her forehead dropped to the hand she put to it. Thinking about him made her heart hurt, and that wasn't how it was supposed to be.

"Love isn't about when it's easy," her mother said in her ears.

"But does it always have to hurt this bad?" she asked the

empty fire station beyond. "Because I don't think I can stand it if it does."

The fire was small. One truck. Two holes. Three hours. By eleven o'clock they were backing back into the station. The men around Jeff talked happily, glad to be home and hoping that would be the last call for the night.

"A shower's going to feel really good right now," Bob said. "You know you could've warned me about that flower bed."

"How was I supposed to know you were going to take a mud bath in it?" Zack asked as Bob lifted his mud-caked boots from the floor. "I'm thinking, flowers, dirt, water. What did you think it was going to be, a rock garden?"

"Ha. Ha."

"It's stand down time, everybody," Gabe called from the door as he slid out onto the concrete below. "First one to the showers, first one to bed!"

"Hallelujah!" Zack said, jumping down. "Don't anyone get in my way! I've got a date with dreamland."

Jeff slid out of his seat in the middle as Bob, Zack and the rest of the crew shuffled off to the showers. However, Gabe stayed back to go over the engine in case that wasn't the only call for the night. When the others were gone, Jeff stopped. "You need some help?"

Gabe looked up as he flipped across the ladder brackets and laughed. "That's a dumb question."

"Just thought I'd ask. I can pull that cotton down and get a new one up there."

"And Bob was worried about what the academy sent us," Gabe said, shaking his head. "If you're offering, I'm not saying no."

With a hit on the engine door, Jeff went around the back, his boots clumping loudly on the floor. It wasn't a problem helping Gabe out. Sleeping would be the bigger problem anyway. A hand up, and a hand up, and he was up top, pulling the one hose they had actually used down.

"I'm going to go get out of these boots," Gabe called. "They're killing my feet."

Jeff nodded his acknowledgement and went back to work,

sliding the hose down the back of the truck. Maybe if he worked a little while longer, he would be so tired he would be able to fall asleep. That would be a new phenomenon. He hadn't had a good night's sleep since…

That's when in the middle of the dead quiet station he first heard the sound. Soft, pitiful, like a muffled sob. His hands stopped as his gaze swept across the room in instant concern. The moment he saw her huddled on the stairs next to the wall in the darkness, he knew who it was. The hose, already halfway down, dropped to the concrete unaided. His turnout gear was still in the truck, there was a hose he had promised to replace lying on the floor, but all his brain could say was that she was needed him right now. She needed him, and all else fell away.

He jumped off the truck, and in three strides he was at the stairs, but his steps slowed on the climb up when she looked down at him. Tear-streaked and care-worn, her face held only sorrow and fear.

"Lis?" he asked softly when his foot found the step two down from her and he slid first to a knee and then all the way down on the step in front of her. She was wrapped around herself, pulling her knees in so closely to her chest that he wondered how she could so much as breathe. Tenderly he reached out to touch her as the sorrow in her eyes knotted around his heart. "Have you been here the whole time?"

She looked at him and gulped back the tears as she nodded. "I couldn't leave."

"Oh, baby." He tried to get closer to her, but the steps weren't making that easy. "Why didn't you go home?"

"I… I had to know you were okay," she said as the tears overtook the words.

"Oh, God, I'm sorry." When he reached up to brush the hair from her temple, the clasp around her knees broke, and she squeezed her eyes closed, fighting the flood right behind her eyes. She turned to him, and for a moment her head dropped onto his shoulder. He kissed the side of her hair as he held her gently. "I'm so sorry."

Pain was all he saw in her eyes when she finally pulled back from him. "I'm sorry," she said brokenly. "I can't do this. I've got to go."

In the next breath she stood, and her feet carried her past him down the stairs. "No, Lisa, wait." He tried to grab her hand, but she yanked it away from his grasp as he stood. "Can we talk about this?"

She never slowed down. In fact, she narrowly missed knocking right into Gabe when he reappeared from the hallway.

"Lis…a," Gabe said in surprise, following her with his gaze as she opened the station door with a snap, walked out, and slammed it behind her. Then Gabe's gaze traveled up to Jeff who stood in stunned speechlessness on the stairs above. "Oh, no."

Twenty-One

"Okay, that can't be good," Gabe said when the walls stopped ringing from the echo of the slamming door.

"What makes you think that?" Jeff asked in sarcastic fury. "Everything in my life is always so almighty perfect, why should my love life be any different?" He walked over to the engine and snapped the latch on the door before climbing into the cab and throwing his turnout gear to the floor below.

"Why didn't you go after her?"

"Because she's right, Gabe. She is. She doesn't need this. She doesn't need any of this." He slid out of the cab, jumped to the floor, and slammed the door. "She doesn't need to be sitting at home waiting for the phone to ring, knowing the next time it does might be worse than the last time it did. She doesn't need that. She doesn't."

"But you need her."

"You don't think I know that?" Jeff asked harshly, not at all caring who happened to walk in and hear. "But it's killing me to see that look in her eyes. It's just one freak second away from catching up with us, and she knows it."

"What is? The work?"

"The fire," Jeff said, straightening so that he stood toe-to-toe, staring at Gabe from point-blank range. In exasperation he shook his head and stepped away. "They don't give medals to the wives, you know that? For bravery in the face of a life they have no control over. They don't hand out medals and give speeches for that." He put his gear on the rack. "No, but it's the wives who hold it all together at home. They're the ones who go to the funerals and the hospitals, hoping that next time it won't be them. And they're the ones left to take care of the family when something does happen."

He worked with the coils of hose that wasn't cooperating and then stood and slammed a hand against the side of the truck. "Damn it." His hand went up to his face to stop the emotions from pouring out of him. "I can't ask her to do that. I should never have thought I could."

"Jeff, this whole thing…"

With one yank Jeff pulled the hose up from the floor. "I'm going to go wash this thing out." He walked over to the door to the washtub, where he stopped and turned. "Don't worry about me. Okay? This might take awhile."

Slowly Gabe nodded, and Jeff pushed the door open and stepped through it.

Tears had never burned so fiercely. Lisa's eyes hurt from their relentless trek from her heart to her eyes and out onto her cheeks. The lights ahead of her on the freeway blurred as she reached up and swiped the newest batch away, but they were followed immediately by their replacements. How many had she already cried? Hundreds? Thousands? And yet there were that many more stacked up and waiting for a stray thought to hit her.

She sniffed them back and gripped the steering wheel. Confusion reigned in her brain. No thought could stay with her for more than a few moments at a time, and too many of those thoughts centered on what she was driving away from— who she was driving away from. Like he might actually be standing there, she looked in her rearview mirror, and a ghost from what seemed like a lifetime ago stood there, hands in his pockets, watching her drive away. The tears washed over her like a gigantic wave bent on sweeping her right to the bottom.

He had put too much soap in. The suds told him that, but he didn't really care. If he could've dove into them and disappeared forever, he would have. Everything he had told Gabe was true, except for one thing. He had made it sound far too easy to let her go. That was a rip, a cleave, that would never heal, and he knew it. It was a wound destined to bleed from this point until forever and beyond. And he of all people knew about the forever and beyond part. He'd been living it ever since that firefighter had set him on the ground under the night sky kissed by fire and smoke and had run back into that house.

They said the bedrooms were too far gone at that point, the structure too unstable, that Bruce Melio should never have gone back in, and yet Jeff knew why he had. It was because of the pleadings of a 17-year-old kid who knew no better.

Jeff wiped the edge of his cheek with one wet arm. The roof was weak. The fire had already eaten away the attic by that point. They knew that. He didn't. All he knew was that the two people he loved most were in the middle of those flames, and he pleaded for their lives. A memory ripped through him—a picture of him standing by his mother as the fireman handed a flag to Mrs. Melio, who crumpled over it like a can under a boot. He remembered the two little kids, too small to really understand, watching as their mother was led from the graveyard where their father now lay.

That was the moment that Jeff had decided that this was his destiny. That was the moment, in fact, when he had shattered his own mother's heart into ever-smaller pieces although she wouldn't know it for nearly a decade. That was the moment that the course of his life was forever set, and now in the face of that memory, he felt powerless to assimilate where duty to them stopped and love for Lisa started.

Through the long nights after the accident, he had lain awake thinking through all the things he could've done differently. Yes, he had felt more helpless and bitter in those hours than most feel in a lifetime. Yet not one moment of that could match how he felt when he looked into Lisa's frightened, pleading eyes now. He had to let her go, let her get on with her life. It seemed impossible. It felt impossible, but somehow he had to find the strength to walk away. She deserved that much.

"This may be just a job to you," Lisa said Tuesday afternoon as she faced down Kurt and Joel who stood before her desk like prisoners before a firing squad, "but this is my life. I'm not interested in half-done, shabby-looking, useless trash. Now when you've got this

278

office supply campaign ready for someone other than a two-year-old, I want to see it. Until then…" She shooed them out with both hands.

The weekend, extended for Labor Day, had been spent trying to dig out from under the piles of paper on her desk. True, it needed done, but that wasn't why she did it. Everyone else was going to picnics and parties and fireworks shows. Lisa had never gone to those when she had the inclination. Now, she definitely did not.

All those things smacked of having fun, and that already loathsome concept was made worse by the fact that it now seemed to be a one-way-ticket to thoughts of him. At all costs, she was avoiding thoughts of him.

When they were gone, she sat back for one second and then pulled herself forward. She would not give in to the thoughts stalking her. Not now. Not ever.

If Jeff could've kept his mind on the information the teacher was presenting in the hazmat class, it would've helped. Not that anything had helped since she'd walked out the door, but he could always hope. Once at home, he poured himself some water. Too tired and too frustrated with himself to make supper, he grabbed a bag of chips, sat down on the couch, and turned on the television. By now he knew the routine, either he would go to sleep on the couch sometime around 4:30 or eventually he would talk himself into going to bed and lay there until the sun came up, telling himself the whole time to just go to sleep.

He hoped it was a go-to-sleep-on-the-couch night. He hated the others. Just as he was settling in, the phone rang, and totally against all reason, he jumped up and rushed over to it, hoping it might be her. "Hello?"

"Mr. Taylor?"

"Yes," he said as his heart fell.

"This is Zane's Jewelry. Your ring is ready."

Spiraling down, his heart plummeted. Why couldn't life just go away and leave him alone?

"Mr. Taylor?"

"Umm, yeah. I'm here. I'll try to get by and pick it up as soon as I can," he said, not meaning one word of it.

"It'll be ready when you are."

As he hung up the phone, the word 'never' drifted through his mind.

Thoughts of Jeff were never far away from Lisa although she had made it a habit to camp out at her office instead of going home. Two days she had actually gone without sleep. When she did go home, even turning on a light was dangerous, so she mostly left them off. The darkness was good company. It felt safe, like maybe she could hide there, and life wouldn't notice she was missing.

At work her temper was getting shorter and shorter so that all she had to do was walk into a room, and people ducked for cover. There had been a time in her life when that would've felt like power, but now it just felt lonely. She had called Haley who basically said, "I told you so." And so, finally, by the end of September she was right where she had always thought she wanted to be: dealing with everything on her own. The only problem was she now hated every single moment of the life she had always thought she wanted.

"Taylor?" Captain Hayes asked, walking into the truck maintenance room as Jeff stood replacing the tools he had used to change the oil.

"Yes, Sir?"

"I was under the impression that Lisa would be sending me the schedule for the conference thing any time now, but I haven't heard anything from her. She didn't take a trip to Bermuda or anything, did she?"

Jeff went back to his task. "I wouldn't know, Sir."

"Uh-huh." Hayes nodded. "And the fact that she won't return my calls? You wouldn't know anything about that either, now would you?"

"No, Sir, I haven't talked to… her in a couple of weeks."

"Uh-huh, well, if you could get her a message for me, tell her that it's going to be hard for me to be there if I don't know when I'm supposed to be there."

Jeff nodded. "I'll try, Sir."

Hayes stood for a moment, grunted, and walked out just as

Gabe walked in.

"Does the fact that we're in here working on the truck, and they're out there playing basketball not seem at all fair?"

Jeff hadn't really thought about it. Working on the truck was something he could still lose himself in, and today more than most days he wanted to do just that. As of this evening he would be one step closer to full-fledged firefighter, but there wasn't a part of him that really cared.

"So, what did Hayes want?" Gabe asked as he threw the rag he'd just wiped the grease from his hands on to the table. However, the motion was a little too hard, and it slipped off onto the floor. Instantly Jeff leaned down and retrieved it.

"I don't know, some dumb thing about the conference."

Gabe stopped and looked at Jeff. "You still haven't talked to her?"

Jeff shrugged. "I've been busy."

"Man, you can be so pig-headed when you want to be. You know that?"

"Thank you very much."

"That wasn't a compliment." For a moment Gabe rearranged the tools, and then he stopped. "You know she probably feels the same way."

"What way?"

"Like the rest of life isn't worth living if she can't be with you."

"I'm flattered."

"No, man, you're a guy who's trashing what could be the best thing in your life, and for what? A stupid job?"

"You want me to quit?"

"No."

Jeff turned to the workbench. "Well, she does."

"Do you?"

"No. Yes. I don't know. I don't want to have to think about it anymore. Thinking about it is getting me nowhere."

"And not thinking about it is getting you... umm, where?"

Jeff just glared at Gabe and slammed another tool onto the wall.

"Why don't you call her? Maybe talking will get you somewhere."

"It never has before," Jeff retorted. "I don't see how it's going to help much now."

"Well, it's worth a shot."

But Jeff knew better. Even if he could come up with the words, he could never say them— for more reasons than he could name.

The machine was blinking when Jeff got home the next morning, and he hit the button.

"Mr. Taylor, this is Zane's Jewelry." Jeff closed his eyes wishing life would just go away and leave him alone already. "We still have your ring. Please remember after 30 days it becomes property of the store. Thank you."

"No. Thank you," he said sarcastically as he punched the off button.

"Don't even start," Lisa said on October first as Tucker sat across the desk from her. "I'm doing the best I can here, and I only have two hands."

"What about the other six out there?" He pointed to the door.

"Useless," she said with a shake of her head as she clicked across the screen on her computer and then down the schedule which should have been printed a week ago. Every entry went right through her heart. The travel agency. That was Jeff's idea. He had sat right there in that chair... "Ugh," she growled at the screen. "You said we got 700 applications?"

"So far," Tucker said. "We're getting more into the office every day. Somehow I don't think they noticed the September 21st deadline."

"Apparently."

"Vera was trying to keep up with them, putting the kids in the sessions they asked for and stuff, but then this audit came up, and she got pulled off, and now..."

"We've got 700 applications for 500 spots, no idea which came in first because someone forgot to put a registration date on the form, and two weeks to figure it all out."

"Basically."

"Where are the applications now?"

"Most of them are in my car."

"Most of them?"

"Hey, I lugged two bags over here. I thought that was doing pretty good."

Lisa exhaled slowly, feeling like the second coming might happen before she got to leave that office again. "Fine. Bring them up."

Jeff was putting it off. He was putting everything off—life mostly. The ring, now lying on top of his dresser, wasn't helping. It stared at him like a judge set to pronounce sentence at any moment. Still he couldn't put it away. He'd tried. But even the darkness was sad without it lying there. So he had relented, and now it sat there—a permanent resident that was going nowhere.

The clock on the wall read 10:30. It was too late to call her. She was probably asleep anyway. However, that afternoon Hayes had asked and again Jeff had promised. Until then he had always been a man of his word— always done what he said he'd do—no matter the cost to himself. But this cost seemed far too high a price to pay.

Trying to find something to do other than sit and watch the clock all night, he stood and went to the bathroom. The stubble on his face blared how pitifully he was managing without her, and although shaving at night seemed rather strange, he pulled out the razor anyway. There was no reason to look like the return of the wolfman even though that's what he felt like.

The phone in the kitchen rang, and the razor slipped. "Ow! Crud!" Bright, red blood sprouted from the cut, and Jeff grabbed for tissue even as the phone rang again. He raced for it and grabbed it just before the answering machine did. "Hello?"

"You're there," the female voice said in surprise, and Jeff's spirit lifted.

"Where else would I be?"

"I figured you were working," she said, and his mind slipped across the fact that it wasn't Lisa. "I was coming up with all these brilliant things to say to your answering machine."

"Eve."

"Yeah?"

He tried to push the disappointment down. "Oh."

"What?" she asked with concern.

"N… nothing. I just thought you were… someone else."

"And this someone else wouldn't have light brown hair, nice legs, and wear a lot of dress suits, would she?"

The exhale was a little too loud. "Did you need something?"

"Oh, no you don't. We were talking about you."

"Not a good subject."

"And Lisa?"

"Worse subject."

"Oh, man, Jeff. What happened? Things were going so good."

He sat down on the barstool heavily and dabbed at the cut on his chin. "Life. Life happened. Just like it always does."

"So, what? You're taking a break?"

"Yeah, a permanent one."

"Permanent?"

"No seeing, no talking. Not for the last month at least."

"And you're okay with that?"

"Do I sound okay with that?"

"No, you sound pathetic."

"Yeah, that's pretty close."

"Well, then why don't you call her?"

"Because I wouldn't know what to say."

"And that's different... how?"

"Ha. Ha."

"I'm not laughing."

He wasn't either. "No, really what were you calling for?"

She sighed. "To check on some friends who I was really hoping could cheer me up."

"Oh, boy. You called the wrong place for that."

"Yeah, I kind of figured that out."

His brain enumerated the excuses of why he hadn't called Eve even as his heart said there was no excuse. "So, how're you doing?"

"I've been better. You know last weekend marked the eleventh week he's been gone."

It seemed like a blink to Jeff, and yet he knew for her... "What're you doing Sunday?"

"Sunday? Not much I guess. Church with my parents at nine, football with my dad after."

"How about I pick you up at noon, and we go do something?"

"Like what?"

"Your choice. I'm sick of looking at this place. Please, Eve. You'll be doing me a favor."

"What about Lisa?"

"What about her?" he asked, not seeing any connection.

"Are you going to call her?"

He dabbed at the drying wound on his chin but said nothing.

"I'll make you a deal," Eve said teasingly serious. "You call Lisa, and we'll go out on Sunday."

"But…"

"And don't flake out on me either. I'm going to want details. Lots of details, and I will ask. Okay?" She waited. "Jeff?"

"Yeah, okay."

"Great. Then I'll see you Sunday."

When he hung up with Eve, Jeff sat looking at the phone, knowing if he walked away from it now, it would be Sunday before he got up the nerve to try again. With an exasperated sigh, he reached for the receiver, dialed her number, and waited until the answering machine had gotten all the way finished speaking before he hung up. Somehow he had forgotten how much he missed that voice. It wrapped around him like a warm, thick blanket on a cold, dreary night.

He looked at the clock and wondered what she was still doing at work. It was after eleven already. She was at work. He knew that much. "Work and home, that's my life." Words from a different lifetime floated through him, and he smiled sadly as they slid through his consciousness. Picking up the phone that time wasn't nearly as hard as it had been the first. In fact, if he was honest, an illogical excitement snapped him into its clutches as his fingers dialed. He felt like he'd lost his mind, and yet he felt more sane than he had in a month.

Envelopes sat in incoherent stacks all over her office as Lisa stood in the middle of them, shrinking before the hopelessness that stared her in the face. There was no way to make any sense of any of this. There couldn't have been thirty opened envelopes. The rest made her want to cry, so much so that when the phone rang at nearly eleven-thirty although she knew it was a wrong number, she jumped for it. "Matheson Agency. Lisa speaking." A moment of pause, and she thought the caller might hang up rather than acknowledge their mistake.

"Lisa?"

"Yes?"

"Hi," the voice said, winding through her. "It's Jeff."

Suddenly she couldn't breathe, and the room felt at least ten degrees warmer. "Oh, Jeff. Hi." She started to sit down in the chair because her legs went numb beneath her, but the two stacks of envelopes lying there sent her right back up again. "Oww! Oh, no." Like a nightmare she could do nothing about, she watched one stack teeter, and then the letters slid one-by-one to the floor. "No! No, no, no, no, no." They kept falling anyway until only three out of the 30 were left in the chair.

"What are you doing?" he asked with concern.

"Ugh! Trying to do the impossible," she said in surrendered exasperation. "And it's not working." Under the desk she crawled gathering applications as she went. She stacked the ones she managed to round up back on the chair, and as she put her hand on the chair to pull herself up, she blew at the loose hair from her forehead in frustration. Her gaze slid around the room as she collapsed onto the carpet. Putting her back against the wall, she shook her head. "This is hopeless."

"What?"

"The youth conference. I've got all these envelopes, and I don't even know where to start, and I haven't gotten six hours of sleep in the last three days. Right now, I'm about this close to totally losing it."

His side went silent for a moment. "Would you like some help?"

"That would be nice," she said, meaning from her employees and not together enough to realize what he really meant.

"It'll just take me a minute to throw something on, and I'll be there," he said in a rush of words.

"Be… here…? Wait. What? Oh, no. I didn't mean…"

"Sit tight. I'll be there as soon as I can."

Lisa was sure Jeff hadn't meant the sit tight comment literally, but that's all she could do. After she hung up, she leaned back against the wall and stared straight ahead. It must be her imagination or a hallucination. She couldn't have just said what she had. More than that, that couldn't have been his answer. Her hand went up to her hair, but it was too late to fix it.

A shower? Make-up? A sandblaster? It would take at least that much to make her presentable again, but she had none of that, and he was on his way.

"Oh. My. Gosh," Jeff said when he pushed her door open and saw her sitting on the floor, the bomb blast around her clearly apparent. "What in the world happened?"

"Welcome to my nightmare," she said as if she was tilting on the edge of sanity, and he arched his eyebrows at the tone in her voice.

"What is all this?" Slowly he stepped over the piles of envelopes, into the room, and over to where she sat. One foot wrapped under the other, and he sat down on the floor next to her.

"This," she said, holding up an envelope, "is the result of letting someone else do something for you. You see this?" She thrust a handful of papers into his hands. "See, no application date. None. Nice, huh? Really great."

He took them from her and looked through them slowly.

"I've got 762 applications at last count, and not a date on a single one of them."

"And the date's important?"

"It's first come-first serve, and I've only got 500 seats!" Like it was him who had made the mistake, she lunged for his throat, gripped it in her hands, and shook him hard. Then she let him go, smashed her palms against her forehead, and slid them down slowly. "This is a disaster."

"I can see that," he said softly. His brain reeled through the problem, cart-wheeling over solutions that had no hope of working. "These didn't have the envelopes?"

"Jan, Pat, Vera, somebody trashed them at Cordell Enterprises. Why?"

"Because the envelopes should have a postmark on them, so you could conceivably..."

A moment and her eyes widened in understanding. "Oh, my gosh, you're right." She jumped to her feet and grabbed a stack of letters from the chair. One at a time she picked through them. "September 5. September 17. September 3. Oh, thank You God."

The chair caught her on the way down.

"Yeah," Jeff said, laying the stack of papers in his hand down beside him and picking up a small stack of envelopes next to him. "Now all we have to do is sort through them, put them in order, open them up, and…"

She waved at him with both hands to get him to stop. "One thing at a time." Quickly she pulled something off of her desk, and then, as though it was the most natural thing in the world, she stood, marched back to his side, and sat down. Her fingers flicked the object up. "Box?"

He smiled at her. "I'd love one."

About 3:30 a.m. Lisa yawned a small yawn, followed instantly by a larger one, and Jeff looked over at her even as she tried to squelch them.

"You look wiped," he said gently.

"Gee, I wouldn't know why," she retorted, picking up another stack to start sorting it as she leaned back onto the hardwood of the side of her desk. Her fingers went back to work trying to get September 7 to follow September 4. She was zoning out. She felt it. With a stretch she tried to open her eyes wider, but that just brought on another yawn.

"Here." Jeff reached over to take the stack out of her hand.

"What… what're you doing?" Without a response, he took hold of her arm and lifted her from the floor.

"You're not going to be good for anything if you don't get some shut-eye."

"But I can't…" Not listening to the protest, he led her from the room. "But there's…" Through the dark office they walked until they got to the conference room on the other side. She lowered her gaze skeptically at that room. "What do you want me to sleep on— the table?"

"I was thinking the carpet, but it's up to you," he said with half of that smile playing on his lips.

"I don't have time for this."

"And when you collapse from exhaustion tomorrow, are you going to have time for that?" He worked the black shirt atop his white T-shirt off as he knelt on the floor next to the wall. "Now, here. I know it's not the Hilton, but…" When his hand touched hers to pull her down, life thudded to a stop. "Come on," he said, his eyes gentle. "Just a few minutes."

Reluctantly Lisa sat down and then flipped her hair over the shirt on the ground. Her cheek felt its warmth instantly, and all the fight in her vanished. Her eyes closed, and sleep swept over her. That's when she felt it. His hand. Warm and soft lying across her arm.

"Get some rest."

"Maybe just a few minutes," she said already drifting away. "But don't forget to wake me up."

"I won't."

When her mind finally surrendered to the pull of sleep, her last thought was that he still hadn't moved from that spot, and she hoped he would just stay there right next to her forever.

Jeff waited until her breathing slowed and found its own rhythm. In the darkness of the room, he was surprised he could see anything, and yet her beauty could pierce even the blackest of the black. He sat for a few more minutes and then pushed up from the floor, catching the edge of the table for balance. With one more look down, he stepped from the room and closed the door softly behind him.

A look at his watch verified what he already knew. Quarter-to-four, and they still had a mountain to get through. Back in her office, he folded himself onto the carpet and smiled. She was crazy to think she could've tackled this on her own, and she was just crazy enough to have pulled it off too. He picked up a stack and got back to work.

It was the front office door that Lisa heard first. It jolted her from the marvelous dream she was having of them sitting in some field together flying kites. Slowly she yawned and stretched. That was when she remembered, and causing a head rush, she sat straight up and looked at her watch. It was almost eight. Why hadn't he hadn't awakened her?

"Jeff?" Sherie said in surprise when she opened the door and found him rather than Lisa in the inner office. "What're you doing here?"

"Working," he said as his fingers threw the envelopes into the five stacks surrounding him, one for each week in September.

"Oh," Sherie said, and although it tried, her voice couldn't quite make it sound like that was the exact response she had expected. She looked out into the front office. "Where's Lisa?"

"Sleeping," Jeff said, flipping three more letters into one of the piles.

"Oh." Sherie nodded. "Okay." She started out.

"Oh, Sherie, do you have any more of these boxes somewhere?" He held one up.

"Maybe..." Her attention jerked outside the door as shock descended across her features. "Lisa?"

"Don't say it," he heard Lisa say, and he smiled at the sound.

One more small stack and all they had to do was get the weeks in order. When she walked in, Jeff's heart said how much he had missed her over the last four hours.

"I'll get some coffee," Sherie said uncertainly, and she left.

"Sleep well?" Jeff asked.

Lisa sat down in a heap right next to him and dropped the shirt into his lap. "You were supposed to wake me up."

He smiled at her. "It's that whole kissing a sleeping princess thing. I knew how much you hated that."

"I didn't say you had to kiss me." Her face scrunched together. "There are other ways to wake a person up, you know." Then she really looked at her office and stopped. "You're almost finished?"

"Ten more," he said, flipping through the last stack in his hand. When the last of them hit the piles, he sighed and scooted back against a chair and wiped his hands over his eyes tiredly. "Now, all we have to do is get each week sorted." With a small yawn, he picked one stack up and righted the envelopes. "These we don't have to worry about. They're all last week in September, so we can put them over here, and use them only if we have to." That pile landed next to the wall.

"Coffee," Sherie said, walking into the room, and after she had handed them each a cup, she pulled the box from under her arm. "And here's your box."

"Thank you very much." Jeff set his coffee to the side and picked up another stack of envelopes. "I say we start here, last week in August and work our way forward."

"We," "our," Lisa was waking up enough to catch onto those words, and her heart was suddenly asking why he was sitting in her office, not offering to help but helping. "You don't have... work or something today?"

"Nope. It's your lucky day. I'm off until Saturday morning."

Thursday to Saturday? She ought to be good and insane in that amount of time. "You really should go home and get some sleep." Lisa heard the phone ring in the outer office, but her mission at the moment was to get him out of hers. "I'm sure you're exhausted..."

"Lisa?" Sherie said through the intercom, "Zebra Carpets on line one."

With a tired shake of her head, she pulled herself up from the floor and grabbed the phone. "Matheson Agency. Lisa speaking."

"Good, you're there," the voice on the other side said. "Terry forgot to call you about our staff meeting today."

"Staff...?"

"We've got some concepts for promotions we want to bounce off of you."

Her hand went to her hair, and she knew with one touch why Sherie had looked at her so strangely when she'd come out of the conference room. "I really don't..." She stopped and sighed. "What time is the meeting?"

Without watching her, Jeff watched her. One person standing beneath a mountain of problems and trying to deal with all of them on her own. She had strength and determination in spades, but delegating had obviously gotten lost somewhere along the way. When she hung up, his gaze traced over to her. "Problems?"

"You could say that. I'm supposed to be at Zebra Carpets at ten o'clock." Her shoulders fell forward under the weight of life. "But I can't leave now. Look at this place."

"Tell you what," he said gently, holding her up with his gaze and voice as he stood and walked over to her chair. "You go home, grab a shower, get you some non-wrinkled clothes, and then go to your meeting. We'll handle things here."

"But what about…?"

"We'll handle things." Carefully he lifted her from the chair by one arm. "Now, go, and don't worry about us."

Exhaustion was good for something, he thought as he laid her purse over her shoulder and led her to the outer door before pushing her through it. At least she was too tired to argue coherently. "Drive carefully."

With only a small wave of acknowledgement, she walked away. When she closed the outer office door, Jeff looked at Sherie like they were on a secret mission together. "How fast can you make a database?"

"Ten minutes depending on what's in it," she said, lowering her voice.

"Fabulous. This is what we need…"

Why she was going to Zebra Carpets when it was obvious she should be working on the youth conference, Lisa couldn't clearly tell. She drove home and showered, which felt really good. Then she put on clean clothes, which felt even better, and wrapped her hair into a twist. When she was finished, she actually felt like living again, which was a downright miracle. Grabbing her purse, she trekked to her door and back down to her car. The sooner she got this over, the sooner she got back to the office, the mere thought of which was sending the butterflies in her stomach swirling.

Her arm still felt the heat from his hand lying there the night before, and her cheek still felt his shirt curled beneath her. Most of all her heart still felt what it was like to be in his presence again, and no matter what rationalizations she tried to use on herself, none of them were working. Despite the space and time she had managed to put between them, he had never moved from his place in her heart, and she was beginning to get the sinking feeling that he never would.

Every computer in every room of the Matheson Agency was manned by an employee diligently entering information into databases configured for the week he or she was working on. Every so often Jeff would get out of Lisa's chair and go around to check on them, but that really wasn't necessary, they were all intent on getting this done quickly and accurately. When he sat back down in Lisa's chair after one such round, a quiet smile washed over him. Somehow, sitting here, he felt her presence. It was like sunshine on a dark soul, and it felt wonderful.

The GTO sitting on the third level was hard to miss when Lisa pulled back in at twelve-twenty. So he was still here. Simultaneously her mind said that was horrible, and her heart said it was fabulous. At the door to her office, she took a breath, wrenched the doorknob, and stepped resolutely inside. Sherie sat at her desk, and despite the audible snap of the door, she never looked up.

"I'm back," Lisa finally said, peering around the ultra-quiet office with concern. "Everybody out for lunch?"

"No, the guys are in the back. Jeff's working on your computer." Sherie took a bite of her sandwich without ever really looking up.

"My... computer. On what?"

"Database," Sherie said, setting one paper to the side and scrutinizing the information on her computer closely.

Lisa arched her eyebrows. "O... kay." Without another word, she walked to her office door and peered inside. Sherie was absolutely right. There sat Jeff surrounded by the blue window at his back, looking very much like Sherie had—totally engrossed in what he was doing. "Knock. Knock."

He looked up, and some part of her deep down said she liked that look in his eyes. "Back already?"

"It wasn't as bad as I thought," she said, swinging her purse into the chair opposite the desk and noticing that there were no longer envelopes stacked everywhere. Slowly she followed her purse into the chair. "What'd you do with the envelopes?"

"Collating."

"Huh?" she asked, wondering what rabbit hole she had fallen down.

"We're putting them all in this database Sherie came up with so we can collate them and put the kids in the workshops in the order they applied. Much easier than doing it on paper." Still his attention seemed riveted to the screen.

"And Kurt and Joel?"

"Third and fourth week," Jeff said. "I've almost got this first week done, Sherie's on week two, and once that's done, all we have to do is put in the earlier ones and shuffle."

She felt like she was shuffling but not the items in a database. At that moment Kurt appeared at the door.

"I got three done," he said. Then he stopped when he saw Lisa. "Oh, hi."

"Hi," she said, turning to look at him doubtfully.

"Great." Jeff pulled the stack of non-enveloped papers out. "Put these in a separate one, and we'll be in business."

Kurt took the papers and disappeared as Lisa looked after him in astonishment. "How did you get him to do that?"

"What?"

"He got something done."

"Of course he got something done—that's the point, isn't it?"

Yes, it was the point, so why did she have so much trouble getting it accomplished? "So, can I help with this little project of yours?"

Instantly he looked up. "Oh, I'm sorry. You want to finish this?"

"Not really." Her smile came although she wasn't sure she wanted it to. "How about if I finalize the workshop schedule so when you're ready to collate, it'll be ready too?"

"Good plan."

On wobbly legs she stood and walked over beside him at the computer, taking the mouse from him. When he looked up, she was only inches away, and she felt his gaze. "Just let me print out the stuff I have, and the computer's all yours." The edges of her skin melted under his gaze.

He wanted to say something. She felt it, and yet he recalibrated his attention back to the computer. In seconds the printer was working its magic. When it was finished, she took the sheaves back around to the other chair. "Don't mind me. I'll just be over here... working."

Twenty-Two

Taking turns sleeping in the conference room, Jeff and Lisa worked all of Thursday and most of Friday. By seven o'clock, the schedule was finished, the applications were collated, the two lists had been merged, and Sherie had even verified everything with each speaker and every school. Alone, Lisa never could have accomplished it, and yet with the army he had amassed for her, that and so much more seemed possible.

"So," Jeff said as Lisa put the finishing touches on the poster mock-up on her computer.

"So," Lisa said, immediately stifling the yawn that jumped to her throat. Her gaze didn't want to look at him in that chair, knowing the next time she looked it would be empty.

"You want to go get some hot dogs or something?" he asked as if the fragile limb he was standing on might break.

She looked over at him. With everything she had, she wanted to accept, and yet she knew that accepting would put her right back where she'd been the month before—talking herself into believing they had a chance. "I'm beat. You're beat. You've got work in the morning." Her hand clicked to save the document. "I really think we'd better call it a night."

Not really looking at her, he nodded. She wanted to say something so he wouldn't look like he understood exactly what she was saying.

"Can I walk you to your car?" he finally asked.

Knowing she should say no, her heart took one look at him, smiled, and said, "Sure."

Making each step last as long as he could, Jeff walked with her to the parking lot. There was nothing his arms wanted more than to reach over and take her in them, but he knew that wasn't what she wanted out of this night. It hurt, but he was willing to respect that so long as she let him walk beside her and didn't tell him outright to get lost. Seeing no other option, he dug his hands into his pockets lest they betray his best intentions and reach out to her.

"I guess things are going well at work," Lisa said, bringing up the one topic he knew she didn't want to talk about.

"Yeah, pretty well. I start aircraft rescue on Monday."

Her gaze jumped over to him. "You're already through the hazmat thing?"

He looked at her in surprise and nodded. "End of September."

"Oh, congratulations. One more rung up. Huh?"

It felt like six rungs down. "Yeah."

"Is the truck running again?"

"Better, finally. I thought Gabe was going to blow a gasket before I finally figured out it was the fuel injector." He smiled. "Never hurts to know a little about engines."

They walked up behind the GTO.

"Well," she said, burying her gaze in the darkness at their feet, "I guess this is good night."

"I guess." But he didn't move. His spirit had anchored his feet to the asphalt.

When she looked at him, it was with unnervingly soft eyes. "Thanks for everything. I would've been sunk without you."

"I'm always just a phone call away," he said gently. "If you've ever got an office-full of envelopes and no idea what to do with them."

She smiled. "I'll keep that in mind."

He didn't know why, but standing there looking at her, Jeff couldn't help himself. Carefully he bent forward, and with a touch on her arm, he kissed her cheek. "Take care."

Looking positively bewildered, she nodded, turned for her car, got in, and waited for him to shut the door. "I'll see you."

"Yeah," he said, and sadly he pushed the door closed. His gaze couldn't even watch her drive away as he stood there helpless in the face of the end.

Work the next day held no fascination for Lisa. She didn't want to work. In fact, she had sent everyone home saying they should have a Saturday off for a change. No, all she wanted to do was sit in that chair and feel him wrap around her. Over and over her rational side said that she had been down that road already. It led only to heartache, and yet she asked the walls if that was true, then what was this hole in her heart that felt so painfully unfixable? It felt like an ache that could sweep her under at any unguarded moment. Everywhere she looked, he was there, but not just in the office but in her heart and her spirit as well.

All she wanted was to spend one more minute with him. One more and then one more and then... Pulling her knees, clothed in denim up into the chair with her, she spun the chair, and her gaze slipped to the rain falling outside her window. The first cold rain of the winter with spring so far away it was merely a promise and nothing more. "God, I don't know what to do here. It's like I can't live with him, but I can't live without him either... I was doing just fine, you know, before You sent him into my life. I was doing just fine. I was... well, not exactly happy but..." Her mind drifted back to those days; however, instead of the take-charge, can-handle-anything person she thought she'd find there, all she saw was a woman desperately trying to win the attention and affirmations of everyone around her—and failing miserably.

In her mind's eye she saw herself rushing to the next meeting, zapping anyone who got in her way, and criticizing herself over every little detail that wasn't perfectly in place. Only now did she feel the loneliness that followed that woman everywhere, and Lisa cringed away from her. One small tear slipped over her lash and down onto her cheek. Until him, life was one long string of forgettable moments, but with his entrance into her life—every moment had suddenly become one that she wanted no more than to hold onto forever.

"This is insane," she said, righting the chair, wiping her eyes, and standing up. There had to be something more productive than sitting around an empty office crying all day.

Gabe had tried to ask about the situation, three times already, and although Jeff was able to put him off, he wasn't nearly so successful with his own heart. He couldn't explain it, but being with her made him feel alive in a way he hadn't felt in many, many years. As the clock wound around to five, he thought about Eve. It would be nice to talk to someone—even if he already knew which side of the fence she would fall on. He laughed softly at that, a small gust and he could as easily as not end up right beside her on that side.

Nowhere. Not one single place could Lisa go that he didn't follow her. Not to her apartment, not to the little café down the street, not even to the streets themselves. As she walked, the mere sight of the walk sign yanked up the loneliness. Driving, the thought of that clutch and all its inherent problems knifed through her heart. At the park oblivious to the darkness and the rain, she got out and walked over to the tree as her heart flew with the memory of his kite into the sky. Leaning against the tree as the cold rain dripped around her, she closed her eyes, trying to breathe. The farther she ran, the closer he got, and for the life of her, she couldn't figure out how to run any faster.

"I called you Thursday," Gabe said that evening as they sat at the tables long after everyone else had gone on stand down. Jeff didn't look up. His mind was too heavy to let him. "I thought maybe we could hit the racquetball courts or something, but I guess you were busy."

Slowly Jeff nodded.

"You know it might help to talk about it," Gabe finally said. "I'm not Ashley, but I can do a mean imitation of her. 'Now, Jeff, this is what you should do...'"

Frustrated, Jeff scratched his head. "I wish somebody could tell me what to do."

"Well, what're your options?"

"Homicide or suicide."

Gabe's eyebrows shot up in concern.

"I try to make this work, and end up killing her. Or I don't and end up killing myself," Jeff clarified plaintively. "Great choices, huh?"

"Isn't there a middle ground?"

Jeff shook his head. "Not that I see." He cracked his fist on the table. "Ugh, if I could just get her out of my head…"

"Do you really want to?" Gabe asked.

For a moment Jeff thought about that question and then lifted his gaze. "No."

"I love him," Lisa said two seconds after the door swung open to reveal Eve standing on the other side of the threshold in a bathrobe and pink slippers.

"Lisa, you're soaking wet."

Forlorn and trembling, Lisa hadn't even noticed that fact. "What am I going to do, Eve?"

Gently Eve reached out and took hold of Lisa's arm to pull her into the apartment. "First of all we're going to get you dry so you don't catch pneumonia. Then we're going to get you something warm to drink and have a little chat about making absurdly illogical choices."

"I thought I could do this," Lisa said later as she sat on Eve's couch, drinking the mocha-flavored coffee and pushing her still-wet hair back with her fingers. "I really did. I thought if I just kept going, kept working, kept moving, that I would forget about him."

"You're asking a lot from work," Eve said skeptically.

Lisa raked her hand across her damp nose in frustration. "Then he came the other night, and all my plans just blew up in my face. Now all I can think about is where he is and how he is and how much I want to see him again." She took a small sip of the coffee, which did nothing to warm her frozen insides. "I can't even think straight anymore. It feels like I'm going crazy."

"It feels like you're in love."

Lisa shook her head and closed her eyes, laying her head backward on the couch back. "I'm just so confused."

"About what?"

"About everything—where I want this to go, why I can't get him out of my head like I've done all the rest of them. I've never seen myself with someone like Jeff. Jeez, I've never seen myself with anyone—much less someone like Jeff. I mean he's sweet and kind and completely wonderful…"

"Yeah, just the kind you want to throw back."

"But he won't talk to me," Lisa said in frustration. "And then there's this whole fireman thing which makes me completely nuts." Eve nodded slowly, and Lisa's heart fell when she realized she shouldn't be laying this on the one person who understood all too well. "I'm sorry. I shouldn't…"

"No," Eve said softly. "It's okay." She sighed and then looked at Lisa. "When I first met Dustin, and he told me he wanted to be a fireman. I thought, 'Oh, cool. Saving lives. Making a difference. Awesome.' Later, of course, the fact that in order to save those lives he had to risk his own occurred to me. But by then I loved him, and there was no going back."

"But how did you do it? How do you say, 'Go ahead, put your life on the line every day, and I'll just sit back and hope it all works out for the best.'"

"Well, I did some of that too, but early on we made a pact to spend every moment we could together. That way if something ever did happen, we would know we hadn't wasted time being angry with each other over the job." Eve exhaled. "See, a lot of people live their lives taking for granted that they're going to have a tomorrow. Dustin and I never did that. We were thankful for every minute we had together." The words stopped for a moment. "I have no regrets."

"But he's gone. Aren't you angry about that?"

"I get angry, and sad, and terrified, but mostly I'm just thankful that even if we didn't have forever on this earth together, we had the time we did. Because of Dustin, I know what love is— I've felt it. I've experienced it. I know the highs it can take you and the lows it can drop you, but I have to tell you if I had to do it all over again, even knowing what I know now, I'd do it all again in a heartbeat."

Lisa shook her head slowly. "I don't know if I can have that much faith."

"There are more things in this world than what we can see, Lis. Like that night of the fire. I'd never been gone when he was on-duty before. It was like an unspoken vigil I kept—sitting here in the dark waiting for that door to open the next morning. Then my company wanted me to go to Dallas that weekend. I didn't want to go—not because of me but because of Dustin, but he wouldn't hear of me staying here. I had to 'take the next step up' and if going to Dallas would help me do that, then that's what he wanted me to do.

"He took me to the airport, and right before I got on that plane, he took me in his arms, and he told me that he loved me forever. I can't explain it, but I think he knew."

"You never got to say good-bye," Lisa said with understanding.

Softly Eve smiled. "We didn't have to. It was never good-bye with me and Dustin. It was always until I see you again. That was Dustin's idea because I had such a hard time when he'd leave at first. So we didn't say good-bye, we always said, 'until I see you again.' And it's true, too. I know there'll be a time and a place somewhere down the line that fires don't happen and people don't die, and we'll be together again. Until then, I know his love is with me every day."

In theory it sounded so good. In reality it sounded more difficult than anything Lisa had ever done.

"You have to learn to let go," Eve said. "Life will take its course with or without you grabbing the wheel and trying to force it to be one way or the other—all that does is make your arms hurt. Let go and trust that whatever happens, it's for the best."

"That was for the best? Dustin dying?"

"From my little perspective it doesn't always feel that way, but I don't see the bigger picture either. I have to trust that in the bigger picture it makes sense—that it was for the best."

"He was lucky to have you."

"We were lucky to have each other." A soft peace slid into Eve's eyes. "Think about that, Lisa. You may not have tomorrow. Do you really want to spend the time you do have pushing Jeff away?"

In the middle of her heart, Lisa knew Eve was right. If he died tomorrow, what would she have gained by not being with him today? Would it make the cut of his loss hurt any less? When Eve smiled and said it was time for her to get some sleep, Lisa nodded, thanked her, and then curled under the blankets on the couch. No, she decided as the questions ran through her again. If he died tomorrow, she would regret every single second she had spent keeping them apart. Every single one.

As a peace offering and to say, "I'm sorry for not being here for you like I promised," Jeff stopped off at a flower shop on the way to Eve's Sunday morning. She wasn't expecting him until noon, but the night at the station—minus his brain—had been quiet. He had gotten enough sleep. What he needed now was to talk to someone who could make his heart believe he was doing the right thing by staying away. It didn't feel like the right thing, no matter how many times he'd tried to explain to himself that it was what she wanted.

At the apartment he grabbed the yellow rose from the seat, ran his fingers through his hair, and took a breath. Seeing Eve, understanding the pain he was keeping Lisa from would be exactly what he needed, that would be enough to make his decision solid. Of that and only that he was sure. On the doorstep, he checked his watch as he reached over and rang the doorbell. 7:38. He dug a hand into the denim and brown suede jacket pocket and waited. No answer. Again he reached over and hit the doorbell, listening this time to be sure it had rung on the other side.

"I'll get it!" he heard the voice in the second before the door swung open. Wrinkled T-shirt, faded jeans, sleep still hanging around her, Lisa stood there, and his breath snagged.

For a six whole seconds all he did was stare. "Lisa? Wh...?"

Her eyes widened in total shock. "Jeff. What're you doing here?" Slowly her gaze slid down from his eyes to his shoulders to the rose in his hand.

Awkwardness dropped over him. He tried to smile, but it fell halfway to his face. "Umm, I didn't know you were..." He looked past her into the apartment. "Is Eve here?"

At that moment Eve strode out, hair up in a white towel, white bathrobe, and pink slippers. "Who is it, Lis?"

"Umm," Lisa said as though she couldn't quite decide if it really was who she thought it was.

"It's me," Jeff said carefully stepping into the room as scenarios of how and why Lisa was standing on that doorstep raced through him. "Umm, I thought if I came early..." One thumb ran down the length of his nose. He glanced at Lisa, a move which took his heart to his shoes. "I didn't know you were going to have company."

Eve laughed. "I didn't either." She turned and went into the little kitchen. "I only got enough donuts for me. I didn't know I was going to have a party." She threw the little box onto the table. "But you're welcome to them. There's milk in the frig. I'm just going to go get ready." With that she turned the corner to the stairs and disappeared up them.

"Oh, man, I'm sorry," Jeff said, breathing the words more than saying them. "If I would've known you were…"

"No, no." Lisa shook her head quickly. "It's me. I didn't tell Eve I was coming. I just showed up."

He wished there were sensible words to ask her why.

"Nice flower," she finally said, nodding at it.

When he looked down, he hardly saw it. "Oh, yeah. I brought it for Eve. I thought she… probably hasn't had some in… awhile." He was having trouble breathing and swallowing and thinking.

Lisa nodded. "I can put it in some water for her—if you want."

Slowly the rose came up, and he handed the stem over to her. He watched her take it, and he followed her past the little table into the kitchen. There he leaned on the counter and put his hands in his pockets. "So, you've been here all night?"

"Since about one," Lisa said, and concern traced through him. Watching her was like watching his soul and yet not being able to touch it. She was busy getting a vase and filling it with water. "Eve didn't tell me you were coming."

"Yeah." He scratched the side of his ear. "Well, I wasn't supposed to be here until noon, but she mentioned church, and… well, we had a good night at the station, so I thought… maybe it would be a good idea to just come on over." How good of an idea that was, he couldn't really tell at the moment.

"Perfect," Lisa said, turning with the rose positioned flawlessly in the little vase. She set it on the table and sat down. Pulling her foot into the chair with her, she looked up at him.

Absolutely, his brain said, looking at her. "So, were you planning to stay all day?"

"I don't know. I hadn't really planned anything," Lisa said. The waves of her hair drifted down around her face. "You?"

"For awhile. I was going to take Eve out to eat or something, spend some time with her."

Lisa nodded, then reached over and popped the donut box open. "Want one?"

He shook his head. At the moment his stomach was in too many knots to eat. "I'm not really hungry."

Silence descended between them as Lisa set the box back down. She didn't bother to take a donut either.

"So, how's work?" he finally asked, fumbling for something to talk about.

"Good," she said softly. "Thanks to you." Her gaze swung over to him as she shook her head. "I still don't know how you did it."

"Did what?"

"Got my employees to be competent for a change."

His face fell in confusion. "I didn't do anything."

"Yes, you did. When it's me, they couldn't put one foot in front of the other without falling over themselves. With you, they're like... brilliant. I don't know how you do that."

"I trust them," he said gently.

She seemed to coil back at that statement. "I trust them."

"No," he said carefully. "You expect them to make a mess of things and so they do. Besides they know it'll never be good enough for you, so they don't bother to do it right."

"But that's their job."

"It's not about the job. It's about trusting someone else to handle something."

Her gaze dropped to the table. "Trusting isn't really my strong suit."

"Doesn't mean that has to be true forever. Take Sherie, she came up with that database in about five minutes. Would you have let her do that for you, or would you have done it yourself figuring she couldn't do it right?"

There was no answer.

"See, Lisa, it's not a question of letting them do it poorly. It's a question of trusting them enough to make them want to do it right. Right now, you've set it up so they don't own their work. You do. It all comes back to you because if they screw up, they know you'll fix it."

"But it's my company."

"And you have every right to run it the way you want. But as long as you run yourself into the ground fixing their mistakes, they're going to let you."

Lisa thought about that a long minute. "Well, how do I not

make everything mine?"

"Little steps," Jeff said. "The first time I walked on duty, do you think they put me in charge of a call? No way. They gave me one job to do. I did that job. I learned that job, and when they knew I could do that, then they started shifting me around to the other jobs. I'm not ready yet, but one day I want to be the one running a call. It's not all or nothing. There can be steps along the way."

Steps along the way. Three forward, four backward. That's what it felt like with them, but at least this was better than avoiding each other at all costs.

"Don't tell me you don't like donuts," Eve said, turning the corner from the stairs, and Jeff's gaze snapped up to her. Fully dressed, hair done, and heels on, she looked the epitome of the fashion industry he knew she so loved. Dustin would've been in awe as always, and Jeff smiled at that thought.

Jeff straightened with the knowing look Eve gave them. "What time did you say church was?"

"Nine." Eve pulled a sugary pastry out and took a bite. "Well, if you're not going to eat them..."

Slowly Lisa stood, and Jeff wasn't sure that he liked the sadness in the hunch of her shoulders. "I'd better get going."

He nearly moved to stop her, but at the last possible second he held the protest back.

"Oh, you don't have to," Eve said, nearly choking on the donut piece in her mouth. "You could go with us."

However, Lisa shook her head. "I've got some work I've got to get done."

"On Sunday?" Eve asked in horror.

"Yeah," Lisa said, and Jeff's heart fell at the thought that they wouldn't get to spend the day together. Lisa went into the living room and gathered her things. "Thanks for everything, Eve."

"Sure, girl." Leaving the donut on the table, Eve went to Lisa, and put an arm over her shoulder. "Anytime." Eve's gaze lowered. "Think about what I said. Okay?"

In slow inches Lisa nodded and then backed away. The fight to keep the tears and emotion at bay was obvious. So was her intention to get as far away from him as fast as she could. "I'll see you later."

"Drive carefully," Jeff called after her as she stepped out the door. His heart splintered the words across the pain in the final look she gave him.

Who could focus on anything? Lisa asked as she drove back through the streets now kissed by the golden sun of autumn. Driving, breathing, living. It all felt so hard. Everything had felt so incredibly hard since... that phone call. Yes, that phone call had changed everything for her, yet what had it really changed between them? The illusion that she was in control? Her fingers gripped the wheel, white-knuckled. Facing that realization pulled her ego to its knees.

Yet it was true. Until that moment she had believed she had the power to guide where she was going in life. Since that moment she had been rudderless—adrift in an angry sea that was bent on pulling her down into its depths. "But I don't know how to let go," she pleaded. "I don't know how, God."

However, God was apparently busy because there was no answer. In frustration she reached down and flipped on the radio.

"He doesn't call you to understand everything in every moment," the preacher on the radio said with that same lilt that all preachers on Sunday have. Frustrated, Lisa reached for the button. "When Peter stepped out of that boat, do you really think Christ required that he understand how it was happening—how he was able to walk on water?" Lisa's hand slipped back to the steering wheel as her heart tripped over the words. "No, all Christ said was, 'Come.' All Peter heard was, 'Come.' And he did. As long as Peter kept his eyes forward—on the God who loved Him infinitely and would never allow the winds and the waves of doubt to overcome him—as long as Peter did that, those waves had no power over him.

"It was *only* when Peter stopped looking at our Lord. It was *only* when he looked down at the waves and only when he saw the wind. It was only when he stopped trusting Christ and started trusting his own understanding and his own power that he began to sink. And he cried out, 'Lord, save me!' Of course, you know the story. Jesus stretched out his hand. He took hold of Peter, and what did He say? 'Oh, ye of little faith, why did you doubt?'

"That's where the story stops, and we chide Peter, 'Why did you doubt? Christ was right there. He would've kept you above the waves if you would've just…' Just what? Not tried to handle the situation on your own? But don't we all do that? Don't we all look around and freak out because the wind and the waves are too much for us to handle alone? Of course they are. But they have no power if we keep our eyes on the Christ standing before us, and in every moment Christ is always before us. He is already there— where you fear to go. He is already there, and He has made it safe for you to pass.

"But instead of looking at Him, instead of trusting Him, we look around and we see the wind and the waves pulling at us. They throw us off balance and threaten to drown us. It's when we think we have to handle all those things on our own that we begin to sink in doubt and fear, and we cry out, 'Lord, save me!' Just like Peter did. But the truth is the same for you as it was for Peter. All you have to do is keep your eyes on the Christ before you, the Christ—who loves you infinitely and would never allow the winds and the waves of doubt overcome you. When you do that, the waves, the winds—they have no power so long as you keep your eyes on Him and His plan for your life. So, then the question is, when He says, 'Come,' what is your response?

"Do you instantly look at the wind and waves and say, 'No way, how can I, are You crazy? ' Or do you step out of that boat and walk toward Him with confidence, knowing He will take care of everything else?"

Lisa's chest felt as if the air had been going in, stacking on top of itself until there wasn't room for any more. What had Jeff said about small steps? About trusting? What had Eve said about letting go? In different words, they were all saying the same thing—she, the perennial ice queen who could handle everything on her own, was kidding herself that she was going anywhere on her own power. No, she was stuck, right where she had been all those long years before when she had vowed that unlike her mother, she would never fall into the trap of needing someone so much she couldn't let go and then have them let her down anyway.

That vow, so sensible at the time, had cost her time. It had cost her being close to anyone, letting anyone get close to her. And it had nearly cost her a life with the man she loved. Of course, one decision didn't banish all the other doubts, but if she kept her gaze on God's plan for her life instead of on the waves and the wind around her, His power could become hers and together…

"Okay, God, I'm ready. Show me the first small step," she prayed, and for the first time in a forever of prayers, she felt like Someone had actually heard.

"You're awful quiet," Eve said as she and Jeff sat by the big bay windows of the restaurant. Then she smiled. "Not that you're ever very loud."

The words running through Jeff's head pulled thoughtfulness to his face. "I was just thinking about what the guy said in the sermon today—you know, about how if Friday had been the end, then the cross would be a symbol of tragedy instead of the symbol of hope." His fingers went up and drifted across the metal cross at his chest. "We always want it to be Sunday, don't we? We don't want to go through the Fridays of life, but the resurrection of Sunday would mean nothing without the tragedy of Friday."

"I don't think I'd ever thought about it like that either," Eve said softly. "I kind of feel like I'm at Saturday now—waiting, not knowing what's coming next. Sometimes I think what's coming will be Sunday, and sometimes I'm afraid it's going to be another Friday."

Jeff nodded. "I've been at Saturday so long, I'm not sure I'd even recognize Sunday anymore." He held up the cross. "Mom gave me this."

"At the academy," Eve said, and Jeff nodded. "I take it she wasn't thrilled about the fire department thing."

"No. She didn't understand. She thought I had a death wish." He shrugged. "Maybe I did."

"What does she think now?"

He breathed in the question. "I don't know. I haven't seen her since she left that day. I thought it'd be easier for her if I stayed away."

Eve twirled her fork on her plate although she didn't seem to see the food there. "How would that be easier?"

Jeff wasn't eating much either. Food had lost its allure. "That way, she wouldn't have to think about me every day and remember everything she's lost."

"Your dad and Kit."

Slowly he nodded. "She blamed me for it."

"No, she didn't."

It would've been nice to believe that, but he knew better. "Yeah, she did, but even if she hadn't, she should have. I killed the two people she loved most in this world. I did, and she never forgave me for that." He sat back and closed his eyes against the pain that admission brought up. "If I'd just put those dumb rags away like she told me to… Why was that so hard? But no, I had to throw them on the bench like a spoiled little brat. Kit could go to the party. I couldn't. It seemed like such a big deal at the time. Now…"

There was only softness in Eve's eyes. "You were a kid."

Anger slashed over him. "Yeah, a kid who should've known better. A kid who did know better. Oily rags and a water heater flame don't mix. I knew that, but that wasn't what I was thinking about. Not to even mention that propane tank Dad had told me to move six times already." Jeff sighed softly. "But I was too busy as usual, with my own life. Too busy to worry about little details like that. And then Mom was left with me—the one who didn't have the funny stories to tell. The one who couldn't tell a joke to save his life. The one who was a terribly poor substitute for her favorite."

"Jeff…"

"It's true." He stopped her protests with one look. "It is. Do you know she didn't get to tell them she loved them? She didn't. She told me that one night, that all she wanted was to hear them say it and to be able to tell them one more time that she loved them. I took that away from her. And because of my stupidity, she'll never have that chance again."

"And what about you?"

His eyebrows furrowed. "What about me?"

"You're still here. Why doesn't she tell you she loves you?"

He didn't answer. He couldn't.

"Jeff…?"

"She'd never bothered to before, why would she strain herself now?"

"But…?"

"I never quite fit into her plans," Jeff said, his gaze settling on his fork with the admission. "She was supposed to go back to work after Kit. International finance—that was her dream. She was on the fast track to being the vice president of her company. Then she got pregnant with me, and her whole life changed. I guess she had

309

a lot of trouble because she was in bed for like the last three months of it. When I finally got here, I was a pretty sick little kid. If it made you sick, I caught it. We were in the hospital more than we were home. Daycare was out, so finally her work had to find someone else. Eventually I grew out of that, but her career was shot by that time. I can always remember Dad trying to make me not notice how she felt about me. He'd take me out, to do things, fly kites, fix cars, but I knew. It wasn't hard to notice. On Saturday mornings I'd hear them in the kitchen all laughing and talking, and I'd know that the second I stepped through that door, the fun would be over."

His gaze never lifted from the table. "Then I burned the house down, and as bad as it was before that, things were worse after. She'd scream at me for every little thing. If supper wasn't ready on time or if I left my car too close to the fire hydrant, or a hundred-thousand other things. I tried, but..." He exhaled. "I went to business school. I thought that would make her happy. Dad always said he wanted his sons to graduate from college. Kit never got that chance, so I went even though I didn't really want to. That day I stood on that stage, I looked out across that whole auditorium of thousands of people, and there wasn't one face out there I knew. Not a single one." He laughed softly. "She still wouldn't know about what I'm doing now if it wasn't for Dustin."

"The letter."

Jeff nodded. "I think he wrote more of it than I did. I never would've had the guts to put it all on paper. Honestly I figured she'd trash it the second she got it anyway." His thumb traced over the cross. "She told me to tell them not to call her if something ever happened because she couldn't handle another funeral. Then she gave me this, told me good luck, and left. I haven't seen her since."

"You know she thinks about you every day."

"I doubt it."

"And every day she wishes she had done things differently, and that she could have another chance."

"Yeah, right. And you know this how?"

Eve looked at him. "Because I know how it feels to push away just when you need to be there the most."

In the darkened apartment as the lights from below traced across his ceiling, Jeff lay watching them. One day their time on this earth would come to an end. There was no surer bet in the world. She would leave him, or he would leave her, but regardless of the circumstances, the opportunity to say those words would forever be gone. How many times had he wished that Dad or Kit could come back for one moment and give her what she so desperately wanted? Yet his own heart wrapped around those words like a dog hording food. True, she had never said them to him, but he hadn't said them to her either. If the opportunity evaporated before his eyes, would it be her he blamed for that, or...?

His gaze slipped over to the clock. It was late, and yet how much later was it getting with every tick of that clock? Would he have tomorrow if he didn't take the chance tonight?

Pushing the idea ahead of him, he swung his legs out of the bed and dragged them through the hallway to the phone on the counter. It was one phone call, and yet it was so much more. A slow button at a time, he dialed the number and waited through the rings. When it clicked, his heart clicked with it. "Hello?"

Time froze around that voice. "Mom?" He fell through the word, his heart plummeting ahead of him. "Umm, it's Jeff."

"Jeff, what's wrong?" He heard the concern flood through her voice.

"Nothing," he said softly. "I just wanted to call and tell you that I love you."

The words rang on the wires between them followed by a long moment of utter silence.

"You...? Oh, well, I love you, too," she said slowly with surprise lacing the words. "Where are you?"

"At home."

Another long moment of silence. "Are you still... with the...?"

"Department? Yeah. I still am."

"Oh."

His brain fought for something to say. "Are you still...?"

"Liquidating estates," she said slowly. "It keeps me busy."

He wound an elbow up to the countertop. "How are you?"

"Good. I'm going on a trip to San Marcos with some friends next week."

"Oh, yeah? That sounds like fun."

"Yeah, it does." The wires buzzed loudly between them. For a long moment he waited, thinking, hoping that she would ask about him, but finally she said, "Well, I'm sure you've got other things to be doing. I'd better let you go."

"Yeah." The word hurt. "I guess."

"Take care of yourself, okay?"

"I will," he said, willing strength into his voice. "You, too."

When he hung up, the center of him ripped in two, and he laid his forehead on the corner of the wall. She could do that. Just hang up and go on with her life. She could, but somehow he couldn't. He needed someone he could love, someone who could love him in return. He needed that, and of every single person on the face of the earth, there was only one person who fit that description. Closing his eyes, he picked up the phone and dialed the number. He had to swallow the protests in his head. Strength was in the asking. Courage was holding out a hand and trusting that she would take it. Faith was believing that Sunday would follow Saturday as Saturday had followed Friday—if only you held onto the hope long enough.

The phone clicked. "Hello?"

"Lisa? Hi, it's Jeff. I need to see you."

Twenty-Three

"What is up?" Lisa asked in barely concealed panic when she opened her door at nearly midnight to find him looking like he was about to jump out of his skin at any moment.

"I'm sorry. I know it's late, but this couldn't wait." Jeff ran a frustrated hand through his hair.

Slowly she opened the door wider. "Come on in."

He stepped past her, and she felt the pent up energy flowing off of him. When she closed the door and turned to him, he hadn't moved as far as she had thought. He was standing there, two feet from her, and if ever she had felt out of control, this was it.

"So what's the emergency?" The concern in her narrowed her gaze like a laser.

With one look at her, his body shook slightly. "This isn't right." Quickly his hand grabbed hers. "Here, sit down."

Uncertainly she let him lead her to the couch where she sat, but still he didn't calm down. Instead he paced back and forth in front of her. She watched him—back and forth, back and forth. "Whatever it is, you can say it. I'm a big girl, I can handle it." *Well, me and God*, her heart said, and she smiled. But his pacing continued. "Look, Jeff, it's okay. Really." One of her hands caught his as he passed, and he looked down at her. She tried to get peace into her eyes. "It's okay. Really. Whatever it is, you can tell me."

A moment. A nod, and slowly his body slid onto the couch next to hers although the jitters didn't leave. It took him a long moment even then to say anything. Finally he let out a long breath.

"I've known how I felt about you for a long time now, but I've had a hard time putting it into words."

"Yeah," she said as worry for him brushed her heart, and she kept her gaze trained only on him.

When he looked at her and smiled, some of his nervousness slid away. "Before I met you, I didn't have much luck with girls. They didn't understand me. I didn't understand them. At least that was my excuse. The truth was I knew that sooner or later I would do something to ruin anything that got started, so I just didn't start. I stayed in my little hole and hoped no one would notice me. It was easier that way. Then you came along, and all of a sudden that little hole wasn't nearly as comfortable as it had been before. I can't explain it, but for the first time I felt safe with you—like I mattered too."

"You do matter."

He put a finger up to stop her. "Shh. I need to say this." She nodded wordlessly, and his finger dropped away. "There are seventeen million reasons why I should've just walked away from this thing right from the beginning, but I couldn't. I couldn't because you make it safe for me to live, to be myself, even when I don't think 'myself' is all that great. I like who I am when I'm with you, but I think that I haven't been honest with you about who that is."

Her gaze searched his profile as he let go of her hand and took a breath. He closed his eyes to get the words out. "I didn't become a fireman to help or to save lives. I became one because I was trying to make up for something I did." His voice faded out, and her spirit fell with concern. He looked right at her then, and nothing in her could look away. "When I was seventeen, I got careless with some rags I was using on my car. My mom told me to put them away, and at the time I was mad at her, so I threw them on my work bench and left."

The words slowed. "I heard the box drop. I can still hear that thud in my head, but I didn't go back to pick them up. I was mad, and I thought I had every right to be, so I left them there and walked out.

"Mom had a meeting that night. She had just left, and Dad and Kit were working on some computer program Kit had brought home from college. I went to my room and slammed the door planning to mope there all night." All the words stopped as he sat squeezing the pain from his eyes and trying to breathe. Finally he sucked in a ragged breath and forced himself to continue. "It all happened so fast. There was this unbelievable explosion. I didn't even know what it was at the time, but it knocked me off my bed. When I hit the floor, all I could think was that whatever had happened was bad.

"By the time I got to my door, there was fire and smoke everywhere. I couldn't see anything. It was just all smoke and flames, but I knew where Dad and Kit were working. It was in the direction that all the flames were coming from, so…"

Lisa knew him, and she knew what was coming although he didn't speak the words immediately. The nightmare hung there between them, so close she could feel the heat and the terror of that seventeen-year-old boy knowing his family was in danger, and yet helpless to get them out.

Unshed tears clung to him. He beat them back. "I went as far as I could into it, but the smoke was just so thick, and the fire was everywhere." He shook his head. "Finally I got down on my hands and knees and started crawling, yelling their names, listening for them so that maybe I could find them. I don't know how long I crawled like that. It could have been minutes. It could have been hours. I heard something once, and I tried to get to it, but when I got to where I thought it was, there was nothing there—at least I couldn't see anything. All I remember is knowing that if I didn't get to them, no one else would."

He exhaled slowly. "The next thing I remember is the fireman dragging me out onto the lawn. I looked up, and I remember how bright the stars were. Then I remembered why I was out there and who was still in the house. I begged the guy to go back in and find them. That's all I could think, 'Get them out. Please, just get them out.'"

The words stopped for a long moment, and then he shook his head. "He shouldn't have gone back in. It was too dangerous. I know that now. He shouldn't have gone back in, but he did because I asked him to."

Softly Lisa put a hand on Jeff's knee which he obviously didn't feel as he fought through the memories surrounding him. Still, she wanted to let him know, she was right there for him—whether he realized it or not.

"I remember watching the roof cave in," he said as if he was seeing the scene before him now. "That whole section just collapsed into this huge ball of flames." Haze took over his voice. "He'd just gone in… just had time to get right in the middle of that thing when it fell. I sat there on the grass, and I knew he wouldn't make it out, they wouldn't make it out, and it was all my fault."

"He was a fireman, he knew the risks," Lisa said, trying to make it better, but knowing all too well the other side of the fireman's story.

"And he wanted to help because I'd asked him to." Jeff's head fell forward. "Just like Dustin."

That name shattered across her heart. "Oh, Jeff, that wasn't your fault."

"That night, I yelled at Dustin for help," Jeff said only hollowness in his voice. "There were these three people I found trapped, and I thought we could get them out. I couldn't do it alone, so I called for help, and Dustin came. If it hadn't been for me, he would be at home with Eve right now."

"Oh, no, Jeff, that's not true. It was an accident."

"I heard the ceiling fall," he said, the words broken and splintered. The tears began to fall for real then. "I heard it… and I should've gone back right then. If I had, maybe…"

Seriousness drilled into her. "No, now you listen to me. You had no control over that ceiling. You had no control over where he would be when it fell. It was an accident."

"Just like the rags?" Jeff asked, and bitterness seared the question. "They were an accident too. Right? An accident that never would've happened if it hadn't been for me."

Gently Lisa slid over to him and pulled him into her arms. His head dropped onto her shoulder. "Okay. Now, you listen to me, Jeff Taylor. There are things in this life that we can't control. Things that make no sense while we're here. But you can't blame yourself for them, and you can't spend your life trying to right the past by torturing yourself now. Helping people is who you are. It's you—not who you're trying to be, not who you want to be. It's you, and I love you for that. But putting these obligations to help on yourself because it's going to change the past doesn't work. It's won't. It can't."

His head moved side to side. "I just wish I could get them back."

Love for him slid through her. "Of course you do because you care."

"I wish I didn't. Life would be a whole lot easier."

"No," she said softly. "Pushing people away because they might hurt you doesn't make things easier. It just makes you lonely and miserable. Believe me, I've found that one out the hard way."

He exhaled, sat up, and put his elbows on his knees. Then he dropped his face into his hands. "I'm so tired of hurting. I'm so tired of waking up every morning thinking that maybe today I'll do something to make it go away, and climbing into bed every night knowing it's all still the same."

Lisa laid her hand on his back. "You're still punishing yourself, torturing yourself for something you had no control over. You're still holding onto fear and pain that's keeping you stuck right where you were when that fireman put you on the grass. But pain and fear don't move you forward, Jeff. They're holding you in that moment."

"But it happened. I don't know how to get it out of my head, how to make the memories stop."

"Have you ever tried forgiving yourself?"

His head shook slowly. "Look around at all the hurt I've caused. How can I forgive myself? People hate me because of the things I've done."

"No, they don't. They don't hate you, but even if they did, does anyone hate you more than you hate yourself?" Lisa watched him, knowing the answer to that question. "It's not easy, but after you've taken responsibility, there comes a point when you have to step out of the boat and let go."

He looked at her in confusion. "Huh?"

She laughed. "It's something I heard on the radio. Life's not easy—for anybody. The wind and the waves are right there all the time waiting to knock you over, but the point is you have to step out of the boat anyway. You have to trust God enough, to believe that He sees the bigger picture and would never let the wind and the waves get the better of you."

Jeff laughed softly and then sighed. "That sounds great, but I don't know how to do that."

"Small steps," she said with a smile. "Just like you told me. You have to take small steps. Take the first step, then He'll show you the next one." Neither of them moved for a long moment. "So the question is: what's your first step?"

When he looked back up, his gaze caught hers, and she could see the confusion and the interminable ache in the depths of them.

"Could you hold me?" he finally asked softly.

If that was the first step, the others should be the easiest of her life. Her arms slipped over his shoulders. "As long as you need me to."

Delegating. It was a word Lisa had heard only in the context of reading the dictionary definition. On Monday morning however, as she sat at her desk staring at the stacks of work in front of her, she thought about him. Small steps. If he was willing to take a few, then what excuse did she have? She picked up a stack of folders, laden with information, and walked into Sherie's office.

"These have been on my desk for six months now," Lisa said, "and I don't think I've even looked at them. Would you do something with them?"

Sherie looked up blankly. "What?"

"File them, trash them, whatever needs done with them."

"O…kay." The stack landed in Sherie's hands.

"And I've got six more stacks just like that one, so when you're finished with it, you can come get some more."

Perplexed, Sherie nodded, and Lisa went back to her office. Now to give Joel his assignment.

The classes, the information, somehow they all felt different today. Small steps. That's what Jeff was taking today by coming to class, not to somehow change what had already happened, but to move forward with his life. A life that he now chose because he wanted to—not because he felt he had to.

As the lecture continued, Jeff thought about Lisa, and the truth was he couldn't imagine moving forward without her. However, although she hadn't run the night before, he still had no idea if her stance toward their chances of being together had changed. His pen slipped across the paper unguided. He needed to find that out. He needed to know if they were destined to be forever friends or if she would step out of the boat with him and ask for more. And the only way to find out was to ask.

"Knock, knock," Jeff said at 5:30 as he stood outside her office door, rapping it with his knuckle. However, when he opened it, he wasn't at all sure he was even in the right office. Her desk was... clean. He could see the wood it was made of. There were no files, no folders threatening to slide off, only her computer and a few pieces of paper, lying there, and life shifted at his feet.

"What? Are you checking up on me?" Lisa asked from behind him. Jeff spun around to her. Her smile was lit by the glow in her eyes.

Stunned, he took the sight of her in. "I thought I must have the wrong office."

"It looks that way, doesn't it?" she asked teasingly. She stepped past him, through her door, and around her desk.

"Where'd all the files go?" he asked as he followed her in and sat in the chair.

She shrugged. "Ask Sherie."

"Sherie?" he asked uncertainly. "And you're all right with that?"

"Hey, I have a place to put my mouse now." She picked up the gray object and laid it down. "I'd say that's a good first step. Wouldn't you?"

"Sounds like it."

"So, how about you? How was class today?"

"Good. We went over the different kinds of seating in an airplane," he said as he folded his hands in front of him. "I never knew there were so many. Bi-seats, tri-seats, seven across. Planes with both, different configurations and combinations, and you're supposed to know what each of them have just by knowing what kind of plane it is."

"Why?" she asked as if she really cared.

For one second he hesitated, knowing the road that question led down. "Because if one crashes, you have to know where the passengers are, so you know what's worth going into and what's not."

Her gaze fell from his face. "So that's what this class is about—crashes?"

He nodded. "By next week we'll be out on the runway doing drills, running scenarios."

It was clear she was working through what he was telling her.

"What about work?"

"I'm on Wednesday and the rest of the week."

"Isn't that going to be tough—going to school and working?"

"It's not so bad. I did it last month, and it was okay. But then…" He pulled himself up with his elbow and looked over at her, hearing the words but not getting them all the way to his mouth.

She looked up at him, puzzled. "Then… what?"

He leaned his head to the side. "Well, I've got this other project I'm working on this month, and it's going to be taking up some time too."

"Oh, yeah? What's that?" she asked as if she genuinely had no idea.

"You," he said softly, gazing right at her, and her gaze swept over him. He looked at her, and the words he had been saying for a month but only in his head tumbled out. "Look, I know what you said that night at the fire station, on the steps, and I know why you said it. I know this isn't what you expected. And I know I don't have a choice but to give you one, but I still have to ask if you think we can find a way to make this work… us work? Or are you going to give up no matter what I think?"

For the longest moment of his life she said nothing. Finally she looked at him. "Well, what do you think?"

He laughed softly. "What do I think? Well, I know what I know. And what I know is that as hard as I've tried to make myself believe differently, I love you, Lisa. I have ever since the first minute I saw you. I've done everything I can to tell myself it's not going to work, that you don't need me like I need you, that you'd be better off without me, but the truth is I want this to work more than anything I've ever wanted in my life. I want you in my life, and I want to be in yours. That's what I know."

She sat in silence just blinking at him.

"Say something," he finally said, hoping his heart could take her next words.

"I don't know what to say," she finally said. "I thought I did. I thought I would, but now that I'm here, I don't."

"Well, what do you want to say?"

Breath slid from her. "I want to say, 'Jeff, you're the most wonderful person I've ever been with, and I'll do whatever it takes to make this work.'"

320

His heart slid through his chest. "But…"

She was still looking at him even as she shook her head. "But how can I be sure love is enough? I mean I want to believe it is. I want to, but I'm not sure I can."

"Why not?"

"Because I know reality now. I've seen it, and it scares me to death. It scares me that I can't just say, 'I don't want this' and walk away from you. It scares me that every time I see you, I have a hard time holding onto the reality that there might not be a next time. It scares me that I could be right that if I don't take this risk, I'll regret it forever. But it also scares me that I could be wrong when I feel like nothing can touch what I feel for you. What if it can? What if I trust this, and it's gone tomorrow?"

"What if you don't and it's gone tomorrow?" he asked. "Will that make it any better?"

She closed her eyes, and he saw her struggle. "I don't know. I just don't know. I'm so confused. My mind's all jumbled up, and I don't even know where to start sorting it out."

Slowly he stood, stepped around the desk to her chair, and sat on his heels in front of her. For the first time in a forever of hours, he felt completely at peace. Even if she didn't trust their love, he now did, and he knew it was enough. His fingers brushed over the hair at her temple, and her eyes opened. Her gaze searched into the depths of his heart.

"I'm not asking for now," he said as he gazed into the fear in her eyes. "I'm asking for when you're ready. Lisa, I want you with me. I do. I want to spend the rest of my life with you, and you need to know that if I have to wait forever for you to be ready, I will because I have no other choice. You're the one I'm meant to be with, and there'll never be anyone else. So when you're ready, I have a ring for your finger and a pillow for your head and a heart to hold yours forever. When you're ready, they're all waiting right here for you. Just say the word, and they're yours."

As she sank into his arms, peace had never felt so real. She was with him already, whether she knew that or accepted it or not. They were together—tied by an indestructible bond. There was no reason to deny it any longer, and the more Jeff trusted that, the more peace flooded his soul until all of life opened around him. He kissed the side of her hair. "I love you, Lisa, and I always will."

Being in his arms, it was the surest way to lose touch with all the rationalizations Lisa was clinging to for fear she would inextricably fall through the point of no return. Sure, Eve had said pushing him away would only lead to regrets, and she knew that was true. But still, something in her said losing him wouldn't kill her if she just held onto the belief that he wasn't her life, that she wasn't his—that together they weren't better than they were alone, that without him, her life could go on.

Although all her scrambled brain waves were telling her this made no sense, her arms wouldn't let him go. They clung there, holding him, clutching to him. She didn't want to let go, but if she admitted that… Fear surged through her. She was destined to lose. If she loved him and lost him, she lost. If she didn't love him and he walked away, she lost. Everywhere she looked was loss and heartache.

"Take your time," he said as the tears overtook her. "It's not now or never. It's now and forever."

But all she could think was, if only it were so easy.

That night as Lisa lay in bed, rolling until the blankets were in knots around her, she reached the point of the cracking of her sanity. "Ugh! Why is this so hard? I thought love was supposed to be easy."

"You're making it hard because you won't trust," a voice from the darkness said.

"I know, I know. Step out of the boat, but how can I do that? The boat is safe. Out there isn't."

"Don't let it fool you, Lisa. The boat's in the waves too."

In her mind she looked around. The voice was right. The little boat she was so furiously clinging to was being smashed at on all sides by the winds and the waves. "But I don't know how to do that. I don't know how to trust like that."

"Let go. Just let go, and believe I'll be enough to hold you up."

Her body hurt. Searing pain screeched through her as she held on, fighting to right her world on her own.

"Until you trust, love is just an illusion. Love can't live where there's no trust."

"But what if I fall?"

"If the possibility of falling were not there, trust would not be necessary. If you could do it all on your own, love would not be necessary. If trust and love were not necessary, there would be no need for other people or for Me. But those things are not true, and you know they aren't. They are manufactured beliefs that you thought would keep you safe. But they won't. You know that now, so let go of them."

"I'm trying."

"No, trying is not doing. Doing is doing. Let them go, Lisa. You can't hold onto them and be free. It doesn't work that way."

Squeezing her eyes closed against the shards of pain slashing through her, her own words drifted back to her. "Torturing yourself by holding onto fear and pain is keeping you stuck right where you are." And where she was, was in a sinking boat, clinging to beliefs that were holding her back from really living. Slowly her stifling grip eased from the fear she had held so close to her heart for so long. It was the fear that said people would always let her down, that she could trust no one, that alone was better than being hurt. But as she let go, she realized that alone hurt, too. That fear wasn't keeping her from getting hurt it was keeping her in the hurt—permanently.

The handhold on the boat slipped from her grasp, and after one small drop down, she was floating, sustained by a power that was not her own. On her own she had struggled and fought to make life safe for herself, never really feeling the safety she so desperately sought. On the wings of this power, however, she was safe. She could feel it even now. It wasn't a mere feeling. It was a part of her. Simple as that.

"And Jeff?" she asked, knowing the answer would be there.

"What does your heart say?"

Her spirit laughed. There was no question about that.

Lisa called him the next morning the moment the sun broke through her window, but he was already gone for work. She called him at the station when she got to work, but they were out training. That was all right, she thought as she laid the phone in the cradle. Some things are meant to be said in person anyway. All day she thought about him, and all day her thoughts were not those of fearing for his safety, but of knowing that he was with her no matter what.

So, when the clock wound around to after five, she gathered her things and drove home to get ready. It wasn't a date, but it felt like the biggest one of her life. With her hair down and the soft, pastel blue dress, swirling at her ankles, Lisa took one more look in the mirror. Accepting at a fire station wasn't exactly her idea of romantic, and yet in a strange way it made more sense than accepting anywhere else.

As she drove through the streets, she remembered the day she had run away from this life, but it wasn't with the guilt she had thought she would feel. To be where she was now, out walking on the waves, it was necessary to have been in that boat first. Without trust there is no love, and without risk, love would mean nothing. Without the wind and the waves, walking like that would not be the miracle she now felt it to be.

She checked her watch when she got out at the fire station. 7:22. Stand down time. With a snap she opened the station door and stepped into it. However, in the next breath she realized the station was empty. No trucks, no people.

"Hello?" she called, but no one answered. Her gaze dropped to the waves at her feet, and for one moment the fear returned. "No," she told herself firmly, "Jeff's worth trusting, and so is God." Resolutely she looked back up. That's when she heard the door open down the hallway. Her feet carried her forward. "Hello? Is somebody there?"

"Yeah," the voice said from depths of the hallway. When he broke into the station, Dante smiled broadly. "Well, if it isn't Lisa. How are you doing?"

"Good. " She reached up and wrapped her hair over her ear. "Where are the guys?"

"Call out on Bayland Street—a residential. I've been listening to the radio. It must be pretty bad. It's taken a couple houses out already."

Determined to keep her newfound faith with her, Lisa kept her gaze up off the waves as she nodded. "Is everyone okay?"

Dante shrugged. "Far as I know, but they don't usually broadcast injuries over the scanner."

"Oh," she said as her heart begged her to go see Jeff. "Where did you say that was again?"

"Bayland. But I'm sure it's all blocked off by now. You won't get within a couple of blocks of there."

"Yeah." She nodded. "That's okay. I was just wondering." She smiled at him. "Well, take care."

"You too."

Quickly Lisa strode out into the late October air that now seemed cooler than it had before. Her hands wrapped around her bare arms. It was a fire—like all the rest of them. Bad, kind of bad, really bad. Did it really matter? They all held tragic possibilities for the men called to fight them. In her car, she tried to tell herself to go home. Dante was right, she couldn't get within a couple blocks anyway. Yet her heart said Jeff was there, and he didn't know what she now did.

Driving through the streets slowly, Lisa thought about him as she stopped at a red light. In front of her car, people streamed into the street, dutifully obeying the Walk sign, oblivious to the fact that it was now flashing Don't Walk. They hadn't even noticed. She hadn't noticed. But he had. He. Jeff. The man who had turned her whole world upside down and then rearranged it into a pattern she would never have thought possible.

"You know I'm not supposed to go," she told the empty car around her as her fingernail tapped out a fast beat on the steering wheel. "You know that, right?"

"Yep, just like I know you're going anyway," came the reply from her heart, and she smiled as she turned the corner.

"Yep, just like I know I'm going anyway."

Three houses had been lost. The charred shell of the middle one was hardly recognizable in the fading light. The other two could be rebuilt, but the middle one would never again stand as it had before that day. It was ashes now. Lost forever. Jeff wondered about the people who had lived there. How would their lives change because of that one moment in time? He sent up a prayer for all those whose lives that single moment would touch, all those now and all those in the future who couldn't even see this moment as it passed into the night.

As he pulled the once-white cotton hose, now grimy black, from the rubble, he wondered if anyone had prayed for him that night so long ago. They must have for it wasn't without a whole lot of help that he had gotten to this point. He thought about that kid who had sat alone on that lawn late into the nights that followed the fire, and in his heart, he wrapped an arm around him and told him that although Friday seemed all around him, there was a Sunday in his future. All was not lost as it had seemed to be in that moment. All was never lost—if you were willing to hold on until Sunday.

The pavement at Lisa's feet seemed as inconsequential as air. It flowed by her strides in great lengths of black-blue hardly noticed but for the slap of her strapped sandals on it. Fear had nothing to do with it—only a desire to see him so overwhelming that nothing could stand in her way. At the scene boundary, she slipped around a bush and past the edge of the perimeter as if it wasn't even there. Across the carefully manicured lawns, still green despite the season and the growing darkness falling on them, she ran. Her spirit flew before her, pulling her forward until she felt like she was soaring. When she finally broke through to the trucks, it took only one glance at the fireman standing on the asphalt feeding hose up onto the truck to know beyond a doubt that everything he had said was true. He was with her always, and she only had to trust enough to recognize that.

"Jeff," she said as she stepped from the curb. When he looked over to her, it was a mix of surprise and concern that flashed through his eyes.

"Lisa?" He stepped over the hose as she flew the last three steps into his arms. Holding her, the strength in his arms flowed into her spirit as the world around them dropped away.

All she wanted to do was hold him, to let him know that at every step from here on out she would be right there at his side. She asked no more from life. No one gets a guarantee, her heart said, and despite the hard shell of his fire suit, she pulled him closer to her as a stream of tears slid down her face. *You have this moment and only this moment. What you do with it is your choice.*

As those thoughts poured through her, she pulled back from him and ran her hands over his grime-covered, soot-stained face, and no face had ever held so much promise. "I'm so sorry," she said as she gazed right into his eyes. "I wasted so much time."

"No," he said, smiling softly. "You're here now. That's all that matters."

"I love you," she said, the emotions choking out the words, "and more than anything in the world, I want to be the one you spend your life with."

Confusion and then slow understanding slipped over his features. "Does that mean…?"

"Yes," she said, nodding until her head could have tumbled right off her shoulders for the motion. "It means yes."

His eyes closed in disbelief at the words, and in the next breath she was once again in his arms—jumping through the point of no return like it was a simple mirage. A moment or a hundred thousand. Whatever God gave them, she would stand right at Jeff Taylor's side. Then in the moment when God called one of them home, she would look back with no regrets for she would have spent all the time from that moment to this loving with complete trust. And that was the only measure of love that ever truly mattered.

Epilogue

Kids milled about all across the hard concrete floor of the Civic Center. The Second-Annual Cordell Enterprises Youth Leadership Conference with 750 kids in attendance had been a resounding success. Even better than the first one the year before, and that understanding brought a smile to Lisa's heart.

A whole year had come and gone since they had stood on that street and held each other. Yet it seemed a lifetime. Lisa's hand slid across the top of her growing stomach as she drifted away from Mr. Cordell who was already talking about who they should contact for speaking at the conference the next year. She slipped over to the little group gathered at the side of the stage and took her place by Jeff's side. It was a given, if he was in the room, that's where she wanted to be. As close as one body could get to another. Spirit-to-spirit they were one, and in four months they would be three. Her heart filled at the thought.

"Well, you did it again, Lisa," Dante said as she lifted Jeff's arm and slid under it. It had been far easier to talk the station into sending its three top firefighters in place of a solo captain this year. Dante, now a trainer; Gabe, the station's newest lieutenant, and Jeff, the latest firefighter to be promoted to driver. She couldn't imagine life without them.

"Yeah, thanks to you guys and a mountain of great help," she said with a smile. "I could never have pulled this off by myself."

"Modesty," Eve said with a nod to Jeff from where she stood two steps up on the small set leading to the stage. "I knew there was a reason you hooked up with her."

"Yeah," he agreed as his gaze found Lisa's. "Not to mention the fact that she's beautiful and strong and brilliant and…" His lips found the edges of the skin at her neck, and she laughed in embarrassment.

"Would you behave yourself?" she asked as her hand pushed him back.

"I don't know," he said, pulling back to look into her eyes seriously. "That's a pretty tall order with you around."

"And you said he was shy," Lisa said to Eve.

"Hey, I'm not taking any responsibility for that one," Eve said with a raise of her perfectly-manicured hands. "He was when I met him."

"And that was before or after his brain transplant?" Dante asked from his position at Eve's side.

"Before," Eve said, nodding. "Definitely before."

"Umm, excuse me," a voice said from behind Lisa, and when they turned, Jeff's hold on her shoulders broke free.

The young face, so familiar and yet indistinguishable from the hundreds of others Jeff had seen that weekend, gazed at him, expectant and yet hesitant.

"Can we help you?" Lisa asked as the wheels of Jeff's head struggled to put that face with a time and a place.

"Yes." The gaze behind the dark glasses fell. "Well, kind of. Umm, I just wanted to come and say thanks." The kid held out his hand to Jeff. "I never got a chance to that day on the bridge."

A breath and all the pieces fell into place. "Parker?"

The young man nodded as Jeff shook his hand. "I couldn't believe it when I saw you up there today. I've been trying to find you for a year now to say thanks, but I guess there are a lot of firefighters in Houston."

"A few," Jeff said with a smile. Then he noticed the close presence of a friend at his elbow, and he turned to look at the man who had looked much older now than when he had first run up on the bridge that day. "Hey, Parker, you remember, A.J., don't you? He was the paramedic that day."

"Yeah," Parker said as he realized who the man standing next to Jeff was. No hat and looking decades instead of a simple year older, A.J. held out a hand. "Sorry, I didn't recognize you."

"That's okay," A.J. said with a soft smile. "I'm just glad you made it." The two shook hands. "So, you came to the youth conference?"

Parker nodded. "They said the emergency teams would be talking, and since that's what I'm wanting to go into when I get out next year, I thought it'd be a good idea to come check it out."

"Go into?" Jeff asked, tilting his head to the side curiously.

Parker's gaze fell to the floor. "Well, I haven't exactly decided yet—fire, police, rescue. Something like that."

The edge of Lisa's hand touched Jeff's arm, and he knew her thoughts without her speaking them.

"That's great, Parker," Jeff said sincerely. "It really is, but do it for you okay? It's too tough to do it for someone else."

A question and then understanding slid through Parker's eyes as he smiled at Jeff. "I'll remember that."

"Hey, Parker!" someone called from the auditorium edge.

Parker's gaze jerked to the side, and he turned back to them hurriedly. "My ride's leaving. I'd better go."

Jeff pointed to the program in Parker's hand. "Any time you've got questions about the field, give me a call. If I can't answer it, I'll find someone who can."

"I appreciate that," Parker said, holding out his hand again. "And thanks... for everything."

When Jeff shook the hand, he once again felt the potential in its warmth. "You're more than welcome," Jeff said with a nod.

Parker turned back for his group, and Jeff had to take a breath of thanks himself. A life pulled back, one of the ones that made the job a calling to be heeded rather than a nightmare to evade. A life. A single life, and suddenly it all seemed worth it.

"So, what do you say, anybody up for some dinner?" Gabe asked still standing on the stage steps next to Dante and Eve.

"Who's paying?" Jeff asked, raising an eyebrow.

"You are of course," Dante said teasingly, and he wrapped an arm over Eve's shoulder and smirked at her. "Don't you think the ones who talked us into this thing should pay?"

"Cool," Eve said, laughing. "Dinner's on Jeff and Lisa."

Lisa looked at Jeff with teasing concern. "I hope you brought your wallet."

"I hope you brought your dish gloves," he said.

"Typical man," Eve said, shaking her head. "They conveniently forget their wallets every single time."

"It's okay," Lisa said as she ducked under the arm Jeff held out. "I didn't marry him for his money."

"Good thing," Dante said.

Jeff turned and smiled at her. "Yeah, good thing."

Her eyes beamed at him with the promise of forever. At that moment his vow in life shifted from a promise to protect and serve others—to a new pledge: for as long as he lived, he would protect and serve the woman who had stood by him in the midst of life's greatest turmoil. Not because he owed her, but just because his love would let him do nothing less.

As the others started out in front of them, Jeff held Lisa back gently. His grasp around her shoulders tightened. "Hey, you did good today."

Softly she looked up at him, belief in all their future held shining in her eyes. "No, we did good."

"You're right," he said, pulling her to him heart, body, and soul. "We did good."

Deep in the Heart

Chapter 1

"Please, baby, please, just get me through these gates and up to that front door," Maggie Montgomery pleaded with her '77 Chevette even as her gaze took in the enormous circle drive that led its winding way up a hill to the cream mansion with the stately pillars beyond. "Oh, Lord, what am I doing here? This has got to be the craziest thing I've ever gotten myself into."

Trying not to think about how her beat-up navy blue two-door looked on the grounds that were perfectly manicured right down to the yellow and red rosebushes, Maggie steered the car around the concrete that was edged with white stones the size of her dresser back in her dorm room. At the apex of the circle, she put the car in park and heaved a sigh that might well be her last.

With a push she resettled her glasses on her nose, grabbed her two-page resume and shouldered the door open. "Just breathe," she told herself as she stood on legs wobbly from the three-hour car drive. Pine Hill, Texas and the Ayer Mansion seemed a million miles from Gold Dust Drive in Del Rio. It was still Texas, but the similarities stopped there.

Of course, she was in her best dress, a floral print that was a size too big. That was better than the heels, which were at least two sizes too big. They were the best Mrs. Malinowski could do on ten minutes' notice. The grace of God alone had gotten Maggie this far, and truth be told, she wasn't at all sure how much longer His patience with her would hold out.

"Listen, Holy Spirit, I know I'm probably over my quota by now, but please... Please, let me get this. I don't know what I'll do if I don't." The remaining two dollars in her purse crossed her mind, pulling her spirit down. Defiantly she squared her shoulders and pulled herself to her full five feet, seven inches.

Every step was pushed on by a prayer. The six wide steps up to the front door nearly did her in, but finally, after 17 years of struggling just to survive, she was here—one knock away from something more than a minute-by-minute existence.

She reached up and rang the doorbell. The wait was worse than the walk. Nervousness raked her hand up her purse strap. Seconds slid by, but nothing happened. What now? Should she ring it again? She looked back at her car and fought the fear and desperation rising in her.

Just before she bolted from the whole idea outright, the door clicked and then opened. On the other side stood a small, Hispanic woman dressed head-to-toe in white.

"Hello," Maggie said, corralling her purse strap even as she held out her other hand. "I'm here about the nanny position."

"Doesn't anyone know how to follow a simple order anymore?" the bellowing, jowl-ridden, over-paunched, balding man at the desk fumed, shaking his head even as he continued to make notes. "I built a whole company, put in oil wells across this state—Midland, West Texas, South Texas—even three in the Gulf, and now my own son can't get one simple solitary task carried out without messing it up."

"Dad, it's not that big of a deal. Q-Main and Transistor will be ready for the track in two weeks. We just need a little more time with Dragnet. He's not where he needs to be yet." Keith Ayers fought the urge to shift in his chair. Laid back and nonchalant was by far his best bet with his father. That much he had learned so long ago, he couldn't clearly remember when it had happened.

One-on-one, head-to-head confrontation had never gotten them anywhere. He clasped his dirt-stained hands in front of him and set his stubble-strewn jaw. His dad was tough, but horses weren't his specialty. They were Keith's.

Racing a thoroughbred, especially one with as much promise as Dragnet before it was ready was the best way he knew to ruin one permanently. No amount of blustering changed the fact that Dragnet simply wasn't ready. "I talked to Ike this morning. He's thinking we can bring Dragnet up for a real race sometime in July."

His father exhaled hard, clearly not pleased with the assessment. "I paid $250,000 for that animal, and I don't like watching my investments sit around eating me out of house and home."

The fact that house and home weren't exactly in jeopardy

crossed Keith's mind, but he wisely chose not to say that. "Would you prefer to sink a $250,000 investment by racing him too soon? Trust me on this one, Dad, a little patience now could hold out big rewards later."

His father scowled, his expression sinking into his jowls. "I didn't build a billion dollar empire on patience." Then he nodded. "You've got two months."

May? That was too soon, but it was all Keith would get, and he knew it. "I'll tell Ike." He started to stand and felt his father stand as well. Never. Never a good sign. "Uh, I know my way out."

"Yes, but you also know your way back in. That's what concerns me." The laugh that accompanied the statement tried to pass it off as a joke, but it felt more like a knife to Keith.

His father followed him right to the door and out. "So, have you heard from Dallas? How's she doing at Yale? Law school going okay?"

In the hallway Keith replaced his beat up, loose straw cowboy hat back over the blue bandana stretched across his head. "Good," Keith answered with the obligatory nod. "She should be back for Spring Break. Graduation's in May. Hayden & Elliott after she passes the bar."

"To infinity and beyond. I like that," his father said with the first smile Keith had seen from him all afternoon. At the staircase that wound to the upper floors, his father stopped, looked up it, and smiled. "Well. Well."

Keith's gaze followed his father's up the carpeted-just-so steps, and although he first noticed his stepmother next to the railing, he stopped dead when he saw the young lady descending between her and the wall.

"Of course you will get time off occasionally," his stepmother, Vivian, said. Her suit dress was perfectly pressed all the way up to the ruffled collar that ringed her neck like a flower. That was Vivian, always impeccable lest anyone see she wasn't perfect. "However, I need you to realize that this is basically a 24 hour, seven day a week job."

"Oh, yes, Ma'am. That's not a problem," the young lady with the mesmerizing head of chestnut brown hair which was falling out of the clip she had in the back of her head said. She pulled the strap of her purse up onto her shoulder. She was coming down, trying to keep her gaze on Vivian out of respect and attention, but she clearly could've used the banister Vivian was using as her own. The descent was anything but graceful, more halting and awkward. In fact, she was having so much trouble keeping up with everything that it was two steps from the bottom before the young lady with the dark glasses and cascading tresses even noticed there were others watching her descent. Her glance from Vivian to the two men standing at the bottom threw her attention from the concentration she was obviously exerting to get down the stairs for one moment too long.

As Keith watched, one step from the bottom, disaster struck. He saw it as it happened, but it was like it was in slow motion. She stepped down with her left foot, but her shoe planted awkwardly in the plush carpet. Her ankle turned, and like a puppet falling to the stage, her body pitched forward with a jerk.

"Ahh!" Her scream lasted all of two seconds—the exact amount of time it took for him to realize what was happening and reach out to snag her downward motion, which would've pitched her unceremoniously to the hardwood floor of the entryway had he not stepped between her and certain humiliation.

"Oh, watch…!" It was all he got out before she thwacked into him. "Ugh!" The impact of her body on his didn't so much as move him although it was significant enough to jar her glasses askew. It was only the clasp of his hands on her arms that kept her from bouncing off of him and ending her descent on the floor next to him anyway. When her unscheduled tumble came to a complete stop, she was sprawled across him from his shoulder to his arms, which supported her without effort. In fact it felt more like holding a weightless butterfly than anything.

"Oh! Oh my gosh! I'm sorry. I'm so sorry." Mortified, she yanked herself upright away from him although she looked as unhinged from the encounter as he felt. His insides were dancing with amusement and fascination as he watched her disentangle herself from him and wobble on the uncooperative shoe once more.

"I'm sorry. I'm so sorry." She was standing, readjusting her dress, her glasses, herself. "I don't know why I'm so clumsy today. I…"

"Are you all right?" Keith asked, gazing at her as if he'd just fallen under an angel's spell. His hands stayed out to catch her again if need be.

"Yeah… Yes. I'm fine." Perturbed with herself, the young lady shook her head quickly and resumed her attempt to look like she belonged there, which she didn't. At all. And somehow, he kind of liked that.

He smiled at her, but she was clearly doing her best not to look at him. "You sure?" But she had resumed her concentration on Vivian.

"Conrad," Vivian said with no small amount of a frown at the ineptitude of her current interviewee, "this is the young lady I told you about. Maggie Montgomery. She's come about the nanny position."

"Oh, yes," Keith's father said. He extended his hand to her, which she shook even as she continued to fight to get herself under control. "It's nice to meet you Ms. Montgomery."

"I have explained to Maggie," Vivian continued, "that she is on a six month probation period. Anything not up to our standards during that time will be cause for immediate termination."

Maggie's gaze fell to the stairs, but she pulled her head up and looked right at Mr. Ayer with a forced smile.

"And that's acceptable to you?" his father asked.

"Yes, sir. It is." She looked like a proud filly with her chin up and her hazel eyes flashing determination.

"I suppose you will need two weeks to let your current employer know you are leaving," Vivian said with a sigh, and Keith couldn't help but notice the dramatics. She should've been an actress.

"Oh," Maggie said, and he heard the note of concern. "No, Ma'am. I can start as soon as you need me to." She pulled her fingers up through her purse strap. "I can start now… if that works for you."

"Wonderful," Mr. Ayer said. "That's what I like. Someone who can make decisions."

"You don't mind starting today?" Vivian couldn't hide the pitch of excitement.

Maggie turned to her. "Right now is fine if that's what you need."

She was intriguing, mesmerizing, captivating. And yet just why that was, Keith couldn't accurately tell. She was nothing like the girls he'd been out with. They with their debutant good looks and impeccable manners. No, this one, this Maggie Montgomery, looked more like a nervous, high-strung pony. Proud and strong, and determined not to be broken by anyone.

"Well, then," Vivian said smartly. "Let's go meet the children."

"Good luck, Ms. Montgomery," his father said, extending his hand to help her down the last step. "It's nice to have you."

All the air had gone right out of the room as Keith's gaze followed her down the hallway and out of sight in the direction of the children's wing of the estate.

"What're you still doing here?" his father asked, surveying him. "I thought you had horses to train."

"I'm on it." With that, he exited the main house and descended the front steps. There in the driveway sat a car that Keith couldn't even be sure still ran. It looked like it would be a better fit for a junkyard than in front of his parents' house. As he started past it, the thought occurred to him that it belonged to her. Her. Maggie Montgomery.

"Well, it will be an interesting two weeks anyway." With a knowing smile, he strode on. He shook his head at his own joke. They never lasted more than two weeks. Never.

In fact, he wouldn't have lasted more than two weeks but for the simple fact that they couldn't get rid of him. He was a member of the family—whether they liked it or not.

"This is Peter," Mrs. Ayer said, indicating the small boy with the blond hair, sitting at the table coloring slowly. "And this is Isabella." She picked the little girl with the bright blond curls up into her arms.

"Hello, little one." Maggie reached a hand out to the soft little face. "You are a sweetie-pie."

Mrs. Ayer slid the little girl back to the ground and planted her hands on her hips. "Dinner is promptly at 6 p.m. They are to be dressed and ready no later than 5:30. Inez will be able to fill you in on the rest of their schedules."

Maggie nodded, taking in the information with the sense that even perfection wouldn't be good enough.

"If you'd like some time to get settled, I can get Inez to watch the children for a few more minutes."

"Oh, no. I think I'm fine." Then she remembered. "But I do

need to move my car. It's still out front."

Mrs. Ayer sighed with disapproval. "Very well. You may park it over at the guesthouse. It's just through the back, down the lane, and off to the right."

"It'll only take me a few minutes," Maggie said, trying to assure her new employer that she was competent enough to handle all of this.

"You may as well bring your suitcases in as well. Your room will be at the top of these stairs, right next to the children's rooms."

"I'm sure I can find it."

"Inez!" Mrs. Ayer called out the door.

"Yes, Ma'am."

Maggie couldn't clearly tell how the maid had been able to answer so quickly. It was as if she had materialized there from thin air.

"Please watch the children while Ms. Montgomery gets her things settled."

Inez bowed slightly. "Very good, Ma'am."

Once more Mrs. Ayer surveyed Maggie, and the fact that she didn't believe this would ever work traced through Maggie's consciousness. "If you need anything else, let Inez know."

"Yes, Ma'am."

"And now you'd better get that car moved before Jeffrey has a cardiac."

"Yes, Ma'am." Something told her she would be saying that a lot now. Pleading with her heels to cooperate long enough to get her back to the car and then back here, Maggie hurried out. The early afternoon Texas sun beat down on the outside surroundings. After having been in the comfort of the mansion's air conditioning, the combination of humidity and heat hit Maggie like two fists.

She got in the car and took her first real breath. "Oh, thank You, Jesus." Except for the unceremonious stumble into the hired hand, the interview had gone as well as she could've hoped for. "Ugh. How clumsy can you be, Maggie? That was a good one." Forcing herself not to think about it, she pumped the accelerator and twisted the key to get the little car started. Then she carefully backed up so she could go down the back drive as Mrs. Ayer had instructed.

With a frustrated swipe, Maggie pushed the trail of loose

strands of hair from her face and then blew them back up when they didn't stay. Carefully she drove around the house, which was enormous no matter which angle it was seen from. Her heart pounded in her ears as the car slipped into the grove of hulking trees. Trees seemed to be everywhere. Somehow she had expected them to dissipate beyond the mansion, but if anything, they got more massive and thicker the farther she drove.

"Did she say right or left?" Intensely Maggie scanned the areas on either side of the driveway that had narrowed to a trail. "This is great. I get lost on my first day."

Then just ahead, off to the right, through the knot of trees, she caught sight of the place. When she got closer, Maggie sucked in a gasp of air. If this was the guesthouse, they certainly treated their guests very, very well. Sporting orange-tan brick with blue-gray accents, the house had a bevy of inlets and cutouts. There were enormous windows, and wraparound accents at the corners, and an inlet door that looked like it alone cost half the national debt. "Wow."

Wide-eyed in awe but trying to keep her mind on her present mission, Maggie surveyed the small hill of a lawn, the flowerbeds, and every inlet for some clue as to where she was supposed to park. She turned her gaze up the trail. Surely there was a garage somewhere. "Oh, Jesus. Help." The trail dovetailed with a small perpendicular drive just beyond the house, and carefully she turned there, hoping maybe this was right. In fact, there was a garage, but the moment she pulled up to it, she had second thoughts. What if someone needed in or out of that garage? If she was parked in the way, that would be a problem.

Twisting her mouth as she tried to find an answer to this dilemma, her heart jumped into her throat when her gaze caught movement in her driver's side mirror. Fear jerked her head around just in time for her to see the hired hand with the blue bandana sticking out from under the ratty cowboy hat come striding up the side of her car. For a moment she felt better, but it was only for a moment because the reality of being out here alone with no knowledge of the terrain if trouble struck with a guy who felt like the Rock of Gibraltar did nothing to calm her nerves.

She swallowed hard. Very cautiously she reached up and locked her door, praying the others were already locked.

"Hey," he said when he got to her window. His easy smile

spread across his face as she rolled down her window just far enough not to be rude. "Fancy meeting you here."

It was impossible not to notice his biceps, which looked like massive tree trunks streaming down from the ripped-off sleeves of his denim shirt. In a fight, she would lose without him even trying.

"Hi." Panic smashed into her, and her lungs constricted around it. "Umm… Mrs. Ayer said I could park here, but I'm not sure where she meant." Anxiety had never meant what it did at that moment.

"Oh, she did. Did she? Well, that figures." He laughed, which threw her incomprehension devices into full-throttle. "Na. It's okay. Swing around back here. We can put it in the barn."

Maggie nodded although no real signals were getting to her brain. She rolled up the window and backed onto the driveway so she could follow him down the increasingly narrow trail. From behind, he was all denim, save for the bent, straw cowboy hat and those arms. "Oh, dear God, I don't know about this. Please tell me if I should be doing this." But as far as she could tell, God was not giving her any other options.

At the end of the drive, mercifully, the trees broke their hold on the surroundings, and she drove out into a clearing and down a gravel road over to the building he had called a barn, but like everything else here, 'barn' didn't quite do it justice. He swung the two doors open and stepped back so she could drive in.

Crossing from outside to in, the darkness enveloped her eyes so that it took her longer than it would've seemed necessary to make it safely into the building. Once inside, she shoved the car into park and then had to corral her fear to gather enough courage to open the door. "Oh, God, be with me. I'm asking here." Busying herself, lest he see just how scared she was, Maggie got out, went to the back, and unlocked the trunk. With a heave she pulled her lone suitcase out, praying it wouldn't fall apart at her feet.

"Oh, here. Let me get that for you." He reached out for it even as he stood at the door that stood open.

"No. I can get it." She tried to swing it out of his reach, but with a soft smile and a wink he took it anyway.

"It's half a mile back to the house," he said. "In this heat you'll be French fried by the time you carry this thing all the way back."

Her heart was beating so loudly, her brain didn't have a

chance to put up a logical argument, so she nodded, ducked her head, and stepped past him. The bright sunshine beyond the door attacked her eyes, and she squinted as he closed the barn door behind them. Everything in her wanted to take that suitcase back and run, but barring humiliating herself against his strength again, she saw no way to do that. The gravel at her feet was playing havoc with her heels, and she fought to keep her balance and stay up with his strides as they started up the incline to the guesthouse.

He wasn't tall exactly. Maybe a couple inches taller than her but no more than that. But the solidity of everything about him swept the air from her lungs just the same.

"So, you work here?" she asked, willing her voice to stay steady even as her shoes threatened to pitch her into the sharp white rocks at her feet just as they had pitched her into him at the mansion. The thought made her ears burn.

"Yeah. As little as possible." There was that smile again, and if she hadn't been so nervous, it might have had a chance to do serious work on her insides. "I run the stable operation up the way."

"Stable?" Her brain was having trouble processing anything.

"Horses."

"Oh."

They made it back up to the trees, and uneasiness pushed into her consciousness again. She looked around, and the trees seemed thicker now, closing in on her, blocking all escape routes.

"I hear you're gonna be on the pay roll too," he said.

"Oh, yeah. Yeah, I am."

"Well, you must be downright impressive. Most of the time they won't let anyone within shooting distance of this place that doesn't have security clearance from the Pentagon."

They had made it to the main road and headed back to the mansion. Crossing in front of it now, the guesthouse was even more impressive going by slowly—if that was possible. Maggie fought not to gawk at it, but it wasn't easy. "I passed my background check, and I had a personal reference from the Dean of Early Childhood Development at A&M Kingsville." She sounded like she was defending herself, and she hated that.

"Impressive." And he actually sounded impressed. "So, you're from Kingsville then?"

"Del Rio." Her heel picked that moment to twist out from

under her. "Ugh." Thankfully, she caught her own balance this time, but it was a close save. "These stupid shoes."

Skeptically he surveyed her feet. "They don't make walking look all that easy or that safe."

"Tell me about it." She continued walking although he had slowed down in deference to her struggle.

Shaking his head, he pressed his lips together in earnest concern. "Why don't you take them off? You're gonna kill yourself on that last quarter up the hill."

"Oh, yeah. Like I'm going to walk into the Ayer mansion barefoot. That should make a really great first impression." Sarcasm dripped from her spirit. Who would even make such a dumb suggestion?

He glanced behind them. "Well, nobody comes down this road but me. They ain't gonna see you anyway, and besides, I'll warn you before we get too close."

Maggie still wasn't so sure, but her ankles were starting to protest rather loudly. "Okay, fine." She reached down for one shoe but had to scoot her other foot around to keep her balance. She reached out for something solid and met his arm coming the other way.

Smooth skin under her palm ripped sanity away from her. How in the world had she gotten here? Sweat beaded out of her back, and she was quite sure it had nothing to do with the humidity. Quickly she removed first one shoe and then the other. When they were off and she was once again on solid footing, she had to admit it was a good idea, even if her breathing was no longer working properly.

"You got it?" he asked, eyeing her seriously.

"Yeah." She forced a knot of a smile on her face and started walking. The pavement would've been burning hot had it not been shaded by the millions of leaves above them. Just then a breeze swept through the branches and right over them. "Ah." The sigh of relief was automatic.

"So, you're an early childhood education major?" he asked as they made their way back up the road. It didn't take long to understand what he meant about that last quarter of a hill. If it was any steeper than this part, she was in trouble.

"Yeah. I graduated in December. This is the first permanent thing I found."

"Well, we're glad to have you. I'm sure Pete and Izzy will keep you on your toes."

The question of how familiar he seemed in referring to the children traced through her, but before she could voice that thought, he looked at her, and that scattered her thoughts like the pieces of a shattering window.

"So, are you up for the 24-hour thing? Most people hear that and go running for the exits."

She shrugged, and it took a solid breath to beat the sadness in her chest down. "I like the idea of having a roof over my head. It's worth a little work to have that."

He nodded, head down, concentrating on walking. When she looked over at him, she fought not to notice how rugged and tanned his face was. In fact, with that face and that body, he looked like he belonged nowhere else other than out in nature, taming some wild beast. His whiskers were more than a five o'clock shadow. They were a dark emphasis to the sheer masculinity of the rest of him. With a glance he caught her looking at him and smiled. Lines of amusement appeared on either side of his face. "What?"

"Oh. Nothing." She ripped her gaze away from him. "I just hope I don't do anything to mess this up."

When he looked at her again, the smile that was already beginning to get to her was a soft and encouraging. "I think you'll be just fine."

Buy **Deep in the Heart** now
on
Amazon Kindle:

http://www.amazon.com/Deep-in-the-Heart-ebook/dp/B005LVVIIG/ref=sr_1_1?ie=UTF8&qid=1336659766&sr=8-1

The book reviewers are calling:

"Absolutely Amazing!"

About the Author

A stay-at-home mom with a husband, three kids and a writing addiction on the side, Staci Stallings has numerous titles for readers to choose from. Not content to stay in one genre and write it to death, Staci's stories run the gamut from young adult to adult, from motivational and inspirational to full-out Christian and back again. Every title is a new adventure! That's what keeps Staci writing and you reading. Although she lives in Amarillo, Texas and her main career is her family, Staci touches the lives of people across the globe with her various Internet endeavors including:

Romance Novels:
http://ebookromancestories.com

Books in Print, Kindle, & on Spirit Light Works:
http://stacistallings.wordpress.com/

Spirit Light Books Blog
http://spiritlightbooks.wordpress.com/

And…

Staci's website
http://www.stacistallings.com

Come on over for a visit…

You'll feel better for the experience!

Also Available from Staci Stallings

In Print

The Long Way Home

Eternity

Cowboy

Lucky

Deep in the Heart

To Protect & Serve

Dreams by Starlight

Reunion

Reflections on Life I

Reflections on Life II

Ebook Editions

Cowboy

Lucky

Coming Undone

Deep in the Heart

A Work in Progress

A Little Piece of Heaven

A Light in the Darkness

Princess

Dreams by Starlight

Reunion

To Protect & Serve

Made in the USA
San Bernardino, CA
09 January 2016